Tomorrow is a River

By
Peggy Hanson Dopp
and
Barbara Fitz Vroman

J. Phunn Publishers

First Printing — May 1977
Second Printing — November 1977
Third Printing — September 1978

ISBN: 0-931762-00-6
Library of Congress Number — 76-52054

Printed in U.S.A.

The authors are grateful to all who lent support, guidance, and assistance in the preparation of this book: to Niki Adam Casimiro who helped in giving birth to the book; to Dr. Helen Corneli, University of Wisconsin-Stevens Point, Natalie Bassett of *Choice*, Arlene Buttles, Journalist-Author, and especially Professor Robert Gard of the University of Wisconsin-Extension, all of whom offered invaluable suggestions for improvement; to Sharon Vroman Kaehn whose labor of love included typing the manuscript; to Marjorie Eichelberger, Martha Jones, and Sylvia Poullette who read the manuscript for structure and grammatical form; to Jeri Bross who contributed technical suggestions, research corrections, and infinite encouragement; to our husbands who lovingly smoothed our paths while we were in the creative throes, and to the writers and authors who went before us and recorded the historical facts we used to recreate the times and scenes of this book.

The works we drew from included:
"Wisconsin" by Robert Nesbit
"History of Chicago" by Bessie Louise Pierce
"Chicago" by Edgar Wagonknecht
"Chicago and the Great Conflagration" by Elias Colbert and Everett Chamberlin
"Fire at Peshtigo" by Robert Wells
"History of Waupaca County" by J. Wakefield
"Soldier Life in the Union and Confederate Armies" by Phillip van Doren Stern
"Lincoln For the Ages", edited by Ralph G. Newman
"The Army of the Potomac: A Stillness at Appomattox" by Bruce Catton
"A Pictorial History of the Civil War Years" by Paul M. Angle

To the memory of my father,
William Edwin Fitz,
who climbed mountains
all his life,
and always urged those
he loved to reach
for the highest peaks.
              Barbara Fitz Vroman

To Pop and the 7 Angels,
   You listened for
      forty years.
It is done.
Rejoice and be
   exceedingly glad.
              P.H.D.

TABLE OF CONTENTS

PART I

THE TOMORROW RIVER COUNTRY

Tomorrow is a river
  that flows through yesterday
  to bring us today . . . . . .
  the only day there really is . . . . .
  the Now!

Learning this, we neither look
  to the past for comfort
  nor to the future for opportunity.

1

During the night the engineer had cut the speed of the train knowing that deer and other wild animals crossed the track in the darkness. The cars did not rock as much, nor did the steam and soot penetrate the interior as much as in the day when the windows were opened. But Caroline Quimby could not sleep or even doze fitfully as most of the passengers seemed to be doing.

Her body was growing heavy with her second pregnancy, and the weight of her five year old son sleeping across her knees added to her discomfort. Her body ached and her eyes burned with weariness, but every time she started to slide into sleep she was besieged by images of Prudence Wainwright. Prudence laughing—Prudence standing in the vestibule of the church, the sun shining through her lavender parasol lighting up her fair hair—Prudence scabrous—Prudence screaming. Struggling to escape the images she would jolt back to wakefulness.

The young woman's bonnet-framed face was pretty without being extraordinary. The dark blue eyes, regular nose and childishly sweet mouth would be noted with pleasure in a crowd and then forgotten. Not so the man sleeping next to her whose head was cradled against her shoulder. Even slackened with sleep, his was a face of startling masculine beauty that once seen tended to persist in the memory. The curling dark hair and tangle of effeminate eyelashes that rested on his cheek were balanced by a bold nose and strong chin. It was the face of an actor or Don Juan, but the man's clothing proclaimed his status a clergyman.

As sunrise began to aureole the spring fog hugging the Lake Michigan shoreline, a stir went through the coach.

"Chicago—we're getting near Chicago—"

1

People sat up yawning, stretching, rustling, craning to see out the dust smeared windows.

The locomotive sounded, and the child, Danny, awoke frightened and began to whimper.

"Shhh, Danny-lamb, we're almost there," Caroline soothed, shifting his weight to a more upright position so he could see out the window as he became more awake.

The Reverend Adam Quimby was rousing too. He smoothed his hair and brushed at his suit before turning his eyes to his wife. He smiled a still sleepy smile.

"You and Danny are so covered with soot you look like chimney sweeps."

The half-hearted smile she started to give back to him changed to an expression of wonderment as the train broke through the fog to higher ground and the sights of the city began to unwind before her eyes.

"My word, Adam!" she cried, "whatever is that—it looks like a wall of gold—"

He laughed. "Just the sun hitting new lumber. Lots of building going on—Ann wrote you that."

As far as they could see, lumber was stacked from six to thirty feet high on either side of the river banks and the Chicago River itself was a jostle of lumber schooners edging their way to deposit yet more.

The illusion of a fairy city rising from the mist, surrounded by golden walls, was broken as the train carried them over a series of giant piers strung over the mud flats along the lake front. Now the squalid slums packed with immigrant shacks, cheap saloons and rotting garbage were exposed to their view.

People were opening windows. The air that rushed in, still tinged with morning coolness, bore a smell of mud, smoke, livestock and garbage.

Through the open windows they could hear the ships and barges blasting at each other for the right of way or for bridges to open. Pigs squealed and cattle bawled from the confines of pens near the packing plants, and the huge elevators lining the banks added to the cacophony with the wheeze and whistle of steam lifts.

Danny stared out the window with his finger in his mouth, never having seen so much concentrated activity in his young life. The docks were aswarm with stevedores, dressed in bright unorthodox clothing, unloading barrels of sugar, molasses, rum and whiskey. Their cheerful curses sounded musical on the morning air as the train slipped by.

As it groaned and shuddered to a stop at the new stationhouse,

2

Caroline felt a glow of happiness for the first time since leaving Providence. Above the rounded roof of the building the rigging of great ships and the smartly furling flags of foreign countries could be seen, but Caroline's eyes were elsewhere.

"Look! There's Ann! and Bromley!"

Adam lifted Danny from her lap and together they divided the parcels and carpetbags that comprised their luggage and allowed themselves to be absorbed in the crush of people forcing themselves toward the opening door.

Ann Thornton, dressed in rich ottoman silk with a matching bonnet, was waiting with outstretched arms to gather her sister into her embrace.

"Carrie. I think I may hug the life out of you, I'm so glad to see you. And Adam! And—oh, no, this can't be my baby-bunny grown to such a man!"

Danny slunk behind his mother.

"Good to see you, Adam," Bromley said. "Let's get the ladies home. I imagine you would all welcome some breakfast and a bath."

Bromley led them expertly through the assemblage of women in belle skirts, gentlemen in tails, trunks, dogs, wicker hampers and children to where the carriage waited.

"I choose breakfast first," Adam said, "but I have a good idea Caroline is going to plunge into that bathwater like a duck into a pond."

Adam's exuberant good mood lapsed into silence as they moved north from the river away from the mud to a tree lined avenue with handsome houses set in orchard-like settings. Not the least impressive was the one up to which the Thornton's carriage drew.

"Ann, your home is beautiful!" Caroline exclaimed. "To think I imagined Chicago being—well, like Sioux City. I thought you would be living in a log cabin."

Ann laughed. "Nearly everyone thinks of us as wild and uncouth, Carrie. You're not the first. But we're second generation Chicagoans and we're becoming very lah-de-dah!" The little toss of her head accompanying the speech was a parody of herself.

"I hear you're making a fortune as a railroad magnate, Bromley," Adam said. "Very far-sighted of you to get in on the ground floor."

"It's only begun—" Bromley said.

"Come in—I'll fix you a hot bath the first thing," Ann promised Caroline.

"Ohhhh, ohhh," Caroline sighed as she later lowered herself into the copper tub filled with steaming water. "Don't tell Bromley, but I never want to ride another train. They go fast beyond belief, but every bone of mine aches."

Ann handed her sister a warmed wrapper when she was ready to step from the tub, and put a cup of tea into her hands.

"Bromley is showing Adam the stable and Danny is quite happy in the kitchen with Bridget—so you and I can have a chat alone and get caught up," Ann said, guiding her sister to a comfortable pair of chairs.

"Caroline, I still can not believe that Adam would give up his prosperous church in Providence to become a circuit preacher in the wilds of Wisconsin. Whatever prompted him to make such a radical decision?"

Caroline looked into her cup.

"Well—he thought about it—for a long time."

"But *now,* when you are with child? Why, *now*?"

"Oh—many reasons. He's excited about saving souls. He wants to reach the unchurched—the lumbermen, the savages—"

Ann noted that her sister was speaking evasively and avoiding her eyes.

"There's more to it, isn't there, Caroline?"

"Oh, Ann," Caroline found herself blurting, "Adam was *asked* to leave."

Aghast at having betrayed her husband, Caroline jumped to her feet and covered her lips with her fingers.

Ann was shaking her head in disbelief. "How could they possibly ask Adam to leave? He is the most powerful preacher I have ever heard. Even five years ago when I was there for Danny's birth, he had doubled the congregation. I know it has been growing ever since. Why, Carrie? Why?"

Caroline paced toward the fireplace. She was shivering as if she were cold. She found she could not tell Ann about Prudence Wainwright. Was it loyalty to Adam that silenced her or simply that she could not face the pain of talking about it?

"Adam feels he did nothing wrong. He believes this is God's way of forcing him to go out into the field," she said.

"And what do you believe, Carrie?"

Caroline sighed. "I only know it is hard to leave everything and go off to a wilderness. Adam gave me so little time to get ready. We could bring so little. I had to leave Grandma Fletcher's rocker, and the clock Mama left me—" she broke off for a moment, then went on apologetically, "I do not mean to sound full of self-pity. You know I would rather be with Adam in a wilderness than with anyone else in a king's palace—"

"Yes, I know," Ann said, "but I shudder at the thought of your

4

trying to cope in that harsh unsettled country. In some ways you are still such a child."

"Oh, Ann—don't you start that, too."

"Too?"

"When we got off at Fort Wayne a terrible man sat at our table."

"Yes?"

"He told Danny that wolves eat little boys in Wisconsin and made him cry. And then he told Adam, 'That one won't last long on the frontier.' Meaning me."

"Oh, dear—"

"Adam was furious. He asked him to leave our table. The man said, 'Well, count them—you'll find two or three tombstones for women to every man—and this'n here she hain't sturdy.'"

"Good grief," Ann said, "He really was horrid. But never mind. God takes care of his angels."

"I'm not an angel or a child either," Caroline protested.

The maid came at that point to announce that the gentlemen were waiting for the ladies in the breakfast room.

"At least I will have you and Danny here with us a few months while Adam readies things. What a joy that will be," Ann said as they started down the stairs.

At supper that night, seated at a table arrayed with laces, china and silver, Adam chided Bromley, "I don't know as I should leave Carrie and Danny with you, Brom. A circuit rider's life is not an easy lot. Watch that she doesn't get an appetite for all this luxury."

He thinks as Ann does, that I am soft and childish, Caroline thought. She looked across the table at him with fierce devotion, pledging silently, *Whatever we must face, I won't fail you, Adam. I promise.*

Bromley changed the subject, addressing himself to Caroline. "Adam looked at a number of stallions today, Carrie. He lost his heart to a black one. I tell him it's wiser to buy one in Wisconsin, but he's made up his mind. He wants this one."

"The horse will be his constant companion, Bromley, and will have to travel some hard places, they tell me. So if he has found one he takes to, it may be worth the trouble to have him shipped."

Adam shot a somewhat triumphant glance at his brother-in-law.

"It is a fine animal," Bromley conceded, and turned his attention to his steak. There were times when Caroline had the feeling that Bromley did not like Adam although he was always faultlessly polite.

In the morning Adam and Bromley went to buy the horse. When they returned, Caroline, Danny and Ann went out to the stable to view the new acquisition. The horse had cost considerably more than the young Quimbys could afford. When Caroline heard the figure,

5

she understood the silent disapproval that had emanated from Bromley the night before.

"Adam, I swear he's worth every penny!" Caroline declared, partly as defense against what she felt was Bromley's silent censure of Adam's extravagance and partly because she was truly impressed with the beauty of the animal. He had slender forelegs that rose powerfully into shoulders of muscular strength, a sweeping arch of neck and a polished coat.

"I'm going to call him Ebonite," Adam said, boyishly leading the horse this way and that to show him off.

"Can I ride him?" Danny asked, jumping up and down in excitement.

Adam laughed and vaulted his son onto the horse. He led the pair in a trot about the courtyard a couple of times.

Caroline felt a jealous pang as she watched her husband's hands move lovingly over the horse's withers. For the next months the horse would be closer to Adam than she would.

2

Adam and his guide Cricket McGuire huddled under their skin robes near a dying fire. A south wind blew over the campsite causing the embers beneath the grey ash to blaze brightly in the stone encircled fire pit. From the near depths of the pine forests a hoot owl sounded.

"I'm gonna get some shuteye," Cricket said. "Day after tomorry we oughta reach the Tomorry River."

In a minute he was snoring.

Adam stared up at the sky. Pine needles, growing in dense masses above him, screened out the stars except for an occasional glimpse when the wind shifted through the branches and caused a soft soughing. He tried to sleep and couldn't. He was gripped with an excitement beyond anything he had ever known. Here he was under Wisconsin skies. He envisioned himself carrying the gospel, the first circuit rider to head into the wilds of central territory. His hand reached under the knapsack he used as a pillow and sought his crisp new Bible, ready for a lifetime of pilgrimage. He fell asleep with it clutched in his hand.

When he opened his eyes again, it was to the sight of drifting ground fog refracting the early morning sunlight. Cricket was already breaking camp. He thrust some jerky and a cup of coffee into Adam's hand. As soon as the unceremonious meal was consumed, he said, "Let's head north. The brush is so cussed thick in here we'd better lead the horses."

The land seemed to grow more hostile as they walked. A feeling grew in Adam that wild and dangerous things lurked in the underbrush and thick shadows of rock outcroppings. He thought of snakes sliding through the tall grasses, and tales he had heard of the savagery of Indians. He was secretly relieved when they gained the well traveled road that signaled their approach to the city of Oshkosh and they could remount their horses.

Oshkosh, which had begun as a trading post named after a Winnebago Indian chief, was a supply center for an increasing number of settlers pushing into the wilderness.

The great Lake Winnebago shimmered under the noon sun, and the waters made lapping sounds against the marshy shores. Reeded plants, cattails, and pickerel-weed moved in the wind or under the weight of the red-winged blackbirds. Ahead of them the city beckoned and bustled. Adam felt his eagerness being restored.

They ate and rested at Oshkosh. Then Cricket forged on leading the way through barely discernible forest trails toward the land of the Menominee Chief, Waupaca. By the next morning they had reached the Tomorrow River.

The beauty about them was virgin and haunting. The river from which the area drew its name ran through the land wild and free, foaming up into white river rapids and then spreading into deep, placid areas with tree branches hovering in green cordons above the banks. Coveys of birds and wild animals constantly startled Adam as the horses roused them from their cover in the underbrush.

On the third day they arrived at the lodge of Pete Tartoué. His Indian wife's venison proved to be as good as Cricket had bragged it would be. Tartoué was a genial host, regaling Adam with legends of the Menominees, Pottawattamies and Algonquins far into the night. A small knot of white settlers had formed several miles up river at Waupaca Tartoué said. Adam might investigate that site, or, if he wished, he could put a cabin up near the Tartoué's.

Adam inspected the nearby land. He found a spot with large birch trees hanging over the river and a natural falls. He was pleased. The site was near enough to the Tartoué's to neighbor but not near enough to intrude. Their lodge was within walking distance but not sight.

Cricket and Pete agreed it was a good choice, and the next day the three men cut the first logs that would form the Quimby house.

*　　*　　*

"Oh, dear, it is so near the time for the baby to come," Ann lamented when the letter summoning Caroline and Danny arrived in late May. "Are you sure you want to go into that wild country?"

Caroline laughed. "Of course I am not sure. What with talk of wolves and scalpings and smallpox—" She grew sober. "I don't really have a choice, you know."

"Promise me if you are ever in want, you will let us help."

Caroline thought of how proud Adam was and how he would hate accepting anything from the Thorntons.

"All we will need is your prayers," she said.

Bromley insisted on accompanying his sister-in-law and her small son from Chicago to Fond du Lac where Adam was waiting. When Caroline saw her husband from the coach window, she stumbled over her skirt hem in her eagerness to hurry Danny out, and then Adam was lifting her from the steps into his arms.

"Oh, Adam, it's so good to be in your arms again," she whispered.

"It's all I can do to get you in my arms," Adam teased, stepping back to survey the two months of girth that had been added during their separation.

"Where's our horse?" Danny asked. He had been thinking about the stallion all during the journey.

"We left Ebonite home, but we'll soon be sailing on a steamboat. That ought to be adventure enough for you," Adam said, as he swung his son up for an embrace.

Before Bromley departed, the two men arranged for Caroline's luggage to be transferred to the steamship "Peggy" which would take them to Gill's landing.

Twilight was falling when the "Peggy" was fully loaded and ready to depart. Adam led his wife and son up the gangplank, a steadying arm tight about Caroline's waist, for the plank was thronged with other passengers embarking with them.

Caroline's eyes were wide with interest as she viewed Indians, lumbermen, new settlers and their families, fur traders, and a good sprinkling of domestic animals—chickens in wooden crates, dogs, goats, and a pig carried as if it were a baby in the arms of a Norwegian man who spoke no English.

Captain Arne Anderson had a curling blond beard and penetrating eyes that studied the waters ahead and around them with the con-

8

centration of a chess player. When those eyes rested on Caroline, they paid a silent compliment in spite of her well rounded girth. She smiled back shyly.

The Captain pointed out things of interest to the passengers as the boat made her way upstream slowly.

"Dis is Injun country, do' recent dey've packed da most of 'em off to a reservation," he said. "Ya see da leddle houses over dose mounds on da bank dar? Dose is graves. Da Menominees put da leddle white flags on top of da houses to mark dere burial grounds."

Caroline craned with the others to see the curious little log frames that were numerous along the banks.

The banks of Lake Winnebago were lined with majestic pine trees for miles and miles. Occasionally there would be a stand of oak and maple with a few birch trees near the water's edge, or the scrub of hazel bushes and elderberry; but soon the strong refreshing scent of pine would take over again.

The boat stopped at Winneconne and picked up six more passengers. Two were white men each with a bag of flour on his shoulder and another held firmly in a calloused hand.

"Yust look who's here," greeted the Captain, "Sammy Shaw 'n his brudder. How ya been?"

"Got our wheat ground the first day, Cap, but we sure wish you had another boat on these waters. It takes too long to come down and have our wheat ground and then have to wait for you to git it back home," Shaw complained.

The Captain laughed. "Ya're a born belly-acher, Sammy."

The four other passengers were Indians. A wizened Indian chief and his crippled grandson were accompanied by two braves. As the boy was lifted onto the ship by litter, his eyes met Caroline's for a moment.

She was horrified when she heard Adam's resonant voice carrying across the deck in a tone of accusation.

"—'And the sins of the father shall be delivered upon the children unto the third and fourth generation of them that hate Me'—Behold how the depravity of the father has been delivered upon this innocent child—"

No, Caroline thought, *oh, please, no.*

One of the frontiersmen was shaking his head in agreement. "Hain't it a fact though."

"Cain't say I agree!" Sammy Shaw set his burden of grain down with a thump on the deck. "Cain't see the Lord would take anything out on little children."

"Are you challenging the Word of God?" Adam demanded.

9

"He's right. It does say that in the Bible, clear as clear," a woman passenger agreed. "I read it myself."

"I got some Bible larnin', too," Sammy bristled. "What 'bout that passage where Jesus said it warn't the crippled man's fault nor his parents' fault—"

"You think you know more'n a preacher, Sam Shaw?" a burly man called Edgars asked. He got up and moved threateningly toward Shaw.

"Now ya all cut it out!" the Captain shouted. "Dere'll be no free-for-alls on my ship. I'll toss da lot of ya overboard if dere's one more word."

Adam said no more, but Caroline could see that he was pleased to have injected his first influence into the thoughts of these frontier people. He believed that hidden sins were revealed through the events that marked each day. To him, the sudden loss of a neighbor's cow, the fiery burning of a barn struck by lightning, the birth of a marked child were evidences of the accusing finger of God pointing out those guilty of secret sin.

Caroline thought her husband divinely inspired. She did not dare to argue theology with him. But for her the bloom had been taken from the journey. Thoughts of Prudence Wainwright swept back to plague her. She saw again the raw open grave in the melting March snow. She sat again in the cold church her fingers turning blue while the deacons decided.

"Ya aren't feelin' ill, are ya?" the Captain asked.

"Oh—oh, no, I'm fine," she said, embarrassed that the Captain had noted the sudden whiteness of her face.

The steamer moved through Lake Poygan into the closer shorelines of the Wolf River. Indian activity could be seen in isolated places along the banks. Smoke rose from tent like teepees; a few dark skinned women were seen gathering rushes. They stopped to stare as the steamer puffed past.

At Fremont most of the passengers disembarked. The Quimbys were among the handful of people who remained on board until the ship drew up to Gill's Landing. Danny pushed closer to his mother and she took his hand.

A small knot of people was waiting to board the ship for the return trip. Caroline looked with curiosity at the women. They made her feel overdressed in her blue traveling gown with matching bonnet. Without exception they wore faded calico with coarse shawls thrown over their heads.

The Norwegian with the pig got off first followed by the Quimby family.

Night was closing in as they walked to the boarding house the

10

Captain had recommended. The house proved not only rustic but none too clean. Caroline had to lift her skirts high to avoid the tobacco wads strewn on the rough floor, but she found she was grateful for the bubbling stew set before them on the split log table and for the feather tick on the second floor.

3

Adam had arranged for the family and their goods to be taken by canoe to their home on the Tomorrow River. The birch bark craft looked frail, and Caroline contemplated her bulky pregnant self with some misgivings as she was told to get aboard. But with Adam's help she negotiated the hazards and her trepidation was soon lost in rapture of the beauty through which the canoes were transporting them.

Adam piloted the canoe, pausing now and then to point out some landmark. Danny rode behind them, in a canoe paddled by an Indian. At first he prattled with excitement to the stern looking figure in the helm; but when he received only unintelligible answers, he grew sleepy and sat nodding, stupified by the rhythm of the canoe and the heat of the sun.

A few deer could be seen having a last drink before settling down for the day in some grassy cove. A racoon was washing his food in the clear water before eating it. Otters were playing on the banks and sliding down into the water.

Communications between the Quimbys and the Indian were limited, but he understood when they needed a rest or food. He found shelter for them at night and seemed able to catch fish upon demand.

Dusk was settling on the second day when they reached the Tartoué lodge. Caroline groaned as she tried to stand on legs kinked from hours of disuse, but Danny darted up the bank like a jackrabbit and Adam had to sprint after him.

The lodge had log walls and a rounded roof covered with mud. A shed had been added on one side and a lean-to on another, giving it a long rambling appearance.

A dark-skinned, smiling man, whom Adam introduced as Pierre

11

"Pete" Tartoué, appeared on the stoop and invited them inside.

After the boarding house Caroline did not know what to expect. A strong smell of wood smoke, bear fat and drying onions assailed her nose as she stepped inside; but the sight that greeted her eyes surprised and pleased her. Thick fur rugs partially covered the board floor. Brightly woven Indian rugs shared wall space with guns, snowshoes and a quiver of arrows. A roaring fire in the stone fireplace that claimed one whole wall illuminated the dark rafters from which Indian baskets and dried strings of onions and peppers hung.

"Welcome," said a voice that was deep for a woman.

Caroline turned and found herself facing a striking Indian woman. She was taller than Caroline, regal, with coarse dark hair plaited in Indian style. She wore moccasins and a calico dress.

"*You* are Kemink," Caroline said, reaching out to clasp the Indian woman's hands.

"And you are Caroline," the Indian answered. "We welcome you to Tomorrow River."

"Hey! You got a boy!" Danny cried when an Indian boy about his size emerged at this point from behind his mother's skirts.

Like his mother, the boy wore white garb and moccasins, with beads around his neck.

"What's your name?" he inquired of Danny. "D'ya want to catch fireflies?"

Caroline and Kemink agreed after a moment of consultation that they could go firefly hunting if they stayed in the clearing. Adam and Pete went off with clubs to kill some pigeons for supper. They were back in a matter of minutes with several birds.

Kemink roasted the pigeons on a spit and Caroline watched fascinated as she made "dough gods" of unleavened bread and baked them on oak chips set near the fire.

There was no cloth on Kemink's table and she served the food upon tin plates, but it tasted delicious to the tired travelers.

As soon as he had eaten, Danny fell asleep two fireflies still clasped in one warm hand. And Caroline was tired enough to postpone seeing her own cabin in favor of a night's sleep on the balsam boughs covered with deer hides which Kemink provided.

In the morning while Danny and the Tartoués were still asleep, Adam led Caroline through the woods along a path alive with birdsong until they reached the place where he had built their cabin.

"Oh, Adam—"

Caroline viewed the great birches, the ring of pines, the cascading waterfall showering from a granite outcropping with breathless pleasure.

12

Adam drew her inside the cabin, the pride of accomplishment glowing on his face.

The cabin was small and crude but nicer than she had expected. There was a fireplace, not as large as Kemink's but with a wide mantel to hold books and dishes. Adam had built a trestle table and benches and a trundle bed for Danny. There was a lean-to bedroom for the two of them and a row of pegs on which to hang things. The room was sweet with the scent of new wood and fresh sawdust.

"Adam, it's nice. Really it is!"

They clung to each other in a burst of happiness.

The rest of the week was spent "settlin' in" as Pete called it. By the weekend Caroline's dishes were on the shelves, the bed was covered with her handmade quilts, her copper teakettle was steaming on the fireplace and Adam had fashioned her a new rocker.

She felt contented as she tried the rocker, not as lovely as the one she had had to leave behind but sturdy. Adam kept pacing about the room.

"Adam, what is it?" she asked, hurt that he did not seem to be sharing her sense of bliss.

He came and knelt beside her nuzzling his head against her.

"Caroline, I know you've only gotten here, but I want to start off on the circuit tomorrow. It's taken me weeks to get this place in order and now I'm tearin' at the bit to be preaching. Can you understand?"

She could not entirely stifle her disappointment. They had been separated for so long.

He leaped to his feet.

"This is where I belong, Carrie, on the frontier!" he said in an excited voice, "Think of it—a new beginning. A new ministry that will be mine to mold. I will not be stifled at every turn by a passel of sour-faced elders."

He was pacing about the cabin in an agitation of emotion. "I will be to the new frontier what Paul was to the Romans. I'll carry the Word to those whose souls are crying for it. I will convert and baptize, wed and console—"

"Adam—you couldn't stay just until the baby is born—?"

"Oh, come—there's still a month before the baby's due. I'll be back in plenty of time."

The note of impatience in his tone was a warning to her.

She bowed her head. "Yes. Yes, of course. You must go."

The following morning Caroline smiled and waved goodbye bravely assuring Adam all would be well. But she felt a sinking sensation as the sound of Ebonite's hooves died into the forest.

13

The woods around her sighed and creaked in the wind, enormous and enigmatic. She felt dwarfed in the shadows of the huge trees. Danny hugged her knees, as if he too sensed the loss of protection that went with Adam.

Caroline jumped at the sound of a breaking branch.

Swaying branches parted to reveal—not a hungry bear as she had feared—but Kemink and her little son. The boy's inexperienced feet had snapped the twig. Kemink came on velvet moccasins. On her face was a smile; in her hand a crock.

"I have brought milk from our cow," she said. "You will have need of fresh food while Adam is gone. If you would like, I will show you where to fish and where there are berries."

"Oh, yes—I would like," Caroline said. She did not care two figs for the idea of fishing, but having company for a time had marvelous appeal.

The women lowered the crock into the well to keep the milk sweet and then with their children in tow started for the berry patches.

Where Caroline saw only suntipped leaves dancing in the wind, a path strewn with pine needles and a fringe of wild flowers, she was amazed to see that the Indian woman saw tales of the past, present and future written as clearly as in a book.

"A squirrel and a marten fought here," Kemink told the boys. "See, the squirrel got away."

Caroline saw only a slight disturbance of foliage, a disarrangement of twigs and a few tracks.

"Ahhh, the bears have come down early from the north. That means the strawberries are ripe in the east meadow," she said, stopping to inspect a crushed place in the grass that Caroline would never have noted.

Kemink knew just where the tangled blackcap vines grew most thickly, in which hollow the wild strawberries were the sweetest, and at which bend in the stream the watercress crowded crisp and abundant, which berries were poisonous and which were not.

By the time they returned to the cabin it was twilight, and Caroline was loaded with woodland riches. But far more important—she knew she had a friend.

14

4

It had rained lightly during the night and Caroline opened the door of the cabin the next morning to air redolent with the scent of freshly washed green foliage, the deep fertile humid scent of the earth and the ripening fruitfulness of June. She felt a sense of exultation rise within her as she realized that her forage with Kemink the day before had laid many of her fears to rest. She could look at the forest now without terror running through her in secret currents. At the same time she knew that it would be some time before she would venture out into that strange enticing world alone.

Caroline had barely washed her face by the well when Kemink arrived with a crock of milk, an act which would become a daily ritual.

As each day passed, Caroline marveled more at the capacities of her new friend. Kemink could predict weather conditions with amazing accuracy. The number of acorns in a squirrel cache, the rings around the moon, the fur on a caterpillar told her secrets to which Caroline was deaf and blind. She could weave reeds and grasses into baskets and jars, mats and rugs. She knew how to make jerky and tan hides and dry berries. And it was not only Indian wisdom that Kemink shared with Caroline. She had lived in the white world long enough to have learned many frontier skills of which Caroline was still ignorant.

Kemink could not read the books that sat on Caroline's mantel, but she was not without literature of her own. When she spoke, her words were like poetry. Caroline noticed that whenever she told the same story twice it was with exactly the same words and intonations as if she were reading from an inner book.

From Caroline, Danny and Kemink's son learned of "Hickory, Dickory, Dock" and "Daniel in the Lion's Den." From Kemink they learned of Tubata, the owl, and Wabus, the rabbit, and of Feather Woman, the Menominee maiden who fell in love with a star.

The two women managed to be together part of each day. Over the churn or the hoe they opened their hearts to each other. Caroline learned that Kemink's deepest sorrow was for her people. In a series of treaties the Menominees had been forced to exchange their traditional hunting and fishing lands for money. The latest treaty, finalized in 1852, had been signed by Chief Oshkosh. His people had forced him to sign out of fear. They had been told if they did not comply they would be sent to live west of the Mississippi on the land of the Crow Wing. Though the government represented this land as abundant and rich in game and other resources, the tribe knew it was worthless. As the lesser of two evils, they ceded away the last of their acreage for the price of thirteen cents an acre and allowed themselves to be removed to a sandy, unproductive reservation in the Tomorrow River country.

The government had arranged for some white couples to live among them and teach them the rudiments of farming. Many of the Menominees, who had been catholicized, were making a valiant effort to learn; but the land was too poor and their means of equipment inadequate.

The Thunder people of the Mitawin lodge, (Kemink's branch), who still clung to the old gods, had no intention of farming. Small bands continued to migrate to the traditional hunting and fishing areas where they could "live before the sun," as Kemink put it. But the fur trade with the French and British on which their livelihood had depended since the seventeenth century had passed. Game had diminished to the point where hunger was a constant spectre, and worst of all, a disproportionate number of what should have been their finest young men and women were debauched with whiskey. They cared only for their government allotments and their bottle.

Kemink often told the story to the two boys.

"In this land—" Kemink would begin, her long fingered hands gesturing at the wilderness around them, "—the Menominee, the Winnebago, the Pottawattamie, and the Ottawa received the grace of the Great Spirit. Here did our chiefs hunt the elk, the bear and the wolf and the buffalo. The land was to the heart like a poem to the ear, undulating, forested softly with generous oak, the slender birch and the always pine.

"Here was the land good to all comers. Each season brought fresh feasting for every creature. The maple leaked her sweet juices in the spring. The rambling blackberry brought her fruit to dark succulence for both bear and man. In the fall the marshes rustled with the great song of abundant rice.

"Then came the white man—at first like a few melting drops of snow in the spring, but soon a steady stream, and then a raging torrent sweeping his Indian brother from his path. No longer did the buffalo skirt the lake trails in the dusk. The sturgeon grew scarce beneath the ice. The steel plow cut our mother earth, and the steel pick dug into her innards for iron and ores. As the old order was destroyed, the Menominee lands were taken from him piece by piece.

"Kemink, daughter of the great Chief Pow-wa-ga-nien, has found happiness at the side of a man with white blood. But to my people the

16

white brother has brought only sorrow. Where now are the great nations of the Algonquin tongue? Where are the Chippewa, Ojibway, the Ottawa, the Pottawattamie, the Kickapoo and Illinois?—The Sauk, the Fox, and the Mascouten? All but remnants have been driven from our land. Gone—gone."

The two little boys listened round-eyed. The real pathos of what she was saying did not fully penetrate, but the emotion and drama with which she told it pleased them. They liked to hear the sonorous roll call of the Algonquin speaking tribes, the Chippewa, Pottawattamie, Kickapoo and Illinois.

One day, Pete was present when Kemink related the familiar saga. Later he made a point of telling Caroline in private, "Most of what Kemink says ees true. Her Indian heart and pride tell her eet ees all true. But eet ees not zo.

"When Father Alloues arrive here in 1669, he leave the first written records. He found the once powerful Winnebagos and Menominee tribes almost destroyed by pestilence and war. Perrot, a French trader, tole heem there were fewer than forty braves left in the entire Menominee nation.

"The rest had been keeled in inter-tribal wars. We took care of them as eef they were our children. We gave theem guns to defend theemselves and we succored their womeen and children through winters when they would otherwise have died of famine—and the Menominees flourished and grew again until they were a nation of thousands—"

"But it *is* true that we have taken their lands—have we not?" Caroline asked.

"The land does not belong to eeny man. Eet belongs to God," said Big Pete.

"Still—" Caroline protested, troubled, "certainly by prior right it belonged more to them than to us—"

"Land does not belong to eeny man who cannot defend eet," said Pete with conviction. "Thees land belong to heem who loves eet and heem who sweats upon eet and heem who dies for eet eef he must."

Though Caroline could not accept in her heart Pete's 'might makes right' philosophy, she soon learned that the truth about the Indians varied with whoever was speaking at the moment. There were those who loved and revered the Menominees and felt they were an innately noble and gentle people who had been victimized by whiskey and injustice. There were plenty of others on the frontier who saw them as savages with no redeeming features.

"They starve and die in the winter because they are too lazy to forage in the autumn—" was the scathing remark she heard. "No other tribe has so desecrated itself with drink as the Menominees."

When Caroline told Adam, at a later date, of what Pete had said, he responded, "True enough. But Pete neglects to explain that the reason the Menominees had nearly been extinguished by the Iroquois was that the Dutch had given that tribe guns."

For herself, Caroline knew only that Kemink was one of the most inspiring people she had ever met.

Kemink's son and Danny became so inseparable that the little Indian boy picked up the nickname of Dan-Pete, designating his relationship to both his father and Danny. The long Indian name Kemink had given him was almost forgotten. To the Quimbys, Dan-Pete he would be for the rest of his life.

As the child within her grew more forceful each day, Caroline spoke to Kemink of the apprehension she felt. Danny's birth had been arduous. At the end the doctor had given her laudanum to escape the pain. She wondered how she could manage if the doctor did not come in time. If Adam did not get back. If—

Kemink was comforting. "Before was your body ignorant of birth," she said. "Now it knows well the pathway. The trail that has been broken is easily traveled."

Caroline was reassured by the knowledge that Kemink would be with her. But still, the dreams of Prudence Wainwright that plagued her, were entwined now with dreams of labor and open graves and tombstones. She woke up sweating and clutching at her stomach.

5

"Won't Papa be surprised when he comes home and finds all these berries dried for winter?" Caroline said.

She and Danny had been berrying in the cool, wet smelling morning. By noon, both buckets were brimming. The sun had dried the grass along the ditch bank, so they sat there to enjoy the bread and milk they had brought for a lunch.

"Why does Papa have to go away?" Danny asked. "What is he doing?"

"He's saving souls," Caroline said.

"How do you save souls, Mama?"

"Well, Papa doesn't really save souls. Only God can save souls, but Papa helps."

"How does Papa help?"

"Oh, land!" Caroline said, laughing. "I think I'll wait and let your Papa answer that question."

Her laughter ended in a moan.

"Whatsa matter, Mama?"

"Must have been bending over too long," groaned Caroline, rubbing the place in her back where she had felt the twinge.

Hearing the swish of a tail among the brush, Caroline shushed Danny and told him to watch and be very still. As she had hoped, after a moment a squirrel appeared. Made brave by their stillness, he darted forward, grabbed a crust that Danny had left in the grass and scampered away.

"Maybe we could tame a squirrel like that someday," Caroline said.

"I'd rather have a pig," Danny said. Dan-Pete had recently taken his friend to see their spring litter.

"No doubt we'll have to have a pig," Caroline agreed. She and Adam both had a firm conviction that God would provide for them, but she wondered now if the people along the circuit route were being generous to the young minister. Since the common practice was for people to give produce, she suddenly had a mirthful picture of Adam arriving home with a pig in his arms and potatoes poking from his pockets. She started to giggle and again found her laughter ending in a gasp of pain. There was something down to earth and convincing about this twinge.

It's still too early, she tried to reassure herself, but she began to fold up the napkins.

"I think we'd better be getting home, Danny."

"There's lotsa berries left," Danny protested. "We could fill the lunch basket."

A third twinge struck. Caroline tried to stand up and sat down hurriedly, biting her lip. Danny's young brow screwed up in concern.

"Whatsa matter, Mama?"

The twinge passed. She stood up and picked up the berry pails.

"Nothing to worry about, but we should start home."

They had not gone far down the trail when Caroline stopped and clung to a small tree, almost spilling one of the berry pails. When the seizure had passed, she said, "Danny, will you run on and fetch Kemink for me? I'm going to keep coming slowly, but I need Kemink. Tell her to come right away."

"I thought Kemink couldn't come 'til milk time."

"Danny, *just go.*" There was an unusual sharpness in Caroline's voice.

"Shall I take the berry pails?"

Slightly recovered, Caroline took a deep breath, shaking her head.

"Don't bother with the pails, Danny. Just run, hurry please." Then calling after him as he darted on ahead of her, "Danny, stay on the path now, don't turn off for *anything.*"

The flash of his blue shirt was soon lost in the profusion of branches and Caroline, feeling the grip of pain in her back again, stood still, wondering already if she had done the wrong thing sending so small a boy on such a long and lonely path.

She tried to lengthen her stride on the path, but she found herself halted every few lengths by the pains. At last she sat down in a small clearing, took off her sunbonnet and ran her sleeve across her moist forehead.

"Baby, I guess you are determined to be on the way," Caroline lamented. She had hoped the twinges were false labor pains, but their severity convinced her this was not the case. Closing her eyes against tears that wanted to overflow, she whispered, "Oh, Kemink, please hurry—"

Danny scuttled down the pathway to the cabin. Obedient to his mother's command to hurry, he by-passed the temptation to stop at a willow grove and cut a whistle the way Big Pete had shown him; and when he reached the cabin, he felt hot from hurrying and thought of stopping to get a drink from the well; but he went on, consoling himself that Kemink would give him a drink when he got there.

"Hey, Dan!" called Dan-Pete as the small white boy reached the curve in the path. "Com' 'ere."

Dan-Pete was standing by the river bank, beckoning.

Danny approached, curious to see what Dan-Pete was up to.

"I'm catchin' rabbits," Dan-Pete said.

He showed Danny how the noose would pull tight when the unsuspecting rabbit stepped into it. The boys were absorbed in practice for some time before a shadow falling over them caused them to lift their eyes to Kemink, towering above them.

"Where is your mother?"

"She's in the woods," Danny said jumping up, feeling guilty now that he remembered why he had come. "She's got a pain in her back, Kemink, and she wants you to come."

"Where in the woods?" Kemink asked with a note of urgency that even a six year old could sense.

"We were berrying where you took us yesterday—" Danny began,

20

starting to feel anxious.

"Stay here and play. If it becomes dark, go to the cabin and wait there until your father or I return," Kemink instructed Dan-Pete, and then she was gone.

Kemink knew the immediate woods area the way a captain knows his ship. She did not stay long on the trail but loped swiftly through the low underbrush.

*   *   *

There was nothing Caroline could do but cling to the small pine tree beside which she lay, straining and resting during the onslaught and departure of each effort of the child-birth throes and pray between contractions that Kemink would hurry.

A timber wolf padding down a deep path on the other side of the pines paused, catching the warm earthy scent of the woman in travail. Leaving the path, she stealthily skirted the pines and moved into the underbrush. The she-wolf would ordinarily have avoided human scent, but she was in dire need. She had recently whelped, and her mate, who under normal conditions would have brought food to her den, had been killed. Weak from hunger, not daring to stay away from her pups too long, she was obliged to overcome her fear of the human, encouraged by the scent of helplessness.

Caroline, lying on a bed of pine needles, her face wet with sweat, had launched into full-scale labor. Her attention was so absorbed by the recurring waves of pain undulating through her, she did not at first hear the small sound of leaves crushing beneath the wolf's paws.

Her breath swooshed from her lungs as she suddenly found herself staring at the wolf whose eyes were chilling gold-grey triangles above a tongue that laved over shining, back-curved fangs. Her fingers clutching the pine tree numbed, and a scream wrenched from her throat.

Kemink, hurrying through the underbrush, halted for a moment as the scream reached her ears. Her pulses began to pound because it was not the grunting, gutteral scream of a woman enduring labor, but a scream of sheer terror. Kemink began to run again when she heard the second scream. *Wolf,* she thought with a sinking heart, for now she saw clearly the impression of wolf footprints in the mossy earth.

The Indian woman knew that unarmed she was no match for a wolf. She lifted her head and gave the call of a hoot owl. Through the branches she could see Caroline prone by the pine tree and the wolf stalking along the edges of the clearing. She grabbed a branch and cracked it, at the same time giving again the call of an owl.

The wolf paused, listening.

Kemink waited tensely for an answer to her hoot, which she knew would come if there were any Menominee or Winnebagos around. She repeated the call as she moved cautiously closer to Caroline.

The wolf turned her head, listening.

Again Kemink paused and called, this time in rapid succession.

From the other side of the pines she thought she heard an answering hoot, but she was not sure. To her horror, she saw that the wolf was settling back on her quivering haunches to spring. She rushed into the clearing as the beast bared her fangs in a pre-spring snarl. Just as the wolf leaped, Kemink tugged violently at a bush, tearing it loose and sending a dozen stinging twigs into the animal's snarling face.

The wolf swung her head at Kemink, forgetting Caroline. Kemink dropped the branch and raised her arms in front of her face in an instinctive gesture of protection as she felt the form of the wolf hurtle toward her. She heard simultaneously a faint whistling sound and a thud like a clod of earth hitting the ground. She opened her eyes to see an arrow still vibrating from the ribs of the wolf's body arched in a death convulsion. The animal gave one last dying snarl, revealing foam flecked teeth.

"Sashwatka—" Kemink breathed as a tall brave in leggings and loin cloth stepped into the thicket to draw his arrow from the wolf's body.

"I heard your call."

For a heartbeat they looked into each other's eyes. Sashwatka was a shadow from her Indian past, one of those long-legged braves of the pack from which her husband would have been drawn had she not chosen to marry Pete.

Sashwatka bent quickly, lolled the wolf's head to the right and left and then nodded toward Caroline. "Care for your friend. The wolf is dead." And as silently as he had come, he was gone.

Caroline, who with a moan of relief had fainted for a moment, was reviving to her agony. Kemink knelt beside her murmuring reassurances.

"Ohhh, Kemink," Caroline panted, "something is wrong."

"All will be fine," Kemink comforted her. "All will be well now. I will help you."

Though she kept up her reassurances and brought all her Indian knowledge of childbearing into play, as the hours passed and she watched her friend growing weaker and weaker, and the shadows grew deeper and deeper towards darkness, Kemink was secretly disquieted. Caroline was right. The baby was not presenting properly.

Caroline was no longer moaning. She lay with her eyes closed, limp as death, her hair in strings from sweating.

"Kemink—" she whispered through swollen lips," I can't—anymore."

"You can," Kemink said sternly. "This baby *will* be born." But inwardly she agreed with her friend that she could not go on. The baby must come at once if the life of the mother was to be sustained, for Caroline had begun to hemorrhage.

She closed her eyes in prayer then knelt closer to Caroline and felt for the baby's head. She tugged and pulled, wrenching a fresh facet of screams from Caroline.

Her fingers, slippery with blood, lost their grasp. She tried again, pulling *hard*. There was a sound like the soft breaking of a branch, and then as suddenly as the bush had come free when she had tugged it to use against the wolf, the baby came free, almost bursting into her waiting hands and arms.

In the darkening woods, Caroline and Kemink heard the cry of a newborn baby.

Danny and Dan-Pete decided to try some fishing when they had tired of the rabbit snare, but Danny's heart wasn't in it. The feeling that something was wrong with his mother filled him with anxiety. As darkness began to close about them and neither Kemink nor his mother returned, he felt like crying.

"I want my mother," he told Dan-Pete.

Dan-Pete stared at him. "You look like you gonna cry."

" 'N what if I am?"

Legs apart, arms akimbo, Dan-Pete assumed a heroic stature.

"Indian boys don't cry."

"I'll bet they do too," Danny protested.

"Nope," said Dan-Pete with certitude. "Indian boy start to cry; mother do this."

He leaned forward and pinched Danny's nostrils between his fingers.

"Stop breath. Stop crying," Dan-Pete said.

"Yah, I guess that's right," Danny had to agree. He remembered now that once when Dan-Pete was stung by a wasp that was exactly what Kemink had done, shut off his air so he couldn't cry. Then she had tenderly put cool mud on the spot and talked to him in Algonquin, which was their special love language to each other.

23

"How com' Indians can't cry?"

"Mother say small Indian cry wrong time could cost life. Sometime rattlesnake, sometime wolf, sometime bear, sometime enemy around. Indian must learn to be quiet."

"Well, I'm glad I'm a white boy and can cry if I want to," Danny said.

"Danny, you feel like crying, you go ahead," Dan-Pete said generously. "I won't watch."

He turned his head. The truth was that he felt like crying himself, and he hoped that Danny's tears might make Caroline, Kemink, or at least his father materialize. He was no more used to being away from Kemink for long periods than Danny was used to being separated from Caroline.

"No, I ain't gonna cry," Danny said, scornful now that he had been challenged. "Just *little* white boys cry."

"Hey, let's go get something to eat," Dan-Pete said in sudden inspiration.

Together the two boys foraged in the darkening lodge and found corn bread, honey and milk. Since they couldn't locate a knife to slice the bread, they dug it from the tin with their hands without compunction. They dribbled the honey in a sticky mess over the bread, over the table, over their hands and over their shirt fronts. Eating was comforting.

Outside, Lily-Thing, who was not under any obligation to be either a brave Indian or a brave white boy, began to bawl mournfully.

"Cow wanna be milked," Dan-Pete said wisely through a mouthful of corn bread and honey.

Danny forgot for a moment to be lonely and worried about his mother. Excitement filled his eyes.

"Kin we milk her, Dan-Pete?"

Dan-Pete shrugged.

"Don't know. We could try."

The two boys wiped their sticky hands on their pants and climbed up to the peg where the milk pail hung.

*   *   *

Following the birth of her daughter, Caroline had shared one wan but triumphant smile with Kemink and then had slipped into unconsciousness.

Alone in the woods, dark now except for the darting fireflies and the first thin shafts of moonlight, Kemink wondered how she would get Caroline and the baby back to the cabin. Before she could lift her head to hoot for help, Sashwatka reappeared. As Kemink had hoped, he had stayed nearby.

He lifted the limp form of Caroline and preceded Kemink down the path toward the cabin. Carrying the newborn infant wrapped in her apron, Kemink followed.

When the tall Indian had settled Caroline on her own bed, she roused, murmuring, "Dannee—"

Kemink followed Sashwatka to the door.

"My husband will see gifts are sent to your lodge in gratitude for this day," Kemink said.

"The daughter of Pow-wa-ga-nien owes me no debt," Sashwatka replied before disappearing.

"Danny?" Caroline called again.

"He is with Dan-Pete. I will go for them at once," Kemink said. Concerned about the two small boys herself, Kemink did not wait to get Caroline into her nightdress or to bathe the baby, but lighted a lantern and hurried away, carrying the infant still wrapped in her apron.

* * *

"It's harder to milk a cow than it looks," Danny said.

Dan-Pete was seated on the stool, holding tight to the pail, while Danny squeezed diligently. Lily-Thing stomped her hind leg, swished her tail and cast baleful glances at the pair of them. Though they had been trying for some time, only the bottom of the pail was covered with milk.

"Lemme try again," said Dan-Pete.

Just as Dan-Pete set the bucket down to trade places with Danny, Kemink appeared in the shed. Her teeth were a smiling white bow in her dusky face.

"Come here, Danny," she said softly.

He advanced slowly, feeling suddenly shy.

Kemink drew aside the corner of her apron-wrapped bundle to reveal a fuzzy red little face with squinched-up eyes.

"This is your sister."

Danny looked at her thoughtfully.

"She ain't as cute as a baby pig."

"I'd rather have a sister than a baby pig," said Dan-Pete, staring with fascination over his friend's shoulder.

"Come, we must go back to your mother," Kemink said.

The two boys gave each other uneasy glances, remembering the honey-crumb mess all over the kitchen table and floor; but when they got to the lodge, Kemink made no comment about the mess that greeted her eyes. She was wondering what had detained Pete. He had gone with the fur traders to unload a wagon of pelts onto their barge, but she had expected him back long before dark.

The tallow lantern cast only a feeble light on the path, and the woods, now completely dark, was filled with night noises.

"Hold tight to my skirt," Kemink said.

Danny walked along the dark path clinging to Kemink's skirts, while Dan-Pete hung to his shirt tail; and mingled with the cry of wolves and the hoot of owls was the mournful bellow of Lily-Thing, miserable and indignant because she had not been milked.

If Danny was not greatly impressed at first with his new sister, both he and Dan-Pete were highly impressed with the dead wolf. The following morning Big Pete let them accompany him when he went to see if the animal was still there. The boys watched as he deftly skinned it out.

"Big Pete said it was the biggest she-wolf he ever seed," Danny said in excitement. "Her paw prints were like saucers."

"Saw, not seed," Caroline corrected, not wanting to talk about the wolf.

When the pelt was cured, Big Pete would send it as a gift to the lodge of Sashwatka.

Caroline, regaining her strength under Kemink's devoted care, was dressed in a white lawn nightgown, her dark hair tumbling over her shoulders. She sat up among the pillows to nurse her new daughter.

"Ahhh, she's wet," Caroline laughed, as she felt the dampness seeping through the baby's blanket. "Fetch me a diaper, Danny, and I'll change her."

Danny brought one of the white squares Caroline had so carefully hand hemmed before the baby's arrival and then scampered away.

Caroline had been smiling and humming as she unwrapped the blanket. Suddenly her face altered.

"Kemink—" she called in distress.

Kemink, who had been outside drawing water knew before she entered the cabin what had caused the distress in Caroline's cry. She had been expecting it, for it was she who had been bathing and caring for the baby.

Caroline looked up at her friend, her blue eyes darkening, the way a forest darkens when the sun departs.

"Kemink—there's something *wrong* with her. Her arm hangs limp. It isn't *normal*."

"Perhaps it is the fault of Kemink," whispered her Indian friend. Then Kemink told Caroline of the soft sound, almost like the breaking of a sapling, before the baby was born.

26

Caroline put her arms around Kemink and kissed her.

"Oh, Kemink, you must never, never blame yourself. Both of us would have died if you hadn't helped. And I've never heard of anything half so brave as facing that wolf all by yourself. I'm sure it isn't anything *you* did. The arm doesn't seem broken in anyway. It is more as if—more as if it were deformed."

Caroline almost whispered the last words, remembering how Adam's face had looked that day on the steamship when he had said, "That man has committed some horrible sin or this would not have been visited upon his son."

"The arm will grow well and strong," Kemink said, restored by Caroline's love to her usual faith and optimism.

Caroline rewrapped the baby and held her protectively close.

"I believe, too, the arm will become all right, but—oh, Kemink, Adam has strong feelings about deformities." She told Kemink things she had never confided in anyone before, not even Ann. She told her how Adam's belief in the avenging finger of God had gradually led into firey denouncements of members of his congregation. Sabbath after sabbath, the parishioners had cowered in their pews as Adam's oratory hung over them like brimstone waiting to fall—never knowing who would be next. One by one, the deacons had come to call, trying to point out that Adam might be employing too much zeal in his efforts to convert his flock. Caroline could remember Deacon Fieber best, his long, knobby knees drawn almost to his chin in his earnestness, imploring Adam to read again the story of the woman taken in adultery whom Jesus refused to condemn. But Adam would not listen; he believed in what he was doing—and so there had been Prudence Wainwright.

"Never a lovelier girl lived," Caroline told Kemink. "She was at that time about sixteen, beautiful inside as well as out. Sometimes we used to have taffy pulls or Bible readings at our home for the young people and Pru was always so sweet and laughing, I quickly came to love her. And Adam, too, was attracted to all her brightness and seemed to take pleasure in having her about—until—until—she was stricken with a strange malady. Her lovely young face became afflicted with a scabrous skin condition that no amount of salvings seemed to clear. Her parents carried her about to many doctors and still no cure was forthcoming. You can imagine how terrible it was for such a fair young girl to become suddenly hideous. Pru began to hide in her room. She gave up her plans for becoming a teacher—but the final blow was—" Caroline broke off. She still found it almost unbearable to talk about. "—was—when Adam denounced her from the pulpit, implying all manner of terrible things about her. The next morning they found her in her bedroom. She had hanged herself. Not long after, Adam was asked to leave." She went on to confide in detail all that had happened on the steamship that day, even to her own chilled feelings at seeing Adam exhibit so much hatred for a man he didn't even know.

"It will be different with his own child. Perhaps the great good God has even sent this child to teach him compassion," Kemink suggested.

"No," Caroline said with unusual vehemence, "I can't believe God wants my child to be imperfect, Kemink. I will not believe that of God—for any reason."

"His ways are not our ways," said Kemink, who though converted to Christianity and devout, was often filled with unanswerable questions about the deity.

"Kemink," pleaded Caroline, "please don't mention this to Adam. Perhaps if we keep it from him for just a little while, the arm will get well and there will be no trouble over it."

"I will say nothing," said Kemink. She had never told Caroline, but there was something about Adam that troubled her. There was some element in his character that had kept Kemink at her distance. She was always formally polite to him but, in some way she could not explain, watchful. He was not like Pete who was open and easily read. He was like many people in one skin, like murky water in which indistinguishable things were hidden.

So the two women made a pact of silence concerning the baby's deformity.

Two weeks after the baby's birth Adam returned to the small clearing where he had built his home. He came thundering along the path on his black stallion, and to Danny's delight, reached and scooped the child onto the saddle with him for the last few canters that brought them to the cabin.

"That was fun, Papa!" Danny bubbled.

Caroline, who had come to the door of the cabin still in her nightgown but with a long fringed shawl wrapped around her, was not so pleased. It looked to her like a dangerous thing to do. She was far too happy to see Adam to scold, however. She waited to be swept into his arms in her turn.

He smelled of sweat and dust from the trail, and he had a rough stubble of black beard adorning his cheeks, but to her he was beautiful.

"We got a baby sister," Danny said, stealing Caroline's prerogative. "And she was borned in the woods and there was a huge, big-as-a-house wolf, 'n this Indian had to kill it, 'n Big Pete skinned him—"

"Whoa—" said Adam, "one thing at a time." He turned to Caroline,

"My dear, I'm sorry I didn't make it back in time. But thanks be to God, you seem well—and the baby?"

"She is a beautiful little girl," Caroline said, her eyes not quite meeting his. "Come and meet your daughter."

She lifted the baby from the cradle, and laid her in his arms with apprehension.

He looked at her, his face handsome even with stubble, and smiled, well pleased. "Her hair is black like mine," he said, stroking the silky thatch on the baby's head with a forefinger.

"Ye—ess," Caroline said, smiling back. He did not seem to notice the slight shakiness in her voice, but a moment later as he gave the baby back to her, he said, "You don't seem quite yourself. Was it so bad?"

Danny popped up between his father's knees.

"Our baby was born in the woods and a wolf almost got them."

"Caroline, did you really face such an ordeal? What is this Danny keeps saying?"

"It's over, Adam," Caroline said, "The Lord kept us safe. We owe a debt to Kemink. She risked her life for the baby and me. At first I dreamed every night of wolves coming through the windows. Now I am not afraid anymore, but I still don't like to talk about it."

"Poor, poor, dear," Adam said, pulling her onto his lap, stroking her hair. "I never dreamed I wouldn't be here in time."

Cuddled in the strength of Adam's arms, Caroline would have felt completely happy if the secret of the baby's deformity had not hung between them. She almost opened her lips to tell him, but just at that moment Big Pete arrived bearing a gift of trout he had caught in the river, and the opportunity passed.

7

Though Adam did not bring a pig home in his arms or potatoes in his pockets, he did bring a saddle bag of newspapers, periodicals and a letter from Ann, picked up at the post office in Weyauwega.

Harriet Beecher Stowe's "Uncle Tom's Cabin" was being serialized in one of the papers and the Quimbys and Tartoués spent several evenings together with Pete and Adam taking turns reading the story to the group. The last installment with Liza fleeing over the ice floes one breath in front of Simon Legree left them hanging. They would have to wait for the next sheaf of mail for the conclusion.

They were all anti-slavery to begin with, but the story made them feel more so. All the same, Big Pete shook his head with disapproval as he laid the paper aside.

"Thees woman helps light zees flames of war," he said "She adds anger to zee emotions already exploding in zee hearts of Northern people against zee southern slave holders."

"She only speaks the truth," Adam defended the author.

The controversy in Nebraska and Kansas over slave territory seemed to give credence to Pete's misgivings, but they were young and happy and there were lighter things to think about.

Caroline was delighted to find Ann had sent her a Godey's Lady Book. Hoop skirts were coming in, and Caroline ohhed and ahhed over the fancy drapings and ribbons that decorated the great belled skirts, but she decided they would scarcely be appropriate for frontier life.

She did become fascinated by a bonnet with a heart-shaped brim, which she envisioned made of wine velvet with a pink watered silk lining. When she mentioned her desire to make the bonnet it earned her a rebuke from Adam.

"Are you like the saloon girls in the lumbercamp towns who think of nothing but "fripperies?" I thought you were more spiritual. It distresses me to find that your mind, too, is more on velvet ribbons than on the condition of your soul."

Caroline was hurt, but she tried to examine herself and determine if the rebuke was deserved. She could not help remembering the women at Winneconne and Gill's Landing in their worn gingham housedresses with coarse shawls thrown over their heads. Did helping their men in this wilderness take every ounce of energy so there was none left for "fripperies", as Adam called them? Was this what Adam wanted—for her to become one of those worn-faced women in men's shoes? Was it really so wrong to want fluffy petticoats and ribbons and violet scent?

Caroline felt rebellious, but she did not challenge Adam. She slipped the Godey book under some quilts in a corner of a chest with a sigh. Even if Adam had approved, the bonnet was out of their reach. Adam had told her the night before that most of the other circuit riders he knew were unmarried men because few could afford a wife and family. The average wage was eighty dollars a year. And Adam had not only not come home with a pig, but after a month of work, he had brought home virtually nothing else. Caroline was mostly concerned because of their need for a cow. She had hoped that Adam would be able to supply enough money to at least purchase a heifer calf.

"We can't expect Kemink and Pete to share their milk with us indefinitely," Caroline told Adam. "They won't take a cent in return, and I know that it does represent a sacrifice to them, for they have a calf to feed and need the whey for their pigs."

"Then you must stop accepting milk from them," Adam said.

"But Adam—how am I to continue nursing the baby if I don't have milk to drink—and what of Danny? We would have no butter or cheese—"

"You must have faith that God will supply us."

"Yes, Adam," Caroline said, ashamed of her lack of faith.

Adam had many tales to tell Caroline after his month away. She listened with eager attention to his exciting narratives.

He told her about one young couple who had been waiting eight months for a preacher to happen by so they could be wed. The poor girl let out a whoop like an Indian when she saw him coming up the trail, Adam said, and reappeared before he could dismount, wedding dress clutched in one arm, her swain in tow with the other.

Caroline was touched by his tales of the many old people who hung to a thread of life until he arrived at their bedsides because they longed to speak to a preacher before they died.

There were those who could not stall death for the arrival of a circuit preacher. Adam found that death had stopped in many of the homes he had visited, and often he was asked to accompany the family to the burial ground where he delivered a few words at sites marked with crude crosses or stones.

If there were a depressing number of deaths from cholera, pneumonia, smallpox, whooping cough, diphtheria, snake bite, malnutrition, consumption, and childbirth, on the frontier, they were at least well balanced by a yeasty birth rate. Everywhere he went Adam was besieged with requests for baptism.

Since he was not of any particular sect, he had no prejudice against baptising by either sprinkling or immersion and catered to either belief, so he often baptized entire communities of adults as well as infants.

Caroline could not help laughing when Adam told how he had almost drowned himself and a three hundred pound woman while trying to baptize her near the falls at Waupaca.

There was only one subject that Adam waxed eloquent upon which Caroline did not enjoy hearing and that was the condition of sin that prevailed in the lumbering communities that had spawned in the north woods.

As he related to Caroline tales of the lumbermen's Saturday night sprees, "drunken orgies" Adam called them, it seemed to Caroline that Adam's whole demeanor changed. His eyes took on a hot glow; the blood climbed red in his throat and cheeks; he paced back and forth in agitation, only stopping to strike a table or to pound on a door in emphasis.

"They have women, Caroline, that they use for nothing but *lust*. There are as many brothels as there are saloons. The women shamelessly bare their breasts and powder them white. They expose their legs, sometimes up to the *thigh*, clad only in *thin* black stockings. They *reek* of perfume and, God pity them, of *whiskey*. They offer their caresses to any man who pays—"

Caroline, rocking the baby as she nursed her, felt her cheeks flush.

"Really, Adam, if you insist on describing every scandalous detail, you're going to scandalize *me*," she protested.

To her surprise, Adam flung himself at her knees, and looked up at her with burning eyes, "And if I cannot even confide in you, how am I to rid myself of these flaming images of sin that torture my mind?" he asked.

She quickly said in a consoling voice, "Oh, Adam, but, of course, you must tell me. You must always tell me anything that bothers you. Only—you seem so unreasonably upset."

"Unreasonably upset!" He bounded to his feet in anger. "How can you be so little concerned that hundreds of men and women are committing bestial actions, defiling themselves, forsaking God, heading themselves into eternal damnation? Are you so selfish, Caroline, that you care nothing for the soul of your fellow man?"

"Oh, I do care, Adam, I truly do," Caroline protested, stung once more with her constant failure to live up to Adam's standards of spiritual perfection.

"They drink until they vomit or lie in the sawdust streets like dead. They have unholy dances at which they stomp and shout and embrace those shameless women without conscience. They fight constantly, sometimes with knives, their passions inflamed by these Godless red-lipped women. It is so common for them to jump on each other with their caulked boots that the resulting scars are now called logger's smallpox—" Adam ranted on.

Caroline, looking at her husband's livid transfixed face, told herself she should be proud of his fervor, but at the same time it frightened her. Each time something would set him off anew on a tirade about the lumber communities, she would try to divert his attention to something else, usually earning his anger for her efforts.

When he had run out, temporarily, on the subject, he always ended on the same words, "Ahhh, Caroline, the harvest is surely white and the laborers are few. We must have revivals in those logging camps. We must teach the ungodly the fear of God."

And Caroline would be ashamed that she had felt frightened and repelled by his rage and would feel humbled by the depth of her husband's calling.

Nevertheless, she was always glad when he had returned to a more tranquil mood.

Caroline was daily gleaning and pickling from her small garden. Stripped to the waist under the hot July sun, Adam worked to dig a root cellar for her pickle crocks, squash, and potatoes. She watched him—black hair hanging in wet curls on his forehead, his cheeks dimpled with a smile as he in turn watched Danny trying to emulate his skill with a shovel—and felt inundated with love.

Lying at night by his side in the still heat of the cabin, she watched the moonlight trace the swell of his chest, his handsome profile, and she could not forbear saying, "Oh, Adam, *I am selfish*. I hate for you to go away again. I wish I could have you with me all the time."

For once he did not scold her for her spiritual shortcomings. He turned in the darkness and reached for her.

She truly meant what she had said to him, and yet when the time came that she had to pack his saddlebags with fresh clothes and provisions, she was surprised to find herself filled with relief. Only after he had gone did she fully realize what a strain the long hot week had been, how desperately afraid she had been that at any moment he might discover that their daughter was not a normal and perfect baby.

Adam himself had christened and baptized the baby, Felicity Faith, for his mother and hers.

"You would think it was December the way you have this baby wrapped up," Adam had teased.

Caroline froze inside with terror that Adam would discard the concealing wraps as he dipped in the basin and baptized the child. When he handed the baby back to Kemink's waiting arms, still safely wrapped, Caroline had to blink back tears of relief.

Dan-Pete found it hard to say "Felicity," so he called the baby "Firefly," and before long the infant was Firefly to everyone.

After Adam had left, Caroline hurried to Kemink. "Kemink, we must find a way to make Firefly's arm all right before Adam comes home again. Adam must *never, never* know."

She understood in part now why Adam's fervor frightened her so.

What if that fury and fire were directed against their own imperfect child—what then? Caroline wept a week of held-back tears on Kemink's sympathetic shoulder.

8

Caroline believed in miracles. Each night after she had tucked Danny into his bed she knelt beside her own on the splintery wooden floor and prayed earnestly that Firefly's arm would be healed. Yet for all her faith, some tiny part of her remained skeptical. In the morning, she would creep toward her daughter's cradle with a pounding heart, and draw her covers aside—expecting *what? Do I really believe that some morning her arm will suddenly be normal and perfect?* she asked herself—and returned to her prayers with renewed anguish, saying, *Father, help my unbelief.*

Once Caroline told Kemink about Brother Billy Devine and how he had healed a cripple at a revival meeting, and Kemink said, "Yes— we have such men among our people, too. The one most famed in our legends and our songs is Walking Iron. All the tribes in the northwest made journeys to the sacred ground of his great village situated where now is New London. All enmity between tribesmen was laid down when they stood on Walking Iron's holy ground. Many claimed great healings. His followers were thousands and his wives numbered in the hundreds."

Caroline, who had been listening earnestly, blinked at the last statement, but held her tongue. Kemink had explained to her once before that polygamy had arisen in Indian tribes during periods of grim necessity when so many braves had been killed in war that the bereaved widows and children had to be enfolded in the name of mercy. When Caroline had protested piously that the resources of the tribe could have been shared without polygamy, Kemink had looked at her with pained eyes and said, "Should all those women then have been deprived of the love of a man—and the young women of children? Is not love also a necessity?" And Caroline, feeling on delicate ground, had retreated into silence. She did not share Adam's compulsion to convert all others to their way of thinking—and besides, did not Christians revere the memory of Solomon who had had, it was said, a thousand wives?

Kemink augmented Caroline's prayers with poultices made from potent herbs she had learned of in Indian lore, and both women took turns massaging and exercising the little arm.

At times when Caroline nursed the baby, she could not keep hot tears from falling.

"H'cum you cry all the time when you look at Firefly?" Danny asked perturbed.

At first, Caroline had tried to keep Danny from noticing the useless arm for fear he might let the truth slip to Adam. It soon became clear that this was impossible. If July had been hot, August was stifling that year. Firefly broke out with prickly heat from being wrapped up so much. Caroline bathed her often with cool water to ease the rash, and Danny noticed the arm and wondered about it.

"Her little arm is not quite right, Danny," Caroline said, "but let's not say anything about it to Papa just yet. Maybe it will soon be better, and then we won't have to worry your father about it. All right?"

"All right," Danny said.

Now with Firefly to care for, Caroline was busier than before. Cucumbers and tomatoes were ripening in the garden, and Danny helped her with the picking and pickling. Water had to be drawn and heated almost every day to wash Firefly's diapers and aprons.

Some days, when every gust of hot wind seemed to bear a new swarm of mosquitos from the forest, when Danny and Dan-Pete got in one of their rare quarrels, when Firefly, usually good, cried from the heat and the insect bites, when Caroline's back ached from hauling water and wood and she burned the bread, she would brush slipping loops of hair from her hot face and fight back tears of loneliness for Adam.

But there were other days when the white diapers blew freshly in the faint puffs of breeze and the last crocks full of pickles and brine stood in rows in the root cellar Adam had dug, Caroline would feel a sense of pride and accomplishment. "Oh, Adam, I *am* going to make a good wife for you!"

Kemink still brought milk each day despite the fact that Caroline had dutifully told her Adam said they were not to accept it anymore.

"Adam feels we must rely on God to supply our needs," Caroline said.

"And who is to say that God is not supplying them?" Kemink asked with a slight smile as she set the milk containers down.

After that, Caroline did not feel she could refuse the milk, though she knew that the pastures were drying up and that Lily-Thing gave a less plentiful supply than earlier.

The woods were full now of curling orange and brown tiger-lilies. The bright flowers attracted Danny who brought armfuls of them to Caroline until she had to suggest they should leave some to decorate the woods.

If there were swarms of mosquitos, there were also swarms of butterflies. The small yellow ones particularly seemed to descend like pale gold clouds on the dusty path to the well. Propped in her cradle, Firefly followed the fluttering brightness with her eyes.

Watching, Caroline sometimes knelt by the child and held her good arm down, hoping that the baby would make an effort to reach toward the fluttering insects with the other arm. But the long-lashed blue eyes would turn toward Caroline, and Firefly would dimple and coo at her mother, forgetting the butterflies, her arm hanging useless as ever.

At least, she told herself, Adam would not be home for another two weeks or so. By then the poultices Kemink was applying might work improvement—or perhaps the exercising. So she lived from day to day with hopes—and from night to night with pleading prayers.

*   *   *

Adam was finding that July and August were not easy on circuit preachers. In many places the dust rose up around him in clouds as he rode. His black alpaca suit was powdered with it. His hair felt stiff with it. His usually impeccable white shirt was soiled and gritty. His feet burned inside his boots and perspiration crawled in itchy streamers from under his hat band.

More than once, when he stopped to pass the time with a farmer and to deliver the Word, he was handed a hoe or a pitch fork. A preacher who couldn't help pitch up a load of hay or hoe a few rows wasn't considered "worth his salt" in that region; so, though physical labor had never been Adam's forte, he doggedly complied.

By the end of July he had calluses on his hands and blisters on his heels, and by the time August came he was cranky and worn out with the heat, no fit state for a preacher. He decided to head home early. He thought of the cool waterfall playing behind the cabin, a natural shower, of the shade trees spreading out from the forest and of Caroline and decided that even Jesus had withdrawn at times to gather His resources.

At the end of the third day's ride toward home, Adam came upon a fresh running stream with a cabin beside it. An old man was sitting by the bank fishing. The water winked blue coolness, inviting the dusty, weary preacher. He dismounted, his body aching, and led his horse toward the old man.

36

"Hello, Brother," he said.

"How'se yerself," the old man returned his greeting. He was grizzled and snaggle toothed, but he gave off an air of vitality rather than decrepitude. His bronzed arms still swelled and bulged with muscles. His shoulders were broad and erect beneath a tattered shirt splattered with tobacco juice.

Adam took off his hat with a sigh. "Would you mind if a tired preacher stuck his feet in your creek?" he asked.

His horse was already sluicing up water.

"Stick away," the old man said.

Adam sat down on the bank beside the man and pulled off his boots, dumping out the accumulated sand from the day's journey.

"Circuit rider, hey?" the old man said.

"That's right, Brother. I'd be glad to share the Word with you over a little supper."

The old man laughed. "Yer welcome to stay fer supper, but I hain't got no soul fer ye to save."

"Everyone has a soul," Adam said, his tone grave.

The old man chortled again. "Wull, iff'n I ever had one, I sold it to the devil a long time ago."

"You will not find it any laughing matter if you end up in eternal damnation," Adam said, his sternness riled by the old man's inane laughter.

The grizzled codger only laughed harder.

"M' name's Leviticus. Leviticus Jones. Y'see, I had a Bible reading mama, too. But most folks just call me Levi." He extended a battered hand.

Adam took it gingerly, which amused the old man even more.

"I reckon I'm a heap more tolerant o' you then you are o' me, son, but thet's unnerstandable. You hain't lived near as long as me ner suffered near as much."

Adam started to roll up his cuffs so he could put his hot feet in the cool stream.

"Ahh, lad, take off your duds and take a good dunk," the old man advised. "You probably still got a piece to go, hey?"

"I'm settled in the Tomorrow River," Adam said, deciding that the old man was right and starting to unbutton his crumpled shirt.

"Ohh, ye-ah, over by Pete Tartoué. Right pretty country. Wull, ye jest go ahead and rinse yerself off lad, and I'll go heat us up some stew."

The creek was deep and cold. Adam splashed away half his weariness along with the dust and came out refreshed. He found a clean shirt in his saddle bag and brushed his alpaca pants back to some semblance of neatness. After wiping the dust from his boots, he replaced them and once more felt like the Reverend Adam Quimby.

Levi came out of the cabin bearing a dented and blackened sauce pan in one hand and a smoked up granite coffee pot in the other. "Too hot to eat in the cabin," he announced, setting the utensils down on a rock.

He made another trip to the cabin returning with a loaf of bread, two tin cups and a cracked soup bowl.

He handed the bowl to Adam.

"He'p yerself. I eat right out o' the pot myself. You go first."

The possum stew in the dented kettle looked unsavory to Adam.

"To tell you the truth, this heat has ruined my appetite," he said. "I'd be pleased just to share your bread and a little of your coffee."

The old man chuckled. "Don't think y'd like possum, hey? Bet you been eatin' it all up 'n down this region and niver knew the diffrunce."

Using his bread as a shovel, he dipped heartily into the kettle, filling his cheeks out and chewing with gusto.

Adam poured himself a cup of coffee and tore off a moderate hunk of bread.

"Make me a fair livin' here trappin' muskrats," the old man said, nodding toward the creek. "Make me enuff to keep in booze and terbaccy and fer the rest I kin pernair live off the land."

He wiped his gravy-stained mouth with his shirt sleeve and reaching into a back pocket brought out a whiskey bottle. He uncorked it, took a swig and passed it to Adam. Adam was surprised at the sweet, almost enticing odor it had in the clean open air. Always before he had associated liquor with the fetid smell of saloons up north. Adam pushed it away aggressively.

"You forget, sir, I'm a man of the cloth. I do not imbibe."

The old man chuckled richly again.

"Ye think summer's hard on a circuit rider, do ye, lad? Y'jest wait 'til winter. Ye'll be passin' this way again and I shawn, son, ther'll come a time when ye'll be glad o' possum stew and a little o' the snake bite, too, ye mark my word."

He went off into his insane cackle.

Discomfited, Adam swallowed the last of his coffee, rose and put on his hat.

"I'm much obliged for your hospitality, Brother," he said. "I'm refreshed now, and I'll be on my way. I'll pray for you."

"I'll be seein' ye, Laddie," the old man said, taking another swig from his bottle and watching with squinted eyes as Adam swung onto his stallion and headed down the trail.

38

9

Adam arrived home just before noon. He found the cabin empty except for Felicity, asleep in her cradle. He smiled to himself at finding the cabin empty, surmising that his wife had just stepped away for a moment and anticipating how he would surprise her when she returned. With a sigh of pleasure, he tossed his hat on a peg, slipped off his cravat and unbuttoned the top three buttons of his shirt.

When he was home, Caroline always tried to keep a clean cloth on the table. He noticed that she had set plates for herself and Danny on the bare table, but there was a bouquet of tiger lilies that gave the simple setting a festive air.

Small feet began waving above the edge of the cradle, and Adam heard a gurgling from within that signified his daughter was awakening.

With a smile, Adam bent over the cradle to inspect this newest addition. Although the baby was almost three months old, he had seen little of her.

From the shadowy depths of her hooded cradle, the baby dimpled back at him, one hand and two pink feet waving. Caroline had dressed her in a sleeveless shift because of the heat. Adam lifted her from the cradle into a shaft of sunlight—and froze. Felicity, unalarmed by this black-haired stranger, continued to gurgle, but Adam no longer heard her. His gaze was transfixed on her dangling arm.

"My God—" he said, "my *God*—"

He almost dropped the baby back into the cradle the way a woman might quickly divest herself of a worm she had picked up by mistake.

Felicity, so abruptly abandoned when she thought she was going to receive attention, let out a wail.

"No—" Adam said, "No—no, no, no!"

He staggered toward the cabin door. "CAROLinnne!"

She was rounding the corner of the cabin, her feet bare, her skirts still tucked up, tendrils of curls slipping about her sun-warmed face and shoulders, her hands clutching the bowl of cress she had just gathered. Her hair was backlit by the sun and there was an expression on her face like that which might have been on the face of Eve when she was turned away forever from Paradise. For years afterward that picture of her was to remain burned in Adam's memory.

She looked at Adam standing in the doorway, his face white, eyes boiling. She heard Firefly's gasping, outraged screams—and she knew that Adam *knew*.

She set the cress down, wiping her damp hands on her apron.

"She's—she's *deformed*." It was a hiss.

"Ohhh, Adam, *no*. She's not deformed. Her arm isn't quite right, but she's bright and beautiful and—"

She rushed toward him, full of yearning, wanting to be comforted and to comfort; but he raised his arm as if to strike her and she drew back, confused and afraid.

He advanced on her, caught her shoulders with brutal fingers.

"What sin have you hid from me, woman? What secret unspeakable thing have you done that such a thing should be visited upon our child? Speak to me—tell me—or I will shake it from you as one shakes venom from a snake."

"Adam—I've done nothing—nothing—" Caroline cried. The face before her seemed an apparition. The blood had come flowing back into Adam's face in a purple stain; his eyes were gashes of fury, the veins in his strong neck stood out.

"Adam, stop, *stop*," Caroline cried in terror. He was shaking her until her hair came loose and lashed across her eyes, and her teeth felt as if they were coming loose.

Suddenly he flung her from him so hard that she went sprawling in the dust. She looked up at him, unbelieving.

He was heaving like a winded horse. He looked at her lying in the dust, her hair a tempest, a trickle of blood starting to curl along one cheek and gasped.

"Caroline— Oh, God forgive me."

He fell to his knees beside her, raising her out of the dust. He burrowed his head against her breast, his hot tears falling on her knees.

"Forgive me—forgive me—forgive me—"

"Yes, Adam, yes, yes, yes—" She could not control her sobbing.

He lifted her to her feet and brushed the tangled hair from her forehead. He led her to the well, dampened his handkerchief and started to wipe her face. They could hear Firefly still screaming in the cabin.

"I—I must go to her, Adam. You frightened her. She'll rupture herself crying."

She slipped past him to the cabin and lifted the screaming baby into her arms, soothing her, rocking back and forth as she paced the floor murmuring, "There—there—now, now, Honey Lamb. You're all right."

After a few long quivering sobs, Firefly allowed herself to be pacified at her mother's breast.

Adam came into the cabin. His face had a strange pallor as he stared at Caroline and the baby with a burnt out look, but his voice was quiet.

"Caroline, I beg of you, confess to me what deed caused this—this terrible thing. If you but tell—if you but repent—I will absolve you, *whatever* it was. God will absolve you."

Caroline shook her head helplessly.

"Adam, I didn't—nothing that I know of—if there were—"

"Don't *lie* to me!" he cried between clenched teeth. "Don't place abomination upon abomination!"

"Adam, I've *never* lied to you, *ever*!"

"Yes, you lied to me!" He came close to her. He was shaking. Even his hair was shaking. She clung to the baby, her eyes widening with fright.

"You lied to me with silence. You never told me."

"Only because I was afraid, Adam—" she was sobbing so her words were scarcely understandable.

"You were afraid because you were filled with guilt. In the name of God, I exhort you—confess what thing you did that marked this child!"

"Adam, I did nothing. I swear to you—"

"Blasphemy," he flung at her. "If you were innocent of wrong doing, would not you have told me at once of this child's mishapen condition? No—you breathed not a word. Indeed, you contrived that I should not know. You—and that Indian bitch. She must have known, too."

For the first time, Caroline felt anger flame through her.

"How dare you speak like that of Kemink! I owe her my life— the life of our child. Adam you're being *unspeakable*."

He prowled around her, glaring at her almost with hatred.

"Yes—I remember now. Even when I christened this child, named her after my own mother—you had her wrapped like a mummy so that your sin would not be revealed to me, heinous in its form of twisted flesh—"

"Adam, for the love of God—"

"Don't evoke the name of God unless from your knees in repentance," he screamed at her.

She stood straight and tall, the baby still suckling at her breast, the tears drying on her cheeks.

"Adam, I am going to tell you for the last time—I have done *nothing*."

"The child isn't mine, is she?" Adam said. "That's what it is."

"Now it is you who should ask forgiveness of God, Adam!" Caroline said, "to say such a thing to me—to imagine—"

"I loved you. I *worshipped* you. And now—even now—I am so weak in my feelings, so helpless before that in you which draws me, that I would forgive you—erase it all from my memory, accept even this bastard child as my own—if *you would tell me the truth*."

"Adam, would you have me tell you a lie to gain forgiveness for something I didn't do?"

Somewhat regaining her composure, Caroline disengaged Felicity from her breast and laid her back in the cradle. Rocking the cradle with one hand, she turned and faced Adam.

"How could you think these things?" she reproached. "I have never been with any man but you—never *wanted* any man but you. You yourself noticed how the baby favors you."

"Then why didn't you tell me? Why did you keep the child's condition from me?" he raged.

"I told you before Adam. I was afraid. I was afraid because of the way you acted about Chief Pottwattie's son."

"Who was it, Caroline? Deacon Williams? He had black hair—yes, yes, and he was always looming about you, too."

"Adam!"

He came to her and clamped his fingers about her shoulders.

"I know my own conduct, Caroline. I am pure before the Lord. The fault is in you. *Must* be in you. I swear to you that if you do not this minute tell me—the entire truth, however terrible, I will turn and walk out that door and never return to you. Do you understand?"

"Adam, you're hurting me," she moaned.

He released her, picked up his coat, and pulled his hat from the peg where he had only so recently flung it happily.

Bruised, shaken, stunned, she stumbled toward the door after him, but the sound of receding hooves was already echoing from the forest trail as something catapulted into her arms.

"Danny—" she said, realizing he must have witnessed the whole scene.

"Mama, mama," he cried, "Won't Papa ever come back?"

She hugged him against her pounding breast, struggling to make her voice calm.

"Papa's just upset, he'll come back," Caroline said, and even in that terrible moment, believed her own words.

10

"Adam will come back. I know he will," Caroline told Kemink, as she had told Danny. But days turned into weeks and he did not return.

Late September came, bringing winds that were suddenly brisk and cool, bearing the scent of drying grasses. The plum trees turned red, and in the garden the potato and squash vines shriveled.

Caroline moved through the days automatically performing the tasks necessary to keep Danny and Firefly cared for but with some part of her always listening. Twice she heard the sound of an approaching horseman and ran out into the yard, only to find that it was some other wayfarer passing through—not Adam.

At night, what Kemink called "an Indian moon" rose red as fire above the pine trees. Inside the dimly lit cabin, Caroline would hear the lonely, mystical sound of geese honking their way through the dark heavens. Hoarfrost laced the grass at night, and each morning when Caroline arose, the maple trees had grown a brighter gold, a more burning red.

By day tall grasses creaked with leaping grasshoppers, and Danny brought her goldenrod. On breezy days, the air was filled with spendthrift gold, as leaves swirled down from the birch and ash. But the beauty that Caroline would normally have reveled in, only touched her more severely with melancholy.

She found herself shrieking at Danny for no good reason. She could not shake her deep depression. It sat on her shoulders like a vulture. But in the beginning of October something happened that forced Caroline to push her own troubles into the background.

Caroline, sitting up in her bed, thought at first she was imagining it—it was almost like a throbbing in her own head—but the sound increased, an insistent pounding in the night. Indian drums? Up until this time she had never heard them pound their drums—what could it be?

She got up and slipped into her dress. She was fastening the last button when Danny came whispering to her.

"Mama, what's that noise?"

Caroline was frightened. All the stories she had heard about Indians attacking and scalping white people came swarming to her mind. She tried to keep calm for Danny's sake.

"I think it's Indians, Danny," she said. "Maybe they're having some sort of harvest dance. If it were anything that could be of danger to us, I'm sure Kemink would come and warn us."

Stiffly they sat side by side, their hearts seeming to pound with the rhythm of the drums.

"Perhaps it *wouldn't* hurt to bar the door," Caroline conceded.

She barred the door and then tiptoed to the window to see if anything unusual was visible. Cones of fire bobbed here and there through the thicket.

"What is it?" Danny, who had pulled a stool up beside her, queried. "What's those lights, Mama?"

"I think they're torches, Danny," Caroline said, trying to keep her voice from shaking. Now the stories she had heard of Indians burning out settlers assailed her.

Oh, where was Adam? Where was Kemink? What was happening? The lights seemed to pass out of sight but the drumming went on and on—boom, boom, BOOM!—boom, boom, BOOM!—boom, boom, BOOM!

Caroline could not stand the fear and aloneness another moment. She decided that whatever the cost, she would go to Kemink.

She told Danny to dress; and while he obeyed, she wrapped Firefly in a shawl.

"It's dark enough to hide us but not so dark that we can't find our way if we go with care. You must be as quiet as you can possibly be, Danny."

"Y'sum," he said.

She got her grandmother's sterling teaspoons and her Bible and put them in her apron pocket, a measure of her state of apprehension. She was not sure that the cabin wouldn't be burned behind them.

Caroline unbarred the cabin door, and quietly the trio slipped into the darkness athrob with drums. It seemed to Caroline it took an eternity to find their way. Every snapping branch, every dry leaf that crunched beneath their feet sent a swirl of panic through her. But at last they saw the reassuring bulk of the Tartoué lodge outlined by the starlight. Danny started to bolt forward, but Caroline caught at his shoulder.

"Wait—" she whispered, hoarse with fright, for she perceived now that the lodge was surrounded by Indians, some carrying torches.

44

Were the Tartoué's under siege, and if so, what could *she* do about it?

She had little time to deliberate, for suddenly a hand was laid on her shoulder. She looked up to find herself staring into the face of an Indian. She gave a strangled gasp and felt her knees weaken. The expression on the Indian's face was not unkind and the hand that slid from her shoulder to her arm was persuasive but not rough.

They were escorted forward to the lodge. Indians, who stood on each side of the door with torches, turned aside to let them enter. There were more Indians inside, both squaws and braves. Some of them were painted black. In their center stood Kemink, though Caroline did not at first recognize her for her skin too was blackened. She stood immobile with eyes that did not see.

"Ke—mink?" Caroline faltered.

Still her friend did not seem to see or hear her. Caroline's eyes followed the Indian's glance to the bed in the corner. A dark form lay among the coverings of wolf and fox pelts. One of the Indians holding a torch lifted it higher.

Caroline screamed and then buried her face against Firefly's bundled form.

The mangled and bloodied body of Big Pete lay on the bed.

Caroline started to shake. The Indian who had brought her into the lodge led her to a bench where she could sit down. Danny came and wormed against her knees, his eyes black smudges in a pale face.

"Mama," he whispered, "is Big Pete—dead?"

Caroline nodded.

More Indians were arriving and outside the squaws had started a keening accompaniment to the drums.

Since Kemink seemed locked in impenetrable grief, and Caroline could not speak Algonquin, there was no one to tell her what had happened. But she was certain that her first thought that the Indians might have done this to Pete was wrong.

The dark skinned people, some half naked, with necklaces of bear teeth and snake rattles, many with streaks of ochre and black painted on their cheeks, may have looked savage, but their gestures, the tones of their voices made it clear to Caroline that they had come to comfort Kemink and grieve with her. Whatever had happened to Big Pete had not come from the hands of these people.

As more and more Indians made their pilgrimage into the lodge, Danny crept closer between Caroline's knees and clutched her arm more tightly. These were not the sort of Indians he had seen in Weyauwega. The Indians there had worn white man's clothes and had spoken pidgin English. He had heard some white men make fun of them. He could not imagine anyone making fun of these men with bare and glistening legs and long knives stuck in their beaded belts.

"Mama, where are all these Injuns comin' from?" he asked nervously.

"I guess they've been around all the time," Caroline said. She had always known that all Kemink had to do was hoot and soon an answer would come back, but she had somehow never imagined that such a multitude of Indians existed all around. How could they have been so invisible all this time?

"I guess it's like the story we read about Elisha, Danny, where God had multitudes of angels stationed in chariots about the hills, but they were invisible to everyone except those God allowed to see. I guess Kemink has her own 'legions of angels'."

She felt Danny relax a little against her. If his mother likened them to angels, he felt the Indians couldn't be anything to be feared.

The lodge was becoming stifling with the scent of many bodies— and of something else, the smell of blood and death that emanated from the corpse.

As the hours ached by, Caroline did not know what to do. Felicity, who had slept through most of the night, had aroused, hungry and fussing and Caroline was reluctant to bare her breast in front of the Indians. She felt she ought to be comforting Kemink and yet felt a strange new shyness. For Kemink's dark-skinned sisters still surrounded her and ministered to her. Caroline felt a pang of jealousy. She had thought she was closer to Kemink than anyone but Pete and Dan-Pete, but now she wondered at all these women might have shared with Kemink during their growing up years. She longed to go to Kemink and embrace her, but she felt that to step through that circle would be to intrude.

Would she offend Kemink and her friends if she slipped back to her own cabin to nurse her baby? As the pervasive odor of death seemed to grow more suffocating, she was also agonized by the thought that as the only white woman in the area, she might be responsible for the "laying out" of Pete. She had never had to face that task.

Caroline sat in a miserable state of indecision, balancing an increasingly irate Firefly first on one knee and then another. Help arrived at the next opening of the door. This time it was not a Menominee or Winnebago who entered but a tall man with reddish hair, dressed in buckskins. He took the scene in with narrowed genial eyes; and after he had stood in silent respect for a moment before the dead man, and had spoken in Algonquin briefly to the assemblage, he came to Caroline. His eyes radiated kindness.

"They tell me yer Miz Quimby, ma'am. I'm Cricket McGuire. I was with Adam when he first come out to this country."

"Oh, yes—yes, he wrote about you," Caroline said eagerly.

"Looks like that young one of your'n wants some feedin'. Why don't you jus' step back there in the lean-to, Ma'am, and see to it. Then when you're done, iffen you could get on a pot of coffee—"

"Thank *you*," Caroline said, and the big man escorted her through the throng that she had been so foolishly afraid to brave. Felicity nursed hungrily and fell asleep again at once. Caroline came back to the room feeling much better that she could at least do *something*, if only make a pot of coffee. She saw that Cricket had bedded a sleepy Dan down on an old wolf hide and thought, *bless the man*.

There were more white people in the room now. Two fur traders who had heard the news nearly as far away as Oshkosh had ridden hard all night to get there, and the big-bearded men were weeping openly at the sight of Pete. Pierre Tartoué had been a man much loved by both Indians and whites.

Outside, the keening and the drums had stopped. The stars were fading into a grey sky that promised morning rain. Caroline stepped outside and took a deep breath of the wet morning, and the fragrance of coffee that was beginning to drift out.

Cricket came out for a breath of air too.

"What happened?" Caroline asked. "You seem to understand Algonquin. Did they tell you how it happened?"

Cricket related the story to her. Pete had gone out to run his lines as usual. Although he did not return when Kemink expected, she was not unduly alarmed. Pete was a garrulous man and if he met anyone, he lost track of time in his enjoyment of visiting. Kemink had simply set his supper to the back of the fireplace to keep warm.

The Menominee who came upon his body told Cricket that apparently a small cub bear had been caught in one of the traps. For some reason, Pete had decided to release the animal rather than shoot it. He evidently had laid his gun aside and was so intent on freeing the cub that he did not see the mother bear descending on him. The strong trapper had put up a tremendous battle and succeeded in slaying the bear. The Indians estimated that the bear weighed close to eight hundred pounds and that the struggle had been phenomenal. However, though he had been victorious over the bear, Tartoué had been so badly mauled that he bled to death before he reached the trail to home.

The grief-stricken Menominees who found him had made a litter for him, covered it with wolf pelts, and carrying torches had borne the body back to the lodge. It was this procession that Caroline had glimpsed earlier. The drums had already warned Kemink that there

47

was trouble, but she was not prepared for the full shock. The drums continued the news all up and down the Wolf, Fox, and Tomorrow Rivers. And now the procession of mourners continued to arrive.

Caroline wept as Cricket related the story. Like everyone else she had loved Big Pete. She had been ashamed to weep before when Kemink refused to cry. Cricket thumped her back and said, "Cry 'er out."

"Cricket," she pleaded, "will you get word some way to Adam? I know Big Pete would have wanted Adam to say the words over him."

"I'll do my best, ma'am," Cricket promised, and Caroline returned to the lodge to pour coffee and prepare food for all who felt able to eat.

She had wondered through the long night where Dan-Pete was. She was relieved to see that he too had been asleep on a wolf pelt and that she had overlooked him in the crush. He sat now, face blackened, cross-legged by Kemink. Her face remained impassive, but her eyes were the suffering eyes of a deer with a shaft in its belly.

Caroline felt uneasy to be cooking in the same room as the corpse. Drawing up every ounce of her determination and love for Kemink, she went to her.

"Kemink—do you want me—do you want me to lay Pete out?"

Kemink took Caroline's hand and squeezed it.

"No, Cricket will do it."

Caroline kissed her friend's hand and returned to her task of feeding the mourners.

Several braves came and took the corpse into the lean-to while Cricket asked Caroline for hot water and soap and fresh clothing. When all had been accomplished, he came back and spoke softly to Caroline.

"It must have happened quite early in the day. He laid a long time before he was discovered. I'm not sure, ma'am, that we can hold off the funeral 'til Adam gets here."

"Perhaps he is already on his way," Caroline said, hope lighting up her eyes. "If the news traveled so swiftly and so far—"

But Adam did not come, and by sundown it seemed wisest to bury Pete. In the last of the dying light, in a slow drizzle of rain, a large assembly of Indians, trappers, fur traders, farmers, and other settlers watched the simple pine coffin of Pierre Tartoué lowered into the ground.

Several Indians of high rank spoke grave and melodious words. Because there was no one else more qualified, Caroline read from her Bible.

When the earth had been piled on Pete's coffin, Rufus Neilson, one of the fur traders who had come from Menasha, stepped up and inserted a sturdy cross at the head of the plot. In the center of the cross, along with Pete's full name, the date of his birth and of his death, Rufus had carved simply "A Good Man."

The Indians and many of the mourners dispersed at once into the dripping darkness, but late arrivals lingered to rest. Only after Caroline had seen to it that those who remained had a place to bed down did she realize Kemink was nowhere to be seen, nor was there any trace of Dan-Pete.

Several of the farmers had brought their wives along, and they were eager to gain her acquaintance. They led lonely lives in isolated cabins and longed to share some feminine talk with her. But Caroline, worried about Kemink, and almost fainting on her feet with weariness, was too heartsick to oblige them.

She searched out Cricket and asked, her face twisted with worry, "Have you seen Kemink?"

"The last I saw her was at the grave. Perhaps she went with some of her people."

"Would she go without telling us—without a word?"

"She wouldn't be responsible for thinkin' straight today, ma'am," Cricket said.

Nevertheless, Caroline and Cricket took lanterns and wandered in the darkness calling for her. There was no answer.

Kemink and Dan-Pete had disappeared.

11

"Ma'am, you look shucked enough to topple," Cricket McGuire told Caroline. "Kemink's a woman of uncommon good sense. I don't think you got to worry about her. There's no floor room left here. Why don't I jus' escort you back to yer own cabin so you can git some shuteye?"

"We can make it alone," Caroline said.

"Wull, Ma'am, I don't reckon ther's sleeping room here fer me neither, so I'd jus' as ruther," he said with an engaging grin. He scooped up Danny, who was so tired he was almost teetering. Caroline, carrying Firefly, led the way and Cricket and Danny followed.

When they reached the cabin, Caroline laid Firefly in her crib, and then turned to light the lamp. As the light flared up, she gave a squeal. Somebody was sitting in the middle of Danny's bed.

"Oh, Dan-Pete, it's *you!*" Caroline said with relief. "Is your mother here, too?"

Dan-Pete looked up at her with huge sad eyes.

"Mother go 'way. She say come by you and stay."

"Where did she go, Dan-Pete?"

"Dunno," the little Indian said, and then he had to pinch his own nose to keep from crying.

Caroline gathered him in her arms.

"She'll be back soon, Dan-Pete."

"Wull, young'uns, do you think ther's room fer me on that bed?" Cricket asked.

Danny and Dan-Pete looked at the tall length of Cricket and at the little trundle bed and after a minute the corner of Danny's mouth curled up and a giggle escaped. Even Dan-Pete managed to smile. Cricket slid off his jacket and gingerly arranged his length on the bed. His long legs stuck out ludicrously. Caroline began to giggle too, and soon all of them were laughing uproariously.

Caroline wiped mingled tears of laughter and weariness away. She felt ashamed of their sudden hilarity, yet she knew the levity had been a blessed release from the tension of tragedy.

Cricket pulled up a rocking chair to accommodate the protruding length of his legs, gathered one small boy on each side of him, and was soon snoring loudly.

Caroline's last thought before sleep was, *Kemink, where are you?* She could hear the rain dripping.

*   *   *

Caroline awoke the morning after the funeral with a deep sense of loss. When the events came flowing back to her, she rose at once and dressed. The bedroom was chilly, and the light that filtered in was grey. Although it was October, it felt like November.

Cricket and the children were still asleep. Dan-Pete was cradled in Cricket's arms and Caroline paused, touched by the tableau. Those powerful arms must have felt very comforting to a little boy who had just lost his father and whose mother had disappeared.

Caroline started a fire in the fireplace, then left a note for the sleepers and slipped off for the Tartoué lodge. In the absence of

Kemink, she felt she should see to the visitors still there.

Millie Whirter, one of the farmers' wives, already had side pork frying and coffee boiling. Together the two women fried hot cakes for the group. Mrs. Whirter's mouth flapped without ceasing. She was a thin woman with a sweet smile that was spoiled by bad teeth.

"Sure is too bad your man didn't git hyar," she said to Caroline, obviously curious. "Folks come as fer away as Shawno."

"Adam would have come if he had got word," Caroline said, keeping her eyes on the hot cakes she was turning.

"What ye say he been?"

"He's a circuit preacher."

"Thet right? Wull tell him to circuit my way sometime, heh, heh, heh!" she chuckled.

Caroline wondered if poor Mrs. Whirter wasn't getting strange from too much solitude. She looked at the other woman with pity. Her scrawny neck was burnt red from the sun and her face was etched with wrinkles, though she couldn't have been much older than Caroline.

Caroline had spent little time on her toilette under the circumstances, and yet she felt an envious wistfulness in the other woman's glance.

It was noon before the last spring wagon rolled away.

"Won't you and yer Adam come by some time. We hain't so fer as all thet?" Millie Whirter pleaded.

The big rough men pressed her hand awkwardly as they left, mumbling thanks for the coffee and the food.

Only Cricket remained, and he too began to fill his saddle bags.

"Wull, Ma'am, I hate to leave yer here alone," Cricket said, "but I reckon Adam will be home in a day er two. I'm feared if I stay it might cause talk."

Caroline was reluctant to see Cricket go, but she was too proud to tell him that Adam might never come back, and that she was lonely and afraid.

"I'll be fine," she lied in a bright strained voice.

He looked down at her, his hazel eyes intense.

"Adam's a lucky man," he said.

He gave Danny his jackknife and Dan-Pete his mouth organ and then he rode away, leaving Caroline alone with three small children depending on her.

The boys were looking up at her as if they realized her frailty.

"Mama," Danny said. "Don't look so sad. Me 'n Dan-Pete will take care o' you 'till Kemink comes home."

"Yes," Caroline said, feeling a rush of love, "I know you will."

They walked back to the cabin, Dan-Pete blowing a sad and form-less tune on the mouth organ.

*　　*　　*

Kemink had walked away from the grave of her husband in a trance and disappeared into the forest. She was not aware of the rain that soon soaked her through or the insects that feasted on her. She hardly noticed when daylight broke again and then dwindled and was replaced by darkness. She made no attempt to find food, and drank water only when thirst became intolerable. She walked until she was exhausted, slept, rose and walked again until she had pene-trated where only occasional shafts of sunlight burrowed through, and there was an eery silence except for the wind that rushed and receded like surf in the tops of the trees.

How many days and nights passed that way she could not have said, but a morning came when she awoke to the smell of roasting meat and wood smoke. She sat up, half dazed, and felt something soft and furry slide from her shoulders. Someone had covered her with a wolf pelt during the night. She stared down at the large pelt, with it's slightly blue-grey cast. She had seen only one other like it, the one Pete had sent to Sashwatka. Even as the name formed in her mind, Sashwatka appeared. He squatted down by the campfire that he had made and tore a good hunk off the meat on the spit and brought it to Kemink.

She shook her head.

"Eat," he said sternly.

Kemink bit into the offering and chewed.

"Mukwagona is half Indian," said Sashwatka. Mukwagona was Dan-Pete's real name.

" I know," Kemink said, swallowing hard. "I have thought on this much."

"When first the white man came, the French and then the British, they were as brothers to us, as kind as fathers. Our wise men coun-seled us to welcome them—'Very soon you will see someone coming over the water. He will be the father of you all; all manner of things will he give you.' And the words of our wise men proved true. Gar-ments and knives and kettles and hatchets did they give to us—and more. They honored our ways and called us brother and took our sisters to their hearts as their wives. And even later when the white man came—still did we call them brother and fought by their side against the Blackhawk whose skin was red like our own. But they do not think of us as brothers. They call us savages—dirty, vile. They want only to push us from their sight and to take our land.

Since the Blackhawk defeat, all is changed and changing. The red man is no longer honored. The white man looks upon us with scorn. Bring Mukwagona back among the Menominees where he will be honored as the grandson of the great Pow-wa-ga-nien. He will be a leader and a chief. Now that his father is gone, if you try to raise him in a white man's world, they will call him half-breed. He will be scorned."

Kemink laid aside the meat. "These past days I have wrestled with these same thoughts, Sashwatka," she confessed. "Day and night I have sought the counsel of the Great Spirit."

"In the last full moon," Sashwatka related, "three Indians camped on the shores of the Embarrass River. A white man named Walter James had come to the lake in his canoe to hunt deer. Maddened by the white man's liquor, they attacked him. He had with him a huge knife. Our people were not armed. He severed the arm of one Indian with a blow. Another that he struck in the head died later. Hatred grows like an ugly flower. Bring Mukwagona back to his own people, to his own heritage."

"Ah, Sashwatka, there have been deep longings in me at this time to return to the teepees of the Menominee. All that you say and more have I sifted in my head. Since his father was a white man, I have settled it within myself that he would have wanted his son raised as a white man."

"Even if he will find no honor, no rest among them? Doors will be barred against him. The maidens of his father's people will turn from him."

"The son of Pierre Tartoué and the grandson of the great chief Pow-wa-ga-nien will not flinch from that which is hard," said Kemink.

"You lay a hard path for him," Sashwatka said, "but he who travels a hard path well, earns greatness of spirit and soul. Be it as you say then, Kemink. But know that the grandson of the great Pow-wa-ga-nien is always welcome in the lodge of Sashwatka."

"Your heart is deep," Kemink said. "I will remember."

He nodded, satisfied.

"Now you must go home."

Kemink laid aside the wolf pelt and rose. But he picked it up and placed it again on her shoulders.

"Winter comes," he said, "and you have a long way to go."

Days later, Kemink walked out of the woods. Her skirt hung limp and soiled, tattered to the knees. Her usually shining hair was dull and caught with brambles. Her face was swollen with insect bites. Around her shoulders she wore a magnificent wolf pelt.

After she had embraced Dan-Pete, who for once lost all his Indian decorum in his joy to see her, she turned to Caroline. She gave neither explanation nor apology. She only said, "Winter is coming. We have much work to do."

"Oh, Kemink, I'm sure Adam will come back soon—I'm sure he won't leave us alone all winter. He'll hear about Pete someway. He couldn't—he wouldn't—"

Kemink was unconvinced. "You must come and live in our lodge. It will be best for us to be together," she said.

12

Other years by the time the first snow fell, Big Pete had one side of the lodge stacked to the eaves with cords of neatly chopped wood, but this year there was no Big Pete. So each morning began for the women with a trek into the forest to search for dead trees, which were easier to chop and drag than fresh wood.

Danny and Dan-Pete took turns caring for Firefly and gathering up kindling bundles.

The mornings were cold and grey now, and the faces of the workers were a bright red in the snappy air. Even Firefly, bundled and re-bundled for warmth, grew a red button nose. Usually by noon a pale sun shone; and the women, warmed by exertion, shed their heavier garments and were able to move more freely.

As evening shadows began to creep beneath the trees and blot out the light, Firefly was put into Dan-Pete's old Indian cradle and hung on Kemink's back while the two women dragged the last heavy load homeward.

Before Pete died, Kemink had had the gift of moving through the most arduous day as if she had all the time in the world. There had always been time to show the boys an interesting plant and explain its properties or to tell an Indian tale.

Now, Kemink talked little except to direct; and Caroline, poor, panting, weary Caroline, often found her a hard taskmaster. Fingers aching with cold, breasts bursting with the need to nurse Firefly, and each foot feeling like another log to drag, Caroline begged to quit a

54

little sooner—just this once. Kemink shook her dark head, eyes searching the sky. "Too soon winter comes," was her short answer.

Danny and Dan-Pete got tired, too, and sometimes whined; but for the most part, they enjoyed the wood gathering. At noon, Kemink made a fire and they toasted bread and cheese over the flames.

When they got home at dark, Kemink still had to milk the cow and do barn chores. Nor did she allow Caroline to rest. When supper was over and the baby fed, Caroline moved a load of things each night from her cabin to the Tartoué lodge at Kemink's insistence. Caroline knew her friend was right and that if Adam did not return soon, she would much prefer to be with Kemink than alone with the children; but it gave her a hollow feeling each time she took a load of things to the lodge, making the little home look more and more bare. She felt a deep sadness as she locked the cabin door to keep it from blowing open in the wind. It made her feel less sure of Adam's return. Her faith was waning, and at night, lying beside Kemink in the strange lodge while outside the wind howled with a new earnestness, the tears that dampened Caroline's pillow were not without bitterness.

Beside her in the darkness she knew that Kemink did not sleep either. She wondered which of them was suffering more. Big Pete would never again throw his great arms around Kemink. That was the ultimate grief, wasn't it? And yet, sometimes hope could be more cruel. She almost wished that Adam *were* dead, then she could at least relinquish all hope and go on. The way things were, some part of her was always tensed with listening, longing, waiting for something that never happened. But no, *no,* she didn't want Adam dead, oh Lord, forgive her—what if something had happened to him? Was that why he hadn't come?—and she turned and tossed in new turmoil.

The next morning dawned clear. Legs planted firmly apart, arms akimbo, Kemink viewed the wood piled in deep tiers almost to the eaves and nodded.

"That is good," she said. "Now we must go to Weyauwega for winter supplies. We will go alone, Caroline. I will have an Indian friend care for the children. We have only four canoes and we will need all of them to take hides and to bring back our supplies."

After the weeks of unremitting labor, Caroline felt like a child told she could go on a picnic. She was surprised at her small thrill of pleasure at the idea of the excursion. She had felt little happiness since Adam had walked out the door. She had a few second thoughts when it was time to turn Firefly and Danny over to the Indian woman Kemink had summoned. A dank odor of past woodfires and grease emanated from her clothing, but Caroline was reassured, when she saw the universal tenderness and motherliness with which the woman soothed Firefly.

Kemink loaded three canoes with hides that Pete had cured. Into the fourth, and lead canoe, she seated herself and Caroline. Caroline had only once before traveled by canoe and knew nothing of navigating one, but Kemink was an expert, and Caroline did well for a novice.

There were places where the canoes glided tranquilly and Caroline felt enthralled by the great still trees reflected in the spreading water, and the sudden flight of birds along the banks. At other times it was hazardous to enjoy the view for every bit of attention had to be focused on getting the canoe safely through barriers of logs and rocks, overhanging tree branches and roaring rapids.

At eventide they hit a rock and the lead canoe was tipped over. Kemink, who had changed to buckskins for the trip, leaped onto the rock; but Caroline, less agile in her long skirts and petticoats, sank slowly with the canoe. Since the water was not deep, there was no real hazard; and for the first time in weeks Caroline heard Kemink laugh.

She helped drag her shivering friend from the water and then pulled all the canoes to the bank and tied up for the night.

Kemink made a good fire, and Caroline took off her dress and petticoat and hung them on a branch before the fire to dry. Huddled in fur it was pleasant roasting herself by the fire while she waited for her pantaloons and chemise to dry.

The coming night was all starshine and river whispers and the cool sweet smell of water and wind. Due to the frost there were no insects to plague them. Caroline felt as if she had been transported back to her girlhood—young and free and unencumbered.

The night grew rapidly cold; and the women wrapped themselves in pelts to keep warm as the fire died to coals.

"It's been a beautiful day," Caroline said.

"Yes," Kemink said, her strong face lovely in the red glow of the coals, "the heart must have comfort."

Caroline understood. Kemink, too, had been carrying a heavy load of grief. For both of them this day, all past and future had vanished. There had been only the blessed *now* of gurgling water, thin November sunlight, and deep quiet forest on each side of the river.

In a short time Kemink's breathing was peaceful in sleep, but Caroline lay awake, watching the water reflect the thrusting stars like wiggling pieces of silver.

"*Adam*," whispered the water—"*Adam*"—but inside of Caroline a new strength was forming. She got up and walked to the edge of the river where the canoes nudged each other in the rhythm of the wind. She stared up at the star flamed sky and said, "Adam Quimby, wherever you are—I'm not going to wait or cry anymore. If I have to, someway, somehow, I'll take care of these children and I'll make it without you. Do you hear me, Adam Quimby—Do you *hear* me? Without you!"

Caroline had lost hope that Adam was going to return, but she had replaced it, not with despair but with resolve. She went back to the campfire, gathered her pelts around her, and slept for the first time in months without tears.

Weyauwega was small by the standards of such flourishing communities as Green Bay and Oshkosh. But to eyes accustomed only to wilderness, the little town was exciting.

There was a feeling of coarse vitality in the growing village which now could boast a post office, general store, two churches, hotel-saloon, a blacksmith shop and both flour and saw mills.

A pack of barking dogs came to greet Caroline and Kemink. A wagon loaded with lumber rattled by, the burly driver leaning back on the reins, shouting a lusty, "Haw! Haw!" A poke-bonneted woman with a string of children paused to give the new arrivals a friendly stare.

Weyauwega had originally been the Tartoué's first camp. Later they had moved deeper into the Tomorrow River country, but Kemink was still acknowledged as the First Lady of the settlement. She was greeted by everyone, and with special pathos because of Big Pete's recent death. Caroline saw a few of the people she had seen at the funeral.

Kemink sought out Mr. Tibbets, owner of the hotel-saloon, who was accustomed to purchasing furs and pelts from Big Pete. He went with Kemink to view the furs in the canoes.

Caroline stayed behind to inspect things in the general store, erected only the year before by George Post. The building still had the smell of new lumber and fresh varnish. Post had started business by getting in fifty barrels of salt and there were a number of bets whether he would ever dispose of such a large lot. He had sold out at the good price of five to six dollars a barrel and now had a flourishing business.

A portly little man with a moustache, a stiff collar and dust guards on the elbows of his striped shirt, he greeted Caroline amicably.

"You have a fine store here," Caroline praised, looking at the large bolts of material, glittering array of tin milk pails, stacks of woolen underwear, and shelves of sturdy work boots.

"Well, I do consider myself progressive," Mr. Post said, with a swagger that showed his pride in the store. It was a far cry from the first frontier trading posts where business had been conducted over rough hewn boards supported by barrels and the goods had been hung from nails on the wall or dispensed from barrels.

There were still many good things dispensed from barrels in Mr. Post's store. A barrel of pickled herring lent its pungent smell on the produce side of the store, along with barrels of crackers, rice, millet, and cornmeal.

"What do you think of the ceiling?" asked Mr. Post.

Caroline craned her head back to inspect the swirls, ferns and flowers of pressed tinplate above her head.

"My, it is grand," she said with proper attention.

"That's not all, either," said Mr. Post. "I'm expecting a plate glass window from Oshkosh any day now."

"You stick a glass window as big as what yer braggin' in the front o' this yar store afore winter, all yer goods is gonna be freezin' like Tibbet's cider las' year," a man sprawled in one of the rockers chuckled.

Post glared.

"Some people just don't understand anything about progress," he said. "If I have to put in another stove, I'll put in another stove. And now my dear, what can I help you with?"

"Oh, could I just look for a time?" Caroline said with melting charm. "I'm with Kemink Tartoué and I'm not sure yet what we're going to buy."

"Ah, yes, a great woman, Miz Tartoué. A credit to her race," said Mr. Post, dropping his voice to funeral tones in recognition of Kemink's recent loss. "My store is yours," he added, following her around and pointing out items he feared she might miss.

"Just let me show you—a lovely lady like you would appreciate this." From under the counter he pulled a delicate china music box. When he lifted the cover, the tinkling strains of a Mozart minuet issued forth.

Caroline touched it wistfully. "Perhaps someday." She turned away to inspect the red flannel underwear.

"I have scent, too," Mr. Post said eagerly, still convinced that a woman like Caroline could be tempted with some of his choicer items.

But Caroline only smiled and shook her head, turning her attention to the bolts of flannel. Danny was growing so fast his nightshirt was up to his knees.

"Perhaps some sewing scissors," said Mr. Post.

Caroline was saved from replying by Kemink's arrival.

"Mr. Tibbets was generous," Kemink told her with satisfaction.

58

"He has taken all the pelts. We will have plenty for our needs. Buy what you feel is necessary," she said. "Our canoes are beached nearby. Will you take our purchases out there, Mr. Post, and bring back Mr. Tibbet's hides for him?" Kemink asked.

"My pleasure," said Mr. Post.

While Kemink bought small barrels of sugar, salt, cornmeal and coffee beans, Caroline purchased flannel.

"Well, now, such a pretty lady. Here—let me give you this as a token of good will—" and with a quick flourish of his scissors Mr. Post snapped off a yard or two of lace. "Make yourself something pretty," he said. He somehow was not satisfied to let Caroline leave the store with only necessities. For all his swaggering ways, he was a kind-hearted man.

"Would you like some gingham for a new dress?" said Kemink, equally kind.

"No," said Caroline, "but could we—could we buy some of that pretty candy to put away for Christmas for the children?"

Kemink nodded approval and Caroline was soon absorbed in selecting an assortment of peppermints, anise and horehound drops.

"Ain't ya Adam Quimby's woman?" the lanky man who had been sitting in the rocker asked suddenly.

"Yes," Caroline said. "Why do you ask? Have you heard news of him?" Her eyes raked the man's face so avidly he shifted his chaw of tobacco from one cheek to the other, looking uncomfortable. "Wull, no ma'am, no I ain't."

"You have heard something haven't you?" Caroline contradicted, catching something in his tone and expression.

"No, ma'am, no. I ain't heard nuthin'," he disavowed.

"Nothing's happened to him? He isn't hurt?"

"Oh, no ma'am. We'd a heard if there was something like that."

But still, she had the distinct impression that the man knew something he wasn't saying.

She turned back to Mr. Post.

"I think that's enough candy, thank you," she said in a voice that tried hard to remain steady but didn't quite make it.

13

The news that Kemink Tartoué was in town spread rapidly. When the women emerged from the general store, they were besieged every few steps by friends and acquaintances. Some wanted to offer their condolences to Kemink. Others urged them to stay on and visit.

"I've jus' this minute taken a pan of honey buns from the oven. Do come and sit a spell," Eliza Dudge pleaded. Her husband, along with Pete had been one of the first settlers in the area.

Kemink greeted them all fondly but gave to all the same answer. "There is snow in the air. The journey home will be longer than the coming. We will return in the spring for a visit."

Caroline was introduced and greeted with warmth. Despite her "declaration of independence" the previous night, she longed to ask if anyone had heard from Adam, but shyness, pride, fear—held her back.

Eventually the two women reached their next destination, the post office. Caroline had written a letter to Ann telling of the unusual circumstances of Firefly's birth, the child's disability and what had happened with Adam. She had not had an opportunity to post it until now.

Among the mail waiting for them, Caroline found a letter from her sister. She opened it on the spot. "—I am having three suits made for the winter season. One of crushed wine velvet, one of brown Ottoman silk, and one of grey watered silk—Bromley used to suffer through the operas, but now he is getting quite fond of them—the social season began with a brilliant open house at the Odettes—" The phrases drifted to her from another world.

Caroline folded it and slipped it into her bodice to read again later.

Kemink had bought a bag of white flour at the general store, but she wished to stop at the grist mill for rye, buckwheat and dark wheat flours. Caroline looked about the building with interests. The shafts of the mill were made of hand-hewn oak and tamarac. The wobble of the machinery occasioned by the crooked shafts was counteracted by tightening pulleys, weighted down with stones. The belts were made of bags, sewn together, and cotton factory cloth.

The first grinding of the mill had occurred on a Saturday afternoon. The following day, it was told, the mill owner attended meeting, and before benediction was fairly finished, jumped to his feet, and taking a handful of flour from the tail pocket of his coat shouted, "Here's a sample of my flour!" He was teased about this for years, but the truth was that most of the settlers were hardly less elated than he was. It had been hard work to do all the grinding at home.

"Don't seem right, you two lovely ladies having to take this trip alone," Mr. Post said, shaking his head as he huffed his way to the canoes beneath barrels of grain, sugar and flour, depositing each with a grunt.

Caroline had the feeling that with a word from either of them, Mr. Post himself would have volunteered to escort them all the way home. *What a good little person he is,* she thought remembering the gift of lace.

She gave him an especially warm handclasp as they parted, which turned him quite red. The last thing she saw as the canoes glided off was Mr. Post sitting on the wagon seat, furs piled dark behind him, his pudgy hand waving and his cheeks glowing.

Turning around to look at him earned a sharp word from Kemink.

"Sit still, friend! If we tip these canoes, half a year's work goes into the river."

Caroline gulped and sat still. She had learned on the way down that canoes can be treacherous, and the thought of the sugar, flour, and grain being tipped into the water was frightening. The loss of their cargo could mean they would not survive the winter. So the trip home was understandably less carefree than the one down.

They were going against the current now, and had to portage at every rapids. It was hard tiring work for the two women to not only carry the four canoes one at a time but also all the heavy provisions. As Kemink had predicted, the return trip took much longer than the trip down. It was late in the afternoon of the third day when they at last arrived at the familiar landing of home. The dark bulk of the lodge was a welcome sight for the day had grown as cold as a knife blade and now with the fading light, icy flakes of snow were falling all around them, melting in small twinkles in the grey water that sloshed against the canoes.

"Winter is here," said Kemink, as she helped an aching, stiff-limbed Caroline from the canoe.

The lodge beckoned, a promise of warmth, the sight of their children, food, drink, and rest—and for Caroline, the release of nursing

Firefly. Though she was weaning her, the task had not been accomplished and she understood fully now why Lily-Thing bawled so when milking was overdue. But the weary thought in the mind of both women as they trudged up the bank with sharp icicles of snow spitting in their faces was that they would still have to cart their heavy provisions up to the lodge that night. At that moment all either of them wanted was to throw themselves on a bed and sleep forever.

In the morning Caroline opened the door of the lodge to a fantasy of ice and snow. Kemink was right. Winter had arrived. Every weed, tree, bush and tuft of grass was locked in crystal, tinkling and creaking in icy splendor at each embrace of the wind.

"Oh, Kemink!" she breathed, "it's—it's stupendous! Come and look!"

Kemink, stirring cornmeal by the fireplace, only smiled. She knew the staggering beauty of the forest dressed in the snow and sparkle of winter, but she also knew intimately, the savagery and cruelty that went hand in hand with the beauty.

Danny and Dan-Pete shared Caroline's enthusiasm. They rolled around like bear cubs in the snow, coming in from their chores wet, red, fresh and ravenous.

The snowfall continued intermittently all that week. By Thanksgiving Day the snow was up to Caroline's knees.

Since there were wild turkeys in the surrounding wood, Caroline had hoped to have one. Kemink voted for wild duck. Danny and Dan-Pete solved the issue by catching a rabbit in their snare. It was their first catch, and the small hunters were proud.

They had potatoes and turnips, wild cranberries gathered from the tamarac swamps, and to the children most marvelous of all, a special kind of Indian corn that popped into big white drifts.

Firefly, still short on teeth, could not eat the popcorn, but she played with it like a toy. She was six months old now with dark ringlets all over her head and a dimple in one cheek like Adam's. Danny had almost crawled at six months, but Firefly, hampered by an arm that wouldn't support her, had to be content with trying to scrunch herself along backwards.

"Never mind," said Kemink, when she noticed the sad look on Caroline's face as she watched her daughter's struggle to navigate. "She will walk early."

For Kemink and Caroline, Thanksgiving Day was heavy with the unspoken names of Big Pete and Adam, but when Caroline bent her head over the rough hewn table covered with her grandmother's Irish linen cloth, set with candles and her silver teaspoons, she bowed her head with gratitude.

Outside the wind howled as each day the snow built its fortresses a little higher; but inside the fire leaped high in the fireplace, the table was resplendent with food, and the faces of the children glowed with the pleasure of the holiday. In the root cellar there was a hogshead of salted pork Big Pete had put up before he died, and potatoes, turnips, squash, pumpkins and crocks of pickles. There was much for which to be thankful.

Along with an inevitable sense of loss and sorrow, both women felt a growing sense of self-esteem at their own courage and strength. Winter had come and they were not afraid.

It was perhaps well that they could not foresee all they would have to face before spring came again.

14

The first time Caroline had seen the Tartoué lodge she had thought it charming. She found it comfortable now, but there was one thing she did miss intensely. Adam, like Mr. Post, had sent away for a glass window for their cabin so she had been able to peer out and see the sun setting above the black fringe of trees, the bright wild flowers and waving grasses. There were two windows and a double door in the Tartoue lodge which gave plenty of ventilation and light in the summer. But because there was no glass in them they were tightly shuttered against the winter, and to Caroline it was like living in a cave. She could feel the weather outside by the sound of pelting snow and hail, the song of rain, the wail of wind, but she could not see the color of the sky or the splendor of sunlight on ice crusted trees. She was always anxious in the morning to bundle into her plaid cape, thick mittens and the fur-lined mocassins that covered her to her knees (a gift from Kemink) creak open the heavy door and *see* what was going on outside.

Every day was a gift of beauty, and no two days were alike.

"I have seen the snow-flashing rainbows like the aurora borealis," she wrote to Ann. "When the sun is up, the world around is so full of glitter and dazzle it is almost too beautiful for human eyes to bear."

It was now Caroline who did the barn chores, fed and milked Lily-Thing, slopped the pig and fed the chickens. Kemink left before dawn to run Pete's trap line.

Many of the settlers took an ax and made extra money by making shingles. But since neither Caroline nor Kemink were skilled with an ax, the only alternative seemed for Kemink to carry on what Pete had done, until spring. His legacy to her had been the lodge, his traps, his guns, and little else. She hoped to trap enough small animals to buy more pigs in the spring. There were always new settlers who needed breeding stock.

Trapping was grueling work even for a woman as strong as Kemink. It was not a pleasant task to pry frozen animals from the clamped, sometimes rusted teeth of the cold metal traps, and to skin them out and dispose of the carcasses. Kemink never complained, but her face was grey and drawn when she came in from a day's run.

Caroline partly enjoyed the barn chores and partly abhorred them. She liked getting outside, breathing the fresh air. There was also something satisfying and heartwarming about feeding the animals, the same sort of feeling one got from caring for a child. The chickens would come squawking and clucking about her skirts the minute she opened the door with their pan of warm water and corn, Lily-Thing would bawl her greeting, and even Mrs. Hog, the pig, would come heaving and grunting to the edge of her boarded enclosure. They became individuals with fascinating personalities as she came to know them.

On below-zero mornings Caroline thought that hell was not hot as rumored—Hell was icy cold—Hell was having to shovel a path before you could get to the barn, then having to shovel a path to the well before drawing icy buckets of water for the impatiently thirsty animals—Hell was stepping in chicken droppings—or having to dig manure from the stall floor—Hell was having every socket in your body feel ready to snap with cold and pain—

Once inside again, there was bread to make, butter to churn, clothes to wash and dry before the fire, lessons to teach and a myriad of other tasks before it was evening chore time.

Caroline and Kemink fell into bed the minute the last supper dish was put away. As Christmas grew nearer, however, they tried to stay up later than the children to work on gifts. Kemink was making each child a pair of mocassins. Firefly's tiny pair was of the lightest doe skin, almost white. The boys' were sturdier with fringe at the ankles and bright beads on the toes. Caroline was knitting heavy mittens for the children and embroidering a sampler for Ann.

"Kemink—do you think Adam will come home for Christmas?"

"The mind should not wear feathers on the head until the eagle has been shot," Kemink replied.

Caroline sighed. She knew her friend was wise, but she wished that just this once Kemink might have said, "Of *course* he will!" however improbable it was.

"Kemink—" Caroline had been rocking in her chair as she embroidered the sampler, but now the rocker stilled, "You—don't think something has happened to him, do you?"

"No," Kemink said. "Bad news travels fast, even in the wilderness." Caroline began to rock again.

"I pray for Firefly's arm—I pray for Adam to come home—and—and nothing happens—" Unexpected tears caught the firelight. "Why doesn't God answer my prayers, Kemink? Doesn't He care?"

Kemink looked into the fire. "I have heard you pray, my friend, and your words would melt the heart of a rock. You pray eloquently. But there is a difference between the prayers of the white men and the prayers of my people."

"And what is that?"

"You do not listen. When a red man prays, he spends much time in silence to listen for the answer."

"I see," said Caroline, and then it was she who stared into the leaping flames.

The day before Christmas Caroline made cranberry and pumpkin pies. She let Dan-Pete and Danny help. The lodge was redolent with vanilla and grated nutmeg. There was an air of contentment with Firefly crooning in her cradle and a kettle humming on the fire for tea. But every now and then Caroline would pause to listen with apprehension to the gathering ferocity of the wind.

The storm had begun at dawn and gathered force all day until now it was a raging blizzard. She thought of Kemink struggling along the forest paths trying to find her way in this maddened white opacity of blindly driven snow and ice.

Although still early afternoon, the shuttered lodge was dark. Caroline lit fresh candles; as if, by the act of making it brighter inside, she could lift her spirits. *If Kemink is not home in another hour I'll go look for her.* She realized even as she made the promise to herself, that it would be a foolish thing to do.

She was taking the pies from the oven, fragrant and perfect, when she heard the sound of horses. *Adam!* The unbidden thought flashed through her mind as she felt her throat constrict.

She set the pie down and hurried to release the bar on the door. A dark, bulky figure, glittering with ice, pushed into the room.

"W'ar are we, Ma'am?" a voice inquired through a muffle of icy whiskers.

"The Tartoué lodge—"

"W'ar at Tartoué's!" the man hollered.

In a moment three more figures half fell, half pushed their way into the room.

Gasping and swearing, they began divesting themselves of their ice-encrusted clothing and boots.

Caroline hurried to use the tea water to make coffee and soon presented each man with a steaming mug.

"We'uz headed to Gill's Landing. Wanted to spend Christmas in Oshkosh and by jeez got los' in the storm," one of the men said. He sent a squirt of tobacco juice sailing into the corner without apology.

Caroline looked at him with disgust. He grinned back at her.

"Where's Big Pete's Indian?" the tallest man asked. He was grizzled like the others but had a more intelligent look about him. His hair was nearly white, worn long in Indian fashion. He had narrow grey-gold eyes with an expression in them that disquieted Caroline. She had seen those eyes before, but she couldn't place where.

"Kemink is out running trap lines. I'm concerned about her. I'm thinking of looking for her, but I'm afraid of getting lost myself."

She hoped one of the men might volunteer to look for Kemink when they had gotten warm, but the tobacco spitter only laughed and said, "No need to worry none. Y' can't freeze no Injun nor lose them neither. They got hide like an animal n' they kin smell their way home."

The other men laughed, but Caroline did not. She got a lantern, lit it, and then went outside and hung it beside the door so that Kemink would be able to see it if she came near. The ice and snow sizzled against the hot glass but the flame continued to flare. She came back, shuddering with the cold, and more than ever worried about Kemink.

"Y' got something to eat?" the white-haired man asked. "We've had nothing since breakfast."

Caroline made dumplings and turnips and brought up berries for the meal.

In the meantime, the men had helped themselves liberally to the pie.

"That's sure nuff good pie," the one called Crater said. He had a pear shaped head, and his clothes were of poor quality, almost rags.

"When I worked in the loggin' camp they had pie ever' meal," he confided. "They cut it in four hunks each pie, and ye could have

66

as much as ye wanted. I niver et nuthin' but pie for days n' days."

"Don't pay him no never mind," said the third man, who had black, grizzly-bear hair on his hands, arms, face and head. "He's foolish."

"I ain't nuther foolish," Crater said.

"You sure got nice boots," Danny said, admiring the polished length of leather of the white-haired man's boots.

"Y' got a good eye, Sonny," the man answered with a smile. "Those boots cost more'n some men make in a year. I won 'em in a poker game."

The two boys gathered close to the men, asking questions.

They were amused and a little cruel in their teasing. One of them showed Danny how sharp his knife was by cutting the buttons off the boy's shirt. Caroline felt like handing him a thread and needle, but she held her temper, deciding that the tobacco spitter was too crude to know better. They seemed jovial and kind enough as they dug with appreciation into the food she had prepared.

After she filled their coffee mugs the second time, Caroline suspected that no one had any intention of trying to find Kemink. Soon it would be dark and the storm was unabated. Wise or not, she felt she had to search for her friend. She went into the lean-to and tied on her fur-lined mocassins. She was reaching for her cloak when she heard a pounding on the door. One of the men opened it and Kemink, her hair white with ice, stumbled into the lodge.

It took twenty minutes to extricate the Indian woman from her sleet-covered clothing. Her hands and face looked as if they had been burned, but she assured Caroline that this was good.

"When there are white spots, then must one worry," she said. As soon as she was free of her outside clothing, she drew Caroline into the lean-to.

"Caroline, these men are bad men. The white-haired one is Omar Pettigrew. Big Pete had dealings with him and bad words with him more than once. We cannot harbor them. They must go."

"But—Kemink—" Caroline protested. "You can't turn them out into a storm like this. That would be murder."

She was amazed when Kemink answered in a voice of iron, "I can—and will. They must go."

15

Caroline looked at Kemink incredulously.

"Kemink—it's *Christmas,* and we're supposed to be Christian women. —how can we turn four men out in a freezing blizzard?"

Caroline and Kemink had never exchanged one seriously cross word—even under trying circumstances. Now they faced each other with growing tension that made them both feel unhappy and uncomfortable. Kemink finally weakened. She said, "Very well, Caroline. They will stay as long as they behave. One false word or move and—" She made a sweeping gesture with her hand.

The women returned to the other room. Perhaps having a good notion of what had been going on, Pettigrew said with sudden gallantry, "Look, Crater, the little lady has her cape on to go out and do the chores. We wouldn't want her out on a night like this, would we? You and Ferkus bundle up and go take care of them."

Crater began to ready himself without a murmur, but Ferkus grumbled under his breath.

"I'll go along and show them what has to be done, Mama," Danny offered.

"It's terribly cold out there—" Caroline said uncertainly.

"I'll dress warm, Mama!"

"I'll watch out for 'em," Crater promised.

So the little boys, Crater, and Ferkus went together to take care of the chores.

The tobacco spitter drew a flask from his back pocket.

"You still look cold, Injun," he said to Kemink. "How 'bout something to warm you up?"

"I don't want liquor drinking in my house," Kemink said, her lips thin.

The man laughed, tilted the flask and drank anyway, passing it to Pettigrew.

"We're still 'bout chilled to the bone Mrs. Tartoué. Think of it as medicinal," he said with a pleasant wink, and tilted the flask in his turn.

Caroline and Kemink did the dishes in silence. They were glad when Dan-Pete and Danny returned from helping with the chores. They had worried that the men or children might lose their way even in the short distance from the shed to the lodge. It was a relief to have the children back in the house safely.

The boys had been promised they could trim the tree. Kemink shelled popcorn and popped it while Caroline threaded needles and showed them how to string first a cranberry and then a popped corn on the string. She looked up to see Crater watching, mouth agape, face yearning. With a smile she threaded a third needle and gave it to him. His fingers were so clumsy he did poorly and yet he looked happy and absorbed, sitting cross-legged on the hearth with the two boys.

The other men had started a game of poker. There was much passing of the flask.

The project of the tree well started, Caroline sat down to rock Firefly to sleep, but Danny begged, "Light the candles on the tree so 'Fly can see them 'fore she goes to sleep!"

So Caroline roped the first strings of popcorn and cranberries in loops about the small tree and then arranged and lit the candles.

The poker players paid little attention to the Christmas ritual going on in the corner, but Crater was transfixed. The tree candles leaped again in bright flames of light in his marvelling eyes, and his mouth hung open even more than usual.

"Ohhh—Ohhh—" Firefly gurgled, reaching toward the dazzling lights with her good arm.

While Caroline rocked the baby to sleep, Kemink narrated the Christmas story in her fine dramatic way. The boys were beginning to droop against each other with sleepiness. Crater sat with his head cocked, listening along with the children.

Instead of bundling them into the trundle bed, Kemink took the boys into the lean-to and she instructed Caroline to bed Firely in their bed. Caroline wondered at putting the children into the lean-to, which was colder than the main lodge.

Kemink snuffed out the candles on the tree and dragged some heavy furs before the fireplace.

"You can bed there," she told the men.

"You all goin' to bed?" Ferkus asked.

"You'll have to forgive us, we're tired," Caroline said.

She followed Kemink into the lean-to and was surprised again when Kemink pulled a chest in front of the door.

"Those men certainly *do* frighten you, don't they?"

"Yes," Kemink said, "they do."

Caroline had not lied about being tired. She thought she would sleep the minute she got into bed, but she found herself listening to the growing raucousness on the other side of the door, the shouts and obscenities.

"They're—they're getting drunk," she whispered to Kemink.

"Try to sleep," Kemink said.

Caroline had almost obeyed Kemink when there was a rasping sound as the door was forced open, causing the chest to scrape across the boards. The red fire and candlelight from the other room leaped into the lean-to and with it came a dark staggering form.

"Hey, brown hair, I won you in poker," the tobacco spitter chortled.

The next moment she found herself pulled from the covers and felt his hairy whisker laden mouth against her face. She felt a rush of terror and revulsion and began to scream and beat on him.

They struggled about in the darkened room, he laughing and she screaming and flailing. Danny was up then, too, beating on him and shrieking.

But it was Kemink who stopped it. The man suddenly felt cold steel against his temple.

He was not too drunk to understand that. He released Caroline.

"Kemink—we can't turn them out into—into that," Caroline said. Even sobbing and bruised, she still felt it would be murder to force the men into the blizzard.

"Get some rawhide," Kemink said, nodding at the man to step to one of the poles that supported the lean-to. Caroline tied the man's wrists behind him at Kemink's bidding and then around the pole.

Kemink herded the other three into the lean-to and Caroline repeated the process.

"He didn't mean no harm. He was jus' funnin'," Pettigrew protested.

Kemink kept the gun trained between his eyes.

"This ain't smart of you, Injun." Pettigrew threatened.

Kemink checked the knots Caroline had made and nodded her approval. She gathered up blankets and children and shut the door on Pettigrew's threats and recriminations.

"You shoulda killed him. He was hurtin' my Mama," Danny told Kemink indignantly.

"No—Danny, no," Caroline whispered, but she wondered what she would have done without Kemink and the rifle. She had always thought herself absolute in her non-violent philosophy, but what would she have done if they had tried to hurt one of the children?

It was a long time before any of them would settle down to sleep.

In the morning, Kemink cut the rawhide and herded the men into their jackets at gun point. As Caroline helped, she looked into Pettigrew's eyes and knew where she had seen such eyes before. They were like the eyes of the wolf that had confronted her before Firefly's birth.

"Now, c'om Mrs. Tartoué," Pettigrew pleaded. It's still mighty cold out there—"

But Kemink never digressed from her intent to get them into their saddles and down the road.

"Don't come back!" she said, sending a bullet zinging over their heads in emphasis.

It was still freezing cold, but the blizzard had stopped.

The incident left a pall over Christmas day. But it was not half so sad as the next day. Kemink had gone out to run a short trap line. She came back in despair.

"They took everything," she said. "They must have circled back during the night. All the flour, all the sugar, all the salt—all the hides—all our supplies"

All the hides that Kemink had worked so hard to amass, all those days of freezing and walking and keeping on—Caroline knew what those furs had cost her friend and now they were all gone.

Pettigrew had kept good his word to make them pay. Lily-Thing, scheduled to calve in March, had virtually dried up. There was little milk. No butter or cheese. Without grains to feed the chickens, there would soon be no eggs.

"We will know hunger before spring," Kemink said.

In the root cellar they found that the barrel of salt pork had been taken, too, but there were still potatoes and rutabagas, and onions.

Two days later, they found a freshly dressed buck on their doorstep.

"Sashwatka," Kemink said.

The lodge was filled with the smell of roasting venison, and the women's spirits rose. But even as Kemink set the things on the table for their feast, a new crisis beset them.

Firefly had caught a cold. She burst into one of her fits of coughing. Caroline picked her up to comfort her. The coughing went on and on.

"Goodness," Caroline said. She looked up at Kemink and the expression on her friend's face frightened her.

"Kemink, *what is it?*" she asked, and Kemink, too stricken to lie, said, "Whopping cough. She's got whooping cough, Caroline."

16

Before the siege was over, all three of the children had whooping cough. Kemink and Caroline took turns nursing. The lodge had the fetid odor of sickness and onions. Onions because Kemink made a cough syrup of honey and onions to ease their croupy throats. Firefly coughed until she turned blue. Kemink showed Caroline how to turn her upside down and with her fingers extract the phlegm from her throat.

Moving in a miasma of weariness, Caroline never doubted the children would get well. Only after all three were on the road to recovery did Kemink reveal the depth of her terror. She had lost two children born before Dan-Pete with the dread malady.

The weather celebrated the children's return to health with a January thaw. The sky remembered how to be blue. Birds, which had been only dark silhouettes of misery in brief rushes above the frozen terrain, found their voices and sang. Snow melted from the trees, the edge of the lodge and shed, sounding like splashing fountains.

Weakened from the long hours of nursing, Caroline felt giddy in the sweet warming air when she went outside. She stood in a daze, listening to the ice sliding from the trees and watching the pale sunlight tinge the snow with gold.

But this beneficent interlude of nature was only a prelude to the worst disaster of the winter for the women. The snow, which frozen and crusted had supported Kemink on her snowshoes, was now rotten and treacherous. As she made her way along her neglected trap run, it gave way beneath her in places, and she would sink to her knees or waist in the melting drifts. The muskrat traps were set along the banks of the river, and one afternoon Kemink slipped on one of the melting banks and slid down to the river, plunging through the sun-thinned ice.

If the accident had happened earlier in the day, it would have been less disastrous, but it occurred late in the afternoon when the sun grew low and the temperature dropped. By the time Kemink arrived back at the lodge, it was dark and she was a human icicle, her buckskin clothing a frozen sheet encasing her.

With sewing shears and hunting knife, Caroline cut the wrappings from Kemink's body. As she cut and pried the frozen mocassins from Kemink's feet, Caroline looked up at her friend with a question too terrible to voice.

"Yes," Kemink said through chattering teeth, "They are frozen."

Danny and Dan-Pete brought tub after tub of snow into the lodge and Caroline, sweating with exertion and fear, rubbed Kemink's legs and feet until at last a pink glow and then a blue-red mottled color came back to the limbs, except for two toes on the left foot.

The following morning Kemink was unable to run the trap line. She had a high fever and the two toes were turning black.

The weather had taken a turn for the worse again. A storm raged and the melting drifts were replenished and refrozen.

Caroline made a bed for Kemink close to the fireplace. She tried to feed her the honey and onion concoction and to get warm tea and broth into her. Alternating between chills and fever, Kemink would break into strange lyrical passages of Algonquin. At other times she muttered incoherently, thrashing wildly.

By the end of the week in spite of all Caroline had tried to do, Kemink had pneumonia, and the frozen toes were putrefying, sending red tongues of infection up the instep. Caroline, dropping the covers, turned away gagging and overcome with panic. She had no one to whom to turn. It was all she could do to keep from giving in to her terror in front of the children. She flung on her cloak and fled outside into the early sullen dawn.

What am I going to do? What am I going to do? she cried. *If I don't get a doctor, she's going to die*—Even if she found the courage to amputate the toes, all her efforts against the pneumonia seemed futile. Kemink was growing worse every day.

Caroline looked at the dark palisade of trees that fenced her in like a prison. If she left the children alone, and started for help, there was little chance she would make it alive. She did not even have a horse. She was encapsuled in a frozen world. There seemed no help anywhere.

She began to sob. Hysteria mounted inside her. How could Adam have done this to her? How could he leave them alone, two helpless women in this wild, savage country. How could he? How could he?— Hatred, blind fury ravaged through her.

"I hate you, Adam, I hate you, I hate you, I hate you!" she screamed, beating against the bark of a tree. But an inner voice spoke sharply to her. *"Stop this! Get hold of yourself. This isn't going to help*

Kemink. Think. What would Kemink do—if it were you lying in there? She wouldn't stand beating against a tree trunk."

What would Kemink do? She remembered the night of Big Pete's death watch she had told Danny that Kemink was surrounded by invisible help, God's angels. Were they there now? All around her? Within shouting distance? Was she, after all, not alone?

She looked around, trying to penetrate the stark black growth of trees, the endless white of snow. She tried to hoot like Kemink, but only a hoarse, broken noise came out. *Dan-Pete!*

Caroline hurried back to the lodge, ran into the lean-to where the boys were sleeping and shook Dan-Pete awake.

"Dan-Pete—get up! Hurry! Come with me at once."

Frightened by her urgency, but obedient, the little boy unrolled from the blankets.

"Dan-Pete, your mother is ill. We must have help. Can you hoot for Menominees to come as your mother would?"

"I think so," said Dan-Pete. He gave a practice try.

"Oh, it sounds right, Dan-Pete," Caroline cried. "Please come outside and try, Dan-Pete. Hurry."

Bundled into his outer clothes, Dan-Pete followed her outside and began to hoot. He hooted until he was hoarse. There was no answer. Caroline would not give up.

"Perhaps, if we go farther," she said. They walked deeper into the undergrowth, until she was afraid they would get lost. But now she thought she heard an answer.

"Ohh, try again Dan-Pete, try again!" she pleaded. Had it only been a mourning dove, the sound of a branch scraping against the snow? No—there it was again.

"Oh, Petey, someone's *heard* you!" she cried.

Dan-Pete hooted again, and this time the answer was unmistakeable and so close they jumped. A moment later an Indian brave stepped through the growth.

Caroline took an involuntary step backward. Now that he was here she was not sure what to do. She couldn't speak Algonquin and he couldn't speak English.

"Tell him your mother is very ill. Tell him we must have a doctor, a white doctor," Caroline urged Dan-Pete.

Dan-Pete spoke in Algonquin and the brave answered.

"He say he wants to see my mother," Dan-Pete translated. The brave was already striding ahead of them toward the lodge. Caroline and Dan-Pete scrambled behind the best they could.

By the time they reached the lodge, the brave was kneeling at Kemink's bedside. The face he turned toward Caroline convinced her

74

that he understood the seriousness of the situation.

He stood up and spoke rapidly to Dan-Pete.

"He say white doctor may not come for Indian. White doctor far away and old man. He maybe would not come even for you. But Sashwatka say write note to doctor and he will get him to come. He say he will send Indian Shaman also."

He was gone so swiftly Caroline did not have time to thank him.

An Indian woman arrived at the lodge. She put on a strange head-dress and arranged poultices on Kemink's chest and toes. She shook rattles and muttered incantations. But all the while she shook her head in a hopeless way. Other Indians began to arrive. They set up a keening.

Caroline found their wailing insupportable.

"Please, Dan-Pete, tell them to stop," Caroline begged. "Tell them your mother needs quiet. Tell them to go away."

They looked at her with reproving eyes, but left the lodge. They stood vigil outside. When one group could no longer endure the cold, they were replaced by another group.

Kemink was burning with fever.

When it was almost dark, she had a lucid moment. The Indian Shaman woman was sitting cross-legged at the foot of the bed, half asleep, wearied with the efforts she had expended. Dan and Dan-Pete were outside struggling with the chores. Caroline was making an effort to get some liquid between Kemink's lips, when suddenly her eyes opened with an expression of recognition.

"Kemink!" Caroline said.

"Caroline—promise—"

She closed her eyes and it seemed she would sink back into the fever.

"Kemink—Kemink," Caroline pleaded.

The dark eyes opened again; the parched lips struggled to form words.

"Promise—take care of Dan-Pete—promise—"

Caroline felt the edge of hysteria rising within her again.

"Kemink—*don't*. Don't talk like that. *You're* going to take care of Dan-Pete yourself. Kemink, don't leave me!"

The glazed eyes, sunk into the flesh, were full of entreaty.

"Pro—mise—"

"Yes, yes, yes,—" Caroline cried, tears scalding her cheeks.

Kemink's eyes closed. There was a strange sound in her throat.

The Indian Shaman jumped up. She made harried motions with a plume and shook her assorted bags with renewed fury. Then she shook her head and went out. Caroline heard the Indians outside start a keening cry.

Caroline knelt paralyzed, understanding. The noise in Kemink's throat was a death-rattle.

17

The light in the lodge grew redder and more dim, as the last log in the fireplace fell into coals. Overcome by emotion, Caroline did not notice the fireplace needed replenishing.

Outside, torches were beginning to flare in the darkness as more Indians arrived to keen and bewail the approaching death of Kemink Tartoué.

Caroline felt hope ebbing from her as surely as life was ebbing from Kemink. It took nearly a day by canoe to get to Weyauwega. It would take even longer by horseback through woods made impassable in places by drifted snow. Sashwatka seemed uncertain that the doctor would agree to come even then—and if he did, how many more days would it take by the far more circuitous route needed to bring a sleigh if the doctor was too old to ride horseback? At best, Caroline might expect the doctor by nightfall the following day if both Sashwatka and the doctor rode like demons. Too late—too late—each beat of her heart said. Why hadn't she thought to call for help in the Indian way before Kemink had sunk so low? Why? *Why?*

Outside the wail of the Indian mourners joined the wail of the winter wind. Inside there was no sound but the rattle of Kemink's labored breathing and Caroline's sobs.

"Please Lord," she pleaded, "don't let Kemink die. Please, *please,* Lord. We need her so much. I can't go on without Kemink. I've tried to serve you. I know I've failed sometimes. But please, Lord, please have mercy. Don't take Kemink away from us—away from her little boy."

The sound of her agonized voice echoed from the walls. She stopped praying—listened, with tears running down into her mouth. What was it Kemink had said—*"You pray most eloquently, my friend—the red man listens."*

She struggled to her feet, moved uncertainly through the semi-red darkness of the room and found her Bible and knelt.

She opened the book randomly with shaking fingers.

In the red light of the dying fire, she read: "Every valley shall be filled, and every mountain and hill shall be brought low, and the crooked shall be made straight, and the rough ways shall be made smooth; and all flesh shall see the salvation of God."

She closed her eyes against the seeping tears and—*listened*. Gradually her tense body drooped with weariness. She stopped sobbing. Her tears dried. She began to have a sense of something warm enfolding her. She had a sudden memory of her mother sewing—looking up from her sewing at her as a child. She remembered the way her mother's love had flowed out to her, intangible yet real. She became aware of a similar feeling of light and warmth and love. Then something else flowed into her—an assurance that *Kemink would live!*

Outwardly nothing had changed. The Indians still keened. The breath continued to rattle in an ever more ghastly and more faltering way in Kemink's throat. The fire had died now and Caroline found herself sitting in the dark. The only thing that had changed was that her fear had been stilled, the way Jesus had stilled the waves of the tempest.

Calm now, she arose and rekindled the fire. It was starting to leap again into a good blaze when the door of the lodge burst open and Dan and Dan-Pete came in, two small frozen figures. Frozen with cold, frozen with fear, frozen with grief.

"Is my mother dying?" Dan-Pete cried. He flung himself against Caroline, his fingers clutching her skirts.

"No, Dan-Pete," Caroline said with certainty.

Slowly he drew his face from her skirts and turned his gaze toward the fireplace where his mother's profile was highlighted by the new blaze of fire.

"You lie to me," the little boy sobbed.

"No," Caroline said with the same conviction. "Your mother is going to get well, Dan-Pete. I feel it."

Danny crept closer and closer until he was standing next to Kemink.

"My mother would not lie to you, Dan-Pete," he said, aggrieved that his friend would dare to question his mother's veracity. "Look, Dan-Pete, your mama is not hot anymore."

The rattle in Kemink's throat had stilled. There was no sound in the room, except the crackling fire. Caroline felt a gradual release of the tight grip on her skirts. Dan-Pete, his eyes enormous, began to shuffle one step at a time toward his mother.

He reached out one small hand with hesitancy and dread touching his mother's cheek. He had touched his father in death, and he remembered that coldness—that forever coldness. True—his mother's cheeks were no longer hot and red with the fires of her fever—but had all fires stilled forever in that loved one?

Tentatively his small fingers stroked his mother's cheeks.

He looked up at Caroline, his eyes brilliant.

"Aunt Caroline—Dan speaks the truth. My mother is warm. My mother lives!"

With a cry of joy he ran outside the lodge and shouted in Algonquin and then again in English, "My mother lives!" He shouted it to the Indians, and the tall black shrouds of the trees, and the thin sprinkle of winter stars, to the snowheld earth and the hooting owl—"My mother lives!"

The Indian keening ceased. There was a babble of voices. After a moment the Shaman came into the lodge. She bent and listened to Kemink's breathing. She touched her skin. She folded back the covers to inspect the poultices. Then she turned and looked at Caroline in a strange way.

Other Indians were crowding silently into the lodge. Craning over each other's shoulders to see if it were true.

The Shaman woman had told them that Kemink's soul was leaving. She could not now with honor claim she had healed her patient when she had so lately passed a death verdict. A lesser woman might have worried about her status at that moment, but this Menominee Shaman was a great woman.

She turned and spoke to the Indians with a low voiced intensity. Then she walked to Caroline and, drawing the many layered necklace she wore from around her neck, slid it over Caroline's head and left the lodge.

One by one the Indians came and removing belts, beads, and bracelets laid them at Caroline's feet.

"What is happening?" Caroline asked Dan-Pete, perplexed. "What did she say?"

"She said you are a great healer," Dan-Pete translated.

"But I didn't—" Caroline protested. "God healed your mother. Not *me,* Dan-Pete."

"They know," Dan-Pete said. "They know it was the Great Spirit, but Shaman woman say you touched by God. You are a healer."

Caroline made the boys go to bed after a simple meal of turnips and dried venison, but she continued to sit by Kemink's bedside.

Toward morning Kemink opened her eyes and smiled. The fingers Caroline was holding tightened for a moment around hers, then Kemink drifted back to sleep.

Caroline could not sleep; she was too suffused with emotion. She went outside and walked under the stars, her feet crunching in the snow. Light was beginning to rim the trees. She felt like a person newly in love. She was gripped by a religious exaltation.

She murmured over and over again, *"You are,* oh, God, you really are!"

Before she had believed. Now she felt she *knew*—and the entire force of her being resounded with that knowing.

In the morning Kemink took nourishment. She smiled at Caroline as her friend fed her.

"I almost did not come back."

"I know. Oh, how I know—Kemink."

"Caroline—I was in a place so beautiful. There were people there— so happy. Little children are not so happy as the people that were there. I wanted to stay."

"Thank you, Kemink, for not staying," Caroline said. "We need you so." She pressed her friend's hand against her cheek.

The following day at dusk the doctor arrived, accompanied by Sashwatka and Cricket McGuire. Doctor William Kennicut was a fusty little man with a barrel tummy. His pale compassionate eyes did not seem to belong in his plump, sagging face.

While he examined Kemink, Caroline told him about the miracle of her recovery.

"Well, young lady," he said skeptically, "I'd be the last one to say that there are no miracles or that faith don't count. I seen too many cases myself where a body ought to a died and just plain struggled on in faith and will power. On the other hand, in pneumonia there is a crisis point. Your friend just plain passed the crisis point and started to get better. At any rate, your miracle didn't seem to extend to those toes. They're gonna have to come off or she'll lose the whole leg to gangrene."

Cricket, watching the color evaporate from Caroline's face, volunteered to help the doctor so she wouldn't have to.

"You jus' keep the youngsters outside with you 'til it's over," the frontiersman instructed.

"Oh, Cricket, how will she stand it?" Caroline asked.

"She'll do fine," Cricket assured. "Doc's got laudanum."

Sashwatka and Kemink talked for some time in Algonquin.

"He'll stay with Kemink 'til it's finished," Cricket translated. "She's pleased 'bout that. She knows it's gotta be done. She hain't afraid."

Caroline and the boys walked outside in the snow, carrying Firefly until Cricket summoned them and told them it was over.

The cabin smelled of laudanum and whiskey when they came in from the cold. Kemink was asleep.

With hands that wouldn't quit shaking, Caroline poured coffee for the men.

"Everything's—all right?" she questioned.

The doctor was looking at her in a strange way.

"Well, Missy," he said, rubbing his chin, "I ain't so sure but what you had yourself a bona fide miracle at that. The length of time that's gone by, those gangrene toes should have sent poisoning at least to the ankle—"

Caroline remembered the streaks of red starting up Kemink's instep.

"But there was no poisoning, Missy, nothing. After I got them toes off, the rest was clean. Either you had yourself a miracle all right or that greasy old poultice that Indian stuck on was a whole lot more potent that I ever gived 'em credit for. It was like them toes was plumb sealed off from the rest of her and woulda dropped off in their own good time, anyway."

The doctor took a slurp of his coffee.

"There is just a heap that none of us knows anything about," he concluded.

18

When Caroline made supper that night, she apologized because there was no coffee. The pot she had made earlier had used up the last she and Kemink had been saving for a special occasion.

"Wull, now—" said Cricket, "Y' got flour, y' got salt, y' got coffee, and y' got sugar and tea, 'n candles, 'n y' didn't even know it. Thet's how I happen to be here in the first place. I jus fergot to brang 'em in."

He took Dan and Dan-Pete along with him to help tote in sacks from his saddlebags which had been stored in the shed.

"How did you know we needed these things?" Caroline asked, overjoyed. The whole family was tired of turnips and potato soup.

"I run into Crater in Embarrass a few days back, and he tole me how Pettigrew and his bunch used you women at Christmas. Crater felt real bad. He said you give him the only real Christmas he ever had. He knew I had been Big Pete's friend, so he 'fessed up to me. He was feared ye might not have enough to get through the winter. So I fetched up this stuff and was comin' this way when I run into Doctor Billy and this Injun feller," Cricket explained.

After all, Caroline thought, their kindness to the motley bunch at Christmas had not gone entirely unrewarded.

In a lower voice Cricket said to Caroline, "We had no idee you two women was out hyar all alone. It's a hard country for a man, to say nothin' o' women."

A muscle trembled at the corner of Caroline's mouth. She looked up from her task of measuring coffee beans into the grinder.

"Cricket—have you heard anything of Adam?"

"Nothin' but rumors. Somebody said he was workin' at a lumber camp. Niver struck me thet Adam would take to thet, though. Ain't heard anything about him running his circuit, though. Several folks was compainin' that he hain't stopped back like he promised. You two have troubles, Miz Caroline?" You wanna talk about it?"

She shook her head.

"You're a good man, Cricket. A good friend," Caroline said, giving his arm a little squeeze before she turned away to get water for the coffee.

Sashwatka had stayed silently by Kemink's bedside until she had regained consciousness. Caroline begged him to stay for supper with the rest, but he declined and left. Although Kemink was too weak to come to the table, she was regaining her strength well and was able to sit propped up in the bed so she could feel part of the convivial circle joined around the table for supper.

For the first time since Thanksgiving, Caroline put on her grandmother's linen cloth, set the table with her sterling teaspoons and lit all the candles. The table looked festive, and Caroline was hardly less flushed with pleasure and excitement at having guests than the children were.

With Caroline engrossed in Kemink's illness, Firefly had gotten little attention of late, with much of her care being put on the two boys who were not always the epitome of patience. She was eight months old now and already taking her first uncertain steps. As Kemink had predicted, she was going to walk young.

She was delighted with the candles, the company, the return of her mother's attention. Holding on to the table, she made a game of tottering first to Cricket and then to the Doctor and beaming up into their faces. The two men were charmed, but Caroline noticed the doctor's eyes studying the limp and lifeless arm.

"She was born that way," Caroline said. "Can anything be done?"

The doctor picked up the toddler and moved her limp arm about. Then he tickled her a little, making her squirm and giggle and set her back on the floor.

"I'm jus' an old wilderness doctor, Missy, and I ain't to be believed one hundred per cent, but I'm afraid the only thing that'll help thet arm is another one o' yer miracles. Luckily it's the left arm. She seems to manage pretty good with her right, 'n with dimples and a smile like thet, someday some young man'll come along and won't notice a thing wrong."

Caroline mentally rejected the doctor's attitude of accepting the affliction and making the best of it. If it would take a miracle, well then, she would *have* a miracle. Whatever the doctor thought, what-every anyone thought, she was convinced God had healed Kemink, brought her back from the brink of death. That same love and power must work for Firefly. *God doesn't will her to be like this,* she thought, looking at Firefly with heart-rending love.

When the dishes were done, Cricket called Dan and Dan-Pete to him and demanded, "Wull, now, ye'all bring out thet mouth organ I give ye and let me hear what ye kin play on it."

Dan looked at Dan-Pete. Dan-Pete looked at Dan.

"We can't play nothing!" Dan-Pete finally confessed.

"Ye can't play nothin'!" Cricket roared in mock outrage. "Now how kin thet be? Wull, then fetch it to me."

Dan-Pete pulled it out of his pocket and handed it over to Cricket.

His big hands swallowed the instrument as he raised it to his mouth. All the boys could see were his hands moving, but where only doleful noises had emerged for them, Cricket filled the lodge with gay melody.

Doctor Billy amused the children by singing four stanzas of "Sweet Betsy from Pike" to the accompaniment of the harmonica.

> "I'll tell you the story of
> Sweet Betsy from Pike,
> Who crossed the wide mountains
> With her lover Ike.
> With two yoke of oxen
> And one spotted hog,
> An old Shanghai rooster
> And one yellar dog—"

The evening was gay. Caroline had not realized how hungry she had been for fun and companionship outside their own small circle. The boys hopped in dances of their own devising to the foot tapping tunes Cricket played. Kemink clapped her hands in time to the beat now and then. The doctor took Firefly in his arms and did a bow-legged waltz.

Adam would have disapproved, Caroline thought with a twinge of guilt. Then she brushed away the thought of Adam and guilt and danced with the Doctor herself.

"We ain't gonna leave you two women so forlorn no more," Cricket promised the next day, as he and the doctor prepared to leave. "I'm gonna check up on you now and then 'n when I can't make it, I'll have somebody else passin' this way look in on ye."

"We'll be all right, now," Caroline said. "It's almost spring."

"I hate to tell ye, Missy," the old doctor said, "but ye don't know much about Wisconsin winters it's plain to see. We get some of our best snow storms in March."

"You mean worst," Cricket affirmed.

It seemed very quiet after the two men left. Kemink still needed rest and the children were shushed so as not to disturb her. The doctor had said she would walk almost as well as ever once she got used to the toes being gone, but she would never be able to walk long distances again, which would rule out continuing Pete's trapline. Kemink was unconcerned. She had lived off the land all her life. She had no qualms that Mother Earth would not go on sustaining her. But Caroline fretted within herself—*how were they to live?* She had given up hope of Adam's return, and without Adam, what reason was there to go on trying to eke an existence on this hard frontier? She knew Ann would welcome her in Chicago. Bromley was doing well; it would be no financial hardship for him to welcome his sister's family into his household. Still Caroline felt it would be unfair to arrive bag and baggage on their door step, but how else was she to manage with two small children to raise and no money or means of support?

Perhaps I could teach—she thought, remembering how she had enjoyed teaching music to people in Adam's congregations.

She had once briefly made the acquaintances of a young lady named Lydia Millerd, who was a teacher in the New London area. Caroline now set about writing a letter to Miss Millerd, inquiring how she got her teaching position. The letter was given to Cricket to mail the next time he stopped by as he had promised.

Three weeks later an answer was delivered to the lodge by a passing farmer on his way home from Weyauwega.

Dear Mrs. Quimby, (Lydia wrote)

In the year 1852, my family moved to the Village of New London.

The village consisted of two families. I was chosen teacher, being the only young lady in town who could devote time to the undertaking.

The next thing to be considered was the certificate. As you perhaps know, teachers are placed under the supervision of Town Superintendents.

The Superintendent came on Sunday. The much dreaded examination consisted of the questions: "Where are the Straits of Bering?" and "How far have you been in Arithmetic?" Grammar and all other studies were omitted, I suppose for the sake of brevity. He asked me to give him a sample of my penmanship. I wrote 'Sabbath morning', leaving out one of the "b's" in the first word, which fortunately did not prevent me from being accepted.

Our own house is sixteen by twenty-two feet, the front part is occupied as a store, while the back part is used both as our home and as a hotel. As there is no room there in which to keep a school, we organized it upon the stairs and kept it there until the weather became warmer.

On the bank of the Embarrass River there is a double log house. Part of it has been used for a warehouse and the other part for a stable. As the weather became warmer, it was found necessary to provide a school room for us, so we moved to the old warehouse, which was obliged to do double duty, for the boat came often during school hours.

The other half of the building is still used as a stable, and in warm weather the flies are very thick, as the oxen are kept standing there through the day. With their lowing and stamping of feet, the unloading of freight, and the occasional visit of an Indian, our school is not a model of order.

There are seven pupils enrolled, but the average attendance is about two and one-half. One of them in particular I am never sure of. He is always here at roll call, but when it is time for him to read, he is generally missing. Being extremely hard to catch, he usually goes without instruction in that subject.

"At the end of the year I received $10, which I invested in real estate that since has brought me $300.

I have written all this to you at length in the hope that seeing how primitively we operate and how few special qualifications I have, you will feel quite sure of your competence to set up and teach school. You struck me as being a genteel and learned woman.

Most sincerely your friend and servant,
Lydia Millerd

Miss Millerd added in a post script that she believed a Miss Chandler was teaching in Weyauwega, but she thought there was no teacher in Royalton and Caroline might possibly seek a position there.

Caroline immediately wrote a letter of application, but as the doctor had warned her, new showers and avalanches of snow poured down the first part of March, making the roads and trails again impassable, and Cricket, who had taken Mrs. Hog to be bred did not return to post her letter.

Lily-Thing gave birth to a fine black bull calf during one of the worst storms. There was rejoicing in the lodge for now once more there would be milk to drink, cream for berries, and butter and cheese. Danny was given the honor of naming the calf by Dan-Pete, to whom the calf was to belong. Danny chose Ezekiel after the Biblical prophet about whom his mother had been reading to them. Everyone's spirits were dampened when Ezekiel developed scours and died.

Looking down at the small black calf, Caroline felt the sadness of mortality and felt anew the helplessness of being a woman in this raw country. How was she to dispose of the carcass? The ground was frozen. When she consulted ever-wise Kemink, the Indian woman said sadly, "Have the boys drags the carcass into the woods, the wolves will do the rest."

Caroline helped the boys wrap Ezekiel in an old blanket, and together they dragged their burden as far into the woods as their strength allowed. She stood with her teeth chattering, icy blasts of snow and wind biting her cheeks while the boys conducted a funeral service of their own devising—and then poor Ezekiel was left to the wolves.

That night, listening to the howl of the wolves and the grief-stricken bellowing of Lily-Thing, who missed her calf, Caroline wondered if spring would *ever come*.

19

The spring of 1857 came at last. The air was an elixir of heady scents, the smell of melting snow, thawing mud, new grass and budding trees and then sweet, overpowering rushes of wild plum blossoms.

Caroline forgot her duties and decorum. She hiked up her skirts and ran barefooted along the river bank, skipping stones like a school boy. She loosened her hair and let it blow free in the wind. She swung from tree branches and balanced her way up the trunks of trees that had fallen in the winter.

Merely to stand outside in the sunlight with no heavy wraps after the seemingly endless winter was a miracle. She flung her arms out, embracing spring with rapture. The woods that creaked with silence and mystery all winter suddenly thrilled with murmurs and stirrings and songs and scamperings and rustlings and matings and births.

Kemink watched Caroline's antics with an indulgent smile. She was still weak, but she was up and around and spent a short time each day turning soil in the garden to ready it for planting.

Caroline had confided her plans of trying to find a teaching position, and Kemink had acquiesced to the other's urging that, if that came to pass, the two families would remain united.

They planned that as soon as Kemink had recovered enough strength they would make the trip to Weyauwega. They wanted to advertise Mrs. Hog's expected litter in *The Weyauwegian*. Kemink said Mr. Post would give them spring supplies on credit on the strength of the litter to be sold.

Mrs. Hog grew more satisfyingly portly every day and every member of the family watched her jealously. Since she contained their entire prospects of fortune nothing must be allowed to happen to *her*.

The Indian woman would be summoned again to watch over Fly, but this year the two boys were to be allowed to go along. Full of excitement and anticipation, they watched Kemink as closely as they watched Mrs. Hog for every sign of renewed vigor. Finally, in self-defense, Kemink set a date. The first week in May they would go, she said, but the last week in April brought unexpected company.

The chores and dishes had just been finished when Caroline heard the beat of horse's hooves in the clearing.

"Must be Cricket," she said, and drying her hands on the towel she had just hung up she hurried to the door. But when she opened it, she did not find Cricket. The man standing there was Adam Quimby.

*   *   *

When Adam left Caroline that fall afternoon, he had been almost out of his mind with the rage of his emotions. Usually he was very careful and thoughtful of his stallion, Ebonite. But he had ridden the poor horse at breakneck speed for miles, spurring his sides ruthlessly everytime the animal tried to slacken his speed.

The sun was hanging low above the trees before he came to his senses a little and realized that his horse was a mass of lather beneath him. Belatedly, he dismounted and rubbed the heaving horse down. While Ebonite rested, Adam took his Bible and settled himself on a large flat stone, turning to that familiar source in hope of some solace and silencing of the turmoil within him. He did not notice until too late that the stone was already occupied. A rattler, basking in the last of the afternoon sun, lay coiled on the rock. By the time Adam heard the warning rattle, it was too late, the snake had struck, sinking his fangs deeply into the flesh of the calf just above the edge of his boot.

Adam stared at the two purpling marks left by the fangs, feeling as if the earth itself had turned against him. The leg began to throb immediately. He knew what he had to do, but he was unsure if he had the courage. Could he cut into his own flesh? His fingers were shaking when he got out his jackknife. The first two cuts were too shallow. Finally, gritting his teeth, he sank the blade deep and the blood came. He had heard that one should try to suck out the venom, but the wound was located in such a way that he could not get his mouth to it.

He thought of returning home, but Ebonite was in no condition for the ride. His leg was bleeding profusely—there might be a danger of bleeding to death—and it would soon be dark.

There was a fork in the trail and up ahead he could hear the sound of the river. He was pretty sure that he was within a short distance of the cabin where he had once stopped and visited with the old man. He pulled his boot back on, took Ebonite by the rein, and began to walk on his throbbing leg. His boot was soon warm and sticky with blood and a dark haze kept drifting past his eyes.

Behind him, forgotten on the rock, the pages of his Bible riffled and blew in the breeze. Years later in moments of depression he would sometimes brood that if it had not been for the serpent striking him that day, his entire life might have been different. Perhaps, there in the late afternoon sun, quiet with his Bible, he might have been directed to a different path.

As it was, he staggered half conscious into the old man's cabin just before dark.

"Wull, Laddie, I didn't expect to see ye again this soon!" Levi chortled, and then had to jump up quickly and grab Adam to keep him from falling to the floor.

The cot he laid him on was rumpled and smelled sweaty, but Adam was too sick to care. The old man propped him up and gave him a tin cup of whiskey. Adam drank. He choked, his throat and stomach revulsed against the fiery liquid, but a gradual numbing warmth spread through him.

Maybe, I'm dying, he thought, and at that moment did not care. He was dimly aware that the old man pulled off his boot and ripped his blood-caked pants to the knee.

"Snake bite, huh?" the old man said. "Wull, ye did pritty good, son, but there's still some poison in thar I'm afeared."

He gave Adam another cup of whiskey. By the time he had gulped it down, the room became blurred and he felt almost pleasant. The old man sat on the edge of the bed, sharpening his knife with a whetstone while he whistled through his teeth. He tried it against his thumb and found it satisfactory. He plunged it neatly into the swollen calf. Adam scarcely felt it. Between the poison and the whiskey he was floating in some dark sphere.

"Nasty," the old man said, making a face at the dark liquid and new blood that his knife had drawn. He got a loaf of stale bread, soaked it in milk and wrapped it around the leg.

"Damn waste o' good bread and whiskey," he grumbled. "Greenhorns always gettin' themself snakebit."

But for all his grumbling, he cared for Adam with a clumsy tenderness for two days while the younger man tossed through various phases of delirium. He even baked a new batch of bread so he could put fresh poultices on Adam's leg. On the third day his patient was improved, though he was still a rough looking specimen with saucer sized shadows around his eyes, and whiskers growing across his cheeks like black crabgrass.

Levi felt of his ears and said, "Hell's bells, you're gonna be awright. You kin go home tomorry 'n I hain't sorry. I'm gittin' tired o' sleeping on the floor!"

"I have no home to go to," Adam said morosely. He felt devitalized.

Levi sat down on one of the chopping blocks he used for stools. He chewed on a wad of tobacco.

"Ye talked about her all the time ye was out of yer head. Go home to her, Laddie. Ye're crazy if ye don't."

Adam turned his head toward the wall.

"She was unfaithful to me."

"Go back home. Beat 'er up. Tell 'er if she ever does it again ye'll kill her—but go home. I left a good woman oncet, and I'll tell ye, Laddie, I've lived to regret it." His rheumy eyes traveled around the shack with its jumble of smoky pans and tatters of clothes hung on pegs.

"Go home," he said again very quietly.

"I can't," Adam said. "I can't."

In the innermost part of his mind Adam did not really believe Caroline had been unfaithful. But he had to try to believe it, because even that was preferable to believing that he had fathered a defective child. To the proud, stubborn young man it seemed that, by presenting him with a deformed child, Caroline had laid an ax to all his aspirations—all his hopes—everything that he was. How could he continue to be a minister when this mark of depravity was visible in his own family? He had been vociferous in his denouncing of such evidence in other families. His views were known and debated throughout the region. How could he face his parishioners when his daughter's condition became well known?

Although he had preached humility to others, he had always believed that a minister had to be without blemish, and in truth, had considered that he was.

If Caroline would only confess to adultery, then he could remain blameless before the circuit community. The child's defect could be laid at her door. He would be considered noble for forgiving her. As it was, he would be a laughing stock. He found that unbearable. But Adam could not face this truth. Full of stiff necked pride, and outraged ego, he found it impossible to go home.

"Wull, Laddie," Levi said at the end of the week, "I'm gonna sign on t'a lumber camp for the winter. I gotta do thet ever now n' then or livin' hyar all alone I'd get queer. Ye kin either com' along or ye kin hev' my diggin's. Take yer druthers."

Listless, unsure of what he wanted to do, Adam went with Levi to New London. In the hotel-tavern, the old man promptly set about getting drunk. Adam sat alone, brooding and depressed.

Halfway through the evening, Levi staggered over to the table with a cup of whiskey and handed it to Adam.

"Hyar, Laddie, ye kin hev some. Ye're still sick. Ye kin call it medicine."

Adam remembered the pleasant blur the alcohol had produced during his illness. His inner pain now was certainly as great as his physical pain had been then. In a mood of despair and self-annihilation, he drained the cup. During the rest of the evening he proceeded to get thoroughly drunk.

He awoke the next morning lying in a mule stable, his clothes foul, his breath reeking of whiskey. His head felt as if two battering rams were having a contest inside of it. But worse—far worse—was the realization he had dealt a death blow to his own ambitions of continuing his ministry. If Felicity's birth had been an ax blow to his aspirations, he had finished the job with his own hatchet.

The strait-laced frontiersman took his religion seriously. A minister who preached far and wide against the evils of drink and then himself got publicly drunk was not likely to be respected in the future. Adam turned his face into the straw and wept.

Levi, asleep next to Adam, awoke to the dusty spears of sunlight filtering into the stable and the sight of Adam's shoulders shuddering with sobs. He sat up (not without a groan for he had quite a head on himself) and laid a spavined hand on his young friend's shoulder.

"Go home, boy," he advised again. "Go home and work it out. It ain't too late."

Adam, ashamed of his tears, sat up, too, covering his face with his hands.

"I don't know what to do," he said.

"I'll fetch some water from the pump to wash up with. Then we kin git some breakfast. Hain't no trouble so bad thet breakfast won't help," Levi said. Holding his head between his hands, he made his way toward the pump outside.

Adam brushed the straw from his clothes and then sought out Ebonite. He laid his pounding head against the horse's warm neck and with his hand searched the saddle bag for his Bible. When he couldn't find it, he searched more thoroughly. It wasn't there. In his mood of humiliation and self-degradation, the loss of his Bible seemed a sign to him.

By the time Levi returned with a pail of water, Adam had made up his mind to go with the old timer to the far north logging camp. He felt as if his life was ruined . . . as if nothing mattered, anyway.

20

For a long moment Caroline looked at Adam. She had longed for this moment—prayed for it, but now that he was there, she felt only a numbness.

Adam took off his hat and stepped into the lodge. His black frock coat was nicely brushed. His linen shirt and stock were starched and snowy. His hair and fingernails were meticulously groomed. The sight of Adam's impeccability filled her with bitterness. *He* showed no signs of having suffered a hard winter.

For his part, Adam saw a great change in Caroline. The soft girlish contours of her face had melted away along with every spare ounce of fat on her body. The shining dark hair she had taken pride in, coarsened and roughened by wind and neglect, was caught back carelessly into a bun at the nape of her neck. Her white skin had browned until she was almost as dark as Kemink. There were lines of pain etched around her lips. Yet she had gained something ineffable. He had left a pretty, clinging girl; he had returned to a woman whose eyes blazed, who moved with a new assurance. This woman was partly a stranger and he felt in her a challenge he had not felt in the pretty girl.

Danny came out of the lean-to with Kemink, and Adam saw that his son, too, was a stranger. This was not the roly-poly little boy who had always tumbled head over heels to greet him. This boy was a taller, thin child who made no motion to come towards him or speak to him.

"Dan—son," Adam said.

"Hello, Sir."

The gulf of a winter when Danny had assumed the chores of a man, when he had often had to take on the entire care of his small sister, when he had learned not to cry from chilblains and not to complain if there was nothing but unsalted turnips and onion soup for supper, loomed between them. Danny was not bitter, but so much had happened to him that he felt as if his father were a dimly remembered figure from a far, far past. He was overcome with shyness.

The room was full of constraint.

Only Kemink was at ease.

"I am glad you have come, Adam," she said. "The two of you will need time alone. I will take the children to your cabin for the night."

"You don't have to do that—" Caroline began.

"Yes, we will go," Kemink said firmly.

She gathered up Firefly and her things while the boys got their own.

"Does this mean we don't get to go to Weyauwega?" Dan-Pete whispered to Danny.

"I don't know," Danny whispered back.

When the little entourage had completed their preparations and left, Caroline and Adam stood looking at each other in silence.

"Carrie—" Adam said, finally, holding out his arms, "aren't you glad to see me?"

"I—I don't know," Caroline said.

"Carrie—Carrie, I've missed you so—" Adam said. His arms closed around her and drew her to him. She was stiff and unyielding.

"You think you can leave us here all winter to get by the best we can and then come waltzing back and everything is supposed to be forgotten," Caroline cried, breaking free of his arms.

"Let me tell you about our winter, Adam. All three of the children had whooping cough. Some ruffians came and stole most of our supplies and one of them—one of them tried—ohhh," she buried her face in her hands.

"Caroline, were you hurt?" He tried again to take her in his arms, but she broke away and faced him with anger.

"And worst of all, Kemink nearly died—and I had no way to fetch a doctor. You think you can go off, forget about us all winter, and in the spring I'm supposed to welcome you back with a smile. I'm to the point where I don't think I care whether you're back or not, Adam Quimby."

"Caroline, Caroline—my poor darling, my own dearest," he placated, once again getting his arms around her waist. "You know I would have come back the minute I heard about Pete's death if I could have."

"And what kept you away, Reverend Quimby?" Caroline asked, icily.

"Caroline, after what happened with the baby—I couldn't face my ministry. I was too torn apart to come home, so I signed on with a lumber company. I swear to you I didn't hear about Pete's death until several months after it happened. By then it was impossible to get out of the north woods. We were snowed in. You know I would have come if it were humanly possible."

His hands began caressing her back, his touch evoking memories of

92

love-shared nights—she could feel the bulwark of her anger crumbling, as vignettes of their life together assaulted her.

She saw herself, all properly bonneted and gloved, sitting in the family pew while the handsome new minister preached a sermon of such passion as that staid New England church had not heard for decades. Sunlight had flooded in dust ribbons through the windows onto the young man's expressive face—his flying hands—and his voice, *that* voice, deep and resonant, stoking emotions inside people's breasts like a poker stirring coals—

"My heart panteth after thee like a hart in the desert"—"withhold not your tender mercies"—"Thou art fairer than the children of men—" Did she only imagine that his dark and burning eyes were holding hers? She had felt a flush of shame that she should think such thoughts in the house of the Lord—that she should imagine—and yet—oh, he *was* looking at her, speaking directly to *her*.

"Miss Stollen, would you do me the honor of taking a ride with me this afternoon?"

She had felt suffocated with pleasure, shyness, delight, fear. A century seemed to separate her murmured, "Why—yes, Reverend Quimby, I should like that very much—" from the actual moment when she stepped into his carriage. All her clothes flung about her room as she tried on first this outfit and then that, not one of which seemed grand enough—inner conversations when her imagination tried to dart ahead and live the encounter before it occurred—of anticipated terror. What if she slipped while getting into the buggy?— What if she were tongue-tied in his presence or could say nothing but stupidities?—What if he found her shallow?—What if—?

In the end she wore a vanilla suit with ruffles peaking from the neck and sleeves, a matching bonnet tied with pink ribbons, eau de cologne of roses, and she had carried a fashionable parasol. She had not stumbled getting into his buggy but had managed it with the greatest grace while the entire congregation watched, following an unusually brief afternoon sermon.

He drove the horses to a huge oak tree and beneath the flickering shade took off her bonnet and kissed her. She had been unprepared. In her wildest imaginings in the darkness of her bedroom, such an occurrence had never tried to tiptoe in. Nice girls never kissed anyone until they were engaged.

"Reverend Quimby—I'm—I'm shocked—I—I—" she had stammered, laying both hands across the ruffles at her throat in an effort to make them stop shaking.

"I should never have presumed, except God has revealed it to me—we're destined for each other. You feel it, too. I know you do," he answered her tentative protests with intensity. "Tell me, Miss Stollen—tell me you feel it too."

In the spring he had asked for her hand. She had stood waiting in the parlor, staring at the ferns in the brown wall paper, her throat so dry she was speechless. How strange to love a man. How strange to be willing to leave her mother and father and Ann to follow this dark-eyed man about whom she still knew so little—to his new congregation—could she really?

They were married in July. The day was so hot she felt faint with the weight of her satin gown and the burning light of Adam's gaze.

It was still stifling when they left in the late afternoon. Caroline's feet were propped on her trunk because the buggy was filled with boxes of pots and pans, dishes and bedding, given as wedding presents.

Adam stopped at nine o'clock in a small town twenty miles from their destination of Springford. They took a second floor room in the hotel, moldy smelling and oppressive in the heat. Caroline tied the heavy curtain back from the one small window that opened over a roof top, but no breeze came in. She could smell dust. Somewhere a dog was howling.

Even after she had taken off her "going away suit" and put on her nightgown (which had long sleeves) she could feel perspiration seeping from her hair.

When she heard Adam returning from stabling the horses, she thought, "I wish it weren't like this—so hot—so sticky, and I'm so tired—"

Adam moved quickly, throwing off his tie, his shirt, his boots without embarrassment. His bare torso gleamed in the moonlight. She stood watching him, one hand gripping the brass post of the bed, her shoulders moist from her long heavy hair. The dog kept howling.

As he came toward her she could feel his desire like heat from a stove. Suddenly she was afraid. She thought wildly of leaping through the little window and running across the roof top—

He touched her gently, so gently she felt fear ebb. His mouth brushed hers—his hands touched her. After a few moments she had not known it was hot anymore—or that somewhere a dog was still howling.

The church at Springford had a sawdust floor and rough pine benches for pews. Caroline taught Sunday school, served tea at the Wednesday Ladies' Circle, started a choir, and got pregnant. Adam promoted box suppers and special services to raise money for an organ and pews. He asked for no improvements for the two bare rooms that served as their home. He thought it his duty to upgrade the church. He would have thought it unseemly to ask for a carpet to cover the splintery floor of their bedroom or an indoor pump so that Caroline would not have to carry water.

His eloquence and fervour were soon rewarded, however, with a larger, finer church in the neighboring town of Granesville, where a gracious old parsonage offered most of the amenities of life. There, in a bedroom paneled with rosewood, Caroline endured the slow agony of Danny's birth. There, on a Sunday in June, the baby was christened while Caroline glowed with the triumph of having presented Adam with a son.

The loom of memories wove back and forth replacing the recent bruising memories with kinder ones. He was, after all, Adam, her husband, the man she loved. What right did she have to withhold forgiveness?

He could feel the rigidity of her back softening. He laid his lips against her throat.

"We've hurt each other, and I'm at fault," he said, "but you can't throw seven good years of marriage away! Surely we deserve another chance."

She found she was crying. She laid her head against his chest in tacit assent. She had spoken her anger—but now all that mattered was that he was home. *Adam was home.*

They slept that night in the oversized bed Big Pete had built, cradled in wolf furs. Adam pried open the window that had been sealed shut for so long and they could smell the river and the new greenness of spring.

After months of separation, they embraced and united with an intensity Caroline had never experienced before. She felt melded to Adam spiritually, physically, mentally, in a shattering oneness. Everything they had ever been to each other was strengthened, re-affirmed, exalted in each other's arms.

I am his—she thought in a way she had never felt before.

Adam was breathing deeply as he drifted into sleep. But Caroline wanted to remain awake to continue to hold and feel this epitome of emotion.

"Adam—Adam—" she whispered, nuzzling his bare shoulder with her lips, relishing his presence, his nearness, "Oh, Adam,—I love you so. Don't ever leave me again."

He roused back from the edge of sleep. "Never," he promised. "I'll never leave you again. I've got the problem all solved."

"What problem?" she asked in sleepy puzzlement.

"Felicity. I've found a place to send her."

Caroline's lips stilled on her husband's shoulder.

"Adam, are you asking me to send Felicity away?"

"Caroline," Adam said. "You're my wife. I'm telling you. It will be best for her—and once she is gone, I can continue my ministry. Everything will be as before—"

In a minute he was sound asleep.

Caroline lay rigid at his side, all the glory of the love that had reunited them turning to ashes.

21

When Kemink returned to the lodge with the children the following morning she was astonished to find Caroline placing Firefly's garments in a carpetbag.

"What are you doing, my friend?" she inquired with foreboding.

"Adam is going to take Felicity to an asylum," Caroline said. She was very pale.

Kemink turned and said something in Algonquin to Dan-Pete.

"She wants us to go," Dan-Pete translated to Dan and the two left obediently.

"Will this place make Firefly's arm well?," questioned Kemink.

"I think not," Caroline said. "Adam will not tell me much, but I gather it is a place for handicapped children."

Kemink looked shocked. Caroline continued to lay the tiny petticoats and pinafores in the valise.

"My friend," Kemink said at last, her voice trembling, "seldom do I offer advice unless I am asked—but I find I must speak in this matter, for that child is as dear to me as my own—"

"Kemink, all that you would say, I know, and everything you feel, I feel a thousand fold," Caroline cried, "I am taking a desperate gamble—because—because—I believe in Adam."

"You believe it is right to send this child away?"

"I would sooner tear my heart out. But look at her Kemink—look at her—"

96

Firefly sat where Kemink had placed her, the sun glistening on her dark curls, her cheeks pink with the fresh morning air, playing with the tassels on her moccasins.

"She would melt the heart of an ogre, and Adam is *not* an ogre, Kemink. He says the place is a far piece. I cannot believe that he can take this darling child on a journey of any length, care for her and come to know her—and then *give her up.* I know Adam, Kemink. Remember, I believed Adam would come home and he did."

Kemink remained disapproving.

"Oh, Kemink, you don't know Adam as I do. He *is* a good man."

Firefly pulled herself up and toddled to her mother, peeking up at her coquettishly. With a little cry, Caroline picked her up.

"Do not do this thing," Kemink said, "I plead with you."

At that moment, Adam, who had been seeing to the horse, returned.

"Do you have her ready?" he asked brusquely.

"Adam, you have not seen much of your son yet," Kemink interposed. "Must you depart again when you have just arrived?"

"The sooner the child is away, the better," Adam said. "There will be time to become re-acquainted with Danny when I return. I can see you disapprove, Kemink, but I know what it best for my family."

He strode to Caroline and held out his arms for Firefly. She clung tighter to Caroline. She could not fully realize what was happening, but she felt the charged emotions.

"Come," Adam said sharply.

Frightened even more by her father's tone, Firefly began to cry.

"M-m—m-m-—" she sobbed, fastening her fingers in the ruffle around her mother's neck.

Adam forcibly drew the child away. Firefly began to scream.

"Oh, Adam, no—not like *this*," Caroline cried. "Wait, Adam—*wait!*"

But Adam, upset, was determined. He grabbed the carpetbag in one hand, clutching the screaming, kicking child in the other, and left. Caroline and Kemink ran after him, but he was already mounted on Ebonite with the screaming child before they could stop him.

"What's he doing to Firefly?" Dan-Pete cried. He darted forward, face dark red, muscles straining in his neck. "You put her down! You leggo Firefly!"

He charged toward the stallion trying to grab the bridle, but Adam had already kneed the horse forward, and the little Indian boy was sent sprawling. Adam did not stop to find out if he was hurt.

Kemink dusted her son off, and felt to see that his bones were intact.

"That was foolish, Dan-Pete, but brave," she said.

"Where's he taking her?" Dan-Pete asked, outraged.

"He's—he's taking her to—on a trip. He'll bring her back, don't worry, Dan-Pete," Caroline said, but her voice was faint.

"Please—don't say anything yet, Kemink," she begged. I can't bear anything more right now."

Kemink turned away from Caroline and walked into the woods. Dan-Pete followed her.

Caroline sank down on the doorstep. Danny came and sat beside her, silent, comforting her only with his presence.

"Oh, Danny—you're such a good boy," Caroline said. The hot tears started to come. "He will bring her back, won't he?"

"Sure," Danny said bleakly.

They could still hear Firefly's piercing screams echoing in the clearing.

Kemink and Dan-Pete returned at dusk bringing a mess of fish.

"Are you angry with me?" Caroline asked.

"I was angry," Kemink admitted, "I am not angry anymore. This world is filled with so much of sorrow, should one friend cause more to another friend?"

Adam returned in two days. Alone.

The day was radiant. A light wind turned the new leaves this way and that to catch and reflect the light of the sun and ruffle the lush new growth of grass. Wild roses were sending up brambles around the foundations of the lodge. But all Caroline saw was Adam—*alone*.

She could not make her body move. She stood leaning her palms against the table until he came to her. Her eyes begged him to tell her that it was a mistake.

"You're back so soon? Where is Felicity?"

"She is in safe hands. I arranged to have another party take her."

"Adam—You can not mean you went through with it? No. I don't believe it!" Her voice rose shrilly.

"Caroline, I know this is hard on you," Adam began, "but you must see this is the only way to handle the situation. The child will be much better off among her own kind."

"Her own *kind*. Her own kind! Are you out of your mind, Adam? What do you mean—*her own kind*?"

"You simply will not face the fact that she is a *defective* child, will you, Caroline? Well, that's what she is, and she would only be miserable among normal people—"

"I think I hate you, Adam!"

Caroline wavered as if she were about to faint, but when he reached to support her, she struck his arm away.

"I never dreamed you would go through with it—"

"Caroline, I thought you agreed—that you understood the wisdom—"

"No, no, no—I thought if you took her on a long trip you would learn to love her."

She reeled around the room sobbing convulsively. He watched her, helpless, wanting to comfort her but afraid of being again repulsed. Suddenly her mood changed. She darted to him and flung her arms around his neck.

"Adam, darling Adam, go bring her back. Please—she's our own flesh and blood, our love made flesh. You cannot banish her. Darling, darling, please—"

"Caroline, do you care nothing for *my* future? Can you not see that this is the only way I can continue in my ministry?"

"Ohhh, Adam. You cannot be this monstrously selfish. I cannot believe it." She drew away from him and sank into a chair. "If you will not go, I will. Tell me where you have sent her."

"I made the decision once and for all. I want no more opposition on the matter, Caroline," Adam said sternly. "If we are to continue as man and wife, there is no other way. I will not have this deformed child flaunted before me all my life. She should have been disposed of before you became attached to her—"

"Disposed of—"

"I mean taken to a proper institution for care, of course—"

"Adam, I am not your wife anymore. I want you to leave, and this time don't ever come back. But first, tell me what you have done with *my* daughter!"

"Three nights ago you begged me to never leave you again—"

"What have you done with her?"

"You know that you love me and I love you—"

"Tell me where she is!"

She leaped up and shook him as fiercely as her strength would permit.

"What have you done with her?"

He tried to embrace her. She slapped him, staggering away to throw herself on the bed, sobbing.

He bent over her.

"Caroline, you are working yourself into a frenzy. Stop it!"

She brushed her hair away from glittering eyes.

"Adam—tell me where she is—"

"Caroline, I do not know, in all honesty. I did not want to know. I had a third party make the arrangements, a man named Omar Pettigrew."

"Ohhh, no. *No! No!*" she jumped up.

"Caroline, what is the matter with you?"

"Adam, that's the man who stole our supplies. A terrible man, a thief—and you gave our daughter into his care. Oh, Adam. Oh dear God!"

"He assured me he would take her to an acceptable home."

"A man like that—he might murder her! Adam, you *must* go in search of her. You've got to!"

"Caroline, the thing is done. Put it in the past. Let's start fresh from this moment," he pleaded.

"Will you go and look for her?" Her voice was steel.

"No."

She closed her eyes, pale as if she had died. He reached out to touch her. She jerked from him with revulsion. He straightened, his face as white as hers.

"Is that the way it is going to be?"

"Yes," she screamed, "How can you expect it to be any other way?"

"Then I might as well leave. There's nothing for me here. But remember—just remember—*this time* it was *you* who sent *me* away."

He stopped at the door, waiting, but she did not look up or call after him.

She fell on the bed, exhausted, waiting in her turn, for the sound of Ebonite's hooves to announce his departure.

Only when the sound came did she get up and begin to run as if by the physical act she could escape the torment devouring her. She ran screaming after Adam.

"Go—go—damn you! I'll hate you forever!"

22

Caroline ran until she could not run any farther, then threw herself upon the ground and cried until her eyes were swollen and she couldn't swallow. When her paroxysms of grief were spent, she turned on her back and watched a blur of clouds.

"Where are you, God?"

There seemed no answer to her cry. The universe seemed oblivious to her travail. The clouds moved serenely on. The branches danced in the wind. An insect crawled up a blade of grass. What did the universe care for the grief and heartbreak of a Caroline Quimby? Certainly the clouds didn't care, or the insect, or the wind—*but God?* Where had it gone, that surety that *He was?*

Caroline had not only lost Firefly, but Adam too, and she had lost him not with one clean blow, as Kemink had lost Pete, but in an ugly gangrenous, festering way.

And the poison of guilt was added to her despair. She had felt such a high resolve that Firefly's malady would be cured after the miracle with Kemink. But in the busyness of her everyday life, she had not taken the time to recapture those conditions of surrender and communication with God that had seemed to lead to Kemink's recovery. Now, she wondered bitterly how she could have let daily chores and her frivolous enjoyment of spring take precedent over Firefly's need for healing.

If she had only done this—if she had only tried that—. Yet beyond all her own self-abuse, the thought remained that Adam could be, and was, the kind of man who could send their daughter away for purely selfish reasons.

Why hadn't she listened to Kemink? How would she ever find Firefly? She must find her—but how?

As the sun climbed higher, the heat burned into her closed eyes. She laid an arm over her face and for a moment almost went to sleep as a certain dull comfort stole over her. The universe went on about its business with little concern for the grief of Caroline Quimby, it was true—and yet, she was part of the universe, one with it. The sun kissed her eyes and arms. The wind ruffled her skirts and hair. She was aware of the clouds that moved and the insects that crawled even if they were not aware of her. One had to go on. One couldn't simply give up because life was so hard.

The thought of Firefly being in the hands of Omar Pettigrew wrenched through her afresh. She must waste no more time crying. Someway, somehow, she must find the child and rescue her.

She rose, brushing off the twigs and grass that clung to her dress. As she walked back toward the clearing the beauty of the day escaped her. The cobalt sky shimmered in torn pieces through the pine boughs. A cardinal soared like winged fire. White daisies nodded about her skirts. She was aware only of her pain.

Danny, catching sight of her the minute she came to the rim of the clearing, came running toward her.

"Mama, hurry up! We got a whole shed full of pigs! Come and see!"

There was no place in her heart for joy, but she allowed herself to be tugged into the shed by his eager hands. She was greeted by the smell of birth and manure and straw.

"Lookit the little black one, Mama," Danny urged. "Kemink says I kin have him. I'm gonna call him Lucifer, Mama."

As her eyes adjusted, she could see the squirm of small pigs crowded about Mrs. Hog's supine form, fighting for their right to suckle, avid for life.

"Nine piglets, not one lost," Kemink told Caroline with pride, as she emerged from a dark corner with a small pig in her hands. She had just finished drying the infant off. "I believe this one is the last but—"

Kemink broke off as she saw Caroline's swollen face, the white dead despair of her expression.

"What is it?" she asked, setting the pig down.

"Adam came home without Firefly."

For a long time Kemink said nothing.

When she spoke at last, it was only to say, "I let the boys watch the births. It is good that they should understand."

And Caroline understood that Kemink would never say, "I told you—", and at that moment there was nothing else she could say. Silently they walked back to the lodge.

The trip to Weyauwega was made as planned. They stayed on with friends as Kemink had promised last fall. But what was expected to be a pleasant adventure had become for Caroline a crusade. While Kemink and the boys shopped for supplies, Caroline went everywhere, including the saloons, seeking someone who might know the whereabouts of Omar Pettigrew. No one did.

"There are not many such asylums in the state, Caroline. Why don't you try writing to the Governor. He might have a list," Kemink suggested.

Caroline wrote letters to all the officials in Madison she could think of who might have the information she was seeking. There seemed nothing left to do then but return home and wait.

The only ray of light on the trip for Caroline was the letter she found waiting from Ann. Ann had received Caroline's letter recounting all that had happened up to the time of Adam's first departure. Her answering letter was full of sympathy, indignation with Adam and loving support.

"We have not been blessed with children," Ann wrote, "and Bromley would dearly love to have you come to us. He would relish being father to Danny, and we would take Felicity to the finest physicians. There must be something that can remedy her condition. Bromley knows what a blessing it would be to me to have you beneath our roof. Don't hesitate to come—We have come to know and love Kemink through your letters. Assure her that she and her son are welcome too."

102

Caroline still had her letter of application to the school board at Royalton. She had not mailed it because her concern had become to find Firefly. After receiving the letter from Ann, she and Kemink agreed that a sojourn in Chicago might be the better choice. The offers of medical help for Firefly were tempting, and Caroline felt so worn out that the thought of being taken into Ann and Bromley's warm care for a time was appealing.

Nothing could be done until Caroline had received some answers to her various letters or in someway had word of Pettigrew. Caroline ran into Cricket one day and confided the story to him. He promised he would ride into Weyauwega each week for mail and, if there was a letter, bring it to her at once. So they returned to the lodge.

Caroline, having lost her fear of the forest, often sought the privacy of the woods when the chores had been finished early in the morning before the others were up, or at sundown, courting a spiritual state she could not describe but that she felt existed.

She watched the frog catch insects on his sticky tongue and swallow them, only to be swallowed a few minutes later in his turn by a snake. She marvelled at the perfection of a baby rabbit only to see it gathered up squealing in the murderous talons of a hawk. All around her was heart-catching beauty—small waterfalls spraying silver pearls into fern lined creeks, birch trees arching white limbs to the sky, meadows turned gold with buttercups—and side by side with the beauty she saw incredible savagery and brutal carnage on every hand. Why did everything prey upon everything else? The theology she had been taught no longer satisfied her. Because one woman had eaten forbidden fruit should all of creation suffer? In the deepness of her hurt and torment she had become sister to every other living thing that knew pain, defeat and annihilation.

She voiced her new doubts to Kemink.

Kemink's strong brown hands stilled at their task of pulling weeds. "Death is part of life," she said. "Unless the old seed dies, the new fruit cannot come." She indicated the garden. But her words could not assuage the unrest in Caroline.

Again and again she would think back to the night of Kemink's recovery and how she had walked through the snow exalted with *knowing*. Why couldn't she recapture that *state of consciousness?* There were times in her contemplations when she seemed on the brink of discovering that which she longed to know, of having everything unfold before her, crystal clear, and then it would all elude her.

She came to only one conclusion and that was that pain was the Gordian knot. Understand the reason for that monstrosity and the knot would unwind. Life seemed to insist that every living thing ex-

103

perience pain. There was no escaping it. From the greatest to the smallest, from the most minute to the most complex organism, pain seemed an inherent condition of living. Did this mean pain was good in some incomprehensible paradox? But if so, why did every living thing seek so assiduously to escape from it? Her mind spun in futile circles. And always, somewhere in the maelstrom of her pain were locked the images of Firefly and Adam.

The last days of July were searing. Grass grew brown and the bare earth bleached white. Danny and Dan-Pete, stripped to Indian loin cloth, spent half their days in the creek. Kemink carried water to keep the garden green and watched the sky.

"In weather like this sometimes are devil winds," she said. "They come from the sky with a roar and eat trees and people."

Night after night Caroline twisted in the hot bed clothes and awoke sobbing.

"Oh, Kemink, I keep dreaming of Firefly. She calls and calls to me. I see her holding out her arm, and I cannot go to her—I cannot reach her."

"We will find her. We will bring her home," Kemink soothed.

"If only I had a horse," Caroline fretted. "I would go everywhere until I found Pettigrew."

In the end, Pettigrew came to her. The two women were washing clothes in the creek when he came riding up. In spite of the heat and dust he looked debonair in a pale manila suit, attire rarely seen on the frontier. He dismounted and wiped the dust fastidiously from his handsome black boots.

Caroline waded out of the creek, her cheeks burning with heat and emotion. She wanted to strike him, but she realized it was to her advantage to remain civil.

"Mr. Pettigrew—"

"At your service, Ma'am. I heard you'd been askin' for me. Seems I have a bit of information you're interested in."

"Is my daughter all right? What have you done with her?"

"Right hot out here," Pettigrew complained, frowning at the sun. "Seems like a visitor might be invited in for a cool drink."

"All we have is buttermilk."

"That'll do."

Caroline drew up a gallon of buttermilk they had set in the well bucket. She hated Pettigrew for playing cat and mouse with her when she was so desperate to know of Firefly's welfare, but she understood from his manner that he wasn't going to be hurried.

Kemink followed and stood in the background as Caroline offered Pettigrew a seat and poured a glass of buttermilk for him.

104

He sipped it with deliberate slowness, his gold flecked grey eyes watching Caroline's strained and anxious face with amusement.

The lodge was dim after the bright sunlight outside. Caroline could smell the strong scent of buttermilk and the wet cloth of her skirts.

"*Please—*" Caroline said at last, no longer able to contain herself. "My husband said he gave our daughter into your care. *Please* tell me where she is."

"You know, my dear, you're looking quite thin and peaked. What you need is a little fun. A pretty woman like you, alone without her husband, too."

"Stop it!" Caroline cried, no longer able to hold back her rage. "Either you tell me where my daughter is or get out of here!"

"Now that isn't a nice way to act atall, especially when one party wants something from another party," Pettigrew said in a nasty tone.

Caroline regained control of herself. She sat down, her eyes glinting. Evidently he wanted to savour his position. All right, she would have to wait.

He inspected his fingernails.

"Suppose I did have this information—what would there be in it for me?"

"We will give you our cow. That is all we have," Kemink interposed.

"A cow for a daughter?" Pettigrew raised his eyebrows. "Not a very good trade, I'd say. You can do better than that. What about jewelry? Do you have any jewelry?"

"Nothing of value," Caroline said, "but I have eight sterling silver teaspoons—"

He laughed uproariously.

"Eight silver teaspoons and a cow for a daughter. You'll have to do better than that."

"It's all we *have*," Caroline cried in despair, "what do you *want*?"

"Five hundred dollars. Not one red cent less. A daughter ought to bring that much in any market."

"But—but—" Caroline said at a loss, "we could not possibly—we do not have—"

"If you want to know where your daughter is—you'll find a way."

"Get out!" Caroline cried, rage getting the best of her again. "Get out! Get out!" She grabbed a broom and began beating him from the room.

"I'm going—I'm going—" he yelled. "But I'll be *back*," he shouted, as he mounted his horse and rode off. "You'd better get the money somewhere, that's my advice!"

23

Caroline's legs were shaking as she watched Pettigrew ride off. She collapsed on the lodge step, still clinging to the broom.

"I will have to write to Bromley. He will send me the money. I do not know what else to do," Caroline said.

Kemink laid her hands on Caroline's bent shoulders. "We will find ways to pay the sum back to your brother-in-law. The important thing is that Pettigrew knows where Fly is and will come back to tell us if we get the money."

"Oh, Kemink, how good you are—and how right you are!" Caroline cried, springing up. "I will write the letter at once."

They decided that Kemink would take the letter to Weyauwega in the morning. She would travel alone to make the best time.

Caroline saw her off at dawn. Usually at that hour everything was jeweled with dew, but the drought had lasted so long that even at that hour, the trees, earth and grass looked parched and withered. The sedges rattle mournfully and the grass crackled beneath Caroline's feet.

Kemink pushed off, guiding the canoe through water tinted pink by the rising sun. Caroline stood watching until she could see her no more.

Filled with weariness, she returned to the lodge and went to sleep, sleeping long past her usual hour of rising. She was awakened by Danny pulling at her arms.

"Mama, wake up. There's someone here."

She had been in some pleasant place where there were no heart rending dreams. She surfaced from her dark retreat reluctantly.

"Please Mama, wake up," Danny went on tugging.

She sat up, wiping damp tumbled hair from her face.

"There's a man to see you. He's brought some letters—"

She was instantly awake. Without stopping to put her hair to rights or to replace her mussed skirt with a fresh one, she hurried outside.

106

A wiry man, weathered face shadowed by a straw hat, was standing by the well holding out a kerchief while Dan-Pete poured a dipper of water over it. The man pushed back his hat and wiped his face.

"Hullo, Missus," he said pleasantly, as he saw Caroline. "Cricket McGuire sent ye some letters by me."

Caroline almost snatched the mail he extended.

There was a letter from the governor's office. Shaking with excitement, Caroline tore open the envelope. *Perhaps, Kemink need not have gone—*

But the letter was a disappointment. It informed her that the governor could not help her.

She let the letter slip from her fingers and attacked the other two the man had brought. The messages were similar. Most retarded or handicappd people remained with their families. Some were placed in insane asylums (she was given a list of these.) A few were placed in charitable homes not related to the afflicted. Perhaps she could find such a family.

"Oh, if only I had one clue to where Pettigrew might have taken her," Caroline said, frustrated.

' The farmer cleared his throat. He was staring at this tumble-haired, agitated young woman and Caroline realized with shame how unceremonious her greeting to him had been.

"Please rest yourself," she invited. "There's a bench in the shade and I'll fetch you some buttermilk from the creek."

"I come on business, Missus," the farmer said. "Ye got pigs fer sale I unnerstan'."

"We let them loose to root during the daytime," Caroline said. "They come up by themselves at night. We could find some easily enough for you to look at though."

"They're down by the river," Dan-Pete volunteered.

Caroline and the farmer followed the boys to the edge of the clearing. The small meadow was spotted with the pink and white piglets, who were growing fat, their skins stretched taut beneath their sparse coarse hair. The meadow, like everything else, was dry and burnt. There wasn't much to root, but with no calf to feed there was plenty of whey from Lily-Thing and the piglets were in good condition.

"Good pigs," the farmer said. "I'd like to have them all, but I don't have the money. I could pay ye along—?"

"I can't say," Caroline said. "The pigs belong to Kemink. She is on a journey. Could you come back when she is home?"

"Wull—" said the farmer, disappointed, "I live clear on the other side of 'Wega—"

"She left for Weyauwega this morning. Maybe you can catch her there," Caroline suggested.

The farmer seemed satisfied with that. Upon their return to the house he drank the buttermilk she gave him, holding the mug in a huge work worn hand. He took off his hat and stared up at the sky which was becoming a sullen blue, compacted with murky clouds.

"Gonna storm," he said.

"Be a blessing, might break this heat," Caroline said.

"Gonna storm bad," the old farmer said. "Ye got a root cellar? If'n it gets any darker, I'd take to it, Missus. 'N I think I'd better hurry me along." He adjusted his hat back on his head. A rising wind bent the brim back and forth. Spirals of dust were starting to blow around them. The farmer mounted his mule and left.

"We'd better get the pigs and Lily-Thing into the barn," Caroline told the boys, but she stood for a moment unmoving savoring the fresh wind that lifted her hair from her shoulders.

A rattle of buckets and the call of "Soieee—soieee—" brought the pigs readily but Lily-Thing was more recalcitrant. Caroline heard her bell tantalizingly close. It seemed just beyond the hedge, but when she emerged from behind the hedge, the bell tinkled in a hollow just ahead—and when she could see the hollow—that irritating bell urged her forward to a small thicket.

A twilight-like darkness was closing around them. The wind had a cat scream to it now and was carrying a mean sting of sand and sharp twigs.

"You boys go back and crawl into the root cellar," Caroline shouted. "I'm going to look in one more thicket for Lily, and if I can't find her, I'll be right along. Hurry now!"

The boys scampered off, almost lifted from their feet by the wind.

Drops of rain pelted Caroline's cheek and neck as she ducked her way into the thicket. She found herself face to face with Lily-Thing's big white head and long lashed brown eyes just as the full force of the storm broke. Sheets of rain slashed her with such force she had to hang onto a sapling to keep her balance.

Lily-Thing, anchored by her eight hundred pound frame, continued chewing her cud and stared at Caroline with what appeared to be pretended innocence.

It struck Caroline funny. She stood shaking with laughter while the rain soaked her hair and plastered her clothing to her body.

"You big dumb cow," she scolded. But she felt revived by the hard cold rain, as if she, like the grasses and trees and earth, had been shriveled and arid. She lifted her face to its life-giving drive in a silent ecstasy.

When it was over, she drove Lily-Thing through a dripping, humbled, storm-sweetened world. The sun came out and a rainbow arched in the clean washed sky, while miniature rainbows took form in trembling drops that clung to spider webs or trembled at the tips of leaves. The drought was over. The world was cool again.

She found Danny and Dan-Pete already out of their shelter splashing about in the puddles that sparkled like carelessly flung jewels in the muddy dooryard.

Caroline had been worried about the garden. She found it somewhat bedraggled by the force of the wind but essentially unharmed.

She gathered Danny on one side of her and Dan-Pete on the other and said, "Look at that rainbow! Do you know what that is? It's God's promise that he will never again destroy the world by water."

Looking at the rainbow, she felt more at peace than she had for a long time.

The week was spent and Kemink had not returned. Caroline was becoming apprehensive, wondering if the canoe might have overturned in the storm, or if Kemink had been taken ill again. She felt enormous relief when she saw Kemink come paddling up the river. Her friend's dark-eyed smile told her all was well.

"I have it," Kemink said as soon as she stepped from the canoe. "I have the name and place where Firefly is being kept."

"But how—where?" Caroline cried in excitement.

"Our friend, Mr. Post, advanced the money. After a little trouble I found Pettigrew and the transaction was carried out."

"Why, how *kind* of Mr. Post."

"I assured him your brother-in-law would repay him," Kemink said, "But yes, he is kind—and soft toward you—"

"Where—where is this place?" Caroline demanded urgently.

"Milwaukee."

"Milwaukee?"

"Come," Kemink said, "I am hungry and tired and we have much about which we must talk."

The candles burned late in the lodge that night. For Kemink to leave the place where she had lived so long with Big Pete, to leave his grave, to leave the support of her own people, was difficult. But the lives of Caroline and Kemink had become deeply interwoven, and it had been agreed that the two families would cast their lot together. They would find Fly and go on to Chicago.

Kemink had sold the pigs to the farmer who had caught up with her in Weyauwega, but as he could not pay cash at the time, they had no riverboat or train fare for the journey to Milwaukee to search for Firefly.

"We will have to sell Lily-Thing anyway," Caroline said, "Won't she pay for the fare?"

"I had the same thought," Kemink said.

The farmer came the following day for the pigs. The boys watched with sad eyes as the squealing shoats were loaded into the cart. The animals had been playthings to them. Mrs. Hog was the last to be loaded, walking on her dainty feet up the plank and thrusting her snout through the slats in the cart as it jolted away. Not only the boys, but the two women, felt as if they had lost a member of the family, and they knew it would be even worse when Lily-Thing was sold. But there was little time to mourn. Everything that could be carried had to be packed.

Because they had to lead the cow, they would have to travel by foot. Kemink constructed an Indian sled which she attached to Lily-Thing. That bovine aristocrat was going to have to help carry things whether she wished or not.

They left in the cool of the evening, after one last visit to Big Pete's grave. As they turned to leave the clearing, both Kemink and Caroline paused and looked at the lodge, their hearts full. They had known much suffering in this forest, but they had known joy as well. They felt they were leaving part of themselves behind.

It was a silent group that walked single file through the woods, each one bearing bundles and packs, Lily-Thing grudgingly bringing up the rear.

Several days later, Captain Anderson thought it a strange group that awaited his steamship. A tall Indian woman dressed in flowered calico with a beaded headband around her braided hair stood behind a small white boy whose arms were heaped with boxes. Beside him was an Indian boy wearing a fringed loin cloth over his homespun pants, carrying bundles in both arms. In the back a slender white woman clung to the rein of a balking, bellowing cow.

The white woman turned the cow over to the Indian woman and approached him.

"Captain Anderson, we don't have the fare, but we were told you sometimes buy livestock and sell the animals in Oshkosh. We were wondering if you would take our cow in exchange for passage to Fond du Lac and money enough to get us to Milwaukee?"

He squinted down at her, finding something familiar in the delicate face, the deep-water blue eyes.

"She's a very good cow," the woman said earnestly. "She freshened in the spring."

Something jarred in his memory, and he saw again a pink-cheeked girl in a blue traveling suit.

"Why—why, Miz Quimby," he said. "It is Miz Quimby hain't hit?"

A shadow passed over her face. She nodded.

"Did ya lose yar husband, Ma'am?" the Captain asked solicitously.

"Yes," Caroline said, "I lost my husband."

"Well—yah, yah—sure, we can arrange something. I'm not in da animal business to be sure. But she does look like a fine cow and I'm apt to come out good enough. You and yar friends step aboard and I'll see to da cow," the Captain said.

The procession filed on board, and Lily-Thing, stubborn and aggravating to the end, had to be urged up the gangplank inch by inch, bellowing protests all the way.

The steamer moved along the shores of the Wolf River into Lake Poygan, past the Indian ceremonial grounds with the strange little bark roofs and white flags. The sun set in a blaze of beauty and fireflies dotted the marshes at dusk as the boat passed through the mirroring waters close to shore.

Kemink and Caroline watched the panorama pass with expressions of poignancy on their faces.

24

When Solomon Juneau founded a trading post on two bluffs above a sluggish river and an almost impenetrable tamarack swamp, there was little indication it would grow into one of the large cities of the world. But the harbor soon made Milwaukee one of the leading wheat ports of the continent. Immigrants swelled its population in unprecedented numbers. When Caroline and Kemink arrived in 1857, three-fourths of the populace were either new immigrants or had foreign-born parents.

The motley throng at the livery stable included thick muscular Germans with round red-cheeked countenances; flaxen-haired Norwegians, Hollanders, wearing wooden shoes and pegged pants; stocky Swiss, and Belgian housewives who had decorated their faces with magnesia paste to appear citified.

Even in this heterogeneous group, Caroline and Kemink drew glances of interest. Kemink, with her dusky skin, beaded headdress and beartooth necklace, caused heads to turn.

There were horses and rigs parked on either side of the street as far as they could see, and it was getting dark. Lanterns and lamps burning in stores ahead cast a patchwork of yellow and gold squares on the mud and gravel street. Unable in the dark to decipher the address of the people caring for Fly, they walked toward the lights.

There was a yeasty smell of beer in the air. Danny and Dan-Pete, hearing the sound of an accordian and the spirited stamping of feet, stared round-eyed through the window of a tavern. Inside they could see girls in gaily colored skirts bearing aloft trays of beer steins, red-faced men laughing and shouting, and dancers who seemed to bounce and fly into the air to an oom-pa-pah blast of music. A polyglot of languages drifted from the door along with the smell of sausages and sauerkraut which had a marked effect on the boys who began to proclaim they were hungry.

"The place is located just off Spring Street," Caroline said, having read her instructions.

"I know how anxious you are, my friend," Kemink counseled. "But it has grown late and we are tired. You do not yet know what you might have to face there. Perhaps it would be well to wait and go in the morning."

"Oh, Kemink, I cannot wait," Caroline protested. "You must understand—"

"I do," Kemink said.

"I'm hungry," Danny moaned.

With the mingled scent of beer and sausage they could now smell fresh warm bread from a German bakery next door to a tavern. In the window was a display of rye and pumpernickel breads.

"My stomach rumbles," declared Dan-Pete.

"All right," Caroline sighed. "We'll eat first."

Merchants stayed open late, and even at this hour the streets were congested with horses, carriages, carts, pedestrians and wagons. Caroline had never seen so many wagons. Brewery wagons, ice wagons, water wagons and fruit wagons tumbled by in endless parade.

They found a hostelry suitable for women and children. Run by a Hollander, it had scrubbed brick floors and tables with spotless cloths. They were served kentje, a dish of cabbage, pork and potatoes cooked with apple cider.

Caroline was too nervous to eat, but she was glad Kemink and the children had pressed to eat first because she had time to arrange for their lodging.

It was past ten o'clock when they all squeezed into a carriage and directions were given to the driver to take them to the address where Firefly was being kept.

112

Caroline's anxious heart outpaced the plodding horse through the back streets. Her pulse raced impatiently. At length they drew up before a dark brick building squeezed between similar buildings. A small lantern burning by the doorway revealed a respectable looking entrance, which reassured Caroline.

Full of food and weary, Danny and Dan-Pete had fallen asleep. Kemink stayed with them in the cab while Caroline stumbled over loose cobblestones to the door. She pounded the tarnished knocker a number of times before the door opened to reveal a small servant girl holding a flickering candle. She was in her nightgown with a shawl thrown across her shoulders.

"Mum, we ain't open to visitors at this hour," she said. She had spotted skin and hair that drooped untidily about her face.

"I'm not a visitor," Caroline said, pushing her way in with determination. "My little girl is here. I've come to get her."

"Plez, Mum, you can't fetch 'er tonight. The Marster don't allow it no way. Come back tomorry."

In contrast to the fresh night air, the hall was permeated with a stench Caroline could not identify.

"Plez, Mum," the servant girl was imploring, " 'E'd 'ave me ears for lettin' you in at this 'our. Won't you plez be off 'n trot back around tomorry? I couldn't let you tak 'er without 'is say. 'N 'e'd tan me fer sure if I was to wake 'im."

"Welll—," Caroline said, her pity aroused by the anxiety on the girl's face. "Perhaps I could come back tomorrow, if you would let me *see* her tonight so I would know she's all right."

"What be your name, Mum?"

"Caroline Quimby. My little girl's name is Felicity."

"Oh, I know the one. She's got a mingy arm."

"Yes, that's right!"

"Wull, Mum, she's right as rain. Pop by tomorry and talk to the marster."

"No," Caroline said. "I shall see my child tonight if I have to break down doors!"

"Shhh, shhh," the little servant said, cringing. "Plez, Mum, keep your voice down! You'll be wakin' 'im yet. Promise to be quiet 'n I'll take you up fer a peek, but you'll 'ave to be quiet or you'll 'ave the whole bloomin' lot of 'em awake an' then there'll be 'ell to pay, I'll tell you."

She went up the stairs ahead of Caroline, her worn, over-sized slippers making flapping noises at each step. As they climbed the stairs the stench Caroline had noted became more pronounced and she identified it as a combination of urine and sour milk.

The servant paused before a door locked with a combination of chains. She balanced the candle precariously in one hand while undoing the chain with as little noise as she could.

"Shhh," she cautioned Caroline as the door swung inward.

The candle's wavering flame cast strange shadows on the wall and turned the children, crowded together in all manner of beds and cribs, into gargoyles. The dead air and the smell of feces and unwashed bodies were so overpowering Caroline gagged.

The servant advanced toward the end of the room.

"There she is," she said, lifting the candle a little higher.

A cry wrenched from Caroline as she saw Firefly sandwiched between a child with a water head and a black child with a hideously pock-marked face. Fly was wearing a yellow nightgown and had been put to bed without being washed. Her hair was matted as if it had not been combed for weeks.

"Fly, *darling*," Caroline cried, holding out her arms.

Firefly was awake, but she shrank back.

"Fly, it's *Mama*," Caroline entreated.

"Shhhh, Mum," the servant girl hushed her nervously. "Oh, limey, you've got 'alf of 'em awake already!" And indeed a whining and mewling was beginning to swell in the room.

"Plez, Mum, take your leave now. You said if you saw 'er you'd be satisfied to wait until tomorry."

"I cannot leave her here," Caroline said in anguish. She caught Fly in her arms and suddenly, as if her touch awakened remembrance, the child buried her head tightly against Caroline's shoulder and flung her arm in a strangle-hold about her throat.

The mewling around them was rising higher.

"Oh, hit ain't no use," the servant girl said with a gesture of despair. "The fat's in the fire fer sure, fer sure. 'E'll 'ear all this."

The words were hardly out of her mouth before a heavy set man in a frayed robe appeared in the doorway. He had a bulging forehead and pale eyes that threw a baleful glance upon the servant, on Caroline, and Fly, like an accusing net.

"What is the meanin' of this?" he demanded.

"Marster, this lady's come fer 'er child an' wouldn't nothin' 'alt 'er, Sir. She come up without me say-so, Sir. I swear she did. Threatened to 'it me if I stood in 'er way," the servant declared cowering.

"We don't accept visitors at this hour, Madam," the man said coldly. "Put that child down and leave at once or I'll have the constable on you."

"It is I who will have the constable on you," Caroline declared, clinging even more possessively to Firefly. "Fetch me my child's clothes or I shall raise such a ruckus as you cannot imagine! Look around you." she cried angrily. Her glance swept the circle of pitiful children, one smeared with feces, some covered with scabs, all of them dirty, their beds filthy.

One of the little boys crawled off his pallet and held out his arms to Caroline. He looked up at her entreatingly. But she could not pick him up without letting go of Fly. He whined, tugging at her skirt.

"Madam, I will not be threatened!" the man said indignantly. "How do I know this is your child? Do you have papers to prove it?"

"She was born on the frontier and I had not yet registered her birth when she was taken from me, but you have eyes. See how she clings to me."

"They all would, were you to pick them up," he said bitterly. "Take that one!" he added sharply to the servant, who obediently picked up the boy clutching Caroline's skirt. He set up a pietous howl as he was carried away.

Caroline's lips were white. "I mean it, Sir, I shall expose this whole dreadful mess if you don't fetch my child's things at once. I will bring the constable."

"Madam, I will not have insults thrown upon me. I'm a pious man. No one else wants these children. No one else will take care of them. I do the best I can on the pittance I am given for their care" the stocky man said, meeting her icy rage with equal outrage.

"Plez, Mum, hit's true what 'e sez," the little servant averred, bobbing up between them after depositing the howling child back on his pallet. " 'E's a good man, Mum, doin' the best 'e can just like 'e said, Mum. See, I was a bum child meself, 'n 'e took me in an' raised me an' give me a job, Mum," she said, raising her nightgown to reveal a clubbed foot. "If you'd just ferget about 'er clothin,' Mum, mebbe we could let 'er go with no trouble. You see, Mum, we never let them outside so they don't have no use for clothin' much. We sold 'er things, Mum."

"I see," said Caroline. She took her cloak off and wrapped it around Firefly. "We'll go without her clothing then."

"Well—you'd have to sign a paper saying you took her," the man said, apparently relieved that there was to be no trouble regarding the clothes. "Otherwise we might be accused of having done away with her. I do the best I can and still I'm forever persecuted—" He went out ahead of them muttering to himself as he started down the stairs.

The little boy had crawled off his pallet again and was trying to get to Caroline. She forcibly shut the sight of him away and followed the fluttering servant girl out of the room.

"Oh, limey, Mum, you've got me in 'ot water now, you 'ave," she said, struggling to get the door locked.

Behind the door the children howled and sobbed.

Caroline closed her eyes. *"I shall never forget this."*

With her arms locked about Firefly, who clung so tightly it was difficult to breathe, Caroline unfastened the brooch at her throat.

"Take this," she said to the servant, "It has a little value. I won't forget that you helped me."

"Wull, Mum, you don't 'ave to do that, you don't," the girl protested, but her eyes shone at the sight of the brooch as Caroline dropped it into her palm.

"For the trouble I have caused you," Caroline said.

"Are you coming or aren't you?" the man called querulously.

"We're coming!" Caroline assured him, descending with the clinging child.

He led her into a small office and pushed some papers toward her. They were documents to attest that she had regained custody of her child.

"If you cause me any trouble, I shall tear them up and declare that you are not the child's mother," he warned, glaring at her.

"I won't cause you any trouble," she promised, weak with relief that he was going to let her take Felicity without further controversy.

He walked beside her and opened the door, as eager to be rid of her as she was to be gone.

She took a hungry breath of night air as the door closed behind her and then fled toward the waiting carriage.

Kemink's arms reached out to take the child so Caroline could get in, but Firefly would not let go of her mother. The driver had to boost Caroline up with her burden intact.

Dan-Pete woke up and grinned sleepily. "Hi, Fly."

The child looked at him with round dark eyes and then hid her face.

Dan-Pete was disappointed.

"Don't she remember me?"

"Thank God, she is all right," Kemink said.

"I pray to God she *is* all right," Caroline said, shuddering. "Oh, Kemink, if you could have seen that place. I pray she isn't permanently damaged in some way."

Cuddling Fly in her arms in the dark swaying carriage, she felt her heart harden against Adam with renewed anger and resentment.

25

The shutters on the window of their rented room kept out the sunlight but not the noise of the awakening Milwaukee streets. Caroline lay with Firefly enclosed in her arms listening to the clop-clop of horses' hooves, the rattle of milk cans, the cheerful oaths of a Sawyer caught in the congestion of wagon traffic.

Danny, awakened by the same noises, came bounding from the cot he had shared with Dan-Pete.

"Mama, kin Dan-Pete and me go explorin'?" he asked, peering between the slats of the shutters at the street below.

"Kemink is going to shop for a dress for Fly. If you boys wash and dress quickly, you may go along," Caroline said.

"Why won't Fly look at us?" Danny asked. Like Dan-Pete, he had made overtures to his sister and received no response.

"She has been gone from us for a long time. We seem strange to her now. In time she will make up to you," Caroline promised, trying to reassure herself as much as him.

The chamber maid knocked on the door and entered with a stack of linen towels and a pitcher of warm water.

"They'll be servin' breakfast in the dinin' room from seven 'til nine, no later," she said in a lilting voice. Already the tantalizing odor of frying bacon was seeping up the stairs.

Within minutes Danny and Dan-Pete had slicked themselves to an unaccustomed shine, their hair plastered to their heads with water, their cheeks red from rough scrubbing.

Kemink braided the last inch of her dark hair, and slipped the coins Caroline had given her into a beaded bag she wore about her neck. After one last eye-measurement of Firefly, she departed with the two boys at her heels.

In a leisurely manner Caroline opened the shutters so she could watch the two well-combed boys and the handsome Indian woman make their way along the street below. It was a bright blue and gold morning, and all along the street shop owners were sweeping the dust from their wooden sidewalks and unshuttering their windows for trade.

Firefly whimpered and Caroline turned back to her quickly, caressing and holding her close.

"Don't be afraid, Fly. Kemink's gone to get you a lovely new dress," Caroline crooned as she washed her.

Fly seemed to enjoy the warm water, the good smelling soap, the crisp towels; but when Caroline got to her neglected hair, there was a tantrum. When she persisted in her effort to undo the tangles, Firefly eluded her and crawled under the bed. Caroline had to pull her from her refuge by force. Kemink returned to find a screaming child being ineffectually soothed by a distraught mother.

"I tried to comb her hair," Caroline explained.

"For you," Kemink said in her soft way, and slid a small package into Fly's lap. For several minutes she continued to howl stubbornly and ignore the gift, but eventually curiosity overcame her and, still sniffling, she bent her head and tried to peer inside. Caroline helped her draw out the apron of cranberry calico and long black stockings Kemink had chosen.

The women refrained from having coffee at breakfast because of their precarious finances, but they ordered bowls of oatmeal with brown sugar and cream for the children. Fly ate as if she were afraid the food was going to disappear at any minute, sometimes supplementing her spoon by dipping her fingers in and stuffing her mouth. Caroline refrained from correcting her for fear of another tantrum.

"It is going to take many steps to get her back to normal," she said to Kemink with a sad shake of her head.

"One step at a time—with love," Kemink said, leaning across the table to catch a blob of oatmeal before it fell on Fly's new apron.

Suddenly Caroline caught sight of a sign swinging in the wind. "Stay with the children, Kemink. I'll be right back," she said.

Milwaukee may have been well on its way to being a great metropolis, but it was still plagued with its rural origins. Caroline had to dodge a herd of swine being driven down the street before she could get across to the pawn shop whose sign she had seen.

The dapper clerk assured her that there was little call for worn wedding bands, dashing her hopes. But after he had squinted at the ring and held it up to the sun, he agreed to give her a small sum.

Whatever she might have felt at parting with the ring was drowned in relief that she had found a way to make up the slight deficit of their train fare. She returned triumphantly to Kemink.

"Now we'll have money to hire a cab to take our things to the station," she said with relief.

After their journey from Oshkosh to Milwaukee, Danny and Dan-Pete felt like veteran travelers and scurried back and forth with pack-

118

ages, up and down the black iron stairs of the train until all their belongings were safely stowed aboard. But the noisy, chuffing, puffing train resurrected all of Firefly's insecurities and she clung to Caroline. The young mother's thin arms ached with the persistent weight and a crick developed in her neck and shoulder, but her heart was full of gratitude. At last she had found Fly, they were all safely aboard the train on their way to Ann and Bromley. Kemink and Caroline gave almost simultaneous sighs of accomplishment as the train lurched forward. They looked at each other over the array of bundles between them and laughed.

The train smelled of soot and herring. A family of immigrants behind them was breakfasting on fish and long dark loaves of rye bread. Outside the windows the sunlit world swarmed past them at a fascinating speed.

"It's unbelievable that before the day is over we will be in Chicago," Caroline marveled.

*　　*　　*

Ann wept when she saw Caroline.

"Oh, my darling, you are so thin—*so thin!*" she cried, holding her sister close, shocked at the way the blue traveling suit hung on her, at the new lines etched on her face, and the roughened hair.

The sisters resembled one another, but Caroline had always been prettier, her features a little more perfect, her skin a shade fairer, her hair a shade richer. Now, Ann, radiant in a fashionable gown of pale green taffeta, her shining hair intricately looped and braided in the newest fashion, outshone her tired sister like an ostrich plumed hat outshines a faded sunbonnet.

"Oh—this must be Felicity—she's beautiful—a beautiful child, Caroline. To think she is so big already—and Danny," Ann was trying to catch them all in her embrace at once.

"Ann, for goodness sake, they're so tired they can hardly stand on their feet. Take them inside," Bromley instructed, swinging the last of their packages from the cab.

"Oh, Brom, if you only knew what a hassle it's been with all this luggage and Fly. The boys have been a wonderful help, but how sweet it is to have a man take over," Caroline said.

Despite Bromley's instruction to get them inside, Ann was now stopping to hug Kemink and Dan-Pete as if she had known them all her life.

When they finally did get inside the house, Dan and Dan-Pete were awestruck and ill at ease as if they had been plucked out of a stable and set down in a palace. Bromley had been doing very well indeed

119

and Ann had refurbished and redone the entire house.

The drawing room sported a white marble fireplace, chandeliers of imported Italian crystal, an Aubusson rug and portieres of pale blue velvet. The settees and chairs were covered in matching blue velvets and silvery brocades. Bouquets of fresh flowers in pastels stood on marble buffets, priceless liqueur decanters and glasses glittered on side-tables along with alabaster figurines and gold filigree snuff boxes.

"Ohh, my—" Caroline said at a loss for words.

"Isn't it lovely?" Ann said happily. "Wait until you see the up-stairs. You'll love your room, darling."

The guests, suddenly feeling like the most ragged of urchins, were swept up the scarlet-carpeted stairway to the upper rooms.

"Ann—it's almost too much," Caroline said, staring at the bed draped in gold satin, the baroque mirrors, the velvet curtains that shut out the late afternoon sun.

"You'll get used to it," Ann said cheerfully. "I'll put Kemink across the hall and the boys will be next door. Oh, I am so happy to have you all!" she said, punctuating her words with hugs and squeezes.

Kemink's room glowed with a satin spread and gilded lamps but the boys' room was more masculine with brass beds and laquered chests.

"Won't you come to me?" Ann coaxed Felicity, aware that Caroline was still carrying the heavy child. Firefly burrowed her head reso-lutely against her mother.

After dinner at a table sparkling with candelabras and crystal; after luxurious baths; after a long cozy talk over hot egg nogs in the library; after the children, buoyed up by the excitement of all that was novel, finally wilted enough to be tucked into beds; Caroline lowered her self slowly into the strange elegance and comfort of a bed made up with Irish linen, goose down pillows and satin quilts.

Thin shafts of moonlight fell across the bed. Tired, she lay wide-eyed, staring at her thin hand resting on the satin coverlet, a small, pale, empty space on one finger where once there had been a gold ring. Outside of the great house of her sister, quieting now as if the building itself fell asleep with all its occupants, she could feel the future days and months and years gathering, waiting to claim her, and she wondered what her life would be like now.

When at last she slept, fitfully, it was to dream of a baby boy chew-ing at the hem of her dress while tears ran in an unending stream from his over-large eyes.

120

26

In the August heat, Levi Jones' shack smelled oppressively of rancid fat and dirty bedding. There was little relief outside. The redolence of the pines was locked in layers of dust. The banks of the river were cracked like feverish lips and the water moved sluggishly beneath a blanket of green algae.

Levi plucked a frying pan from the nail on which it was hanging and stuffed it into his saddlebag.

"Now what did I do with that jerky?" he said out loud to himself.

"It's probably in the teakettle. That's where you kept it the last time I was here," a voice answered from the doorway.

It was Adam Quimby, but it took a full twenty seconds for Levi to recognize him. The usually spotless black alpaca suit was hidden beneath layers of dust, crumpled and ragged. His hair was uncut, his beard a black rage.

"What bit ye this time?" Levi asked. "Musta been sump'n worser'n a snake."

Adam sat down on the doorstep, not speaking.

Levi reached under his bed roll and brought out his bottle of whiskey. He handed it to Adam. This time there was no hesitation. Adam uncorked it and swallowed deeply.

"I thought you was goin' back home, gonna make it go," Levi said, peering into the tea kettle to see if his jerky was there. It was.

"She sent me away," Adam said.

Levi reclaimed his bottle, treated himself to a snort, and then squinted at Adam thoughtfully.

"Looks like it upset ye considerable."

Adam's head drooped into his hands.

"I can't preach anymore—that's what's killing me. It's like I'm wandering around in a woods, lost. Before I was on a clear path. I knew where I was going, what I had to do. I don't know anything anymore."

"You look like you been lost, awright," Levi chuckled. "Bing-ding if you don't look worse'n me."

"I've been living out there for weeks," Adam said, nodding his head toward the sullen, dust drenched woods. "God knows I've had my forty days and forty nights. I tried stopping at settlements for food—work—but they recognized me, wanted me to preach, marry, bury—"

121

He buried his face deeper in his hands.

"I've thought of killing myself—"

"Oh, hell, Adam, it hain't worth that. There's other things than preachin' and there's more'n one wimmen in this world. Iffin I was you, I'd enjoy thet fact while I could. They won't look at ye when ye get old and crusty like me."

Adam raised his face.

"I don't want any other woman."

"Scuddle-duddle," Levi said. "Ever' man wants other wimmen. Ye're half starved, thet's what's wrong with ye."

He tossed Adam a hunk of jerky.

"Eat thet or I'll bash yer head in fer ye and save ye the trouble."

Adam began to chew automatically.

"I used to think when I was still with Caroline that I had to fight against the temptations to want other women."

Levi laughed. "I'll bet ye did. Preachers like ye, good lookin', full o' fire. I'll bet they flocked around like cats to catnip."

"There were—some," Adam admitted, looking down, "I have to admit I took a certain pleasure in it, but of course, I never touched them—"

"Ye mean ye niver squeezed any of 'em up?"

"Of course not!"

"But ye *wanted* to," Levi chortled.

A glazed look of sadness spread across Adam's face. He could not bring himself to tell Levi how he had tried to lose himself in debauchery for a period. He had gotten drunk, had gone so far as to bed down in a barn with a farmer's willing wife. He hadn't been able to go through with it.

"Maybe—" he answered Levi's comment, "maybe I thought I did, but I know now that I don't want anyone but *her*."

How could he tell Levi the way he remembered the silken weight of Caroline's hair spilling on his shoulder in the night, the small warm spot where her hand rested on his ribs—the clean, soap smell of her.

"Iffen ye're thet strung out on 'er, why don't ye go back an' try again?" Levi asked gruffly. He slammed another kettle noisily into his saddle bag.

Adam's mouth tightened.

"A man has to be the master of his own house. She defied me. Turned me out. There's no way I can go back."

"Then stop being such a plum ijiot and fergit her! An' I'm tellin' ye agin, the best fergettin' medicine is another wimmin."

Levi fitted a moldy looking slab of bacon into the saddlebag and

122

buckled it shut.

"Are you going somewhere?" Adam asked, for the first time becoming aware of what Levi had been doing.

"I'm goin' to Californy!" Levi said gleefully. He spat on the floor. "M' brother jus' died and left me a gold mine. What'ya think o' thet?"

"Well—that's something," Adam said lamely.

"Jack was one of the original '49'ers. I hain't saying he made it real big, but he sed the mine hed enuff dust to more'n meet his wants for high livin'. We niver got on too good, but he sez he'd ruther I got it then the rest o' those ugly jokers out there. When he knew he was goin', he had it all drawed up legal 'n sent me a map."

"You're leaving right now?" Adam asked, stunned by the suddenness and feeling a surprising sense of loss.

Levi looked at Adam's expression and laughed.

"I'm too old to run the infernal thing alone. Cricket McGuire is goin' with me. Ye know Cricket?"

"Everybody in these parts knows Cricket. But I'm surprised he'd leave this country—it's like part of him."

"Well, he's agoin' with me. Ye can too, iffen ye want to—iffen ye don't, ye kin hiv this old place. I won't be needin' it anymore."

Adam thought of the winter before in the lumber camp—the sour, clammy smell of men climbing out of bed into twenty below zero mornings in underwear they didn't take off for weeks at a time—the dour silence enforced as they ate their meals—the sheer backbreaking physical strain. He hesitated at the thought of mining. More of the same?

"I hain't got time to linger. Me an' Cricket got to take the steamer from Gill's Landing tonight. But you take yer time an' think it over," he advised Adam. "Thet black horse o' your'n kin catch up with me n' me mule anytime."

"I doubt that mining is for me," Adam said.

"Ye got anything better to do?"

Adam shook his head morosely.

"I'll think about it a little. Maybe I'll meet you later at Gill's Landing."

"The steamer leaves 'round twilight," Levi said. "Iffen ye decide not to show—good luck!" He gave Adam a burly thump, tugged the mule's rope, and left.

Adam finished eating his jerky as if it were a task that had to be done. He spent the next hour washing, shaving and sponging his clothes until he finally bore some resemblance to the well known Reverend Quimby who had so lately made a splash in the frontier community. He spent another hour grooming his horse lovingly.

123

Ebonite was the one constant left in his life.

He did not want to go to California, but the old man's words echoed in his mind—"Ye got anything better to do?" He needed some way to get money. He would still have to support his family even if he never saw them again. He had a sense of being swept along by forces beyond his control.

He was well aware that his cabin was only a short ride away. He could have mounted his horse and been with Caroline in a matter of hours, but things far greater than distance separated them. He mounted Ebonite and turned him toward Gill's Landing.

The first duskiness of night was settling over the little village when Adam arrived. In another mood, he would have admired the yellow glow of lantern and lamp shining from house to house, bright blooms in the gathering darkness, announcing the heartbeat of man surviving in a near wilderness. This night the sight had no beauty for him. His face was set in lines of bitterness as he walked into the saloon. He saw Cricket and Levi drinking at the end of the bar.

"Hello, Friend," Adam started to greet Cricket, but the face turned toward him was ugly. Cricket had had too much to drink. His eyes were a network of frayed red blood vessels and all his features looked coarsened.

"You ain't m' friend," Cricket said.

Adam was non-plussed. He had memories of brotherly companionship with this big man.

"I ain't the friend of any man thet'd leave his woman alone in a country like this."

Adam felt blood pound up to his hairline.

"I left her in the care of Pete Tartoué. How was I to know he'd get killed?"

"Bull," Cricket said. "I'm talkin' about the second time ya left her. Who was supposed to take kere of her then?"

Adam felt a stab of fear.

"Has something happened to her?"

"Well, if it hain't, hits no thanks to you," Cricket said.

"She's all right?" Adam pressed. He realized with sudden shame that he had been so immersed in his own anguish he had never given a thought to Caroline's predicament—or had he in some cavity of his being *wanted* her to suffer?—wanted her to need him so badly that if he ever rode back she would fall on her knees weeping, acquiescent, ready to affirm the position that should have been his right—the master of the household, whose decisions were never challenged, never questioned—accepted inviolate!

"Her 'n the young-uns and Kemink, too, left fer Chicago. She's gonna stay with her brother-in-law," Cricket said.

Adam felt rage.

"Great!" he fumed. "Great! That fancy sister of hers and her pot-bellied brother-in-law never did think I was good enough for her. Fine! Let her live with her millionaire relatives. That's all right. I'm rid of the whole bunch of them, then!"

Cricket looked at Adam with a wild off-kilter glare. "Ye're a damn fool, Adam Quimby. Iffen she was my woman, I'd swim through crocodiles to her."

"Well, she's not your woman!" Adam roared. "What's all this to you anyway!"

"I like her, thet's what. I like her a helluva lot more'n I like you!" Cricket shouted back.

Adam was never sure who swung first. He remembered only the melee of blows, the rage flowing out of him in the hard contact of human flesh, falling to the floor, getting up again, watching Cricket fall across a table, coming up again more viciously—his breath ripping out of his lungs with pain, his mouth filling with blood where Cricket had loosened a tooth—

A gun barrel swung between them.

"Thet's enuff. I hain't havin' my place broke up fer yer amusement. Git outside if ye want more!"

Both of them were sitting on the floor, Cricket's hair across his eyes, blood seeping from Adam's mouth. Levi grabbed an arm of each and dragged them up.

"Niver quarrel over a wimmen boys," he said cheerfully, "iffen you're gonna fight, fight over something sensible. As fer ye, Adam, ye're lucky Crickett wasn't sober. He'd a squashed yer liver."

He dragged them weak and staggering outside and pumped water over their heads. Adam felt hollow. His legs were shaking.

They all started at the sound of the steamer whistle.

"Hit's here! Ye comin', Adam?" Levi asked.

"Cricket doesn't want me to come," Adam said.

Cricket, sobered by the fight and the cold water, planted one of his big hands on the other man's shoulder.

"I reckon I don't kere. I had to get it off my gizzard, but I've made my mistakes, too. We'll start fresh."

Adam led Ebonite up the gang plank with Cricket limping behind him and Levi trailing with the mule.

Adam Quimby, who had ridden into Tomorrow River country flamboyant, arrogant, full of dreams—was leaving, bloodied, humiliated and in defeat—and he was too weary and dispirited to care. He stretched his body across the deck and went to sleep.

PART II

CHICAGO AND THE CIVIL WAR

Trust in the Lord with all thine heart;
and lean not unto thine own understanding.
In all thy ways acknowledge Him,
and He shall direct thy paths.
                                        Proverbs

27

Struggling with all the vicissitudes of frontier living, Caroline had read Ann's letters filled with details of pretty new clothes, parties, trips and social activities, with a feeling that her sister lived like a story-book princess.

As a member of the household, Caroline quickly discovered that if Ann's life was "all roses", it was because of dedicated work by the "gardener". Ann never lifted a pretty hand to wash a dish or dust a table top, yet Caroline learned that she led an arduous existence in her own way.

Charming, gregarious Bromley brought guests home almost every night. Often they would have a "soiree" of four or five couples, then again Ann might have thirty people to dinner. And none of the perfection happened by itself. Ann never had to cook the oysters a la cremeux or the veal di Napoli, but she had to mastermind everything from the instruction of how to buy the best veal to the final arrangement of the place cards and the selection of the right wine.

As the wife of a prominent railroad mogul, she was expected to serve on a dozen charities and organizations in the burgeoning city.

She had, in effect, a small empire to run with many servants under her, including butler, housekeeper, downstairs and upstairs maids, cook, kitchen aids, stable boy, gardener, handyman, and groom. And no allowances were made for imperfection. If the groom ran away with the downstairs maid and the cook came down with pneumonia on the same day, she was still expected to appear in the drawing room that evening with her smile intact and not a hair out of place.

To achieve this perfection, her life was a welter of appointments with the corsetiere, the hairdresser, dressmaker, tailor, florist, wine merchant, confectioner, draper, baker, jeweler, laundry (Dear Mr. Piermont, you are *not* to starch the napkins. Mr. Thornton detests starched napkins. You *are* to starch the bed linens. Mr. Thornton cannot abide limp bed linens.)

Ann was delighted to have her sister in her home only for the companionship they had always enjoyed, but Caroline soon saw that her services could also be used. She was able to take many details from Ann's burdened shoulders. She could order the flowers for the night's dinner party; make sure that the Van der Loefts and the Mc-Gintys were not served Lobster en Coquille twice in a row; and that

129

the visiting French Colonel was not seated next to the American Admiral with whose politics he vociferously disagreed. She could train the new upstairs maid and reprove the downstairs maid for letting dust collect. She could order petit fours for the afternoon tea, show the cook how to get the coffee stains out of the Belgian lace cloth, order replacements for the six Haviland cups that had been broken, fix the ruching that had come undone on one of Ann's dresses and save a trip to the seamstress by taking up a hem. She could arbitrate a quarrel between the stable boy and the groom, pay the iceman and even help Bromley put on his cufflinks when Ann was occupied elsewhere. In short, there was an endless array of things for Caroline to do.

She was glad to help. It made her feel easier about living with Bromley and Ann, but she sometimes pitied Ann for her pressured, hectic, fragmented existence. She sometimes felt a guilty longing for those times of solitude she had been able to claim in the Tomorrow River country and felt a need for time to be alone to work with Firefly. Such time was rare in the active demanding Thornton household.

Deeply in love with her husband, wise enough to value the blessings she had, Ann coped admirably with the irritations and annoyances of her life. Her one area of wistfulness was that she remained childless. She would have eagerly filled this void with attentions to Caroline's and Kemink's children, but Firefly would still have no one but her mother touch her, and Danny and Dan-Pete were a law unto themselves.

After an initial period of being ill at ease in the elegant household, the two boys had found their niche. They adored horses and they naturally gravitated to the stable. The groom, a dour Welshman, at first tolerated them and then came to enjoy them. With Bromley's permission he taught the boys to ride and drive the horses and feed and curry the animals. The stable boy was pleased to push half his work off on them. He taught them how to play cards (to which they quickly became addicted) and how to smoke (which they gave up rapidly.)

If they were not in the stable, they were most likely to be found in the kitchen, especially when there were cookies coming out of the oven.

They also enjoyed sliding down the long curved bannisters, exploring the dark and eery basement, playing pirates, and rough housing in the library with Bromley who allowed them to win their wrestling matches by such unfair tactics as tickling him in the ribs.

They did not like having to wear the velvet suits Aunt Ann ordered for them; going to Sunday School, taking baths every night, eating

130

things Bromley insisted were good for them, not having any pigs, not being able to go fishing, and worst of all, having to wear shoes *all the time.*

Kemink, too, found her niche. As Caroline had taken over many of Ann's small duties, Kemink took over many of the kitchen tasks. At first this disturbed both Ann and Caroline for different reasons. Kemink, not feeling at ease in the grandiose room of satin and gilt, had moved her things into a less pretentious room near the kitchen. When Caroline noted the move and then found her friend in the kitchen peeling potatoes, she was extremely upset. She went to Ann near tears.

"Ann—I know that I am scarcely in a position to complain—living as we are upon Bromley's largess and your generosity, but I will *not* have Kemink made into a domestic. In her own country she is a princess . . ."

"But my dear," Ann protested, "I don't want her in the kitchen anymore than you do. Bridget is the testiest of souls and the best of cooks. I shall have a conniption if I lose her and if she thinks for one moment that Kemink is encroaching on her domain, out she will storm!"

Kemink happened by just as the two sisters were embroiled in their discussion. She chided them both.

"Caroline, would you have me be useless in this household? Would that make me happy?" she questioned her friend. "I, too, must give and work if I am to be content."

Then she turned her dark eyes with equal disapproval upon Ann.

"Have you heard one cross word between Bridget and me? No. And there will be none. Our spirits are in harmony."

And so they were. They made a strange combination—the heaving, grumbling, red-headed Bridget; the quiet, dark, never complaining Kemink. Yet they worked together as easily as a right and a left hand.

Caroline had worried that in the quickly reasserted intimacy between her and her sister Kemink might feel left out. Three is never an easy number in human relationships. But this worry proved groundless. Ann's constant social obligations left ample time for Caroline and Kemink to be together and to keep their relationship healthy.

'What gorgeous hair you have," Ann had cried the first time she saw Kemink's hair loose. "Oh, do let me fix it in the new rat and mouse style!"

But Kemink would not. She stubbornly braided it Indian fashion.

Ann had a number of dresses made for her. She wore none of them. Though for months, place cards with her name were set at the table of the fashionable dinner parties, Kemink would not attend.

"It is not I who choose to make a domestic of her. It is she who chooses to be one," Ann lamented to Caroline.

"Sometimes I feel I was wrong to encourage her to leave her own people," Caroline worried, "but she does not seem discontent. She says when she has learned to read the newspaper, she will come to your dinner parties. I think the truth is that she is proud of her Indian heritage and does not wish to change; at the same time she realizes that her presence at the table might prove an embarrassment to Bromley."

Ann could not deny that some of their guests did view Indians as savages. The Thorntons bumped their moneyed noses hard on the fact that fall. Bromley decided the two boys would start school in one of the finest boys' academies in the city. He was unbelieving when he found that not all his money or prestige could persuade the school's director to admit an Indian child to his hallowed halls. When two other schools turned him down, Bromley was so furious he talked of opening a school himself. Caroline soothed him by convincing him that she preferred to tutor the boys herself. He permitted this arrangement, but periodically erupted over the entire business, always ending his angry monologue by pointing a finger at Caroline and declaring, "You can't teach them yourself forever, you know. They're getting to be big boys. I'll get them in a good school if I have to *buy* one!"

Bromley had also been eager to take Firefly to the finest specialists to see what could be done for her arm. Caroline had begged for a little time feeling the child was still too insecure to be put through exhaustive tests and probing. But by November she was showing signs of becoming the sunny outgoing little girl she was before she had been taken away.

She began to say a few words. At first shy with Bromley, he became her favorite. He took her for rides in the park, plied her with sugarplums and carried her up to bed on his shoulders each night.

Frustrated in her early attempts to gain Firefly's confidence, Ann compensated with gifts and clothes. Caroline did not feel easy about all the expensive gifts, but she knew it gave her sister such pleasure to pick out the velvet hoods, the ruffled pantaloons, the little fur muffs that she could not bring herself to demur.

"It pains me to think that Adam could have treated you as he did," Ann said, "but that marriage, however sad, has left you with a precious treasure, Caroline. I would give anything to have that beautiful little girl as my own."

Bromley summoned a long string of eminent doctors to the house to examine Felicty's arm. The verdict was always the same. They went away shaking their heads. Bromley was not a man to give up easily. They made pilgrimages to other cities, other states. Caroline began to understand why incurable people always spoke of these pilgrimages as "the weary rounds". She grew weary of the trains, the waiting rooms, the hospitals, but most of all, weary of that predictable shake of the head. The diagnosis was always the same. A deadened nerve in the arm was failing to transmit the messages from the brain that would have made the arm move normally. All the doctors could suggest was that the arm be exercised as much as possible to keep the flesh from dwindling away with disuse.

One doctor ordered salt water baths. Caroline and Kemink followed his instructions but no improvement was noticeable.

Christmas came, celebrated at the Thornton household with blazing yule logs, brimming bowls of punch, a fourteen foot tree encrusted with glass ornaments from Germany, and such piles of presents for the children that Kemink and Caroline could only shake their heads.

The Thornton's Christmas gifts to Caroline included a ballgown of cream velvet trimmed with blue lace.

"You shall wear it to our New Year's ball," Ann decreed.

"It's truly, truly beautiful," Caroline said, folding the dress gently back into the box. "I will wear it *next* New Year's. Please try and understand, Ann. I am not unappreciative—it's just—it's as if Adam had died. I need time before I will feel quite myself again. You do understand?"

"Yes," Ann sighed, but she found Caroline's reluctance difficult. She had been so eager to show her Chicago, but Caroline kept saying, "Perhaps later—maybe next month."

"She's almost as bad as Kemink," Ann complained to Bromley when they were settled in bed. "I've had a half dozen lovely dresses made for her but she chooses to wear only the drab ones. She comes to our dinners, but she is so quiet and she always excuses herself early. She has become altogether too fond of creeping away by herself. It's been months since I've really heard her laugh. I can't bear it! She's too young and lovely to turn into a dried up widow. What *shall* we do about it, Brom?"

Bromley laughed and planted a kiss on his wife's worried brow. "We'll do just what she asked us to do. Give her time. She's right, Ann. She's been hurt, she needs to lick her wounds. But in the spring we'll buy her a whole new wardrobe and I'll start fetching some chaps around to lighten her spirits."

"Oh, Brom, what a thing to say," Ann said, giving him a poke.

But secretly she was pleased. After all, it didn't look as if Adam would ever come back and if he did it was doubtful Caroline would have anything to do with him.

Ann lay back in her pillows, smiling and full of plans.

28

In March of 1858, Bromley, Ann, and Caroline took Firefly to Boston for the purpose of having a prominent specialist, who was visiting in that city, examine her. Bromley promised that if Dr. Germaine confirmed all the previous diagnoses, he would finally accept the medical verdict and would not insist on more pilgrimages.

Caroline stood stiffly in a room lined with oak cabinets, and watched as the distinguished-looking doctor went through the by-now familiar procedures.

When he was done, he helped the child dress and sent her out to Bromley and Ann. He leaned against one of the cabinets in a relaxed way, regarding Caroline with tired eyes.

"She is a beautiful child."

"Yes."

"She seems adjusted to her handicap."

"Yes," Caroline said defensively. She wondered if he were trying to tell her that it was *she,* the mother, who could now damage the child by not adjusting. "I would love her if both arms and both legs were incapacitated, but I feel she has a right to be *whole.*"

The doctor continued to look at her in that disconcerting way.

"She *is* whole," he said.

Caroline felt choked by unshed tears.

"You—you want me to accept the condition."

"You must. There is no known cure at this time. Actually, it's a small thing really. If you could see the patients I deal with from day to day—Mon Dieu—" he shook his head. "This child is not in pain. Not even in distress."

He was watching her closely.

She looked away from him.

134

"Doctor—I—I have always believed in miracles. Is that so wrong?"
He laughed softly.

"And so do I. The day I stop believing in miracles I shall cease to be a doctor."

"You don't understand," she said.

"But I do," he said. "I have authenticated several miracles in my time. One woman was from your own Chicago. She had carious bones. There was no hope. She went to a shrine in Lourdes, France and was healed. I went through the most extensive tests when she returned."

"Then you do believe—"
He shrugged.

"I am a scientist. If you could tell me why everyone who goes to a holy shrine is not healed then I would be happier. However, if it would be of any help to you, I can give you the woman's address. I have it in my files. Perhaps you would like to talk with her."

Caroline left the doctor with an address clutched in her gloved hand, feeling a sense of closeness to him as if he had extended an unusual amount of love.

On the way home, Felicity struck her useless arm with her good hand. The child's action reinforced what Dr. Germaine had said. Caroline realized that they would all have to treat and regard Fly as whole if they did not wish her to begin to see herself as handicapped and deformed.

When they arrived back in Chicago, they found the snow that had wrapped the great city was melting and the wind so volatile that you could almost see it as it prowled the streets, hungrily sucking up the last of the puddles.

"Spring is just around the corner," Ann rejoiced. It is time for putting away all sadness. Wait until you see the material I bought for a spring suit for you. And when it is finished, you *will* wear it. And you *will* see every inch of Chicago with me. And you *will* wear your ballgown to the opera. And you *will* attend Mrs. Dormeister's next luncheon—"

"Sounds as if I don't have much choice," Caroline said, then gave a little squeal as Ann showed her the soft rose material. "Ohhh, it *is* lovely."

Ann had it made up with black braid decorating the sleeves and throat and had her milliner make a hat in the newest fashion, underlined with matching material and roses under the brim. Ann was as excited as if she had created a work of art when she saw Caroline in the ensemble.

"Oh, it is exactly right," she enthused. "The color brings roses to your cheeks and makes your dark hair look dramatic!"

And Caroline could not help a smile of pleasure at herself in the mirror. She did look well. Ann had often brushed her hair while they talked and it had regained it's vibrant sheen. Brushed into the newest style, parted in the middle, it framed her face with clusters of curls at each side. The suit showed off her tiny waist to advantage. It was her first crinoline and she laughed as she felt it sway and tilt with her movements.

"Oh, Ann, it makes one feel so free!" she said with delight. "Like a bell ringing!" The fullness of skirts in the past decade had been supported by a dozen petticoats, and it was an exhilarating feeling of freedom to shed them all for a mere pair of pantaloons.

That afternoon at a charity bazaar at Mrs. Dormeister's, many admiring glances were cast at the dark-haired young woman in the rose colored suit, but none so persistently as those of a tall man with blonde hair. She felt his eyes first in the drawing room when Ann and her friend, Doris Dormeister, went on ahead to look at a display of lace. Caroline had paused to inspect the landscape paintings of George Inness. When her eyes flicked upward and caught his scrutiny, he did not look away, but continued to gaze at her without embarrassment. Something about his gaze made her flush. She turned pointedly away and went in search of her friends, but they had finished now with the Belgian lace and had gone into another room. She looked in the west parlor for them and although they were not there Caroline stopped, intrigued with some miniature paintings on ivory. She felt those eyes again. He was leaning against a colonnade looking at her with an expression of frank and intense pleasure.

"Really," she thought in annoyance, but then as she turned away, she had to laugh as the secondary thought came into her mind. "Dear Ann, your suit is much too potent if it's going to have such an effect on strange men."

Her laughter faded, however, and her heart began to beat a little harder as footsteps echoed on the marble floor behind her and she realized he was following her.

She paused in the drawing room, trying to force her attention upon a table of embroidery. Perhaps he would go on. But no—she could feel his gaze and her cheeks burned.

"Do you like embroidery?" he asked strolling over to stand beside her. "Would you consider it a legitimate form of art?"

"This display is rather ordinary, but I have seen pieces that most certainly would be considered works of art," Caroline found herself saying. She looked up into his waiting eyes, startled to find herself

136

speaking to him.

"Excuse me," she said with dignity, and turning she swiftly ascended the stairs and darted into a room with a display of homemade candies. After a moment's hesitation, she decided to buy the children a treat. She could find Ann and Doris a little later. By then the strange gentleman would probably have gone.

The room smelled of chocolates. She peered at mounds of angel-kisses, fudges, nougats, peppermints and caramels nestled on white doilies. She had just decided on a pound of chocolate drops and a box of peanut brittle when she was startled by his voice at her elbow.

"Peanut brittle is one of my favorites, too. Oh, come now. Don't run off again," he pleaded catching hold of her arm as she turned away.

"Please," she said indignantly, tugging her arm free.

"I'm sorry."

He took his hat off and bowed a little, his dark eyes fastened on her with intensity.

"I know you don't know me, and you have every right to be dismayed with my following you about, but there is something about you that enchants me. And if I don't behave in this unorthodox fashion, you are going to slip out of my life and I may never see you again. My name is Baird LeSeure. I am almost, though not quite, respectable, decently rich, and totally charming. Now that we have been introduced, won't you have tea with me?"

There was such a roguish light in his eyes, such a teasing in his manner, Caroline could not remain outraged. She felt a smile tugging at the corner of her lips.

"No, Mr. LeSeure, I cannot have tea with you simply because you have fallen in love with my new rose suit," she said firmly, "and if you are one-tenth as charming as you think you are, you will not follow me another step. I am a married woman with two small children. Even were I available, I would not strike up a flirtation with a stranger at a bazaar."

"Alas!" he said, putting on a very sad face.

Caroline couldn't help laughing.

"You won't even give me your name?"

She shook her head. The attendant came with her purchases, and she left her admirer.

"Where have you been?" Ann scolded when she at last located her. "We've been looking *everywhere* for you."

"I had to run away from a man who was chasing me because he fell in love with my new suit," Caroline said.

Ann laughed. "Oh, I see you've bought candy for the children. You should have told me where you were going."

Despite her adventure with the strange man (or perhaps because of it?) Caroline enjoyed the afternoon's excursion, but all other thoughts were wiped from her mind when she returned home to find a small envelope waiting for her.

"What is it?" Ann asked, wondering at the expression on her sister's face as she read the letter.

"Oh, Ann, it's from Mrs. Louwain, the woman Dr. Germaine said was cured in France at Lourdes Shrine. I wrote asking if I might come and call and she has sent me a gracious letter of agreement. Only it must be tonight because she is leaving in the morning on an extended trip. I hope it isn't too late already. Will you have Charles bring the carriage around for me?"

"Of course," Ann said, "but you haven't even eaten—"

"This is very important to me," Caroline said. She kissed her sister's cheek and was gone with a wild swaying of her new crinoline.

29

As Charles drew up in front of the address she had given him, Caroline thought there might have been some mistake. The building appeared to be a deserted shop with rough planks nailed across empty windows; but on closer inspection she saw there was a light burning in an upstairs window.

"I don't know how long this will take, Charles. Why don't you take the carriage home and I'll hire a cab when I'm ready to return."

"If you say so, Mum," Charles said. He had been grumbling to himself because she had ordered him out during the supper hour, and he was pleased to think he could return to his joint and dumplings.

The stairway that led to the upper floor was so narrow Caroline found her new crinoline hampered her ascent. The landing was lit with a large hanging lamp, and she could hear faint sounds of music.

Mrs. Louwain herself answered the door, a tall figure in rustling dark taffeta and a lace cap. She gestured Caroline to a chair by the fireplace.

138

The room smelled of the coal that was burning and spiced tea that was steeping in a china pot on a small inlaid table.

"It was so good of you to let me come," Caroline said, settling herself with difficulty into the chair. She had not quite gotten the knack of manipulating her hoop skirt.

"My pleasure, though I'm not sure if what I can tell you will be of any help," Mrs. Louwain said, seating herself. By the glow of the fire, Caroline could see now that she was elderly, though her movements had not revealed it. Her face wore the fissures of age with serenity and her hooded eyes had a liquid quality that garnered the light from the fireplace.

"It happened more than twenty years ago; however, it remains forever distinct in my mind," she assured Caroline.

She paused to pour tea into thin, flaring cups. Cradling her cup, she stared into the fire.

"Twelve of us from America went over together on a ship. When we arrived, we were not able to immediately gain access to the holy shrine as we had thought. There were hundreds of pilgrims seeking relief of distresses. We had to wait our turn. I was very ill, and the waiting was difficult for my husband, by nature an impatient man. He was afraid I would die before our chance came.

"There was one man in our group who was not liked. He was not Catholic and to some of the pilgrims this was an affront, and he was what one might call a vulgar man, loud and boastful. He was seeking to have his sight restored. He went on and on about it and to those whose lives were dwindling away, his affliction seemed little by comparison. I didn't share these feelings against him. As I mentioned before I was very ill, often in a state of high fever and sometimes I had—what?—dreams—visions? I experienced a sense of the oneness of all things, and I understood, as the others did not, that this man was part of me, I was part of him, we were both part of something greater."

She set her cup down shaking her head.

"You see, it is almost impossible to say in words what one perceives in a way that is beyond words," she apologized.

"No, no, I think I do understand," Caroline said, "Please go on."

"Well, at last our time came. I was so ill that the transferring of my stretcher to the holy shrine was a blur. I knew that at last I was going, but at the same time I scarcely did know. This man was just ahead of me and suddenly through the fog of my illness I heard him shout, "I see, I see!"

"Until that moment I had hoped to be cured, but I think in my heart I had not really believed that it could be. But—how can I say?—"

She pressed her fingertips together, closing her eyes in search of the right words.

"Because I felt a part of this man, his healing became my healing. When I heard the pure joy in his voice, my doubts vanished. I *knew* I would be healed, and I *was* healed. There is little more I can tell you."

"You've been well ever since?"

"Yes."

"Did it change your life?"

Mrs. Louwain shook her head sadly. "Not as much as I at first thought it would. I wanted to tell everyone I had experienced a miracle. I soon found that it embarrassed most people. Those who did not wish to believe made up their own explanations. I wanted to do something of great service to pay back in some way this marvelous gift of life, but I did not know where to begin. I was caught up in the ordinary cares of a mother and wife. I have done nothing remarkable with my life. My husband was in trade in the store below. He did well and we always gave generously to others, but I have regretted there was not some way I could have given more."

"You *have* given me something," Caroline said.

"I will give you the address where I am going if for any reason you wish to reach me, though I can't think what it would be," Mrs. Louwain said.

Caroline put down the cup of tea she had been too absorbed to drink. She felt a sense of excitement mingled with frustration, as if a door were opening and yet she was not able to go through.

Later in Thornton's library, she paced back and forth as she recounted the conversation to Bromley, Ann and Kemink.

"If you think it will help, we'll take Felicity to France," Bromley volunteered.

Caroline shook her head.

"Oh, Brom, you are so good. There seems nothing you wouldn't do for us. But I'm convinced it isn't *where* one is *physically,* but where one is in his consciousness. Mrs. Louwain had this certainty of healing. I felt the same thing that night with Kemink. There wasn't any outward change and yet I *knew.* The thing I cannot understand is what keeps me from being able to get this surety about Fly. I keep trying but it doesn't come. I do not want to go to France, but I *would* like to go away by myself."

"Oh, Carrie," Ann sighed, "and just when you had started to come out of your shell. I had so many plans. So many things I wanted to share with you—"

"I know, Ann, and I appreciate your wanting to, but Fly is so much

140

more important to me than social engagements."

"Yes, you're right," Ann agreed, "but look, why can't you allow yourself to have a little gaiety for a time? In July you can't imagine how hot Chicago gets. The temperature soars into the hundreds and gets stuck for days. No one can stand it. We usually spend six weeks at our cottage in Michigan. Give me a few more months of your company and then you can go ahead to the cottage and have time to yourself before the rest of us come. How would that be? Someone always has to go ahead and open the place anyway."

"A fair bargain," Caroline said. She would have liked to leave at once, but she felt she owed something to Ann.

That night she dreamed of dark rushes of birds, of a store front with rough planks nailed across it and of a baby boy tugging and chewing at the hem of her gown. She awoke limp and wet.

In the stillness of the night she could hear Ann and Bromley's soft laughter from the master bedroom. She felt a hollowness spread through her. There had been other moments when she had felt it— watching Brom's arm curve protectively about Ann as they started to ascend the stairs—seeing their eyes meet in the special way of husbands and wives—watching Brom's hand seek Ann's.

Adam—

Her eyes felt hot and wet. She prayed to stop wondering where he was—what he was doing. Would she never be really free of him?

30

By May of 1858, even the churches were aflame with political passions. On Sunday mornings Caroline and the Thorntons heard the Dred Scott Decision and the Fugitive Slave Law denounced from the pulpit as atrocious acts which gave into the hands of slavery law, power, and usage while taking away one by one the defenses of Freedom. They were reminded of their Christian duty to stand up for the "moral sentiments of Freedom's battle." The issue was defined as a contest between the divine right and "injustice, inhumanity and national disgrace."

Bromley was repeatedly urged to join one of the anti-slavery groups which had been springing up in Chicago since before 1850. He was in sympathy with their sentiments against bondage of human beings, but Bromley, the soul of conservatism, was put off from affiliation by a wild eyed element that clung to the fringes of most of these organizations. He salved his conscience by frequent donations for the printing of anti-slavery tracts and bulletins which were rampant in the city.

Ann and Caroline were moved to tears by tales of the abhorrent treatment of the black people. They were not a regular link in the underground fugitive slave system, but more than once in an emergency Ann hid a black man among the pickle crocks and wood piles until he could be safely fetched back to the regular link in the chain.

Bromley aligned himself with the new Republican Party which had formed in Ripon, Wisconsin in 1854, and while occasional debates about the merits of Lincoln versus Douglas had been carried on at the Thornton gatherings for years and the threat of secession had come up now and then, the topics now gathered a power and heat that sometimes drove the ladies from the table. All except Doris Dormeister. Doris had a sharp brain hidden beneath her intricate hairdos and satin ribbons. She was a descendant of the venerable Mrs. La-Compt, one of the earliest of Chicago settlers who was said to have had great influence with the Pottawattamies. More than once when the Indians threatened to attack, Mrs. LaCompt had gone to meet the hostile war parties alone, sometimes staying with the Indians for days while she worked to appease their anger. On one occasion, the anxious settlers, weapons in arms awaiting attack, were astonished to see Mrs. LaCompt arrive in the vanguard of the advancing warriors, their war paint changed to somber black in acknowledgement of their change of viewpoint. Her granddaughter exhibited something of the same will and spirit.

Ann found this conduct a little unseemly in her best friend, but Caroline applauded Doris's plucky intelligence and found it sometimes gave her courage to ask questions she might not otherwise have ventured. She had a natural shyness and she still excused herself from the dinner gatherings when she felt it was feasible.

On one such evening when she had declined to come down due to fatigue, Ann came to beg her to reconsider.

"I know you wanted a quiet evening with Kemink, but darling, Bromley brought home an extra man and you know how awkward that makes seating. Won't you please come down?" Ann wheedled.

Caroline found it impossible to say no to her sister, but she was not above bargaining.

"Only on the condition that I can come as I am."

Ann agreed reluctantly. Caroline had her hair drawn back in a simple knot and was dressed in a common day dress of brown messaline.

"More than one of my friends have inquired if you are in *mourning*," Ann chided.

Caroline only laughed, laid aside her book and followed her sister. Bromley and his extra man were waiting at the foot of the stairs to take the ladies into dinner. Caroline felt a shock of recognition as a pair of dark eyes collided with hers.

"This is my beloved sister, Caroline," Ann introduced. "Caroline, this is Baird LeSeure, one of our most charming bachelors."

"I have already heard about Mr. LeSeure's charm" Caroline said with a smile. She refrained from adding "from Mr. LeSeure's own lips."

"Oh yes, his charm is legend, I suppose," Ann laughed, and taking Brom's arm proceeded toward the dining room.

"Is it really you? Then after all it is fate and you have not been whisked out of my life forever," said LeSeure, kissing her hand.

Caroline was female enough to wish that she had slipped into a more festive dress and curled her hair.

"But you lied to me," was the first thing he said to her when they had settled at the table. "You told me you were married."

"I am separated," she said, feeling oddly ashamed. She added, "but I *do* have two children."

"That's fine," he said. "I love children. I have my eye on a manorial place up North which I intend to buy someday, as the perfect place to raise ten children."

"*Ten*, Sir?"

"That way I can have a doctor, lawyer, merchant—"

"Clergyman—"

"No, no clergyman."

"Oh?"

"I'm not a religious person."

"But you believe in God?" Caroline said taken aback.

"Not a transcendent God."

The bite of roll Caroline had taken stuck in her throat. She had heard of atheists, but she had not expected to meet one.

"I cannot imagine not believing in God," she said.

"Have you read Descartes or Spinoza?"

"I'm afraid I have never heard of either."

"Then you must," he said with a smile that took the sting out of the authority with which he said it.

"I still say that it can only lead to economic ruin for both the North and the South," a voice at the far end of the table said so vociferously that other conversation halted, and people leaned forward to see who the speaker was.

Gateway Farrell was speaking, an editorial writer on the Times, a newspaper rumored to have a standing order to "telegraph full all news, and when there is none, send rumors." He had ginger colored hair and protruding eyes.

"My dear, dear Mr. Farrell, you cannot mean to imply that economic considerations are more important to you than individual liberty—that you would support the bondage of flesh and blood human beings for the sake of filthy lucre?" Doris Dormeister protested.

"Madam, you are mouthing the catch phrases of our decade with no real understanding of the hardship and suffering that would occur to this nation if the Southern states seceded from the Union," Farrell countered.

"Nonsense," a hearty looking man across the table from Farrell said loftily. "The South's constant threats of secession are nothing but that—threats. It could not survive without trade and commerce with the North. It's utter stupidity to support otherwise and they aren't *all* stupid."

Ann looked at Bromley with distress. Was yet another dinner party to be spoiled by the discussion of Southern and Northern differences? But Bromley himself had been caught up in the argument and was leaning forward into the fray.

"Would you go so far, Farrell, as to stand behind Douglas on the Compromise of 1850? Would you allow Nebraska and Kansas to decide for themselves on the slavery issue even at the danger of upsetting the balance arrived at by the Missouri Compromise?"

"I am anti-war, sir, above anything else," Farrell said.

"Well, I'll tell you one thing, the people of Illinois are fed up with Douglas," the hearty man insisted, "and not our state alone. Douglas knows it. He admitted in print that he was able to go from Boston to Chicago in the light of his own burning effigies."

"The facts do not support you," Farrell said. "Buchanan was elected on a squatter's right platform in '56. His views coincided with those of Douglas."

"But my *dear*," cried Doris rising out of her chair in distress, "everyone knows how Buchanan won the election in Chicago. It was a scandal! All the saloons in the city kept beer flowing free on Douglas money!"

Now the entire table was into a bedlam of political arguments except, Caroline noticed, Baird LeSeure.

"Have you no interest in politics, Mr. LeSeure?" she asked.

"Do you really think anything said here is going to make a difference?" he asked with a slight smile.

Caroline surprised herself with the answer she gave Baird. "Yes,"

144

she said, "I think it might make a difference what is said here. Ideas are the most powerful things in the world and people's actions are swayed by their ideas and ideals. When enough people believe something, the entire nation is affected."

LeSeure laughed.

"Right you are, lovely lady, but these people have already formulated their beliefs. There is not one of them who would be swayed one tittle by the arguments of the opposition. Their ideas and ideals as you put it, are already set in cement."

"—and yours, Mr. LeSeure?" Caroline said, somewhat offended to hear her brother-in-law and his guests subtly put down.

"—and mine also are set in cement, one of them being that it is a crime to waste an evening on politics when there are beautiful women present. I intend to go to the aid of your sister."

And so saying, LeSeure excused himself and made his way to Ann.

He struck a spoon against a crystal goblet to gain attention. "Come, we're distressing our hostess with ungentlemanly displays of temper—and we're letting all this loveliness," with a nod at the women, "go to waste."

Sourly, for they had been enjoying their spirited conversations, the men allowed themselves to be led into the drawing room for dancing.

Doris Dormeister had also been enjoying the political free-for-all and she made a face at LeSeure.

"Of course *you* don't want to talk about the issues, Bay, because you're a Southerner. Everyone *knows* you have a plantation down South."

Ann sent her friend such a shocked and disapproving look that Doris with a sigh laid down the verbal cudgel with which she had been prepared to beat him.

"I would never *dare* to match wits with you on politics," LeSeure told Doris with a smile. Then he turned his back on her and bowing, asked Caroline to dance.

"I fear I have forgotten how," Caroline said, "but there are so many lovely ladies here tonight I think you will not go without a partner."

"If you have forgotten how, then you must be taught again" he insisted.

Caroline looked around her, embarrassed. Her drab dress was out of place among those of the fashionable ladies in the room.

"I did not dress for festivities. I was going back to my room after dinner."

He held out his arms to her.

Ann was playing a minuet and Caroline found that her feet remembered the steps after all. Her partner's hands were warm and deft as they touched her waist or fingers in the turns and pirouettes. He made a point of looking boldly into her eyes each time they faced.

He is a male coquette, Caroline thought, *sure of his ability to charm any female he sets eyes on. But why should he choose me for his next conquest?*

At each turn he held her more daringly close, his eyes laughing with audacity. She could smell the scented starch of his linen shirt and the wine he had had at dinner. She felt faint with the swift turns and his nearness, and she was angry with herself for feeling his magnetism. She knew by the heat of her cheeks that they were red and that the betraying redness and her inability to meet his bold glance informed him of her intense awareness of him. She could feel that it amused him and that further infuriated her.

A dark, angry sparkle began to flare in her eyes and her chin tilted at an angry level.

I am not some untried young girl who is going to go all aflutter with your attentions, she flashed him a silent message. *I am a woman, who has been loved and hurt enough to be bled free of foolish romantic notions. Find someone else to trifle with—*

As the music came to an end, he bowed, then caught her hand. "Come—now, you must beg me to sing. I want to impress you in every way I can."

"Oh, yes Bay, do sing!" Ann said, eagerly giving him her place at the piano.

He had Caroline's hand in a firm grasp and drew her down beside him on the piano bench.

He began to sing a gay, rollicking and faintly risque song about a French soldier. He had everyone laughing. But Caroline, to whom he was addressing the song, felt her cheeks grow warmer than ever. He had a good baritone and soon the entire company had congregated about the spinet making requests.

"This is the last song of the evening, for my new friend, Caroline Quimby," he announced at length.

Looking into her eyes he sang—"Drink to me only with thine eyes and I will pledge with mine—"

She looked away, embarrassed and bewildered by this unaccustomed attention.

"Or leave a kiss within the cup and I'll not ask for wine—"

When the last of the company had trooped out, Ann looked about the disordered drawing room and gave a sigh. "God bless Bay for rescuing my party. Everyone ended up having a lovely time instead of coming to blows."

"Oh, it was a good argument!" Bromley dissented.

"Darling, don't you think Bay is charming?" Ann appealed to Caroline.

"Yes," Caroline said politely, adding "good night" to avoid further comment.

Later, getting ready for bed, she was swept with a curious feeling of dismay as she realized she could no longer remember the exact sound of Adam's voice or the shape of his face. *But I want to forget, don't I?* she asked her mirror. There was no answer.

She lay awake listening to the clop of horses' hooves drawing a carriage through the dark streets below, the metronomic ticking of the clock on her dresser, the soft breathing of Fly, who slept with her. She was suffused with obscure emotions too painful to name.

Finally she got up and crept through the sleeping house to the library. She lit the lamp on the desk, lifting it up to better read the titles of the books that covered two walls of the room.

"Caroline—what are you doing?"

She turned to find Bromley, wearing a dressing gown the tassel of his sleeping cap bobbing over his nose, peering at her indignantly.

"Ann thought you were a burglar."

"I am sorry Bromley. I did not mean to disturb anyone. I couldn't sleep so I thought I would look for a book. Do you have any works by Spinoza?"

He shook his head. "No. I can send for some if you'd like."

"No, that is not necessary."

"Here, take this one," Bromley pulled one out at random, "If it bores you, all the better—it'll put you back to sleep."

Glancing at the title, "The Care and Breaking of Horses", Caroline suppressed a rueful smile and followed her brother-in-law up the stairway. There was no arguing with his logic.

31

The following day a package arrived for Caroline. Inside was a leatherbound, gold-tooled copy of Spinoza's "On God."

"Look who charmed the charmer," Ann said with a smile when Caroline confessed that the gift was from LeSeure.

"Did you know that he's an atheist?" Caroline asked.

"We—ll, yes, but I think he says that to be shocking, and he is such good fun. Whatever Bay is, he makes things sparkle."

Bromley had had to leave early that morning and the two sisters were enjoying a late breakfast in Ann's sitting room.

"There are rumors Bay had a fanatical love for his step-sister, and that when she died some kind of tragic death he became an atheist," Ann explained, "though I don't know how true it is. Bay is so light-hearted it's hard to associate any kind of tragedy with him."

Caroline had opened the book and was threatening to become absorbed. Ann caught it from her fingers.

"Oh, no you don't! It's too lovely a day to stick your nose in a book. I want you to come with me to see Chicago. You've hardly been around the block all the time you've been here."

"Madam, Mr. LeSeure is here," the downstairs maid interrupted, presenting a card to her mistress.

"That settles it!" Ann said triumphantly. "Bay can drive us about."

LeSeure seemed happy to go along with Ann's wish, and soon the three of them were ensconced in an open carriage with a pair of chestnut horses trotting smartly ahead.

The north side of Chicago at the lake where the Thorntons lived was blessed with numerous gardens. Large trees were already throwing their leafy shadows over the streets, creating a green bower of flickering sun and shadow. The breeze was fresh and titillating, and Caroline, remembering another spring when she had swung from trees like a child, felt something of the same exhilaration now, and was glad she had decided to come.

"Is it not lovely?" Ann said appreciatively. "No wonder they call Chicago 'a city in a garden'."

"It has also been called the 'city of mud'," LeSeure commented as they approached State and Madison streets. Planking had been laid down earlier, but it had been broken up by heavy loads and was in need of repair. The humor of the city's residents was attested to by street signs here and there which proclaimed 'No Bottom Here' or 'This Way to China'.

They made better time when they reached Clark Street where the streets had been paved with wooden blocks. They took circuitous routes at times for some of the streets were obstructed with bricks, lumber, or wooden houses and buildings being moved out to make room for more imposing structures.

With all the signs of new construction, Caroline wondered at vacant buildings and empty stores along the main thoroughfare.

"Casualties of the panic of 1857," Baird explained. "Building was almost a mania until then. When the bubble of inflation caused by

148

outrageous speculation burst, thousands of businesses were ruined and a number of the building projects planned are still waiting to be finished. Things are beginning to recover now though."

Ann, like most of the first Chicago settlers was proud of the city, and she preferred to point out the high school constructed of marble two years before, the elegant Tremont House Hotel, and the hundreds of gas street lamps that illuminated the city at night. Baird, who was not a resident of the city but was only visiting on business, took delight in teasing Ann by pointing out the less desirable features.

As they drew near the river and a noticeable stench began to be pervasive, he said, "Did you know that Chicago means skunk or strong smell in Indian? The Ojibwas said 'She-kag-ong' which means 'Wild Onion Place.' "

"Oh, Bay, it does not!" Ann pouted. "That's just a mean story. Chicago means 'strong.' "

"Well, it certainly has a strong smell," Baird conceded, and Caroline, who had drawn a cologne scented handkerchief from her purse to defend her nose tacitly agreed.

"They also call Chicago 'Queen of the River'," Ann said grandly, ignoring the odor that seemed so offensive to Bay and Caroline.

"It seems that love is not only blind but also devoid of olfactory nerves," LeSeure said to Caroline, casting a sidelong glance at Ann. "This sister of yours certainly loves her Chicago to be so ignorant of what we are gasping to survive. But then—the river has a right to be foul; the sewage of 90,000 people flows into it."

"Oh, Bay!" Ann leaned across Caroline to give LeSeure a slap on the arm. "You know the city has built sewers like mad."

"All of which still drain into the river, dear lady."

"Baird LeSeure, can you not see any of the beauty of Chicago?" Ann demanded, angry now.

"Of course I can! I'm enthralled by the thirty acres of solid cattle and hogs in the Sherman Yards sent here to be butchered and shipped around the country. I go out of my mind at the sight of thousands of bushels of flour and grain arriving every day in your dredged-out harbor. When I see the magnificent steam elevator that has been introduced—"

"Oh, Bay, you make me furious!" Ann declared. "I take back everything I ever said about you being charming."

"Now I am contrite," he said, laughing in a way that made him sound anything but contrite. "Let me make amends by taking you to lunch. You can order the most sumptuous thing on the menu and I promise not to blanche."

"I'm not sure I want to eat with you," Ann said with pretended coolness.

"The Tremont House serves a delicious fowl and wine combination on Saturday—perhaps chocolate eclairs for dessert—?" Baird tempted.

"I can never stay mad at you," Ann gave in, and he turned the horses back toward Lake and Dearborn Streets.

The hotel was an imposing five story brick building towering above all other edifices in the sprouting city. Inside, the Tremont was the quintessence of luxury with mantles of Egyptian marble, damask drapes lined with silk, rosewood and mahogany chairs in the parlors and drinking fountains in the halls.

Baird, a lovely lady on each arm, paused in the lobby to make a cursory inspection of the bulletin board where up-to-the-minute telegraphic dispatches of important events were continually posted.

The board informed readers that the Cook County Democrats had held their convention and had given sanction to the submission of the LeCompton Constitution to the people of Kansas.

LeSeure shook his head at the announcement. "The LeCompton Constitution amounts to a grant of slavery which is sure to prove dangerous to the free settlers of Kansas," he commented.

"So, after all you are interested in politics and you do *not* sound like a Copperhead," Caroline said.

"Ahh, you have found out my guilty secret!" He pretended despair, and then instantly turned to lighter topics as he escorted his companions into one of the elegant dining parlors.

When the tasty entree had been set before them, Ann leaned forward and said to Baird, "You see, Bay, Chicago *is* becoming cultured—" as with a wave of her hand she indicated the linen napkins, the transoms over the doors, the window sashes hung on pulleys to provide ventilation, and the artistic stuccos done by Chicago artists. "When Bromley and I first came here it was impossible to get anything but greasy foods served on smeary dishes and if your appetite survived that, then the spittoons sitting about everywhere and the black beetles crawling on the floor finished off your appetitie. And look now!" she ended with pride.

"Dear Ann, I shall praise Chicago to the skies if it will keep me in your good graces," Bay promised.

Caroline found the chocolate eclairs especially good and when she expressed her appreciation, Baird insisted she indulge herself in another, for which she was soon sorry. Tightly corseted, she was terrified she might disgrace herself by belching at any moment.

"Could we walk a bit?" she asked as they came out of the hotel, hoping to ease her discomfort with action.

"If you have a hearty constitution," Bay said. "The streets of Chi-

150

cago at present are like climbing the Alps. No two at one level."

He lifted one arm as if to ward off an attack from Ann. "Let me hasten to add it only contributes to the delights of Ann's great city."

"You are learning," Ann said, laughing.

The main streets of the city had been only inches above the river level and in the past had been an even worse quagmire in the spring, so silt dredged from the harbor to deepen it for commerce was being used to build up the grade and literally lift the city out of the mud. This resulted in the sidewalks being at disparate levels as the work was in progress.

As they strolled, they stopped several times to watch workers engaged in the engineering process of raising buildings with giant jackscrews.

"Astonishing," Caroline said, impressed, "to think of moving entire buildings intact!"

"They say that when the Tremont House was lifted not a drop of tea in the teacups was spilled and business went on as usual," Ann said.

Caroline's first inspection of Chicago was the beginning of a series of carefree days. Bay's business kept him in the city for several months and he seemed to have unlimited free time to devote to the two sisters. He was a master at finding diversions. He took them to racing matinees at Garden City and Brighton, and encouraged them to 'gamble wickedly' by placing bets in the hope of winning one of the $100 to $125 purses offered each day. He found tableaux, pantomines, pageants, ballets, and acrobatic feats for them to attend. When P.T. Barnum's "Grand Colossal Museum and Menagerie" came to the city, he took the children. Danny and Dan-Pete were also allowed to accompany them to the stereoscopic exhibitions which featured such historical spectacles as the conflagration of Moscow and the lifelike representations of Napoleon's funeral. He called Fly "Her Most Beautiful Highness of Chicago" and tried to win her allegiance from Bromley, but she remained faithful.

Though Dan and Dan-Pete loved Bromley, he was not a hero to them. All his wealth, intelligence, kindness and charm could not offset for them the fact that he was small and portly with thinning hair and glasses. In contrast, they admired Bay's bold swaggering manner and were impressed by his six foot three height and wide shouldered brawn. They took to imitating his walk and using his bantering intonations in their conversation, with droll effect.

LeSeure always addressed Kemink as Princess Kemink and treated her alone with reverence. It seemed impossible for anyone to keep from succumbing to his charm, least of all Caroline.

In the evening he escorted her to hear the Christy Minstrels, to the opera, or to be entertained by magicians who advertised their abilities to controvert the laws of nature. She had never, even as a young girl, had such a time of lighthearted gaiety.

He encouraged her fondness for creme puffs and eclairs and the hollows in her cheeks and shoulder blades filled out. Under Adam's tutelage, she had abhorred all intemperate drink. It amused Bay to try to coax her into "a sip of wine." He flustered her by kissing the nape of her neck whenever the opportunity presented, and shocked her by suggesting that her dress were not decolleté enough. On the whole, he was both toxic and tonic and she could not help but grow fond of him.

She did not realize *how* fond she had become until she came down the stairs to one of Ann's soirees and saw Bay lifting one of the Clement girls' curls to plant a kiss on her cheek. As laughter spilled up the steps to her, she felt a stab of jealousy and anger. She remembered her first estimate of Bay, that he was a male coquette, and was furious with herself for lowering her defenses. He had made inroads on her emotions after all. Then she set aside her anger with a laugh of self-deprecation. After all, Bay *was* charming and he *was* fun; she was fortunate to have been reminded that he was also someone not to be taken seriously. She was able to present him with a serene smile when he deserted the Clement girl to greet her.

Anyway, she thought as she allowed him to lead her in to dinner, it would soon be June; Bay would be on his way south and it was time for Ann to keep her promise and let her go to the cottage alone. The frivolities and laughter had renewed and buoyed her spirits, but there were deeper things within her that demanded their turn. Her holiday was over.

32

The house at the shore turned out to be much larger than Caroline had envisioned when Ann spoke of it as a cottage. Shrouded with dust cloths, tightly shuttered, beset with an unseasonably dreary June rain, it was the sort of house that invited a belief in ghosts.

The man from the village who had brought up her luggage, left her to struggle alone with the task of lighting a fire in the fireplace. She had wanted to be alone, and now indeed she was.

"Don't you want to come with me, Kemink?" she had asked. Kemink was never a distraction. She was one of those rare people who instinctively knows not to intrude. But she had shaken her head firmly.

"I must stay and care for the children so they will not fall upon Ann's busy hands—and besides, I have promised Bromley to plant an herb garden."

Wanting to be alone, already Caroline had been lonely traveling the miles from Illinois to Michigan. Bromley was so good to the children and yet, reasonably, he had his rules, too. Caroline, watching the countryside whirl past the train window found herself thinking that she saw too little of Dan and Dan-Pete these days. In the To-morrow River country the little family had been bound by their needs and their proximity; the two boys, small though they had been, had been bulwarks of that solidity. Now it seemed to Caroline that she only saw them during the hours when she tutored them and for a few minutes before bedtime. Even their meals were taken apart from the adults. And Bromley was talking again about the necessity of sending them to a good school. *Am I too possessive a mother?* Caroline wondered, trying to analyze the rebellion she felt everytime Bromley spoke of sending the two boys away.

At last the flames caught and sent a red glow across the polished floor. Above her the rain made a hussh against the roof. After a cursory inspection of the house Caroline felt better. She made tea, lit lamps, and unpacked the dozen books Baird had sent her and then never given her time to read. She removed some of the dust covers, settled herself into the corner of a sofa with a cup of tea, and began to read an English translation of "Requiel Philosophique". She was soon immersed, gathering darkness, storm, probable ghosts, forgotten. She read far into the night. The pages were becoming blurred with fatigue when she came across a passage in Dumarsais' "De La Raison" Baird had underlined in black ink—

"Reason will never be able to conceive that a wise God should permit man by his follies to disturb his divine plans; that a good and just God would punish man for weaknesses and ignorances which he could have prevented by giving man more strength and more light. Reason cannot conceive that a God full of equity and benevolence should suffer man, whose well-being he desires, to render himself eternally unhappy by the abuse of freedom which he accorded him. A God who has given man reason cannot do or say things contrary to reason or above this reason. A God who was desirous of rendering the human race more enlightened by revelation could not have expressed himself in that revelation in an obscure fashion nor yet have required man to believe mysteries incomprehensible to him. A just God cannot become angry with men for not being convinced of what they cannot understand. An all-powerful God cannot be troubled in his bliss by the actions and thoughts of men whom he himself molded to be what they are. A supremely happy and self-sufficient God has no need of men or of their acts of worship in order to be glorified. A perfectly good and omnific God knows and foresees the needs of his children whom he loves without waiting for them to come begging. Finally, reason will never conceive that a good, just, and wise God could punish eternally with uttermost torments, passing faults committed in time by creatures whom he could have made quite different beings had he wanted to—"

She laid the book aside. She had come in search of God's nearness and the first thing she had done was to bring her fears and doubts into the foreground with this statement.

She replenished the fire, and then went to the door, unbolted and opened it. Wind rushed in, caught and flung her hair, and whipped her skirts in a tangle about her knees. She looked at the sky, which was exploding, tearing into fissures of incandescent white and violent purple.

He *is.* She felt it again, as she had felt it that night of Kemink's near death.

Her face and hair were streaming with rain. She had to struggle to get the door shut and bolted again. Shivering, she knelt by the fireplace. All the questions that had plagued her remained unanswered, the door to higher knowledge still firmly shut, the lock unyielding to her probing—but she felt there had to be an intelligent power. Something designed snowflakes and grew oak trees and made roses smell sweet.

She blew out the lamp and lay down. Please, she prayed, *show me!* And then she slept.

Her days fell into a pattern. In the mornings after her tea, she walked the pale moon-shaped beach that edged the blue and seething lake.

Other families were beginning to come to the resort now, and by ten o'clock clusters of nannies would be gathering with their charges, along the beach. The little girls would go wading and the boys would send paper ships off on the bobbing waves.

She read voraciously the books Bay had given her, Emerson, Thoreau, Goethe, and the Bible. She was like someone searching for a

154

treasure who having found a new clue here and there grows more excited by the minute. It was a stunning revelation to her that not one of the famed atheists whose works Bay had sent to her actually disbelieved in an intelligent all encompassing essence. The target of their malice was man's religious abuses, and the source of their endless inquiry and argument among themselves was not so much if such a divine being existed as whether this being were personal or nonpersonal, immanent within man and the universe or transcendent, far above either. Even Spinoza wrote—"God and only God is—"

When she would look up and realize it was growing late, she would become Martha instead of Mary, cooking supper, taking off dustcovers, washing woodwork and plankings with soda water to freshen the long shut house in preparation for the Thornton's arrival.

After supper she would wash her few dishes and walk again in the darkness, the whispered hiss of waves keeping her company—waiting—waiting.

She had been there five days. The weather had grown so warm she opened the shutters in the main room so a breeze would flow through, flooding all with sunlight and freshness. She was reading Goethe, sitting cross-legged on the floor like a little girl, when suddenly a passage became illuminated for her as if someone had lit it with white flames.

"If you treat an individual as he is, he will stay as he is. But if you treat him as if he were what he ought to be and could be, he will become what he ought to be and could be—"

The phrase jarred loose for her momentarily that tantalizing and beckoning door; she saw into the light beyond.

It's already done—we have only to claim it! She began to cry. She understood now why the door had to remain shut until the soul was capable of sustaining the glory behind the shield. *Fly is not abnormal —she is whole!*

Three days later when the Thorntons arrived, she looked radiant, and the first words she said after embracing them were *"Fly is whole."*

Ann and Bromley looked at each other uneasily. The child had been between them in the carriage and her arm was no different than ever. Their eyes went swiftly to Fly, half expecting that some miracle might have occurred.

Caroline was hugging each of the children. She seemed not to notice that Fly's arm hung limp and useless as ever.

"Is that the ocean, Mother?" Danny was asking. "Does it go clear to England?"

"No, darling—it's Lake Michigan, and it goes all the way to Chicago. You and Dan-Pete will have great fun sailing ships on the waves."

"Mama, Mama," Fly interrupted with excitement, "Unc Bromley bought me candy-nuts while you gone. I sleeped with Kink and Aunt Ann tooks me out ridin'."

"Indeed, indeed," laughed Caroline.

"Kin we roll down the bank?" asked ever adventurous Dan-Pete.

"After you have changed your clothes."

The boys were off in a rush of legs. Only then did Caroline notice the looks on Brom's and Ann's faces.

"She's whole," she affirmed again quietly. "It does not matter what your eyes see. She is healed."

Ann looked at Bromley with a troubled expression. He shrugged and smiled at her. No more was said on the subject.

The following morning, Caroline was half dragged from her bed by an agitated Ann.

"Caroline, you can't imagine what Kemink's doing!" she cried. "You must do something. Make her stop! She is so pure of heart she doesn't *realize*!"

"Whatever in the world—?' Caroline asked, alarmed.

"She's out there in the water—with—with almost nothing on—" Ann said, covering her face with her hands, —"and she has the boys with her in their underwear—and Caroline, everyone is watching them. We'll never be able to hold our heads up againnn—" she ended in a wail.

Caroline flung open the shutters to look out. Bobbing among the blue waves was Kemink's black head, shiny and wet as a seal; now and then a round, brown shoulder surfaced as well as she struggled to uphold two smaller bobbing heads.

"Pray, Ann, do not become so flustered," she laughed. "They seem rather well covered with water. I'll dress at once and go down and speak to her."

When Kemink saw Caroline coming down to the beach, she came out of the water, not at all self-conscious in her wet shift.

"Water's very good," she said, smiling her strong, white smile.

"Kemink, you are getting fat," Caroline laughed, noticing that her friend's body had grown quite round from her own and Bridget's cooking.

Then she tried diplomatically to explain that civilized women were not allowed the same privileges to cavort in the water as Indian maidens. Kemink could be stubborn when she chose, and this time she chose.

156

Wrapping a blanket about herself, she sat down cross-legged on the sand. "Dan-Pete and Dan must learn to swim. There is no one else to show them. I am going to swim. I am going to teach them. To swim is a beautiful thing. There is no evil in it. My people have a saying, 'If your feathers are white, no tongue can make them black'."

Surprisingly, Brom backed her up.

"Ann, she is right. It's a healthy and natural thing for the boys to learn to swim. I used to swim naked in the river when I was a boy. Kemink is a natural creature and should be allowed the right to enjoy the water."

"And would you have me take off my corset and dive in, too?" asked Ann frigidly.

"No, I would not. But that is only because I am a stuffy hidebound person," Bromley said, and hid himself behind his newspaper. "My dear, it says here that the Republican Convention has nominated Abraham Lincoln as their candidate for president."

For the rest of the vacation, poor Ann was obliged to hide her chagrin and embarrassment behind a big hat and to look the other way whenever Kemink took to the waves. Caroline, corsetted and bootshod like her sister, watched Kemink with amused envy. The happy shouts of the boys were music to her. Nevertheless, she felt for her sister, and it strengthened her feeling she should make an effort to find a life of her own and not hang about the Thornton's necks forever. As dearly as she loved Ann, as grateful as she was to Bromley, she was beginning to sorely need some self-determination for both her own sake and Kemink's.

The last night of their stay at the cottage, she dreamed again of the boarded store front and the little boy weeping and chewing on the hem of her dress but this time she awoke in the darkness, not with a sense of travail, but with another of those flashing senses of illumination. She slipped through the darkness to Kemink's bed and shook her friend awake.

"Kemink, Kemink. I know at last what I am to do with my life. You remember those children in Milwaukee?—how awful it was—the way poor Fly was when we got her back? I'm going to start a school for children like that. Will you help me?"

"I am glad we have found our path," Kemink answered simply, and the two women clasped each other's hands in a renewal of their bond of togetherness.

33

On a spring evening in his fortieth year, Louis LeSeure, a Louisiana plantation owner, boarded a Mississippi riverboat to talk to the captain about transporting his cotton bales in the fall. The men grew convivial over fried catfish and a barrel of red-eye, and the night ended with the captain snoring drunkenly on deck while LeSeure enjoyed the favors of the captain's niece.

At sixteen, Marouska Petrosky was deep breasted, with high cheek bones and a full lipped face framed by tow hair. She had never met, never even seen a man like Louis LeSeure—a man who wore a ruffled shirt, gold rings on his fingers, and smelled of cologne much like a woman, a man who spoke as softly as music, and who touched her gently.

At dawn when the effects of the raw liquor had worn off, LeSeure was sorry that he had bedded a girl who was a virgin. He slipped several folded bills under her pillow and went his way, thinking about the incident only if the sight of a riverboat or some tall woman with white blond hair momentarily nudged his memory.

When the girl discovered that she was pregnant, she told no one and tried to conceal her condition under jackets and shapeless clothing. The rummy, cross-eyed captain, who was her uncle, had never paid much attention to her. Seldom completely sober, he noticed nothing amiss.

On a dark and storming night Marouska's time came. While the river rolled beneath the creaky old tugboat, she writhed for hours, biting her lips to keep from crying out, until at last the child was born.

As she lay in her own warm blood, listening to her uncle snoring yards away from her, feeling the pitch and the lurch of the storm-rocked craft, it occurred to her that she could dispose of the child by tossing it overboard. If anyone ever did find the baby and trace it back to her she could say it was dead at birth and she had given it a sea burial. The child seemed to her a bag of sticky wrinkled flesh to which she felt only aversion. Perhaps it was dead. It hadn't cried.

She gathered it up, and rose tottering to her feet, only to have the infant come to life with a lusty scream. She smothered it against her breast to stifle it's cry, and then, too weak to fight the pitch of the ship, tumbled back on the bunk. The baby pressed against the warmth of her breast, began searching instinctively, trying to suckle through her thin blouse.

"So you want that much to live," she marveled, staring in each fresh blanch of lightning at the wriggling mite she had produced.

She felt too weak to rise.

"Well, it is not much—life," she told her infant son. "I don't doubt the day will come you'll curse me for not swingin' you off board to-night—but it was you yourself done it with your bloody yellin' "— and she drew aside her blouse and let the infant nurse, thinking— "There'll be hell to pay in the morning—but there's always hell to pay with him, anyway."

Her decision to keep the child cost her highly. Her uncle now saw her as a whore and no longer felt "bounded to her" as he put it. He let her stay on board the boat only because he needed someone to fry up his catfish and help unload bales and when it suited him he sold her body for whatever he could get.

The child learned early to leap out of his way, and for that matter, out of his mother's way. She loved him after her fashion, but she too, was often drunk now. Sometimes he pleased her and charmed her the way a kitten or puppy would amuse a child. Other times she threatened to "bat the hell out of him" and he learned to keep out of reach lest she make the promise good.

Still, she was his mother and she fended for him the best she could. She taught him to swim and to bait hooks, to clean a fish and fry corn. Though she had no compunction about cuffing him herself she became enraged if any man laid a hand on him.

He learned from her failings as well as her strengths. Someway he survived and by the time he was eight he was tough, aggressive, "rougher than a cob", as she put it proudly. He had inherited her strong bony frame and fair almost white hair, but his eyes were the eyes of Louis LeSeure, dark eyes full of secrets. He had already learned to hold his own with the rest of the little "river-rats," although some were older bullies.

Whatever else Marouska was, she was no coward. She once killed an alligator by forcing a shaft between its eyes—and defended a load of baled cotton with a stove poker when a band of hijackers came on board thinking she would be easy prey while the old captain was drunk. But Marouska never did anything in her life that required as much bravery as the afternoon she took Louis LeSeure's son to him.

She had never asked anything of the Frenchman. She had not even given the child a name, preferring to call him simply "Mate". She had never intended to bother the father and would not have done so if she had not been dying from a disease contracted from one of the rough men she had accommodated. She managed to get LeSeure's name and address and on a slumbering day in August, Marouska and her son walked down the aisle of trees that made a living colonnade to his plantation. Marouska pounded the gold knocker furiously against the carved white door, not because she was angry but because she was afraid she might yet run away

"I want to see Louis LeSeure," she said to the round-eyed black maid who opened the door.

"He in de office, Ma'am, I go see effen he kin see y' all," the servant promised. "Wot yo name?"

"He'll see me," Marouska said as she shoved the boy forward to follow the maid.

From her seat on a divan in the library, Roxelle LeSeure watched with a faint sense of disquietude the haggard young woman and ragged little boy who followed the maid to her husband's study. What in the world could such a pair want? There was something about that child that jarred her.

And Louis LeSeure, looking up from his desk, was startled too. He did not immediately see in this straw-haired apparition of a woman that long ago tow-haired girl.

"I brung you yer son," she said bluntly.

For a moment LeSeure could only struggle with a sense of shock, then he began to feel something else, something unexpected.

He was staring at the boy and he liked what he saw. There was no question the child was his. Dark eyes met identical dark eyes. The full lips were his mother's, but the delicate line of nose, the arch of brow were pure LeSeure.

Unexpectedly he felt pleasure. A son. A *son*. *His son*. He had only one other child, a step-daughter in poor health—a wife incapable of bearing more children—and now, suddenly from nowhere so to speak, at an age when he had given up expectations of an heir, he was being presented with a son! A child of his own blood.

"I wouldn't ask ya to look out fer him," Marouska was saying belligerently, "but I'm in a bad way 'n I can't do it no more myself. He's pert near big enough and tough enough to take kere o' himself, but he's still a minnow and there's plenty that would do him in when I hain't around to take his part. Well, will you claim him or won't you?"

"Cherie," he said softly, embarrassed that her name slipped his mind, "sit down, please. You look exhausted. I'll ring for something cold."

"I don't want no kind words. I want 'yes' or 'no'," Marouska said.

In spite of the pressure she was putting on him for a swift decision, it was some moments before LeSeure spoke. During that interval,

160

difficult as it was for her, he suffered the more violently. He realized that whatever was said next would affect his entire life from that moment forward.

"I want him. I want him!" LeSeure at last assured her, "Now sit down."

He rang for the servant and ordered mint tea. He wanted the boy but he was agitated. To want him was not the same thing as making up his mind to take him. He could see at a glance that there would be no possibility of passing this child off as anything but a son. He could not help staring in fascination. The way the boy moved his head, the shape of his fingers, his scowl, shouted, "I am Louis LeSeure's son!"

The thrill of fatherhood that wanted to rise up in him at these manifestations was stifled by the thought of his wife. He and Roxelle had had a good marriage, not ecstatic, but far more harmonious and rewarding than most marriages. He knew she would be deeply and perhaps irrevocably hurt if he were at this date to unveil a bastard child. But damn it—he wanted this child. He wanted his son.

"What is your name?" he asked the boy gently.

"Mate." The little boy looked at him stoically, his dark eyes revealing nothing of what he felt.

"I didn't give him no real name," Marouska explained.

LeSeure looked at Marouska's shadowed drawn face and understood with sudden horror what her situation was. He was lacerated for a moment at the realization of what one night of his drunken indiscretion must have cost her through the years. It decided the issue for him.

"Cherie, my poor child," he said with the tenderness that she dimly remembered. "You must not worry anymore. You should have come to me long ago. Long ago. I will take care of his every need. And you will have every care, too."

She turned away, feeling the weakness of tears which the cruelest of life's experiences had failed to draw from her ready to pour out at this brush of kindness.

"I don't want nothin' for me. I just want him keered for."

"You're ill. You need medicine—rest—good food," he insisted.

She folded the money he gave her without counting it and tucked it inside her dress.

"You be good now," she said, giving the boy a small punch in the arm. "Ye'll have it good here, Mate."

"Can I get you a carriage?"

"I got a wagon waiting."

"Let me know where you are so I can send you more money when you need it."

"I won't need it."

The boy watched her walk away. LeSeure thought that he must know he would not see her again. He did not cry, but the father noted that the small hands were ridged with white knuckles.

Suddenly Roxelle appeared in the doorway. She stared at the boy, drew closer. Her long white fingers tilted his face up. For a moment she continued to look at him, then she withdrew her fingers as if his flesh had burned them.

"He is your son?"

"Roxelle—" LeSeure began.

"Is he your son?"

"Yes."

She made a small sound like someone getting sick to their stomach, covered her mouth with her hands and ran from the room.

"You are—a surprise to her. It will take a little time," LeSeure apologized to the boy. "I will have to go talk to her. Will you be all right for a time?"

The boy nodded and LeSeure followed his wife.

The child waited a few minutes then set the tall fancy glass down. He did not like the minted tea or this house with the rows of books, flowered rugs and delicate chairs. He thought if he ran very fast he might still catch the wagon. Marouska would knock him aside of the head, but she would be glad to see him for all of that, he bet. But just as he jumped off the chair his father came back. Somewhere he could hear a woman crying with long shuddering sobs. He did not like his father. His face was too white and he smelled like perfume.

"I ain't stayin'," he said and dodged toward the window. A few more minutes and it would be too late to catch the wagon, ever.

"Yes, you are," his father said. He caught him hard. Mate waited for him to rap him one but he only held him gently and looked at him with sadness and love. "For better or worse, you are staying— my son."

He was turned over to the care of Sheba, a negro woman wrinkled and grey as an elephant. She had huge funds of patience, which were desperately needed in the care of her new charge. The process of turning the wild, rough little boy into Baird LeSeure (after Louis's father) was painful for everyone concerned, and would have been even more painful except for Liliane, his step-sister.

Roxelle could not abide the boy and was often cruel to him against her own will. Time and again she would resolve to change her ways— *Mon Dieu, it was not the child's fault, after all!*—but the very sight of him set her "hair on end."

Not so with his step-sister. Liliane loved him on sight. Louis in-

162

vented an early, unhappy marriage, a secret divorce, and an untimely death to explain the sudden appearance of his son. Liliane had no cause to doubt the story and found her mother's sufferings mysterious. Confined to her bed with an illness that progressed with aching slowness, Liliane found her new brother a delightful diversion.

She told him stories, brushed his hair, taught him to play simple tunes on her harp, counseled him, praised him and believed in him. From Liliane he received the first tenderness he had ever known. Her room became a refuge from Roxelle's antipathy, his father's exacting demands and Sheba's determination to see they were carried out. Everything he had learned to his advantage on the waterfront was frowned upon in this household. Sometimes he would cling stubbornly to one of his bad habits just because he felt as if parts of him were being torn away and that soon he would not be himself at all. Twice he was sent away to school, for the plantations were too far apart for the children to walk to a communal school, only to be returned because of his bad behavior.

"Let me tutor him, father," Liliane begged. "He is very quick. He needs only understanding."

Louis agreed and Liliane patiently opened up to Bay the worlds that lived between the covers of books. And when she could teach him no more, it was Liliane who talked him into going back peacefully to the boarding school.

"I know you don't care for the boys there, but darling Bay, you are so clever, so bright, you could twist them around your finger—" she challenged.

On the waterfront he had known cruelty, mayhem, seen the worst kinds of immorality, but he had also seen there a certain spurious honesty. If a man hated you, he said honestly, "I'm going to split your gullet end from end—" The child had been unprepared for the more sophisticated cruelty he met in his boarding schools where polite manners were offered to his face and snickers behind his back, where under the guise of friendship traps were set for his uncouthness and when he stepped into them his friends laughed. When he tried to fight back in the only way he knew, fists and waterfront language, the teachers had called him a "ruffian of filthy mind and manners."

But for Liliane's sake he forgot his worst epithets, brushed his hair, wore a cravat and well polished shoes, and manicured both his fingernails and his manners. He found that his step-sister was right, that he could, by exercising a conscious charm, direct and sway almost everyone to his whim. That mask of polish and charm still hid something that was wild and rough and not quite holy in Baird LeSeure. There was a feeling of something held back and down in him that was part of his attraction. Even in the way he walked there was the feeling of some kind of dynamic energy beaten down but ready at any moment to explode, that gave other people a strange sense of excitement when he was around.

LeSeure had his son initiated into the Catholic faith. Seated in the polished pew with the Gregorian chants rising around him, with the incense and smell of burning candles, the boy felt a hunger for what he vaguely felt all of this meant. His heart was open to accept God in the same eager fashion he had accepted the joy of learning to read and write and cipher—but at the crucial time when his intellect along with his heart might have accepted Catholicism, Liliane's illness reached it's crisis.

Called home from school because of her impending death, Bay refused to leave her side. He saw the final ravagements of her illness— and he could no longer believe in God. It was inconceivable to him that any God, even a monstrous God, could have allowed anyone as gentle and kind as Liliane to suffer such unearned tortures. He had never heard her say an unkind word or do an unkind act. To him, she had given unfailing love, infinite tenderness and confidence. He watched the casket containing her body lowered into the earth with bitterness and unmitigated grief.

When he was sixteen, his father died also. Roxelle met him at the door of the plantation with hatred gleaming in her tear-swollen eyes.

"He left everything to you. Everything."

"Only because you have no head for business. He knew I would see you are never in want."

"I have been in want since the moment you came to this house," she said, and spent the time before the funeral closing doors in his face.

After that, he seldom went home. He searched for and found men he could trust to manage the plantation. He kept a careful eye on the accounts. He saw to it, as he had promised, that his step-mother was never in want. But her hatred was so acidulous that, when he had finished his schooling he knew he would never live in his father's house.

Almost by accident he ran across an old friend of his father's, a woman recently widowed, who was in a state of nervous distress. Not only had she lost her husband, but she had given over his business into the hands of people who had proved to be unscrupulous. Within six months they had run it into the ground. Young LeSeure took her affairs under his scrutiny. Within three months the small company was getting back on it's feet. In a year's time, it was showing an astonishing profit. He had found his forte. There were other widows,

164

but he found that members of the fairer sex were not the only ones in need of the business acumen he possessed. There were men, formerly successful, who were unable to cope with the changes brought by time, weakling sons who had inherited the empires of strong fathers and now did not know what to do with them, strong men who were losing their hold because of illness. He made money for everyone who acquired his services and made himself rich and independent of his father's estate.

He branched out into real estate, transportation and brokerage. By the time he was thirty, he was something of a legend in Louisiana.

"Everyone knows Baird LeSeure, and nobody knows Baird LeSeure," an acquaintance remarked, and it was true. He brought vitality and excitement to whatever social affair he deigned to attend, but he was without family, true friends, or confidants. He allowed no one really near him.

He openly declared his atheism, yet evinced a morality that beggared the attempts of some of the highest churchmen to achieve. His natural brilliance in business made it unnecessary for him to lie, to cheat or connive for worldly goods. He never got drunk because he had a horror of losing self-control. He liked women. He liked the swish of them and the perfume and laughter of them. He liked to flurry them with teasing and attention, but he was not a libertine or a lecher. He had seen men use his mother in cruel and inhuman ways. The acts had burned into his child brain and as a man he had an abhorrence of easy sex. He had known the full range of snickers and innuendoes inflicted on those of suspected birth.

Though he did not realize it, in every woman he met he was seeking a semblance of Liliane. He found many charms in numerous women, but never quite the quality for which he was subconsciously searching. When he had seen Caroline Quimby that afternoon at the bazaar, something in her face reminded him of Liliane. Later, at the dinner party, he had recognized her volatile resistance to his charms, to which almost everyone else surrendered. That had amused him and made her a challenge. Even her primness and puritanism pleased him because it made it more fun to tease and rile her. She had been so thin and sad-eyed when he first met her, it was gratifying to make her laugh, to see her cheeks fill out and grow pink, to unearth her childlike capacity for joy.

When he returned to the South Baird LeSeure found that he could not dismiss Caroline Quimby from his thoughts as easily as he had dismissed other women. He had made up his mind to see her again before he left Chicago, but he had not imagined that he would find himself scrawling her name on sheets of paper, remembering the exact blue of her eyes, underlining passages for her in his books, or suddenly finding himself impatient because his next trip to Chicago was months away.

34

The first thing Caroline did upon returning to Chicago the last of August was to write Mrs. Louwain. It had become clear to her why the boarded up store had recurred in her dreams. The empty store would be a place for her school! She wrote to Mrs. Louwain, outlining her hopes, dreams and plans, taking care to explain she would be able to provide little money for the hire of the building in the beginning.

Mrs. Louwain's answer was prompt.

"—so my dear, after all these years it seems there is a way in which I can 'do more' "—she wrote. "The building is yours. Do whatever you deem necessary to make it habitable for your school—"

Jubilant, Caroline and Kemink descended upon the long unused building with scrub brushes, mops, pails and disinfectants. When they had finished with their marathon cleaning, the building was spotless but far from cheerful. The interior walls were paneled with dark oak wood, the oiled floor was almost black in color, the windows were narrow letting in little light. On the plus side, Mr. Louwain had been a progressive man who had installed gas lights as soon as they were initiated in Chicago.

Caroline and Kemink lightened the building's somberness with white dimity curtains and bright red rag rugs. Charles cut down an old discarded table to a height that would better accommodate young children.

The former storeroom in the back was outfitted with cribs and cots. There was also a room for cooking.

Ann watched all this flurry of preparation with some displeasure. Caroline's sister was not enthusiastic about her new plans.

"Can you not be happy simply living with us?" she asked wistfully. "You have been such a help to me."

166

"Ann, it is something I *have* to do," Caroline said, embracing her sister. She told her again about the condition of the children where she had found Felicity, about the little boy who had been torn away from her in tears, and then ended by reassuring Ann, "We will still be with you for a long time."

Ann tried to be understanding, but she often sighed as she watched Kemink and Caroline, heads tied in kerchiefs, repainting old highchairs, sorting through dusty books bought at junk shops, and pounding dents out of battered kettles bought for pennies.

"If you *must* have this school, at least let us outfit it for you," she begged.

But Caroline was adamant that Bromley was already doing far too much for her and her family.

"And what if you go to all this trouble and then you don't get any children?" Ann questioned.

That worry was dispensed with swiftly. Though the city had a reform school for boys, a House of the Good Shepherd for wayward girls, a poorhouse, several orphan asylums and a relief society, there was no haven for handicapped children. Insane people and other unfortunates were housed at the county poorhouse, following a fire that had destroyed the only hospital for the insane. A discreet ad in the Chicago Times brought a seige of answers. Caroline had expected to take only six children until she found how proficient her skills and sympathy would prove. In the end, she accepted twelve out of over a hundred applicants.

"Oh, I wish I could have taken them all!" she told Ann. "Turning some of them away I saw that little boy clinging to my skirts all over again."

Before the final applicants were accepted, Caroline and Kemink made a trip to Milwaukee. She was still haunted by that baby boy, whom she intended to extricate from that horror-filled house by any means she could contrive. But when the two women arrived in the city, they found the asylum no longer existed. The present occupants, a French teacher and a dancing master, knew nothing of where the former occupants had gone.

Caroline was exceptionally quiet on the way home. She would never be able to rescue the little blue-eyed boy, but in memory of him she would do what she could for others like him. More than her deep disappointment made her silent though. Once she leaned across to touch Kemink's hand and said, "For all we know, if we had been a month or two later, we might never have seen Fly again."

The school was opened on the first day of October. Gretchen, a fourteen year old retarded girl, was the oldest student. She was heavy footed, clumsy, with a mouth that hung agape. Her wealthy step-father had found her presence unbearable. Her mother, a handsome woman, dressed in rustling brown silks and a veiled hat, had sobbed as she told her story to Caroline in a heavy German accent.

"She is a goot girl, a goot girl!" she kept saying. She had had no indication that her daughter would not be welcome until after her marriage. She loved the man, rejoiced in a status she had never enjoyed before—"But, ach, God! Can I turn away from mine own flesh?" she cried.

No one could have understood her anguish better than Caroline. She suddenly saw again, with an inner wrench, Adam's distorted face.

"Don't—don't cry," she had comforted the woman, "we will keep your Gretchen. You can come and see her whenever you want to. Everything will be well."

And well it was. Gretchen's mother was able to pay handsomely for her daughter's care. The girl herself was good as gold, able in many ways; the final dividend was mama herself. Evaline Pritchard did visit her daughter often and made herself helpful in a thousand ways. A checkered apron flung over her fine taffetas or silks, she diapered babies; helped spoonfeed those who did not eat well; sang German songs in a Brunhild voice that awed everyone and taught painting.

"She is God sent!" Caroline declared.

Mrs. Louwain returned at the end of the month, and she too offered her services. Though she looked delicate, she amazed Caroline with her endurance. The older girls were often taken to her apartment to learn the making of soup or the baking of a pudding. Gretchen became her particular charge.

Once more, Dan-Pete and Danny became indispensable. To them it was fun to turn teacher and help someone younger, or less adept, to show them how to trace the letters of the alphabet or help them learn a rhyme. They ran errands, set tables, and carried wood for the stoves.

Even Ann, piqued at being left out, sometimes came down to the school and showed the three students capable of learning them, simple tunes on the piano and worked with them in their copy books.

Felicity, too, was an important personage at the school, as a dispenser of love. Nearly three years old, the practical tasks she could accomplish were limited. But she could squeeze and hug and encourage, which Caroline believed to be as important a contribution as that made by anyone else.

Every bit of the help they had was needed. Two of the children Caroline had accepted were designated by their parents as "demons"

168

and attempted to live up to the name. Georgio was a deceptively beautiful six year old with glowing dark eyes. He was bright at the piano and in his books, but he went into the wildest of rages at the slightest provocation and tried to harm himself or others.

The other "demon" was Margaret. She had lost her hearing during a childhood disease. Now eleven, the frustration of years of being shut off from communication built up towering tantrums in which she did everything from smashing dishes to tearing curtains off the windows. She was thin, unattractive and given to fits of trembling.

Emily was eight, as gentle as Margaret was destructive. She had a pale oval face and long dark hair like a princess in a storybook which she might as well have been, for she lived in some other world. She never spoke or took any interest in the world around her. She would sit for hours unmoving. Dan and Dan-Pete called her the "enchanted girl" and took a special interest in her.

The other girls were Sophie, nine, and Millie, seven. Sophie had a hare-lip. Like Emily, she wanted to crawl away from the world into some dark hiding place, but unlike Emily, she responded hungrily to every crumb of affection and help. She found schoolwork hard but would try with every ounce of her being, the veins in her forehead throbbing with effort. She followed Kemink around like a puppy.

Millie was a charmer, blonde, and adorable, she was subject to frequent attacks that her mother called "fits." The doctors had been unable to relieve her malady.

Millie became the special friend of Thomas. A year older than she, Thomas was in many ways the saddest case of all. His intelligent mind was locked inside a spastic body that refused to work. Millie helped feed him and learned to decipher the sounds he made that others couldn't understand.

There were three four-year olds, all boys: Willis, Paul, and Frederick. Though retarded in most of their processes they were cheerful and loving. Willis was so covered with freckles he looked cinnamon colored. Felicity liked to pat Willis because he would gurgle at her like a baby. Paul's knees got so red from crawling that Kemink made quilted patches on his breeches. Ricky was fat, red cheeked and bald. He loved to eat and Caroline learned that his appetite was her best key to helping him.

The youngest members of the school were twin boys named Herbert and Heine. They had oriental looks in spite of their German ancestry and the doctor had told the parents that they were idiots. The mother was still hysterical about it at times. Next to Millie they were the most charming children in the school. Everyone loved to take care of Herbie and Heine.

169

Caroline went home to the Thornton's after each day of school, taking Dan, Dan-Pete and Felicity with her. Kemink stayed with the children overnight and Mrs. Louwain was available for such emergencies as nightmares, earaches or midnight tantrums.

Ann was often depressed after her visits to the school.

"That poor Tommy—and Millie, it was so dreadful, so horrifying today when she had that attack. I cannot see how you stand it, Caroline."

Caroline did not know how to explain to her sister the intense joy she felt at each small sign of progress. And there were signs of progress along with many frustrations and problems. She felt at times as if she were feeling her way down a dark alley. She was learning slowly through trial and error.

She thought at first that love and reassurance were the answer to Georgio's tantrums but she soon found that the more she caressed and cajoled him the more often he acted up for attention. She tried lavish praise for good behavior and isolation for bad with better results. He hated being shut away from the others, while poor Margaret, who already felt isolated, could not be handled in the same manner at all.

Caroline had not worked this hard since that forever winter at Tomorrow River. She was asleep almost before she got into bed. Adam did not come as often to haunt her in those lonely moments just before sleep. She was absorbed and content.

35

The smell of mincemeat and freshly grated orange rind seeped from the kitchen and invaded the sitting room where Ann, Caroline and Doris Dormeister sat wrapping gifts among a welter of boxes, ribbons and gaily decorated paper.

"Wait until you see my dress! It's a sensation," Ann enthused to Doris. "The bodice is garnet satin and the skirt is one pink rose upon another. I've never seen anything like it."

"She may even outshine Mrs. Potter Palmer," Caroline teased, giving a last plumping to a fat red bow.

170

"Are *you* going to the Palmer ball?" Doris asked.

"No. Not that she wasn't invited," pouted Ann, "but she can think of nothing but her school."

"We're going to have a Christmas program for the parents." Caroline explained. "You should hear the carols. Truly it's marvelous when you realize that Margaret, Tommy, Emily and the babies can't sing, but everyone except Emily contributes. Tommy tries to hum the melodies, Margaret plays chimes and Herbert and Heinie shake bells."

"Am I invited to your program?" Doris asked.

"It's the same night as the Palmer ball."

"Well, I'm not going to miss *that*," Doris admitted. "Some people say that *he's* pushy, but everyone agrees that *she's* devine. They say he's bought two-hundred thousand dollars worth of jewels for her. But she's more than glitter. She's really interested in women's welfare and factory legislation and she knows more about art than anyone in Chicago, I'd say."

"Don't you be running down Potter Palmer," Bromley scolded. He had just come into the room, epaulets of snow on each shoulder, his face rosy as a radish, a large brown package in his hand. "It *takes* push to get ahead. I can remember when Palmer opened his Lake Street store in '52. It was nothing but a frame structure where tobacco chewers loafed with their feet on the railing. He's come a long way."

"What have you there?" Ann asked, curious about the large package.

"A Christmas package from Baird", Bromley said, laying it in her lap.

"Oh, do open it now," Doris begged, "so I can see what he's sent, too."

Ann drew aside the brown paper to reveal a number of extravagantly wrapped packages inside.

"Oh, maybe we should wait—"

"I'm sure Bay wouldn't mind," Doris said, more avid than ever.

"Well, all right. Just to please you." Ann laughed.

She opened her package. Inside a velvet box she found a pendant of filigreed gold surrounding an enameled rose.

"Oh, how lovely! Do look, Caroline, it will go with my gown. The finishing touch!" Ann was holding the pendant against her neck.

"At times, Bay is insufferable, but he does know how to make up for it," Doris conceded, leaning forward to touch the gift with an envious finger. "It's lovely."

She turned her large grey eyes on Caroline.

"Aren't you going to open *yours*?"

Caroline undid the moire bow that decorated the package.

"Oh, it's that naughty book!" Doris squealed. "Whitman's *Leaves of Grass*. I haven't read it myself, but there was an absolute scandal over it when it was first printed."

Caroline had opened the title page and when she saw there was an inscription she tried to shield it, but Doris was avaricious in her interest and quickly leaned forward and read it out loud.

"Every moment that I am away from you is a thousand years. I am embalmed in the torpor of your absence—"

Caroline slammed the book shut.

"My word!" crowed Doris, "I had no idea—"

"Doris, don't be ridiculous," Caroline reprimanded. "Can't you tell by the very extravagance of the language that Bay is teasing me?"

"Well, I wish he'd tease me and send me gifts," Doris declared. "He's an awfully attractive man even if he is a slave holder."

"He isn't!" Caroline protested.

"He's got to be. He's got a fancy plantation down South. I'll tell you that accounts for half of Steven Douglas' politics as well. John Sidell of Louisiana was here in August, and it was all over Chicago that Douglas' slaves down there are all ill-fed and mistreated. As long as he traffics in human flesh himself, how can anyone expect him to uphold the principles of human freedom?"

"You can't believe everything you hear, Doris," Bromley interjected from where he was warming his hands by the fire. "I've heard those reports about Douglas misusing his slaves are not true."

"Well, I was here this summer while all the political shenanigans were going on, Brom, while you were off cooling your feet on the other side of the lake, and I daresay, I know more of what is going on politically than you do," Doris said.

"Ohhh, don't get onto politics," Ann cried, throwing up her hands. But Doris was already "on" to her favorite topic.

"Oh, you should have been here in July, Bromley. There must have been thirty thousand people out to welcome Douglas. You could hardly get through the streets from the Central Depot to the Tremont House; they were so full of milling people. Banners were flying all over the place and buildings were all flag be-decked in his honor. And as if that wasn't enough, the Irish military organization and the Emmett Guards escorted him in his open barouche drawn by six white horses, and *cannons* were *booming*. Can you imagine?"

"No, frankly, I can't," Bromley said, "I can remember when he came to Chicago in '54. The city flew its flags at half mast and tolled church bells to show disapproval of his congressional activities. I was in the public square when he started to speak, and the crowd drowned him out with hisses."

"I remember, I remember!" Doris said. "The abolitionists kept singing, 'We won't go home until morning, 'til morning, til morning. We won't go home until morning, 'til daylight doth appear.' And they didn't either. But you have to give the little devil his due. There were men in that crowd ready to kill, and he stood his ground and kept trying to be heard. He must have been in the square until midnight fighting to get his piece said."

"And all that anyone remembers that he said, was 'Abolitionists of Chicago, it is now Sunday morning. I'll go to church and you go to hell,'" Bromley quoted with a smile. "What did the 'Little Giant' have to say for himself this trip?"

Bromley had read accounts of the speeches in the papers, but he enjoyed egging Doris on.

"Well, he actually said that the black man was not the equal of the white man and that justice could be dispensed by white men as they saw fit. And the crowd cheered him and threw up rockets and the band played 'Yankee Doodle.' I swear it made my blood boil," Doris cried. "To think that Chicago, a depot of the underground railroad, a refuge of fugitive slaves, could endorse Douglas."

"Oh, come on," Bromley cheered her, "according to the newspapers Lincoln demolished Douglas when he spoke."

"No matter what the papers said," Doris lamented, "Douglas is back in the Senate. Lincoln lost on the points of negro equality and the charge that if he was elected there'd be a war of sections. There are a great many people opposed to slavery who don't go along with negro equality, you know."

"Come on, Caroline. If they insist on talking politics, let's go somewhere else," Ann said, catching her sister's hand, "These discussions always end in talk of war and it frightens me to death."

Caroline gave her sister an affectionate pat.

"I'm sorry, Ann, but I have to leave for the school now. We only have two more days to practice for the program. Would you like to come along?"

"Not today. I have so much wrapping left," Ann sighed. "But I'm going to do it somewhere else," she added with a baleful glance at her husband and her best friend.

"Well, the Press and the Times both say there will never be a dissolution of the union, but I'll tell you—" Doris's strong voice trailed them as the two sisters paused in the hall while Caroline put on her wraps.

"Do you really think there will be a war?" Ann asked Caroline with a shiver.

"There will be wars and rumors of war until the end— let not your heart be troubled," Caroline quoted. She gave her sister a kiss on the cheek and was gone.

The day was heavy and dark, but the snow held a radiance of its own. Caroline peered from her fur hood with pleasure at the snow-lined trees, the plumed breath of the horses and the shop windows ferned with ice paintings. Perhaps there would be war. Bay seemed to think there would. He wrote her that he was trying to liquidate his interests in the South and transfer his enterprises to Chicago before the conflict came. The future seemed foreboding. But today was beautiful and she intended to enjoy it.

Before she stepped inside the school building, Caroline could hear Evaline Pritchard's impressive voice singing, "Stille nacht— heilige nacht—"

Kemink, Herbie on one knee and Heinie on the other, smiled from the head of the long table which was covered with plates of Christmas cookies. Ricky had not waited for official sanction. His fat red cheeks were stuffed.

Millie, Georgio, Gertrude and Danny came in a swarm to hug Caroline, all talking at once. She shushed them, indicating Mrs. Pritchard. "Wait 'til the song is over—"

Caroline was instantly alert to the fact that Margaret's thin face was suffused with some special emotion. She had not run to Caroline with the other children, but when Caroline had taken off her wraps and seated herself at the table, the child inched her way toward her, the expression on her face intensifying.

She wants to tell me something, Caroline thought. She had learned during the past weeks that Margaret's tantrums were always detonated by frustration at not being able to communicate something. Kemink had come up with a partial solution. She had been teaching Margaret Indian signs for many things. Margaret had learned to reproduce them and sometimes her needs could be pieced together from these symbolic fragments.

"What is it, Margaret?" Caroline whispered.

She felt in her pocket for a scrap of paper and handed it to the child along with a crayon.

Margaret shook her head and began to tremble in the characteristic way she had when there was something she wanted to say and couldn't.

Caroline took the paper back and drew the Indian symbol of a pointing arrow. Kemink had worked with Margaret on this symbol to teach her to take them to what she wanted.

The child looked at the paper and seemed even more agitated.

174

Caroline understood. There were some things Margaret could not lead them to by the hand.

Evaline's voice was rising, filling the room.

Suddenly Margaret darted around the table and put both of her hands around the startled woman's throat.

"Mine Gott!—" she cried.

"Keep singing," Caroline urged, fascinated. "She isn't going to hurt you."

There was a look of bliss on Margaret's face as Evaline, her voice somewhat shaky, obligingly picked up the melody.

"She must feel the sound," Caroline said.

Slowly, Caroline made her way to the singer and the child.

She wrote "sound" on the paper and gave it to Margaret.

The little girl took her hands away from Evaline's throat and took the paper. She turned it over and drew something before giving it back to Caroline. Caroline studied a long moment before she understood what she had drawn. It was a smiling heart. Caroline looked at the child's face and understood that it was a symbol of *joy*. She wanted some way to communicate her *joy*.

Caroline knelt and drew Margaret into her arms. Her face was wet. There was a stack of presents three feet high under the tree in the Thornton library, but no other present this Christmas would match the one she had just been given.

36

January 4, 1859

Dear Baird,

How can I thank you for *Leaves of Grass?* Doris Dormeister pretended it was scandalous; but I felt if my beloved Emerson gave it sanction, it could not be all that bad. True, Whitman is frank, but perhaps we need more of that. His poetry is so full of the recognition of immortality and God at every hand, that I was astonished you should choose this volume. What answer do you have, my atheist friend, to his lines—" and a mouse is miracle enough to stagger six trillion infidels"?

He writes, "Is it wonderful that I should be immortal? as everyone is immortal—I know it is wonderful—but my eyesight is wonderful— and that my soul embraces you this hour, and we affect each other, and never, perhaps, to see each other, is every bit as wonderful." And it is, Bay, it is! He says things for me that I have felt, and he must say things you have felt, too. It makes one know that there is some connecting linkage between us all.

He writes, "There is something that comes home to one now and perpetually—it eludes discussion and print, it is not to be put in a book—it is not in this book, it is for you, whoever you are—it is no farther from you than your hearing and sight are from you, it is hinted by the nearest and commonest and readiest—"

I have felt that all my life. It is the basis of my faith. We cut an apple for the children in my school and show them the little five-petaled flower in the center. It is always there—perhaps has always been there through countless generations of apples since the Garden of Eden. An unchanging pattern. The acorn unfailingly grows an oak. Spring and summer follow winter eternally. I cannot believe that so much pattern can be an accident, as you do, Baird!

And yet—the darker aspects of life crowd about me too. Sometimes, like Whitman, I am swept with the sheer ecstasy of being. I, too, could cry out, "Press close, bare-bosomed night! Press close, magnetic, nourishing night! Night of south winds!"—but in the very midst of my ecstasy I am suddenly pronged with guilt. How dare I feel such joy, when all around me there is so much suffering pain and bewilderment? How can I dare such wild rejoicing while my brother cries? Like you, Bay, I cannot quite embrace death and evil and pain with the equanimity of Whitman, who preaches that even these are good.

At this very moment one can feel the darkness, that throbbing ache at the root of existence, operating. Our country is dividing into two hostile camps. We sit here in the north and point our fingers at you in the south, declaring, "You are wicked. Slavery is wrong. You must put an end to it. If you don't do it yourself, we will force you to do it!" And the people of the south cry back, "Mind your own affairs! We need our slaves. We take care of them and they are content and love us. We treat them better than you treat the people who work in your factories. Take the beam from your own eye!"

And there are great abuses of human beings in the North. Just this past year the printers in Chicago have organized a union in protest of eighteen hour days in rooms almost without ventilation and at wages that bring only subsistence. Women who must work are in even worse straits. And those who have no work are in the worst condition of all. Business has not really recovered from the panic of '57 and crops were poor last year. It is heartbreaking to see the many people in Chicago this winter who are hungry, cold and scantily clad. You southerners say that at least the slaves do not go hungry.

I remember in the Tomorrow River country how it used to be before a storm. First the sky would darken and then the wind would rise; all the trees and bushes would begin to tremble, there would be dark rushes of birds and the grasses would bow and blow flat beneath the wind. One felt the storm long before it arrived. There is that same mood now like a giant shadow hanging over everything. It frightens Ann so much she has stopped asking Doris to her dinner parties because she cannot bear everyone talking about war. It is hard for people like Ann and me to imagine what it would be like to be caught up in a war. Bromley says if it comes, it is certain to be the worst war in centuries.

It is worse for Ann than for me. When we were children and there was a storm, she was always the one who cried and ran to papa to be comforted. I used to want to look out the window and see all the flashing lights and flailing trees. My school absorbs so much of my thought, feeling, and emotion, that I have little left with which to worry. Ann is busy, too, but her thoughts are more free. Every party and social doing she goes to is permeated with political discussions. Even her milliner was quoting Lincoln's "a house divided against itself cannot stand—" speech.

I cannot tell you how much I have come to love each of the children at the school. I wish you could see the change in Margaret. They had tried to teach her to read and write, but she was so high strung and given to tantrums it seemed impossible. With Indian symbols, Kemink was able to gain her attention and help her communicate. From there she has progressed to the alphabet and simple words. To be able to convey to us what she feels has made all the difference. She has become a joy to have around.

I would like to make such a happy report about our other "demon," Georgio; unfortunately I cannot. He seems such a devious child, always angelic to our faces and manufacturing mischief behind our backs. I have this deep, deep conviction that inwardly we are all perfect, as truly as the pattern of the acorn is perfect to produce the oak. Upon this conviction the entire school was conceived. So it is with shame that I confess how hard it is to erase my image of Georgio as a rapscallion. How will he ever see himself differently, if I cannot? Every day is a challenge.

Our baby twins are over a year old now and still not crawling.

177

They are as good as sunshine, but it is a care to lug them about. They have grown heavy. So we are trying to give them every incentive to crawl. We set bright balls and small sweet cakes just beyond their grasp. Once Herbie cried and I felt so cruel, but they are learning. Firefly does her part by getting down and demonstrating, it is hard on her stockings; but if it accomplishes nothing else it makes them laugh.

Speaking of "Her Most Beautiful Highness of Chicago," she was delighted with the fur bonnet you sent her. She has a natural bent toward vanity and with you and Ann both encouraging it at every turn, I do not know what a poor mother is to do. Ann not only had a blue velvet suit made for her, but also an exact miniature duplicate for a doll. The doll has hair fashioned from Fly's own curls that Ann saved when we cut her hair last summer, and is as close in resemblance to her small mistress as could be imagined.

As for Dan and Dan-Pete—I think of all their Christmas gifts, they liked the lariats you sent most of all. They love horses anyway and have developed great enthusiasm for reading adventures of the western frontier. For a time, they were making a practice of lassoing Fly, so your gift was not an unmixed blessing to the household.

Outside my window the bare twigs are encased in ice but I realize that before long the ice will be dripping off in April rain and suddenly the twigs will be swollen with May blossoms. We will be looking forward to your return to Chicago then. You have been very good to us, Bay. Especially to me, teaching me to laugh again. You are such a good friend—and yet sometimes I feel that you are like life itself—"a puzzle within a mystery." I find myself thinking sometimes, "What is Bay *really* like?"

Affectionately,
Caroline

37

Baird LeSeure did not return to Chicago in the spring as Caroline had expected. The liquidation of his business concerns in the south proved more difficult than he had thought.

"I have signed over all the rights of my father's estate to my step-mother," he wrote to Caroline. "Her resentment of my involvement in her affairs has been a weight around my neck for years. I am wealthy in my own right and have no need of the income of the plantation. I do not feel the release I expected. I am nagged with a sense of responsibility toward that woman. Vitriolic though she is toward me, she is my father's widow. Anyway, for the time being, she is happy to be rid of me. I spent Christmas at the plantation to settle up the ends of our legalities and for the sad task of burying the black nurse of my childhood. Good old Sheba was all that was left to draw me back. I think I shall never go there again—"

Caroline stayed on in Chicago with the children that summer, learning for herself that Ann's description of "smoke rising out of the wooden sidewalks it gets so hot—" was not as far fetched as it sounded.

The school had its first graduation. Gretchen—had learned so much under Kemink's and Mrs. Louwain's tutelage, she had been transferred to the Thornton kitchen. Bridget had grown spoiled with Kemink's help and had grumbled incessantly ever since the Indian woman's skills had been directed to the school. Now, with someone to help peel the potatoes and wipe the plates, Bridget was happy again. As for Gretchen, her round little face glowed with pleasure at her usefulness and pride at the dollar and twenty-five cents she received each week for her services, which was as much as any unretarded domestic was earning. Her mother was relieved to have found a haven for her daughter, and Caroline was pleased because Mrs. Pritchard continued to come and help at the school whenever time permitted.

"We have taken another stormy petrel in as replacement," she wrote Baird, "a child of eight, who stutters so badly he cannot be understood. He is a small pugilist and regularly takes on Danny and Dan-Pete who, in spite of constant reprimands, feel they must defend their manhood. We are learning about the aggressiveness of males through sundry black eyes and bloodied noses. Bromley is talking again about sending the boys to a good school. He is not sure that my school of "mishapen little ones" is the best environment for our own two boys. I disagree. They have learned so much of compassion, of tolerance, of love here, despite their fisticuffs with our new Joshua. I wish you could see how patient they are with our "Enchanted Emily." After months of trying she still does not respond, yet they go on giving. Still—Danny is nine, now, and Dan-Pete soon will be, so I suppose I must give serious thought to Bromley's urging. Danny has a talent for mathematics; he almost knows more than I do in that field. I must not hold them back from possible advantages."

LeSeure arrived in Chicago in October just when the city was seething with the news of the raid of John Brown at Harper's Ferry.

"No man in his senses can say that it is not the most crazy development which slave history of this country affords" Doris Dormeister read aloud from the Press. She had been admitted back into Ann's parlors when that lady had to admit that even without Doris, conversation continued to tilt toward war and politics.

"We desire to see all parties engaged in that bloody event brought to punishment. If hanging is the penalty—hang; if imprisonment— imprison; but give us no accusations of innocent men," she read dramatically from the Times.

"Ahhh, but the poor man was addled," Caroline said.

"At first everyone was outraged, northerners and southerners alike," Bromley commented. "But now the incident is being used politically. Already some of the Republican papers are claiming that the only objection the Democrats have is that Brown was running negroes north instead of south."

"Well, I tell you the way feeling is running, you're a brave Copperhead to dare to come to Chicago," Doris told Bay.

Bay only laughed and as always seemed to avoid political discussions. He was often at the Thornton household, and was free with invitations to every gala event that came to the city. Caroline was not so free to accept. When she did, it was never for herself alone. Baird would find himself with an entire entourage. Heads would turn as Bay arrived at some event with a small boy in each arm, an Indian woman on one side, and an unusually lovely white woman on the other, a gaggle of small boys preceding them, and a few half-grown girls following. He bore it all with humor.

"You're absolutely ruining his reputation as an eligible bachelor about town," Doris complained. "There are rumors circulating that he's a Mormon with two wives."

Caroline giggled. "Actually, I'm doing him a favor. He told me once that he wanted ten children. I am only preparing him.

"Besides," she added with a saucy glance at Bay, "from what I hear, it's not hampering his style at all!"

It was true that Bay did not seem to be suffering from neglect when Caroline turned down his invitations. He was seen all over Chicago with one of the Clement sisters or Nelia Fitzpatrick. Miss Fitzpatrick, reportedly a distant cousin of Cyrus McCormick whose invention of the reaper had revolutionized northern farming, was red of hair and famed of charm.

180

"You are overwhelmed with jealousy?" Bay asked.

"Overwhelmed," Caroline said, sweeping Firefly onto a stool to undo the tiny buttons at the back of her dress.

"Baird, are you in love with Caroline?" Doris pried.

"Of course," Baird said. "Isn't everyone?"

"Doris you are the most terrible woman I know. I cannot think *why* I like you," Caroline said.

"Are you going to come with me to hear Maurice Strakosch's Italian Company at the Rice Theatre?" Bay asked Caroline.

"Oh, Bay, I would love to—but truly, I cannot. Mrs. Louwain will be gone all this month, and the night duty is too much for Kemink alone. But—could you do something else for me?"

"I shiver to ask what."

"Well, it's Georgio. He's become fascinated with matches. No matter what we say or do the moment he is out of our sight he is at them. I can't seem to impress upon him the danger. I thought, perhaps—"

"You think if I would talk to him—"

"Well, not exactly. All our threats and punishments haven't worked. I was thinking of—well, a reward. He has taken a liking to you. Could I promise him a day with you all to himself, if he doesn't play with matches anymore?"

"So you believe in bribing children?" Doris accused.

"Not so much in bribing—as rewarding. We all need rewards, do we not?"

"Do you really believe that?" Baird asked.

"Yes, yes I really do," Caroline affirmed.

"Very well. Georgio gets his day with me if I get properly rewarded."

"What did you have in mind as a reward?" Doris asked with interest.

"Let's see, a proper reward—?" Baird rubbing his chin pretended to be thinking, "Ahh, I know. I'll accept a kiss from you, Caroline. Not one of those chaste little pecks on the forehead or cheek that you and Ann are so adept at dealing out. But a nice, passionate, honest, full-blown, kiss."

"I swear, Doris, you and Bay are a pair," Caroline said with a laughing sigh, "Adam was always trying to make me into a better person, while you are just the opposite, Bay. You always seem to be trying to corrupt me!"

"Well, after you've kissed me, I'll marry you. Will that make it all right?"

"Honestly, Bay, that's the thing about you. You can never be serious two minutes in a row," Caroline laughed. "I'm going upstairs to tuck Fly in."

Ann had come into the room just in time to hear the tag end of

181

the conversation. She was looking at Baird in serious surprise. "But you meant it, didn't you, Bay?" she asked.

He shrugged. "Did I?"

He bent and kissed her cheek. "Save a place for me at the table tomorrow night."—and he was gone.

Caroline was not at the dinner the following night and she did not see Bay again before he left for the south to settle the final transferring of his business affairs. However she heard that he took Miss Fitz-patrick to the Strakosch Company's performance and that Miss Fitz-patrick looked ravishing in green satin.

"You have never worn your white velvet gown—" Ann pointed out delicately. "You know, Caroline, Bay is—"

"I think there is something you are forgetting," Caroline cut in. "I'm not free to consider *what* Bay is. I am still a married woman, Ann."

*   *   *

On December 2, John Brown was hanged in Charleston, Virginia. Passions in Chicago had been inflamed by editorials in the anti-slavery papers of John Wentworth. He entreated the people to assemble as a sign of unanimous public sentiment against slavery, suggesting that business as usual would be inexcusable while a fellow human being was being executed for standing up against slavery.

On the way to school that cold December day, Caroline saw hundreds of people who had followed Wentworth's cry to assemble. They stood in tense groups, like knots in the rope of city streets, waiting for the fateful word to arrive. Some of the groups offered prayers for the souls of the hangmen. When the news arrived by telegraph that the work of the gallows had been accomplished, John Brown, who a few short months before had been reviled by almost everyone, became a martyr.

Within weeks "John Brown's Body Lies A-mouldering in the Grave" became a popular ballad. The song was heard in the streets, sung at fashionable affairs and picked up by school children. Caroline felt the drums of war pounding nearer. Surrounded by her children, Kemink, Ann, Bromley and dozens of friends, she suddenly felt unaccountably lonely. She longed for spring.

38

"Mother, how com' Bay hardly ever comes to see us anymore?" Danny asked.

He was lying on the new May grass staring into the branches of a budding tree, his shoes discarded, his toes wriggling blissfully.

Caroline, jacket and bonnet removed, lay beside her son, her eyes dreamily tracing the pattern of branches through the gauze of their new leafing.

"He's working very hard. Before, when he came to Chicago, it was mostly to make contacts and finalize contracts; now he is laying down the cornerstones for an entire business enterprise and it's much more demanding. Bromley says he is putting in sixteen to eighteen hours a day. It's a wonder we see him at all."

She rolled onto an elbow and stared into her son's eyes. "Why? Do you miss him?"

"Don't you?"

"Welll—yes, I suppose. I'm awfully busy too."

"I know. That's why I was surprised today when you said that just you 'n me could go on a picnic— Was there something special you wanted to tell me or something?"

"Ohhh, Danny." The corner of Caroline's mouth quivered. "That you should say that proves how much we needed a day just to ourselves. Sometimes I feel I get so busy I don't know what's going on in your head anymore. I don't want that to happen. I want us to stay close. I want you always to talk to me about all the important things you think—and even the silly things."

"I'm glad that's all. I thought maybe you were going to tell me that me 'n Dan-Pete had to go away to school like Uncle Bromley keeps saying."

"You wouldn't like that?"

"I don't know. I don't think so."

"It could be an adventure."

"So that *is* what you wanted to talk about."

"No. I just wanted us to be together; but now that you brought it up, we should talk about it. I suppose Bromley is right. You and Dan-Pete should have a first rate education. Only *I* hate for you to go away, too."

"They've got lotsa schools in Chicago."

"They don't want to take Dan Pete because he's an Indian."

Danny shook his head in disbelief.

"He's three times as smart as any white boy I ever met."

"I know. It's hard to understand."

Danny sat up and put his arms around his knees. He was a tall child, but slight, not nearly as sturdy as Dan-Pete, who was several months younger. Sometimes it seemed to Caroline that he was too serious, too reflective for his nine years. His blue eyes looked at her solemnly from under his bangs. "Mother—is my father ever going to come back?"

For a moment their gaze broke; she pulled at a few tufts of the new grass. When she raised her eyes back to his, her face was perceptibly whiter. He had never asked about Adam before.

"I do not know," she said.

"I can't remember him so good. I remember that he used to pull me up on his horse to ride with him. It was wonderful. I wish you'd talk about him sometimes. It's—it's worse than if he were dead like Dan-Pete's pa, 'cuz at least Aunt Kemink tells him about him all the time, so that it's almost like he was still here in a way. But you don't ever say anything about my father."

She ruffled his hair wordlessly, and then finally said, "He was really a very great preacher at his best, Danny. There were things he believed, some of his theology, that frightened me; that I couldn't accept. But he had a great gift for speaking. He could touch people and move people in a rare way."

"What's theology?"

"The study or understanding of God."

"I wish I understood God. Uncle Bromley says there is going to be a war, and I can't understand why God makes war."

"I don't think God does."

"Well, he doesn't stop it and that's the same thing."

"That's a hard question, Danny. Almost everyone asks that question. There are a number of answers that wise men through the ages have thought up or been inspired to give. Some people think one answer is good; some people think another is good; some people don't think there is *any* good answer."

"Like Bay?"

"Like Bay."

"What do you think?"

"Well, I'm not like Bay. I do think there must be an answer, but I haven't found one that perfectly satisfies me yet. I'm still searching."

"What if you never find an answer?"

"Search and you will find, the Bible tells us."

"You're sure?"

184

"Uh-huh. I've always believed in miracles and answers to prayer."

"What are some of the answers that other people think are right?"

"Well, some people think God is punishing man's wickedness."

"But you don't think that?"

"I do think wickedness gets punished. It's like when you eat too much candy, you get a stomach ache. But I cannot imagine God sending the horror of war on purpose."

"Tell me some other answers."

"Some people say God cannot stop the wars and sorrows because he has given man free will. He doesn't want to take away man's right to decide. Like Georgio. We could make him be good if we locked him up in a room and watched him every minute, but we want him to *want* to be good. We want him to learn that he would be happier being good."

"You don't think that's a good answer then?"

"Not completely, because good people suffer too. Maybe we are all going to school here so we can become something greater in the future. And maybe we're just in kindergarten and can't understand trigonometry yet."

"Maybe."

Caroline began to put the picnic things back into the hamper. "I can see Charles coming with the rig. Better help me with this."

"May we drive by Lake Street on the way home and see the Big Wigwam? Bromley says it's all done now."

"If Charles doesn't mind," Caroline agreed.

"I'll betcha he'd like to see it himself."

The Big Wigwam had been constructed to house the Republican convention that was being held in the city. Chicago was filled to overflowing. There wasn't a hotel room to be had for any price, and almost every private home was opening its door to guests. Ann had expected seven house guests, but the company had swollen to fifteen with more arriving each day. There were rumors that people were sleeping on pool tables and saloon floors.

Charles, dour with everyone else, was a soft touch for Danny. He seemed pleased to take them around to Lake Street, but they were hardly on the street when they had to turn aside for a parade. The loudly trumpeting band led marchers shouldering rails in honor of their favorite son, Abraham Lincoln, the rail splitter. Marching right behind them with equal volume and enthusiasm came Seward supporters, their streamers and banners keeping time to the brass band with gay flurries in the May breeze.

Chicago was astir politically. The buildings were festooned gaily with banners and political slogans. There was a rampant air of ex-

185

citement and buoyancy in the crowded streets. The restaurants were blue with cigar smoke; champagne flowed as if it were beer. Even the lake was full of boats loaded with delegates.

Lake Street was so crammed Charles had to withdraw his promise to take them past the Big Wigwam. It would have taken hours to work the carriage through the press. But Caroline and Danny could see the huge building towering in the distance with the inscription over the door proclaiming "For President—Honest Abe; for Vice-President—Hannibal Hamlin."

Darkness was coming as Charles turned the carriage about and started the horses for home. Looking backward, Danny gasped.

"Mother, look!"

She turned back to see the Wigwam ignite, flare, burn white against the darkening night. From turret to foundation it was lit with a thousand lights; in the streets the light seemed to turn into sound as thousands of voices broke into cheers.

The Thornton house was scarcely less quiet when they arrived home. Doris Dormeister, enthusiastic supporter of Lincoln, was holding sway with equally enthusiastic protest from Seward supporters. Each faction was trying to outshout the other.

Ann welcomed her sister with a wan face.

"Wouldn't you think Bromley could have at least stuck to inviting all Lincolnites or all Sewardites?" she complained. "I'm going to be deaf before this convention is over. Why does he have to be so democratic?"

"De-mo-crat? De-mo-crat? Did I hear someone say *Democrat* in this stronghold of Republicanism!" roared one of the guests who had been helping himself more liberally than wisely to the wine.

Ann rolled her eyes heavenward and Caroline giggled. It was plainly going to be quite a night.

The following night Lincoln won the nomination on the third ballot. A message from the floor of the Big Wigwam was sent to the skylight where it was announced to the swarms of people waiting in the streets.

Caroline, Bromley, Ann and their guests were jostled like popcorn between thunderously applauding, sometimes weeping, wild, rapturous crowds of people, while cannons boomed and rockets spilled fountains of fire into the night sky.

In the lurid glow of bonfires, torches, and rockets, Caroline noticed Baird LeSeure leaning against the side of a building. In the midst of so many exuberant people, the expression on his face was curiously

186

abstract and sad. He felt her eyes on him and looked up. Their glances met and held above the seething jumble of the crowd. He smiled slowly. She waved and tried to make her way to him but was forced back. Taller and stronger, he edged his way toward her until he made it to her side. The crowd was half shouting, half bawling, half singing—

> "Oh, hear you not the wild huzzas,
> That come from every state?
> For Honest Uncle Abraham,
> The people's candidate?
> He is our choice of nominee,
> A self-made man and true;
> We'll show the Democrats this fall,
> What Honest Abe can do!"

Conversation was almost impossible.

"Are you glad it's Lincoln?" Caroline shouted to Bay.

He put his arm around her shoulder to shield her from the crowd. "I think he'll do his best to keep the country together, but that in itself could mean war," Bay answered.

Now the crowd had picked up 'Poor Little Doug' to the tune of 'Old Uncle Ned'—

> "Dere was a little man and his name was Stevey Doug,
> To the White House he longed for to go;
> But he hadn't any votes fru de whole of de Souf,
> In de place where de votes ought to grow.
> So it ain't no use for to blow—
> Dat little game of brag won't go;
> He can't get de vote 'case de tail ob de coat
> Is hung just a little too low—'"

The crowd surged forward so forcibly it flung Caroline tight against Bay. His arms closed about her protectively. As her face pressed against the rough worsted material of his jacket, she felt his arms tremble. She raised her face, large-eyed, her heart pounding, but whatever expression had been on his face was instantly concealed. He started to laugh and in one movement swept her into his arms and began to fight back against the crowd.

"We'd better get you out of here before they turn you into Caroline squash," he joked. "If you have seen enough, I'll tell Bromley I'm taking you home."

She nodded.

Riding through the darkness of the quieter residential streets, they could still hear the booming of the cannons, see the light of bonfires and the special white radiance of the illuminated Big Wigwam against the sky. Bay was uncharacteristically silent and Caroline, seated beside his dark, unspeaking form, felt curiously shy herself. She found her mind re-echoing Danny's question of the afternoon before.

Would Adam ever come back? If he did—what then?—If he didn't, where did that leave her? She remembered her last words to him. "Don't ever come back—I'll hate you forever." She no longer tried to deny to herself that the reason for all the wondering had something to do with the man seated beside her. She was acutely aware of his closeness, his masculinity, of his knee occasionally bumping against hers with the sway of the carriage. She wanted to slide further away from him but she knew if she did he would know why and he would laugh at her.

She was glad when they reached the Thorntons and she could escape from his disturbing nearness.

39

The maniacal fever that had shaken the nation in the late 1840's and early 50's after gold had been discovered at Sutter's mill had died down to a trickle by '58 when Adam, Cricket and Levi arrived in California. Many of the towns that had sprung up overnight out of the dust and mud were standing grey and ghostly in the blowing sand and tumbleweeds. But Columbia and her sister city, Sonora, would not suffer this fate. They lay in the mother-lode country and those miners and prospectors who had failed to make it big or who had dissipated what they had gained, could find work at a dozen operating mines in the area; mines so rich it was thought it would take a century for the greediest owners to dredge them clean. So the two communities continued to flourish.

All three men were struck dumb at the sight that greeted them after they had headed out from La Grange toward Sonora.

Levi drew the wagon to a halt and sat staring, while Cricket let out an irreverent string of homespun profanity.

As far as the eye could see, gold diggers had spaded and sifted through every ounce and inch of earth in their search for color. The

188

ground lay bare, lumped over upon itself in sullen waves, brooding, withdrawn and unforgiving as a woman who has been taken in violence, rejecting even the timid tendrils of wild cucumber that tried to crawl out and cover the scars.

Seated on Ebonite beside the wagon, Adam said, "That's the most damn depressing sight I ever saw."

Cricket spat eloquently, and clucked the horses forward through the ravaged miles. By noon the next day they had reached Sonora. Crouched in the foothills, the town was at first scarcely discernible from the rock and earth from which it had come. Schist quarries were becoming a secondary industry in the gold town and there were few buildings that were not built of the crystalline, easily split rock.

The three men were glad to pull into the shade of tall pines and seek rest from the burning sun. In the cool of the evening they pushed on to Columbia, where they were told Levi's mine was two miles north. They were glad of a high moon, for it was well into the middle of the night before they located it on the Stanislaus River. Levi squinted down at the water sparkling in the moonlight and grinned from sideburn to sideburn.

"Hot daggedity! Right on a river. Water is a gold digger's bes' halper," he said with satisfaction.

Adam was not grinning. The crude shelter erected from canvas, timbers and the lateritic red clay of the region made Levi's Wisconsin shack look like a palace. The febrile stench of a discarded animal den rose from the earth floor.

In the month that followed Adam helped Levi and Cricket with the gold mining. As he had feared, he did not like the work. Cricket enjoyed the physical labor. He had a natural propensity and pleasure in working with his hands. Adam watched with admiration the deftness with which the other man constructed new sluice runs from pine boards, the ease with which he sunk a pickax into a fresh slope, the force with which he drove timber. He seemed impervious to things that drove Adam insane. Neither the heartless blinding sun that beat down day after day on the sluice run, the flies that clustered in swarms on the roof of the mine and attacked in black masses buzzing and biting when the men ventured inside, nor the isolation of the claim seemed to affect Cricket.

By the end of a two-month period it was evident the ore they were able to extract from the mine was of such low grade it was not going to support all three of them. Adam was secretly relieved to have a gracious out. He was tired of Levi's sloppy cooking, sick of the shack. He felt stifled and restless. One night he stayed in Columbia instead of riding back with the other two. Levi and Cricket accepted his deci-

189

sion good-naturedly, although they kept assuring him that things would pick up at the mine once they got everything running smoothly.

Adam had no idea what he was going to do. The decision was made for him by a girl named Sally Magee. Billed as "Satin Sal, the Most Gorgeous Gal West of the Rockies," she sang and danced at the newly built Golden Nugget. A Jenny Lind she was not, but she had a way of rolling her eyes and hips and kicking up her heels that brought cat calls and hollers from the miners. She wore black ribbons around her white throat and red garters about her black silk stockings. Her blue-white skin, scarlet lips and harp gold hair came out of boxes and jars. Adam knew that, yet he found himself as vulnerable as any of the others when she undulated out in her plumes and laces and high heeled shoes. There had always been something about that kind of woman which had both repelled and appealed to him.

Sally took a fancy to him.

"You're a real gent!" she told him, casting admiring eyes over his carefully pressed suit, white shirt and handsome cravat, among the sea of scuffed boots, and sweat-stained hats.

"I hear you're splittin' up with Levi and Cricket," she said, seating herself at his table.

"You heard right."

"Whatcha gonna do now?"

"I'm open to suggestions."

"We could use a black-jack dealer. Why don't you try it? Just for tonight. See if you like it. I'll show you."

Sitting down at the green baize table, he took the slippery pack of new cards in his hands. It was a lot easier than crushing ore or panning dust.

In the middle of the evening she did a song and dance. Afterward she came and sat by him during the break in a game.

"How'd you like my act?"

"It's quite an act."

"You bet it is!" she said with conviction. "I made it up myself."

"How'd you get into this?" He asked more for something to say than because he cared.

She threw her head back in loud laughter.

"You really want to know? My pa caught me kissing a boy behind the barn. He's a mean old rat and he sez, 'if that's what you want to do, you might as well get paid for it,' and he brought me into Columbia and dropped me off."

Adam was appalled.

"I can't believe a father would do that."

"Hell, he was glad to get rid of me," she said roughly. "He had

190

ten more like me at home to feed. I'll say this much, Big Jack was okay to me. He sez I was too young and he was gonna hire a buckboard and send me home. But I seen everybody havin' such a big time and the pretty dresses the girls was wearing and I wanted to stay. He sez, 'kin you sing?' and I sez,' I kin sing better'n anyone you ever heard.' So I sung for him and he sez, 'by cracky you kin!' He let me stay and I been here ever since."

She preened. "I'm a belle around here. Look, Big Jack's giving you the sign to get back to work. But come around after and have a drink in my room."

At the end of the night's work Adam went back to her room. He felt embarrassed. The room was cluttered with intimate feminine articles, corsets, stockings, powders and beads. The lamp was turned so low it was almost dark.

"Stay with me and be my man," she said.

"I don't think Big Jack would like that."

"I cleared it with him. He liked the way you operated tonight. He wants you'n he don't care about me. He's got plenty of girls."

Sally stepped out of the black ruffled dress she had been wearing. Her skin gleamed like calla lilies in the darkness.

Adam felt as if everything he had stood for and believed in was suddenly dangling on a thin tenuous string inside of him.

She moved toward him, her walk undulating, inviting. He had the familiar sensation of being swept by forces he could not resist. His mouth went dry but his body began to sweat and throb.

She was standing close to him, the scent of her perfume musky and heavy in his nostrils. She looked up insolently, teasing.

"Unhook me," she commanded, and turned so he could undo her corset. Adam didn't move.

"Don't tell me you've never been with a lady before?" Her expression was mocking.

She undid the corset herself—let it fall. Adam felt the string inside of him break. With a cry almost of anger he grabbed her. She threw her head back and laughed and laughed. He ground his mouth against hers to shut her up. She kissed him back, experienced and knowing, her hands starting to caress the hard ache of his body.

In the morning when Adam woke up, Sally was standing by the window with a drink in her hand, watching him. He felt disturbed. He did not like the idea of her watching him while he slept.

The golden curls that had adorned her hair the night before lay in a tumble on the dresser along with hairpieces, ribbons and jeweled combs. In the wan morning light her own hair looked strawlike, her features without makeup looked coarse and ordinary. Her body was wrapped in a kimono. The dragons on the sleeves wriggled everytime she moved. The room smelled fetid.

Adam felt his stomach convulse. He sat up holding his head.

"You got a hangover?"

She laughed and held the glass out to him. "Some hair of the dog?"

He didn't want to drink from her glass. He shook his head.

"I want a bath and some coffee."

She sat down on the edge of the bed.

"Who's Caroline?"

He winced.

"Who told you about Caroline?"

"You did. You kept yelling for her in your sleep last night."

He remembered his nightmare then. Caroline was going over a waterfall in a canoe. His feet wouldn't move. All he could do was shout and scream to her to jump—but she kept sitting there calmly, her face straight ahead toward the falls as if she didn't hear him. The feeling of anguish and horror that gripped him in the dream returned for a moment.

"Who's Caroline?" Sally demanded again. She ran her fingers over his shoulder. He didn't want her to touch him.

"My wife."

She gave a disgusted sigh.

"Might know when I finally find a gent I want, he'd be married. Why aren't you with her?"

He got out of bed. He didn't want to talk about Caroline. He didn't want to stay in the room.

Sally came up behind him and put her arms around him.

"That's all right—I'm here and she's not. You're gonna be my man."

He unclasped her arms from him. He would have preferred the tentacles of an octopus at that moment.

"I'm not sure about anything right now," he said.

But in the end he stayed on. It was an easy life to drift into. He slept during the long hot California day, rising to the coolness of evening. He could take all the time he wanted for a bath and a shave. Then he would stroll in the streets having his supper at Fritchee's or the Chinaman's. Sometimes he ate with Sally or Big Jack; other times he met Cricket or Levi. He took to smoking long black cigars and wearing fancy waistcoats. After his leisurely supper he would stroll back to the Golden Nugget and seat himself at the green baize table. The player piano would be tinkling, the bartender drying the long rows of glasses in preparation for the night's trade, the lights

192

along the walls turned up to their brightest blaze. Soon the customers would start drifting in, mostly rough miners, a few trappers, businessmen, the local drunks. At seven-thirty the girls would come down and start circulating. The laughter would grow more feverish. The games would start.

An element of danger to his job lent an edge to everything. Irate and drunken miners were not always reasonable when they lost a wad of money which had taken months of sweat to work out of some flea mine. There was a plug-ugly assigned to bounce them if necessary, but a greater risk was acknowledged by the slender little gun Adam had been given to keep in his sleeve.

Adam made more money in a month than Cricket and Levi made in four. The miners nicknamed him "Padre" because he retained the habit of quoting the Bible.

Night after night from his green padded table he watched the panorama of human dreams, greed, sorrow, hope, played. It was four a.m. when the last deck was laid aside and the night's work complete. Big Jack always had a breakfast of tough steak and greasy eggs waiting in the kitchen for himself, the bartenders, dealers and any of the girls who hadn't bedded for the night.

He was a rough-talking and in many ways mean-hearted man, but he liked Adam. He had a shrewd intelligence under his balding pate and he liked to play Adam on politics, religion and philosophy, subjects that few of his customers or compatriots were well-versed on. They talked a lot about whether a war could be averted between the north and south and if not, which side California would join.

When the sun started coming in strong through the dusty windows revealing the stains that never showed at night on the fancy wallpaper, the wads of tobacco spit indiscriminately on the floors, the cracks and haziness in the mirrors, Big Jack would get up and pull the shades, plunging the place back into its realm of eternal twilight. The bartenders would double check the locks on the heavy iron doors which every business place in town found a necessary security against the rambunctious miners, and each one would head for his room, leaving an old coolie to start cleaning up.

The odor of stale smoke and whiskey would follow Adam up the stairs, mingling with the reek of powder and perfume from the girls' rooms. His room was at the end of the hall, large and bare. He made a fetish of leaving the windows open during the night.

If Sally wasn't bothering him he sometimes read for a couple of hours before falling asleep. Sometimes he just lay on the bed staring at the ceiling. To him it was a strange charade he witnessed each night. There was a great deal of laughter and the men kept assuring each other of what a good time they were having—"We sure are hanging one on!—Whooopee!"—and yet they came back again and again with the same hungers, loneliness, unfulfilled emptiness. There was an underlying desperation in their attempts to have a good time.

It was easy for someone like Sally to be a belle in a town where men outnumbered the women fifty to one. The burly miners were driven to dancing with each other, parodying a feminine part by pulling out a trouser leg with ludicrous daintiness between a calloused thumb and forefinger to resemble a skirt, or tying a kerchief about their heads in strange contrast to a bristling beard. Their performances were hilarious—and sad.

A slow sorrow for them built inside Adam. He felt with an ironic bitterness that now when he was no longer fit to be a preacher he finally understood the true meaning of ministering. He saw for the first time that he had never really loved the people to whom he had preached. He had loved his own glory, the passion of the role he was playing. He had looked at people like these miners, saloon girls, bartenders, in hatred, outraged by their sins. Staring at the ceiling on those dim mornings he came face to face with the fact that part of his rage had been against the secret elements within himself that wanted to partake of the very sins he denounced with such vigor. He had been infuriated at saloon girls and lumbermen because they were doing things he secretly wanted to do and would not allow himself. The lights, the music, the red-lipped women had held a forbidden fascination. Only now that he knew intimately and understood how empty that gaiety was did a real sorrow build in him for those men who came needing so much and got so little. In the Golden Nugget Adam came to understand that pleasure is not happiness and lust is not love.

There were times when he wanted Sally more than he had ever wanted Caroline because Caroline's arms had always been open to him. She had hardly known how to say 'no,' while Sally was a master at tantalizing, teasing, withholding, tormenting. But like Shakespeare in his sonnet, Adam found that she was no sooner had than despised. There was none of the oneness he had felt with Caroline. Once his lust was sated he was sickened with Sally's nearness.

Sally knew he did not love her. Completely enamoured of him, the knowledge drove her to shrill, demanding behavior. She wanted constant proof that he cared about her. She was greedy for presents, caresses, his time. He felt that she had only three moods—coy and teasing, shrill and screaming, pouting and weeping. He wanted to be free of her. He was miserable and yet he continued to drift along in the easy stream of the black-jack job.

194

On April 22 word reached him that a war between the states had been declared. Adam felt a strange sense of relief, as if the war was a signal for which he had been waiting. His announcement that he was going to join the Union effort was met mostly with admiration, but Sally's hazel eyes narrowed into cat-slits.

"You ain't goin' " she told him when they were alone in her bedroom.

Adam was determined that no matter how much she screamed and shouted he was going to stand his ground.

"I've made up my mind."

She neither screamed nor shouted.

"You ain't goin'," she said again with calm certainty.

He felt a queasy uneasiness creep through him.

"What makes you so sure?"

"You ain't gonna leave me now," she said. She jumped off the bed, her face flushed with triumph.

"I'm gonna have a baby. Your baby."

40

"I know how you kin get rid of it," Mama Tutu said. She was a heavy set woman with coal black hair and a faint moustache to match. She had been one of the girls in the Princess Saloon until age and fat had overwhelmed her. Now, she cooked for Big Jack and kept the girls in line.

"I don't wanna get rid of it," Sally said. Her body submerged in a wooden bathtub, she looked at her swelling abdomen with satisfaction and waved her toes in the air.

"I thought you told me you never wanted no kids?" Mama Tutu said.

"I don't. But I want Adam Quimby," Sally said. "Hand me that towel."

Mama Tutu handed her the towel, shaking her head.

"I know," Sally giggled, "that'd make most men run for their lives, but Adam ain't most men. With men like Adam Quimby, havin' a baby nails them down. That's the way they are."

Mama Tutu went on shaking her head.

Her skepticism was well-grounded. Baby or no baby, Adam was determined to ride off to the war.

"Not without marrying me first!" Sally shrieked a hundred times a day.

"I can't marry you. I'm already married!" Adam shouted back, flinging clothes into his valise.

"You can get it annulled."

"Annulled?" Adam laughed with derision. "There are two children to prove the marriage was consumated and neither Caroline nor I are under age."

"There are other grounds," Sally persisted.

"Such as?"

"Desertion. She deserted you."

"You can't get an annullment on grounds of desertion, Sally."

"You can! I know a priest in Sonora who'll do it. You don't even need to have her sign a piece of paper. He kin do it."

"You're crazy."

"I'm not crazy," Sally screamed. "I fixed it with him. He's got the power and he'll do it *for a price*."

"No." Adam said shortly. "I don't want a questionable annulment from a corrupt priest."

Sally grabbed the valise he was packing and threw his shirts on the floor and began to stomp on them, screaming, "You will. You will. You will. You ain't leavin' here without marryin' me! I got it fixed with Father Waint."

Adam grabbed her and slapped her.

Sally let out a bellow and went screaming down the hall. Big Jack came charging up the stairs ready to bust Adam in the nose, but when he got into the bedroom he couldn't do it. Adam was sitting on the bed crying.

Jack breathed a pungent word and then added, "Hell, she'll be better off iffen you don't marry her, you cur," and walked out.

By the time Sally was done with her screaming and her tantrums, there wasn't anyone in Columbia who wasn't aware of the whole story. Sally had been right when she said she was a belle around there.

Adam walked beneath a load of derision and criticism, but it was Cricket's remark that sunk to his quick—"I guess Adam makes a habit o' treatin' his women bad."

Adam stood up in the dark corner where he had retreated with his beer. Cricket stood up too, the muscles in his arms flexing at the possible approach of battle. But Adam's intention was not to fight Cricket. He walked past, his face set. When he returned, he had a carriage.

"Get in," he ordered Sally.

She drew back, frightened by the hard whiteness of his face.

"What for?"

"We're going to Sonora to see your priest."

196

"Oh, Adam—" she yelled, laying a stranglehold on his neck.

He unwound her arms. His face was cold.

"Get in."

"Adam, I gotta get dressed. I c'n't go in this—"

He looked down at her nightgown, her swollen, tear-red face, and sighed.

"All right. Hurry," he said more gently.

They rode the four miles, with dust boiling around them. Sometimes she tried to talk. He said nothing. He kept hoping she would change her mind. She didn't.

They found the priest in a flaking adobe church. He was a heavy, sweating man with dark eyes that jerked about in his head. Adam's obvious contempt made him uncomfortable. When he had filled out the necessary papers, he said to Adam in an aside, "You understand we are facilitating this for you because your lady is—because of her delicate condition."

Adam's eyes retained their contempt as he handed the agreed upon sum to the man.

"For the poor," the priest said, as he shuffled the bills with pudgy fingers.

"Of course," Adam said. His tone was nasty.

The priest's face reddened but his voice remained unctuous. "The final annulment must come from higher up so there will be a short waiting period—but there is no need to worry. My superior is a wonderful man, but elderly. Very elderly. He leaves these things to me— Do you understand? And—after all—since you were never married in the church, the marriage never really existed."

Adam hated the man more by the minute.

"I will publish your bans immediately. Then when the annulment comes through, you can be married at once."

They were married three weeks later, the priest's shifting eyes avoiding the obvious condition of the bride.

Afterward, Adam bought his new wife a dinner of tortillas and beans and then they began the ride back. The day was broiling, reminding him of another hot wedding day. He kept seeing Caroline in her heavy satin dress holding her roses—he had been so hungry for her, so excited. He saw her again standing in the middle of the rented room at Springford with her hair curling over her shoulders—

"Are you mad at me, Adam?" Sally pleaded.

They hit a bump and she jounced against him. Her hair was covered with dust; her face looked bloated. She burped, gaseous with the spicy Mexican food, the jolting ride, her pregnancy.

"I'm gonna be si-ick."

He reined the horse in hard. She half tumbled from the carriage, knelt on the bone white earth, her body heaving. He got out and held her forehead until it was over.

She turned and clung to him. He was almost retching himself, from the smell of vomit.

"Adam—are you mad at me," she sobbed.

"No—" he said softly. "No, Sally, I'm not mad at you." It was true. All he felt now was sadness for her and for himself. He helped her back into the carriage.

*   *   *

No man was ever happier to ride off to a war than Adam Quimby. He had saved up a good sum of money as a black-jack dealer. He gave most of it to Sally and promised he would send her more when he got it.

"Phooyah! I know how much they pay soldiers!" she raged. "I'll get precious little, and I can't dance now, y' know."

She wanted him to sell Ebonite and give her the money, but he couldn't do it. Ebonite was the one thing he had left that he loved.

He asked Cricket and Levi to look after Sally while he was gone and they promised.

Sally had a consuming fear that he wasn't going to come back to her. At the last moment she clung to him, half hysterical. "Promise me you'll come back, Adam. Promise!"

He told her he'd come back to her, and then rode off with a wild hope that in the holocaust of the war he would find salvation and purification; that in some way he could rediscover the Adam he had meant to be. And he hoped that if he didn't—he would be killed.

41

"What in the world is happening?" Ann cried as she helped Bromley off with his coat.

"My dear, I'm afraid it's come. The South has fired on Fort Sumter and President Lincoln has called for troops."

Ann started to cry. "Oh, Bromley, I'm so afraid."

He put a comforting arm around her. "I doubt we'll see actual combat in Chicago," he reassured her.

"You won't go off to the war and leave me alone?" Ann pleaded.

"Even were I so quixotic, they wouldn't take me," Bromley said. "I can't see an inch in front of my eyes without these spectacles. I'd be a pretty worthless soldier."

Caroline did not cry like Ann, but she experienced a sudden feeling of great aloneness. As if he sensed it, Bromley drew Ann along and put his other arm around Caroline.

"Come, ladies, war or no war the world must go on. Take this starving man in and feed him."

*　　*　　*

At last Caroline was wearing the white velvet ball gown Ann had bought her the first Christmas she was in Chicago. She had pink tea roses entwined in her dark hair and knew she had never looked lovelier; yet Baird LeSeure had not danced with her once during the evening. The musicians were striking up the final dance and she had to struggle with a sense of disappointment and hurt anger when she saw him bow to Miss Fitzpatrick and lead her onto the floor.

Caroline had not lacked for partners. Dozens of young men, handsome in their blue uniforms, had given her a whirl. But something inside her had been waiting for Bay.

A waiter stopped and handed her a glass of wine.

"I don't drink—" she started to say and tried to hand it back. Her hand was shaking and she spilled some of the wine on her dress.

"This is ridiculous!" she thought, furious with herself. *Of course Bay wants to dance with young girls who are free to accept his attentions.* He has been more than kind to give so much attention to a married, older woman like me.

She dodged into a pantry to sponge the spot on her dress and to avoid several possible partners who had been bearing down on her. By the time the last notes of the song died, she felt she had restored her composure. Her pique was gone. She felt benevolent and grateful to Bay. She assured herself that she *expected* nothing from him. She emerged from the pantry to help Ann say goodnight to the guests, and ran smack into Bay.

"Why, Bay! Hello. I haven't seen much of you tonight," she said with bright gaiety.

"That was my loss," he said, his usual gallant self.

"I was astonished when Ann told me you had enlisted," she said. She had to work to keep her smile from quivering. "You never seemed

199

to want to talk about the war or to care a fig for politics."

He laughed. "So you thought I was the court jester, and it turns out I'm Paul Revere."

"Oh, Bay, that's no answer," she protested.

"Doris says I'm joining the Union Army to be a confederate spy."

"Can't you be serious for a moment!" Caroline scolded, but she couldn't help laughing. "Tell me the real reason."

"What?—and lose all the fascinating mystery I have suddenly acquired?"

At this point Nelia Fitzpatrick came sashaying between them. "I wonder, Bay, if you'd mind dropping me off?"

"I'd be delighted," Bay said, bowing.

Miss Fitzpatrick's green eyes met Caroline's with a brief glint of triumph. "You *are* sweet! I'll just get my cloak then."

Before they could resume their conversation, Ann took Nelia's place. "Bay—will we see you again before you leave?"

"It's not likely, Ann."

"Oh, we *shall* miss you! You've been such a good friend," Ann said. Impulsively she stood on tiptoe and kissed his cheek. "Do send us your address as soon as possible and keep in touch."

"I will," he said, giving her a hug in return. Then he turned back to Caroline. "Aren't you going to kiss me goodbye, too?"

Caroline felt very strange. She wanted to lean forward and kiss Bay as lightly and casually as Ann had done, yet she was held back by the most awful constraint and embarrassment she had ever felt.

His eyes compelled her to meet his glance. Something in them took her breath away. For a heart-pounding moment she had the feeling he was going to take her in his arms and kiss her with wild savagery. Then the fire in his glance died. The moment was gone. He was laughing.

"Write to me, Caroline—"

Before she could reply, Miss Fitzpatrick came fluttering back. Amidst a flurry of goodnights and goodbyes she bore Baird off with her. Caroline was left with a sinking sense of loss.

Usually she helped straighten things after a party but she felt that to be in the ballroom another moment would be intolerable. She gathered up her velvet skirts and ran up to her bedroom. Only when she reached that sanctuary did she realize she was choking with tears.

Did it really matter that much to her that Baird LeSeure was going off to war?

She sat down on her bed, mopping at her cheeks. No, of course not, she told herself crossly, it's everything! All the beautiful young men on both sides caught up in this horrible affair!

200

Turning, she caught sight of herself in the mirror. A young woman with hot, red cheeks, eyelashes spiked with tears, and a pink wound across the front of her white gown. She covered the stain with trembling fingers, as if it were an evil portent.

And where was Adam?—the unwelcome thought assailed her against her will. *Was he, too, riding off to war somewhere?*

*   *   *

The Thorntons, Tartoués, and Quimbys were spending a quiet evening at home. The two boys were bent over their geography books. Bromley was reading the latest accounts of the war. Caroline was making out lesson plans for the older children at her school. Ann, seated near the fireplace, was embroidering yarn flowers on a pillow cushion. Firefly, grown more slender and long legged now that she was nearly five, was sitting at her feet, watching her aunt's clever fingers working the yarn. Kemink was lengthening a pair of trousers that Dan-Pete had outgrown. The clock in the hall could be heard ticking and the smoke whispered up the chimney.

"Let me try it once, Aunt Annie," Fly begged, intrigued by the bright yarns.

Ann handed the needle to the child with an indulgent smile. "Follow the tracing with backward stitches. Remember the most important thing is to keep the thread taut so it doesn't tangle."

Fly's shining curls bent over the hoop of buckram.

Suddenly the assemblage was startled by an emotion filled cry from Ann. "Oh, my Lord!"

Bromley jerked to his feet—Caroline's pen clattered from her fingers—Kemink stared, her bronze skin paling, for it was not apparent to any of them what had elicited the cry from Ann.

"Look!" she cried again. "Look!" Her face was contorted with emotion.

They looked and saw nothing. All three of the children were now looking at their aunt with wondering puzzlement.

"For God's sake, what is it Ann?" Bromley exploded.

"Look at Fly!"

The eyes that had been fastened on Ann turned toward Felicity.

"She's using her left hand—" Tears were pouring down Ann's cheeks.

It was true. Felicity was holding the hoop in her left hand to steady it as her right plied the needle.

In one swift movement Caroline was on her knees hugging her daughter to her. "I knew it! I knew it!" she exulted. "I told you all long ago that she was healed!"

Brom was across the room in a leap, kneeling before the child, lifting and touching her arm.

"How does your arm feel, Fly? Does it hurt to move it like this?" he questioned urgently.

Fly giggled, enjoying all the attention. "It feels jus' like the other arm, Uncle Bromley. I guess it's been helping me do lotsa things only I never noticed much."

"Kin you really use it?" Dan-Pete cried. "Now you kin play ball with us!"

"Let us give thanks," Kemink said. She joined Bromley and Caroline on her knees and motioned for the boys to do likewise.

Caroline experienced an ecstatic love of God. She could not have felt more exalted if she had tried to walk on the water and the water had supported her. In the sudden manifest wholeness of Fly's arm, she felt all her intuitive beliefs made demonstrably real for all time. She was filled with awestruck wonder.

As soon as the prayer of thanks was over, Bromley insisted on making exhaustive tests of Fly's arm. He had her try to carry objects of various sizes and weights, lift things, push things, and twist things.

"Remarkable, remarkable," he kept saying. When he was satisfied that she had done enough, he said, "She hasn't got complete use of the arm, but by George, it's coming. I would say she has regained sixty per cent of normal function—"

"She is one hundred per cent well!" Caroline insisted.

This time Ann and Bromley did not exchange any dubious glances. Bromley was as overjoyed as anyone else that the child's arm seemed normal, but at the same time, he felt uneasy. It was to him unexplainable, mysterious, and rather frightening.

July, 1861

Dear Caroline,

We are camped in Virginia. Up until the end of May all the troops were kept on the Washington side of the Potomac, but the sight of

Confederate pickets stealing closer and closer to the capitol proved unnerving. General Mansfield sent three columns down river to drive them back. Since then we've been working on a line of fortification which will continue into Maryland to protect the Capitol. It is hard physical work, and for a time I had reason to regret how soft I'd grown. Now I can boast that every muscle is hard as a bone and that I sleep on the ground as if it were eiderdown.

My "home" is what they call a Sibley tent. It looks like an Indian teepee. I share it with fifteen other men. We sleep with our feet to the center pole like spokes in a wheel. Having earned the rank of Captain, (no congratulations are in order, my dear, as I think this honor was conferred on me because I am over 25 and able to keep my feet pointing in the right direction at the right order), I am to have a wall tent to myself. I will not miss the snores that presently put me to sleep.

Except for the hardtack (which is supposed to be our bread) we have been eating well. Our cooks rely heavily on beans, but when you are up at sunrise and spend the day in the open air, pork and beef boiled with beans over an open fire, can taste mighty good.

They say that General Scott hopes to hold off putting us into a major battle until we've been properly trained and equipped. I may be able to write you news of battle all too soon, for the Rebs ambushed a troop train and now there is a great lust from the public and the press to draw blood in return.

"On to Richmond!" is the cry in the newspapers and in Washington—and we are the army pointed in that direction.

If I should die in my first encounter, remember—I thought you were ravishing; I loved you madly, and I died with a rose stolen from your dark hair pressed against my heart!

Your Humble Servant,
Bay
Captain Baird LeSeure (Ahem.)

July, 1861

Dear Caroline,

I received with joy your letter telling of Felicity's miraculous recovery. I would like to tell you that it converted me to your way of thinking, but human beings cling hard to their prejudices and the axioms they have personally welded from hard experience. I can only concede that there is much in the universe we do not understand and that there may be powerful laws at work that supersede the ones we have deciphered. If you want to call those superior laws "God," I suppose it is as good a designation as any.

I have had my first battle and it leaves me even more certain that there is no governing intelligence in this universe—or if there is, that it does not share the morals men acclaim. The fact that men slaughter each other like pigs, while each side proclaims they are doing it in God's name and pleading with Him for victory, is as hard to swallow as a salty cork.

I wonder if any battle in history ever started out the way this one did. You would have thought we were on our way to a country fair, Caro. We straggled along the country roads, every man at his own pace, laughing, talking; our flags fluttering at the head of each regiment and our guns the only sign we were an army. We have Garibaldi Guards who wear green-plumed hats; add to that the Fire Zouaves, who wear red fezzes, blue jump jackets, and red Ali Baba pantaloons; and the Highlanders, and you have a circus. We spent half the first day *picking blackberries* and stopping to wade and drink from every stream we came to! I think if I had been an officer above Captain, I would have cried. We made only six miles the first day.

Imagine, if you will, that we were joined the next day by all manner of gigs, wagons, and carriages, driven by citizens of Washington who were riding along for the pleasure of being spectators at the battle, complete with hampers of food and drink. Some of them were high ranking Senators, and Congressmen—and there were a number of ladies as well. One red-headed beauty (she reminded me a little of Miss Fitzpatrick) amused herself by throwing apples to us. They expected a decisive battle that day.

Just beyond Centerville there is a stream called Bull Run; and beyond that was our goal, Manassas Junction, a supply depot for Richmond. Beauregard, the Southern general, was waiting for us on Bull Run's south bank with back-up troops under Commander Jackson. Perhaps, by now, you have read accounts of the battle and know more about what went on than I do. Only after I read the newspapers did I learn we faced 32,000 Southern troops, many of whom had been brought in by rail or forced march. At the time, all I knew was that as far as you could see along the banks of Bull Run, for miles upon winding miles there was a glint of bayonets and rifle barrels in the sun. Our wayfaring picnic was over. We heard our first cannon and musket fire as we were ordered forward.

My regiment was ordered to sneak along the South's left flank. The Confederates have developed a system to convey signals with flags. I believe that something of this sort must have occurred because the element of surprise we hoped for was not there. We immediately encountered hard fighting.

204

Being in battle is strange, Caroline. Not what one imagines before-hand—and I suppose different for every man.

You asked me before I left why I had volunteered. If I had answered you as truthfully as I could that night, I would have said that my motives were purely practical and business-like. The fact that I was long a so-called "Southerner" made me suspect in the eyes of many of the Northerners with whom I want to do business. What better way to demonstrate my fidelity to the Union than to enlist for 'our noble cause'? Ninety days is not forever. For three months service I would purchase good will and banish the 'Copperhead' title that people keep hanging on me. Besides, I am in sympathy with the Union cause. I do not, and never did, feel like a 'Southern Gentleman'. There are things in that way of life I would not defend. I remember slave children forced to stand for hours waving palm branches over my sleeping step-mother. A subtle form of cruelty, but I can still see their eyes. And Sheba, who was as loyal as an old hound dog to her "Marsa," once told me that her only child had starved to death when she had been forced to wet nurse a white child, and had not been able to produce enough milk for both. I have always felt that for every good done for the negro there were two injustices.

Now I am not sure that I am aware of all my motives. They may be deeper than I know. I discovered in battle that war is a crucible—and perhaps one that men secretly crave. I never thought I was a coward; yet, no man knows for sure what he will do in conditions of danger and stress.

Being in battle is both horrifying and exhilarating. I felt I was viewing an unreal nightmare, and at the same time, as if every cell in me was more alive and aware than at any time in my life.

The countryside was beautiful, rolling wooded crests, with here and there a flash of the trickling waters of Bull Run. We started fighting early in the morning, and there were times during that long day when I would suddenly feel as objective as if I had climbed outside of my body and were seeing the scene from some faraway perspective. At those times death and terror seemed incapable of touching me, as if I were witnessing an epic ballet of embarrassing beauty. The dust raised from plunging horses seemed to form and unfold like giant, grey-gold flowers which then lay themselves back onto the earth with the most incredible grace. A man next to me was fatally struck with a mini-ball and I could only stare with wonder because he seemed to soar for a moment like some God-man against the blinding radiance of the sun. Once when I was crawling up a plateau, I looked back and saw what must have been an entire regiment of our forces behind me, but they did not seem to be individual soldiers; instead, I seemed to behold one monstrous, beautiful, sinuous blue being. Perhaps during those moments I was in some kind of shock or extreme fatigue. I do not know.

At other times during that day the war became personal and subjective, and tragic. On the battlefield I discovered how entwined I had become with the men under my command. Three of my men died in the battle. One was a sixteen year old boy. It is strange that I had to come to a field of death to learn that I do love my fellowman.

The grief I felt was genuine and yet I would not lie to you—there was also that day the exhilaration that I mentioned before. I could not deny that I felt a thrill at those moments when we were driving the enemy back.

At one time it seemed our victory was certain. Then a fresh brigade of Southern troops hit our right flank, and Beauregard renewed his attack all along the line. They captured twelve of our important guns, and from that time on the artillery fire grew so heavy we could do nothing but fall back. Our forces became fragmented. We were too green and inexperienced in battle to know how to regroup after each repulse. I am proud that I managed to keep most of my company together; but a large majority of our soldiers lost track of their brigades, officers, and even regiments. Thousands of men were wandering around without command, an impossible situation for an army! As a result, the battle turned into a fiasco for the Union. I understand now that McDowell ordered us to unite and stand at Centerville, but the orders never filtered to me, and I'm sure not to many others. The Southern forces had not suffered the same disintegration we had, and it seemed as if they were coming at us like a solid wall of raised sabers. No wonder many of our men panicked. Our fragmented army retreated through Centerville like bee-stung bulls. Our 'observers' from Washington had remained there in their carriages, eating chicken from their picnic baskets and waiting for word of our 'victory'. They were caught in the ensuing melee. To add to the sense of confusion and misery, it had begun to rain. It was a mess of carriages, horses, army wagons, ambulances trying to evacuate the wounded, terrified civilians and exhausted soldiers slipping and scrambling and crawling through the mud and downpour.

At the worst moments, there are often things to laugh at. The carriage of one of the senators had become so mired in the mud he had to get out and run for his life. He had lost all his aplomb and dignity. The sight of him, with his cheeks chuffing like a bellows, his eyes rolling like billiards, and the tails of his coat floating behind him like banners, started a roll of mirth through my company. One of the men, Alvis Bernardi, composed a song on the spot to the tune of "Yankee Doodle Dandy", which began—"Senator X came down to Manasses to watch us win a battle—a little raindrop came along and knocked him from his saddle—" From that point on it becomes too bawdy to quote to a lady, but it served to set our men laughing again.

That laughter was precious, for we were on the verge of slipping into despair. The area we were leaving was strewn with bodies from both sides. We saw despicable acts born of fear and panic on every side. I saw a man cut a horse from an ambulance bearing wounded and try to ride off with it. A man from our side shot him dead on the spot.

There were also exhibits of unbelievable bravery. Our fiery-pants Zouaves beat back a black horse regiment from Louisiana single-handed. The blood that was shed actually ran like a river in the rain.

We marched all night, and many soldiers are still straggling into Washington today. Muddy, soaked, defeated, bloody, exhausted to the point where many staggered rather than walked—I wondered if ever such a flea-bitten, defeated army was met with such compassion and kindness as we are being given here. The city has been turned into a hotel for us. The civilians came with soup and coffee and bandages and bore soldiers off to the shelter of their homes and porches and sheds. A little girl brought one of my men a bucket in which to soak his blistered feet. A number of public buildings have been converted into hospitals. My men and I are comfortably situated in an old church. Women in the neighborhood have brought up quilts, stews, warm bread and coffee.

Our feeling of 'defeat' is abnegated somewhat by the realization that we at least whomped the Rebs to the point where they were too worn down to follow us all the way and take Washington. But I scarcely need tell you that we have gained a healthy respect for the enemy and you no longer hear comments about how quickly we are going to wind up this thing.

Receiving your letter here was a good surprise. Every time I take it from my duffle and look at it, it makes me smile. It is so like you— It begins so decorously with copybook penmanship, but by the end, the words are coming swift and rushing, all in a tangle with the passion of your thoughts, the t's crossed with wild flourishes.

Deliver a special kiss from me to Her Royal Highness of Chicago, and give my greetings to the rest of the household.

Bay

43

~~Dear Baird,~~ Dear *Captain* LeSeure,

I was happy to receive your letter and read with interest your account of camp life. Though you disavow any merit in the matter, I am impressed with your swift promotion and also alarmed. At this rate you will be a Major General by the end of your ninety days and will be obliged to continue in the war if it is not over!

Bromley was like a small boy when your letter arrived. He is so interested in the war and was bursting to know what you had written. See us now at breakfast. I am reading your letter as I drink my tea. He keeps giving me expectant glances. I do not seem to notice. He begins to make little clearing noises in his throat. Still I do not seem to notice. Finally he can forebear no longer and leans forward, "Well, I say, Caroline, what *does* Bay have to say?" I hope that you will not mind if I share your letters with the others. I could spirit them away to my room to read but that would cause them to make all sorts of silly conjectures.

Ann is relieved that the war scarcely seems to touch Chicago. Oh, I suppose that isn't really true. Brom says that thousands of dollars of goods and supplies are pouring into our railroads and that we will be the greatest supply depot to the Union forces in the entire nation. There is also talk that a training camp may be built here. But for the present time life goes on much as it always has.

I continue to be engrossed with my school. I learn so much in trying to teach. I would know nothing of astronomy were it not that I have to learn it in order to teach Dan and Dan-Pete. Last week we took all the children, even Herbert and Heine, in carriages at night to an open field so that we might see the constellations. I thought of you, Bay. How far away you are and still you must watch these very same stars from your open tent at night. Even Emily looked. Emily, who never looks at anything! Can you imagine the excitement I felt when I saw her face turned up to the starlight along with the others.

Not all our experiences are such happy ones. A terrifying thing happened yesterday. I think I told you before that Millie is subject to seizures—the doctors term it epilepsy. Yesterday she was stricken so violently that I feared we would lose her. They swallow their tongues sometimes while in the grip of these seizures and strangle. We ran for a clothespin to force her tongue down but her jaws were so clamped I could not insert the pin between her lips. The child was turning blue and the calm I was trying to maintain was about to shatter when Kemink came back from an errand. She is exceptionally strong and succeeded in getting the pin into Millie's mouth. Within a few moments the crisis had passed. I still shake thinking about it.

I have had such *proof*, Bay, that a healing principle does exist. Fly is my evidence as she uses her arm freely every day. Still, I am frustrated. It is as if I knew that if I put a teakettle of water on a hot stove it would come to a boil but was in the position of not knowing how to kindle the fire. There have been times in my life when the "fire" has been there, but I do not seem to be able to kindle it at will! I could at times beat my head against the wall when I feel so thwarted, especially when I want to help someone like Millie, and I fail.

Now that Fly is able to use both hands, Bromley is having her instructed in piano. She is practicing a simple setting of "Greensleeves" in the room next to me. Do you not think that is a lovely melody?

Since you never stole "a rose from my dark hair", it must be one of Miss Fitzpatrick's roses you cherish—.

I shall look forward with great interest to "the further adventures of Captain LeSeure"—should you care to share them with me.

Your affectionate friend,
Caroline Quimby

August 12, 1861

Dear Bay,

I had barely posted my last letter to you when we began to hear news of the battle at Bull Run. As stories of the terrible losses suffered there (they say there is still no accurate account!) came trickling in, you can imagine our state of concern for you. How relieved I was to receive your letter and know that you were safe.

I have read your letter a number of times and each time I am freshly moved: Strange that when you were in the South—and now again, I can feel so close to you in your letters; while when you are with me in person, you are a mystery. I can never guess then what is going on inside of you because you are never serious for a moment. Your teasing and joking make you a delightful companion, but often I think they are a mask behind which you hide. In your letters, you are more willing to open your heart.

I tried hard to imagine what the battle must have been like. The nearest I could come to equating your experience was my winter in the Tomorrow River country. Kemink and I were alone with the children. We, too, faced enemies of a sort—freezing cold, loneliness, possible starvation, wild animals. By the first big snow, we had provided ourselves with a plentitude of food and fuel and were self sustaining. I remember that at Thanksgiving, I felt a thrill of pride in our accomplishments.

Some of the newspapers said the retreat was orderly from Bull Run, but there were eyewitness reports from other writers that painted the same picture you wrote us. Bromley is enraged that McDowell has lost his command over the issue. He feels the loss of the battle was not his fault and begs me to ask you for your opinion.

He insists on reading these accounts of battle to us at breakfast although Ann is terrified. He assures us the South cannot prevail in the end, and says our generals are planning to send ships to blockade the Southern harbors, and ultimately, if we cut off their trade with England, they will be without supplies to make war.

Everyday more troop trains arrive in Chicago. Many recruits look so young my heart fails me at the sight of them. A number of prominent Chicago women, Ann among them, are planning a benevolent group to provide these young soldiers with some comfortable place to rest and be refreshed between arrival and departure, an interval which often takes hours and sometimes days. I am very busy with my school, but I, too, will do all I can to help.

Your ninety days must be coming to an end. How grateful we will be when you are home safe.

Ever with concern,
Caroline

P.S. I am not sure it is flattering to learn that when you look at my letters it makes you smile. Please note the careful "copybook" handwriting clear to the end! (It was a frightful effort, and I think it is horrible that *you* write so beautifully.)

*　　*　　*

On the last day of August, 1861, Sally Quimby gave birth to a baby boy. She named him Loratio, after a character she had once seen in a play. She wrote a labored letter to Captain Adam Quimby informing him that he had a son, and that though "I got my figger back, I ain't foolin' around any"—and asked if she should put some of the money he had given her into a gold mine venture that looked promising.

The letter the Captain wrote back was confined to anxious inquiries about the child's wholeness. When Sally wrote again confirming that the child was healthy, Adam sent another letter instructing her to

210

rename the child Garth Aaron after his father and to go ahead and invest in the gold mine.

"He never says nothing about me," Sally complained, crushing the letter with angry fingers. She was having a beer with Levi and Cricket, who had stopped in to see that she was all right as they had promised Adam.

She fixed her eyes on Cricket.

"I suppose his first wife was pretty?" she probed.

Cricket looked at her unhappy face and felt sorry for her.

"Ain't nobody prettier n' you, Sally," he said, but his eyes shifted a little which she did not miss.

"She was beautiful," Sally said with angry intuition.

Cricket sighed. He set his glass down and got up. He didn't feel like lying about Caroline even to save Sally's feelings.

"People got diffrunt ideas about what's beautiful, Sal—but she was to me." He left.

Sally unrolled Adam's letter and began to tear it into pieces, tears leaking down her cheeks.

"I like that damn no-count boy," Levi said, "but he ain't worth those tears, Sally. You believe me." He reached over and patted her hand. "Thet other woman didn't make him happy. I kin swear to thet."

Her face brightened, but then in the back room, the baby started to cry. Sally swore and ground her teeth.

"Ain't never got a moment to myself no more," she raged. But she got up and went back to him. Her expression as she nursed him was bored and rebellious.

44

November, 1861

Dear Caroline,

It was almost worth going to war to receive your letter expressing eagerness for my return; however, I lost my senses and reinlisted for a three year term. Having faced the same perils and grumbled through the same hardships with these boys, I have become bound to them for reasons that somewhat escape me. Their youth has something to do with it. They are *boys,* Caroline. Half of them don't have a whisker to lay a blade to. I have a personal desire to see them through safely, if possible.

Winter has taken over here. It snows and rains, thaws and freezes. The results are mud, mud, mud. Bernardi, our "poet laureate", summed it up in a ballad he calls "Mud and Misery". Actually, our company is well off, for which I take some credit. In spite of the winter conditions, the command has never issued an order to build any winter quarters. The theory is that we are to be ready to move out at a moment's notice. But in fact we continue drilling month after month. It seemed ridiculous to me that men should be suffering from the elements when all around us are fine stands of timber. I ordered shelters built for the men in my command and so did a number of other officers. Now we are relatively warm and comfortable, which makes it seem more deplorable that the greater percentage of the Army of the Potomac is shivering under wet canvas. So many are dying from exposure and illness that we could be in battle without suffering greater losses. Some of the camps were hit with measles during the autumn. Most of the men survived, but it left them weakened. They seem unable to shake off the smallest ailments. Not a day passes without hearing the wailing dirge of a burial party marching by with the latest victims.

So Bromley was indignant with McDowell's replacement? I agree the loss of the battle of Bull Run cannot be entirely laid to his door.

At any rate, the men seem well satisfied with the new commander, General McClelland. They call him "Little Mac", and cheer him roundly when he rides through on inspection now and then on his black charger. My own feelings toward him are mixed. As I mentioned before, I feel the sufferings of the soldiers and many deaths could have been avoided with a few of the right orders from McClelland, but he has shaped us into the semblance of an army, I'll give him that. We could do drill in our sleep. He also seems commendably cautious about risking our lives before we're well prepared.

I had a letter from my step-mother and wish I had not. She had just learned of my "defection" to the Union Army. I believe she feels it was an act of personal vindictiveness toward her.

We have built ourselves a fireplace from a barrel, stones and Virginia mud. We broil fowl over the coals and bake sweet potatoes in the ashes. A nice change from our ever constant beans and hardtack. They say the Zouaves are eating black-snakes made into stew and hash, as the foraging in this area gets thinner day by day.

Days are punctuated by drills, roll calls, duties, care of our muskets

212

and clothing, and scrounging for wood and fuel. Even so, time is beginning to hang heavy.

When I grow tired of other pursuits, I try your stargazing, Caroline. They say what a man truly loves is his. So, I have claimed Saturn for myself. Would you like to visit my planet sometime? It has nine moons. Imagine what it would be like on a midsummer night!

It's intriguing to ponder your idea of a healing principle that could be tapped like the power of steam. At the same time, expecting yourself to be able to heal like the legendary saints is audacious. Could you not be content, Caroline, to be merely a warm, real, flesh and blood woman, subject as everyone else is to the vagaries, pitfalls, weaknesses and blots of the flesh?—Remembering that humanness also entitles you to attendant passions, joys, delights and ecstacies? You seek perfection; perfection is cold and finished and complete. Only humanness is growing and expanding, alive, thrilling to a thousand influences along the way.

You said once, only partly in jest, that I wanted to corrupt you. Perhaps I do. Perhaps I want to leave my sweaty, sooty, thumb mark on the hem of your white gown. A thumb print that will say, "She is alive. She is human. She has lived."

Have a sip of wine for me and dance an extra dance at Ann's next big soiree.

Bay

P.S. You write that I open my heart to you only in letters. It was you who built barricades when I returned to Chicago. I think the only time you're not afraid of me is when at least 1,000 miles lie between us—

* * *

December, 1861

Dear Caroline,

I have looked in vain for a letter from you. Were you angered by the teasing in my last missive? I prefer to believe that it is the impassable condition of our roads that keep me letterless, since almost everyone here is suffering the same fate. You can sink to your knees in mud at fifty spots within a two hundred yard stretch.

The men are bored and I think would willingly take on ten "Stonewall Jacksons," had they the choice, rather than endure one more day of drilling in the rain, and listening to the ceremonial dirges as the latest of the typhoid victims is borne off. When the newspapers report that "All is quiet on the Potomac", they no longer mean it reassuringly, but derisively. McClelland's caution that once seemed commendable is now becoming ludicrous. President

Lincoln has publicly accused him of having "a case of the slows". We are being urged from every side to march again on Richmond. I doubt that anything will happen before the first of the year, though, because McClelland himself has been stricken with typhoid. Reports say he is recovering, but having now viewed the disease at close hand, I can vouch that it is not something one gets over quickly.

Having little else to do in the way of amusement, my men are trying to devise ways to make our hardtack more palatable. Not only is it hard enough to break the best of teeth, but now our supply has been invaded by weevils. When you soak the crackers in coffee or soup, the bugs float to the top, which may be preferable to eating them, but has an appetite defeating effect. While the men fry, boil, stew, crush and grind their hardtack, they dream of the mail finally coming through, complete with Christmas packages from home. For many of my beardless boys this is the first Christmas they will have spent away from home. In short, these Virginia hills seem very bleak right now.

I hear reports that Confederate notes are being counted worthless. A large share of my holdings remain in Southern currency and notes. I'm enclosing some instructions for Bromley to carry out for me if he would be so kind.

There is some hope of Christmas furloughs. I might yet come and claim that extra dance with you. Perchance I don't I'm enclosing a check with the request that you purchase some gifts for the children, Kemink and the Thorntons. We have no shops here.

Oceans of devotion,
Bay

December 21, 1861

Dear Bay,

The homes in Chicago are wreathed with greens and candles. In spite of the daily troop trains, the war seems far away. They say there is no ill wind that does not blow someone good—and dreadful as it is to say, the war has caused this city to thrive. You do not see the crowds of people out of work, hungry and threadbare, that haunted the streets in previous winters. New factories are billowing up smoke in a dozen places. When Charles brought me home from the school tonight, the shops and stores were brightly lit and bustling with prosperous buyers. But oh, at what a price, Bay! For already here and there a death has struck—a son, a brother, a husband.

Bay, you did make me really quite furious with all that blather about white dresses and not being flesh and blood! To want to aspire to that which is highest and best does not make us less than human! Besides, it is not *I* who seek to do the healing. Impossible! Even Jesus said, "Not I, but the Father, doeth the works." But does it make a man less a man or more a man if he utilizes that steam power you mentioned? Perfection to *be* perfection would have to contain all the good things you mentioned to the *nth* degree. If it were cold and complete and sterile, it wouldn't be *perfect*, would it?

I imagine you sitting in your log hut with your barrel fire and your roasting fowl, almost as cozy and comfortable as we, and yet I wish you were coming home to the lighted tree, the turkey and the dressing. Your check was generous and I found lovely gifts for everyone as you instructed—But I was scarcely done with the purchases when Bromley who had been looking into your affairs as you requested, told me you have suffered severe losses because of the money upset. He says the money situation is in such a flux that all the banks in Illinois have been obliged to close their doors. He is writing the details to you that I had not the patience to try and understand. I wish now that I had not spent so lavishly of your funds.

A blessed Christmas to you and to your men, Bay, and may God bring you speedily and safely home.

Caroline

December 25, 1861

Dear Bay,

Christmas is over. The children are so stuffed with turkey and pudding that they have fallen asleep in the middle of the festivities— an unheard of occurrence. And I have crept away to sit by the fire in my room with your gift on my lap to marvel at it again. It was delivered on Christmas eve, wrapped in beautiful silver paper. When I opened it, and found an exact duplicate of a music box I had once admired I could scarcely believe it. I cried, "How could he have known!" Kemink only smiled, but I suspect she must have given you some assist or it would be too mysterious altogether.

I want you to know, Bay, it is one of the most touching gifts I have ever received, and I do thank you.

Caroline

Dear Uncle Bay,

Mother reads us your letters. I hope the war will be over soon. We will be glad when you come home. We had fun at the circus you took us to. Thank you for the very good boots. I like them better than any I have ever had.

Dan-Pete and I bought Emily a locket for Christmas. We wrapped it in a red velvet box. She wouldn't open it. It made me feel sad. Mother says Emily looked at the stars one night. I know that sometimes she looks at me, too. But she will not talk to us.

Georgio and Dan-Pete want to join the war. I would rather be a doctor and save people's lives. But I think you are brave.

Love,
Danny

December 28, 1861

Dear Uncle Bay,

The boots are dandy. They make me very tall. Danny says he does not want to kill anyone, but if the war is still going, I am going to volunteer as soon as I am old enough. I like it when Aunt Caroline reads us your letters.

We had a good Christmas.

Your friend,
Dan-Pete Tartoué

Dear Uncle Bay,

I love the bracelit. I still love Uncle Brom best, but I love you secindt next to Mama, Aunt Ann, and Kink.

Felicity F. Quimby

45

Captain Adam Quimby drew a deep breath of the dawn air tinctured with the smell of boiling coffee and fried bacon. He laughed at Ebonite, who made a chuffing sound as if he, too, were filling his lungs with the clean smell of early spring. The Tennessee land on which they stood was undulating and partly wooded. Some of the fields were already under cultivation and the breeze carried with it the smell of the new turned earth and the Tennessee River, almost visible through a sparse copse of trees to their left.

216

The men in Adam's company were hunched and relaxed, talking and laughing over their breakfast fires. General Grant said there would be no battle at Pittsburg Landing—it was still twenty miles, a good days' march to Corinth where they would take a stand. For one more day they could eat their bacon and hardtack without a knot of fear twisting in their stomachs.

Adam gave Ebonite one last handful of grain, letting the horse nose it from his hand with his big, velvety muzzle, before he squatted to drink his coffee.

"Cap'n, they say General Johnston's the best general they got in the whole southern army. You think that's right for a fact?"

The questioner was a freckle-faced boy from Ohio. His name was Cavanaugh, but the other soldiers called him "Beans" because of his appetite. Like the rest of Adam's company, he had not yet been in serious battle. The day by day accounts that General Albert Johnston was advancing toward them obviously filled him with both apprehension and eagerness.

"Hard to tell," Adam said. "Johnston is first in command of their entire forces, but that could be as much political clout as skill. We *know* Grant is good. He proved that when he took Fort Henry and Fort Donnelson."

"Captain, Sir!" A young lieutenant, urgency in his voice, approached him from the wooded area to his right. "Would you have a word with our picket, Sir?"

Adam wound himself back to his feet and, still holding his coffee cup, advanced toward the approaching picket.

"Sir, I seen some Butternuts peering through the bushes."

"That's to be expected," Adam said coolly. "We've been having skirmishes with their advance forces for three weeks now."

"More than that, Sir. I could hear bugles and I could see a long line of campfires—"

"Very good, Picket. I'll saddle my horse and have a look."

Adam was still cinching the saddle around Ebonite's girth when the first bullet struck. Within a second, the entire area was rattling as if being pounded by a heavy rain.

This is it, Adam thought. *It's here.*

"Take cover!" he shouted to his men, knowing even as he yelled how precious little cover there was to take—no entrenchments had been made and the woods were sparse.

Adam had not time to decide what to do next before a Lt. Colonel came riding into their midst in a stir of dust.

"The Rebs are attacking the front line of our defense in masses. Sherman's orders are to hold the road and the bridge at all costs.

217

We're expecting reinforcements from Buell—we've got to have that bridge!"

He was gone in another burst of dust.

Adam finished cinching Ebonite's saddle and swung onto his back. He drew his saber, a silver flash in the first light of the rising sun. Reining the horse right and left to make an uneven target, he rallied the men into a fighting line. He saw men crumble in death even as they tried to obey his orders.

My God—Adam thought. He could see the Confederates coming now like a dense grey fog from which red fire belched at continuous intervals.

"Fall back! Fall back!" he yelled, wheeling Ebonite.

Few of his men needed the order. They were already running, scrambling, crawling and clawing their way in retreat. He heard the screams of dying men rend the air, high and agonized above the deeper voice of the artillery and muskets, the pounding of hundreds of feet and hooves.

"Regroup! Regroup!" Adam shouted. "Hold the road. Hold the bridge!"

He shouted the same words over and over until his voice was a croak and his lips were so stiff with dust that every time he opened his mouth he choked and coughed.

At times his men heard him and tried to obey. Every time they reformed their line, the confederates would come boiling over the ridges like oatmeal foaming out of a pot—thousands of them, and his men would fall as if they were stacked cards hit by a hurricane—those who survived scrambling frantically to retreat again.

By two o'clock that afternoon the majority of the survivors were backed against the Tennessee River with impassable swamps on each side of them. They had had enough. They joined the hundreds of other Union soldiers who were already cowering and shivering against the banks of the river.

"Give me a flag!" Adam shouted to one of his lieutenants. He unfurled it and raising it like a banner rode back and forth on the bank, pleading in his croaking shout, "Men, for God's sake, for your country's sake, for your own sake, come up here and form a line and take one more stand!"

His men watched him, dull-eyed, apathetic with horror, beyond response. Only one man staggered up the bank toward him—Cavanaugh. His round, young face was so white that every freckle stood out, his eyes glistening with a mixture of hero-worship and tears.

"I'm sorry I run, Sir!" he said. "I want to be worthy of you, Sir—"

218

Adam was touched. Before he could say anything to the boy, General Sherman rode up.

"Soldier, join that company," he said to Cavanaugh, pointing to a group down the road. "Captain, take over Company 13. Their commander has just been killed. They're by the log church at Shiloh—"

Sherman's stock had worked its way from the front of his uniform until it appeared to hang from one of his ears. On the stern and dignified general the sight was so incongruous Adam thought for a moment he was going to burst into laughter—but the laughter died in his throat as his eyes belatedly saw that Sherman's hand was red with blood and there were bullet holes in his hat.

"Yes, Sir!" Adam responded, but his eyes swept back for a moment toward his own men still crowded herdlike against the river bank.

"It's all right," Sherman said with unexpected kindness. "Let them rest. They'll rally when we get reinforcements and yet put up a gallant fight. On your way now!"

Adam felt his own heart thudding with fatigue as he turned Ebonite back toward the battle. He had been fighting since dawn and his body longed to roll down the riverbank and lie with his demoralized men. Pride kept him trotting toward his newly given command. Whether by sub-conscious need or honest mistake, he took a wrong turn and it was dusk before he finally made it to the meeting house at Shiloh.

The scene that met his eyes stunned him. The ground was so strewn with bodies he found it difficult to guide his horse in a path that avoided stepping on an outflung arm or a crushed skull. Even the trees and bushes hung in broken shredded fragments. Nothing seemed to have escaped the carnage of shell and cannonball. And still—the battle raged on.

There was no time for horror or commiseration. A young officer, blood from a head wound streaming down his face, was tugging at Adam's sleeve.

"Are you Captain Quimby, Sir?"

"Yes."

"My God, where have you been? Never mind—thank God you're here now. The marsh hay is afire—the wounded will be roasted in there like pigs. They're screaming for help, Captain—"

"Send in a detail to carry out the wounded."

"I can't, Captain," the Lieutenant was weeping, "I haven't got enough men left to form a detail."

"I'll round up some men," Adam promised. He kneed Ebonite forward—and in the next moment heard a stunning roar and a terrible scream as he felt the world lurch from under him. A warm wave of blood washed him to the thigh and although he felt no pain, he thought with infinite terror—*my leg!—I've lost my leg!*

He lay with his teeth meeting through his lower lip, waiting for the explosions of pain to begin. All he felt was a pattering of rain drops from a breaking storm. At last he forced himself to open his eyes. Even then it was moments before he understood that the blood pumping over his knee was not his own. Ebonite had been hit. His entrails lay strung across the earth. His great eyes rolled toward Adam in numb appeal, while gutteral grunts of pain rolled through his ribs. Wet with blood, and mud, and rain, Adam crouched by the horse, holding the huge head in his arms, sobbing convulsively.

Suddenly a voice spoke above him, a quiet voice, but so filled with disgust it cut through and beneath the thunder splitting the sky, the artillery and Adam's own sobs.

"For God's sake man, how can you sit there crying over a *horse*— when this field is full of dead *men*! I've had three horses shot from under me today. You're an officer. Act like one. Put that poor beast out of his misery and get up and fight!"

It was General Grant who spoke. His face was too covered with dust to be recognizable, but the buff sash of his Major General full dress uniform glowed in the dusk, so Adam knew unmistakably who it was.

Adam had always been an emotional man. At every great crisis in his life he had cried like a woman. Kneeling in the mud at Shiloh, the contempt in Grant's eyes and the tone of his voice shriveled his tear ducts. He rose shakily and drew his pistol. Grant was already pounding off. Adam aimed with care. For one moment he met the agonized gaze of his beloved horse, then he pulled the trigger, his body jerking as if it were his own flesh the bullet was entering. He did not look again at the shining black carcass lying in the rain.

The fire—the wounded—he tried to force his dazed mind back to the battle and realized with relief that the downpour was taking care of the blaze. The wounded might drown; they would not burn.

"This way, Cap'n," the young lieutenant with the head wound was beside him again, "Take cover over here, Sir." He drew him toward a thicket.

"Johnston's dead, Sir. We just got the word for sure. He got hit in the leg and he wouldn't leave the battle. He bled to death on the field. Beauregard's been in command for hours."

Adam looked at him blankly. The fate of the Southern general made no more sense to him at that moment than if the lieutenant had recited a nursery rhyme.

"We don't have to lead any more charges. Beauregard's quit for the night."

That Adam understood.

He tried to speak. No words came so he laid a grateful hand on the Lieutenant's shoulder and then stretched himself full length in the mud, the rain washing the dust into the corners of his mouth. He ran his tongue slowly over his wet, swollen lips.

"You'd better fill your canteen—" the lieutenant said.

Adam opened his eyes. The man was holding his canteen up to a natural spigot made by a large curved leaf.

"You can't fill from the pond," the lieutenant said. "The water—the water's full of blood."

Adam was beyond horror. He closed his eyes again. It was impossible to sleep for the cold. He was shivering now from shock and the icy rain.

"Hear that?" the lieutenant asked.

Adam could hear a high pitched shouting, yelps of joy, echoing in the distance.

"Beauregard's men captured the sutler. They're going wild eating our pickled pig's feet and dates and cheese—I think there was sausage, too."

"Don't talk about food." Adam said. He hadn't eaten since breakfast.

The storm lashed the woods all night. They huddled in the wet and the mud listening to the Union gunboats firing at Beauregard as they brought General Buell's men in as reinforcements.

"We'll fight all day tomorrow, too, I'll bet," the lieutenant said glumly.

Adam thought of Ebonite. He felt as if the best part of himself had died along with the horse. Some long ago time that he dimly remembered, he had wanted to be purified. There was only one thing he wanted now and that was to survive.

One last thought engulfed him. "I wonder if they held the bridge—"

46

June 1862

Dear Caroline,

This is the third time I've attempted to write to you in the last two weeks. We've been hot at it again trying to take Richmond. We've either been on march or in battle. I have been hard put to steal a moment to eat, much less to get a letter written.

Whatever I once wrote to you about the exhilaration of battle, I withdraw. There is no exhilaration anymore. It's bloody butchery. For every one of us killed, we killed two of them, and still they kept coming—and we were forced back relentlessly. We retreated and retreated and retreated.

The newspapers are criticizing McClellan for bringing us by ship down the Potomac to the peninsula between the Yorktown and James rivers instead of overland. But McClellan's plan came close to working. There is no getting away from the fact that he had us lie in for a siege instead of attacking when we reached Yorktown. It is easy to be a good critic when one has hindsight to aid him. McClellan believed that General Johnston's army was there in force. He had us dig so many redoubts the rank and file soldier was calling him the "King of Spades." Then we discovered, after all that digging in, that Johnston had only a token force there that we could have wiped out in an hour had we been given the order to charge. A month too late we found the embrasures were protected with Quaker cannons—logs set up to resemble the real thing—and the Southern forces had long since stolen away to join their main army in defending Richmond. It made McClellan something of a laughing stock. He started us in hot pusuit of our elusive enemy and we caught up with them at Williamsburg on May 5.

We lost 1700 men and five guns that day before Kearny's division finally came up to relieve us. McClellan brought up reinforcements during the night and the Rebs were forced to retreat, leaving their wounded strewn behind them in Williamsburg.

We were loaded on transports then and moved by water to our supply base at White House. After being rearmed, we started westward toward Richmond.

Our forces were so close we could see Richmond, Caroline. Our hot breath on his doorstep made Johnston uncomfortable enough that he decided to attack. He couldn't have picked a better time for his side. The night before, we had a torrential rainstorm. Half the bridges we needed to get our reinforcements were swept away in the raging waters and high winds, to say nothing of the fact that we were up to our knees in mud.

Johnston overpowered some of General Casey's redoubts and was headed for our flank when McClellan ordered General Sumner to cross the river and come to our aid. There was only one bridge left standing that Sumner's troops could use and it had been damaged by the storm, too. Half of the under supports had been washed away, and the swollen river was threatening at any moment to sweep away those that were left. General Sumner has the beetled brow and long silver hair of an Old Testament prophet. There is a certain frailty about him. But there was not one moment of indecision or the over-caution that McClellan seems to suffer from. He had his men on the ready and when the command came, he ordered them across the bridge. It seemed impossible his troops could make it. The bridge was rocking like a cradle. Sumner was the first one on the bridge, his wispy white beard blowing in the wind. The bridge buckled like a sick man's legs, but as the full weight of the troops came thundering on, it actually seemed to steady the blasted thing. It rocked and swayed, but it held. He made it just as Johnston's forces hit our flank.

We drove the Rebs back with Sumner's help. They kept hitting us again and again. It didn't matter how many we killed; more took their places. We kept driving them back each time they attacked until it was dark. We were given the word then that this time we would make the charge. We had been fighting for hours; no one felt like making a counter attack, but we put everything we had into it and somehow, some way, we finally routed them. Johnston was wounded during the course of the battle. He may live but we have heard on good authority that he is one Confederate general we will not have to face again. The war is over for him.

For him—and something like 13,000 others. Three dozen men in my company alone were missing. I had some idea that I might through diligence and caring get my men out of this war alive. I believe I wrote something of that effect to you. I had seen men killed because an officer was drunk at a time of crisis, or because he sent men into a battle with more thought of personal glory than good sense. But I learned that in the thick of battle, there is no sure protection. We were glad to be shunt of Johnston, but it appears this General Robert Lee is no slouch. He's had us on the run for weeks. When the Battle of Fair Oaks was over, I was left with the sorry task of trying to find the wounded and dead of my company. Every barn and house and tent in the area was crammed with dead and dying. Burial details were piling corpses too mutilated to be identified into trenches for mass burial. Those I was able to find, I wrapped in blankets or army ponchos and pinned their names and addresses to their capes so they could be sent home for burial. There were at least a dozen I couldn't find. I did find Bernardi. He was leaning in the fork of a tree as peacefully as if he were asleep. He even had a slight smile on his face. We will have no more of his gay ribald songs to cheer us. Bernardi will be sorely missed. For that matter we'll miss them all—even the

Jonahs and the Beats.

I have no fear of dying, Caroline. I have an inner sense that I'm going to survive. Perhaps this is common—the only way it is possible to go on fighting day after day is to convince yourself that you're invincible. If my sense of immortality proves to be an illusion and I die as so many already have, I would like you to know that my greatest regret will be to not see you again.

Be that as it may, if you were here at my side this moment, I doubt you would associate with me. To put it bluntly, like everyone else in both armies, I'm lousy. Literally covered with vermin. It is an inescapable condition and inflicts the highest officer and the lowliest recruit. You can't wash them out, in fact one is hard put to boil them out, and if on occasion one is lucky enough to get hold of a new uniform and can burn the old (the only sure cure), within two days one is reinfested. Heaven begins to seem as simple as not having any lice crawling in your beard!

Since Fair Oaks, we have been given a respite from battle by more rain storms. We sit bogged in a quagmire of mud by the Chickahominey swamp. The horses are up to their bellies in it and our cannons are sucked to their wheels by their own weight. We're all tired and glad of a rest, but death takes no rest. We are losing almost as many men from malaria as we lost at Fair Oaks in battle. We spend the days digging entrenchments in the mucky-red soup and hoping for reinforcements from Fredericksburg. McClellan keeps sending dispatches to Washington. He is extremely bitter and is blaming our entire situation on Lincoln and his advisors. He feels that if the president had not pulled McDowell back to defend Washington right at the time when he needed the additional forces, that his peninsular plan would have worked. As it is we're still a long way from Richmond.

There is no doubt that disenchantment with the war has set in. Whenever there are men gathered about a campfire there are rancid and complaining comments about how they should have stayed at home, and there is a prevalent viewpoint that the entire war was devised by politicians and businessmen to line their pockets. Those who formerly talked most loudly of "our glorious and righteous cause" are now the quickest to denounce the whole business as a "get rich scheme for the mighty".

A few of the men lay the entire war at Lincoln's feet. In their eyes the war is completely his instigation. They imagine if you could get rid of Lincoln, the entire conflict would magically disappear. I gather that there are enough people back home with the same simplistic viewpoint that the president may have a struggle to be reelected in '64.

It is hot tonight. The mosquitoes are feasting on us and I can hear the frogs croaking in the swamp. If I stare very hard, I can see Saturn. I wonder if there is peace on my planet of the nine moons—.

A somewhat weary,
Bay

P.S. Tell Ann and Kemink that the packages of food are greeted by my entire company with joy beyond their imagining. They wanted to know what else we would prize—onions. A man who has onions is king! And soap and matches, we are so short of matches that no one lights one without first announcing his intentions so that everyone else who needs a light for his pipe, candle or whatever, can crowd close and use it too.

47

June 22, 1862

Dear Baird,

We read of the terrible battles day by day in the news. The reports of large casualties in both Union and Confederate armies, coupled with the fact that we had not heard from you for so long, gave us cause for much anxiety. We thanked God when your letter arrived, but we were sorry to learn that you had contracted malaria. Bromley begs me to tell you he can send you extra quinine if it would be helpful.

In February, eight or nine thousand prisoners captured by General Grant when he took Fort Donelson, arrived in Chicago to be incarcerated in Camp Douglas. Two regiments of ninety-day men raised in Chicago are serving as garrison to guard the camp, but there are a number of veterans as well. We had a group to dinner last night. They told horrendous tales about the Southern soldiers—how they poisoned food and water and crushed the skulls of wounded soldiers of the Union Army beneath their boots.

It is hard to believe. There have been a number of epidemics of measles and smallpox in Camp Douglas. Ann and I, along with other women of the Sanitary Commission, have been spending several hours each day trying to ease what misery and sickness we can. They do not seem like monsters or even like enemies when you hold their thermometers and wipe their feverish brows. Like you said of your men—most of them are so young. They speak with such soft, slow voices, and their eyes are so sad. One night some of them were singing the Southern ballad, "Lorena". Have you heard it? I could have wept for the heartache in their voices.

General Taylor is in charge of the prison now. He is a hard man who withholds the smallest milk of human kindness. Ann and I can understand why the prisoners are burning their barracks and using every means they can think of to escape. We see the conditions he imposes upon them that could be alleviated in small ways.

The burning of the barracks and constant attempts to escape have made the people of Chicago uneasy. Everyone is aware that the prisoners far outnumber the guards. Camp Douglas has been like a smoking volcano in our midst, threatening to erupt at any time. Chicagoans have slept restlessly with the thought of the possible burning, looting and rape that could occur if the prisoners made good an uprising.

The situation is more secure these past weeks, however, since Lincoln issued a call for another six hundred thousand troops. Many of them are being trained at Camp Douglas. The Irish Legion, Van Arman's Regiment, the Railroad Regiment and a dozen other volunteer companies are quartered outside the camp. Tents are dotted all over the surrounding areas as far as you can see and the challenge of sentinels is heard every step for miles.

Dear Bay, how you must have suffered to have lost so many of your men. Tears burned my eyes when I read of Bernardi's death, and I know him only through your letters.

My loss seems insignificant in comparison, but I, too, have had a heartache recently. Do you remember the Joshua I wrote about? Our young stutterer with the pugilistic tendencies? He has run off and joined the army. He is no more than twelve. How he succeeded in being accepted I cannot guess. His mother is furious, holding me personally responsible, and indeed I feel I am, for he was in my care. His father, who is something of a brute (and I suspect a large cause of Josh's problems though I know I should not say so) is actually pleased. The mother wanted to write a letter to Joshua's commanding officer demanding his release but the father would not allow it. I read your accounts of the war, Bay, and I think of that *child* facing such experiences and I feel as if nails were being driven in my palms.

Danny hates the war, but Dan-Pete still views it as something of a glamorous game of trilling bugles and flashing sabers. My heart stops at the thought that he is eleven now and might in another year or two run off as Joshua did. Oh, Bay, you don't know how I pray each

226

day that the war will end *soon*.

One piece of happy news!—Danny found Emily a cat, a beautiful tortoise shell. Danny placed a saucer of milk in Emily's lap and fed Pasha there, so she learned quickly to settle herself in Emily's lap and sit there and purr. Emily strokes the cat! We are so elated—especially Danny, who tried so hard for so long to coax a sign of life from our "Enchanted Princess."

I agree with you that President Lincoln surely cannot bear the entire responsibility for the war. He seems such a good man, sad, tired, and overburdened. I wonder sometimes why he would even *want* another term. They say he has not even a happy marriage, that his wife is given to tirades, and worse—that she's a southern spy. Gossip is so insidious because it is hard not to listen to it, even when it is nonsense—and right this minute, I catch myself helping to spread it. Should I blot those last paragraphs out in black blobs and let you forever wonder as to what they hide? No—you have enough to suffer.

Get well. Come home. We are lonesome for you.

Your affectionate friend,
Caroline

July 1862

Dear Caro,

A note in haste to tell you I received your welcome letter and to assure you I'm still alive.

We have been in hard fighting ever since I last wrote to you. Lee has amassed every Southern soldier he could pull from anywhere and poured them at us.

We lost twenty-two guns and two regiments of men at Gaines Mills. Lee's forces advanced down the left bank of the Chickahominey River thinking we'd retreat down the peninsula. This time it was our forces who gave them the slip instead of the other way around. While they were waiting for us on the banks of the river, we were making a mass exodus from our base at White House through swamp roads.

If you've never been in a Virginia swamp, Caroline, you have no idea what it was like moving thousands of supply wagons, cannons, horses, men and cattle along those narrow muddy roads. I felt like a Moses trying to lead the Israelites from Egypt. Danny and Dan-Pete may laugh at the thought of me as a "cowboy" riding herd on a bunch of cows, but the picture was not uproarious at the time. The scene was closer to a Sodom and Gomorrah, than the freeing of the Israelites. Because of the blockade the Rebs have been suffering for supplies (they haven't had coffee, for one thing, in months)—Our officers had

227

no intention of letting them get their hands on our supplies, so there was mass destruction of everything we couldn't load or transport. Tons of supplies and rations were set aflame—ammunition dumps were being exploded on every hand. The whole area was ringed with fire and billowing cauldrons of smoke. General Casey's division was running train cars filled with supplies into the river at full speed. By now I imagine all the fish from here to the Mississippi have indigestion from eating hardtack and gunpowder.

While we were destroying and loading supplies, the rear of our troops was hit by Southern forces led by General McGruder. They fell back to Savage Station, where Sumner and Franklin were able to hold and keep the road open to White Oak Swamp where the rest of us were already retreating. We had to burn more of our food and supplies and worst of all, leave thousands of our sick and wounded behind. At least we have not come to the point where we have to strip our dead to keep the living clothed, which they say the Rebs do.

We kept burning our bridges behind us. That was one way to slow Jackson up. He seems to have some kind of twenty-league boots. One moment he's in the Shenandoah and then the next he's on our trail. It gave us some satisfaction that he was obliged to stop and build a bridge every time he wanted to cross the Chickahominey.

We lost another twelve guns and many men at Glendale and finally made our last stand at Malvern Hill on the James River. We had no entrenchments but plenty of artillery, and we finally hurt Lee badly. We were in no shape to hit Richmond by that time, but I keep reading in the papers that was what we should have done. McClellan withdrew us to Harrison Landing, our supply base, where there were gunboats to protect us.

The reports that Lincoln is not pleased are substantiated by the appearance of a new co-commander with McClellan, General John Pope. As usual, the battle is being fought and refought with the benefit of hind-sight by every arm-chair general in rank and out. For myself, I feel postmortems accomplish little, but it is clear that the sentiments of the men remain with McClellan.

The most important news I have kept until last. It seems I am not quite invincible after all. One of my ribs got nicked a bit at Malvern Hill. It is not too bad, but apparently is considered serious enough to merit me two weeks leave. I expect to be in Chicago by the fourteenth. I'll send a wireless if there is a change of date.

With eagerness to see you all,
Bay

48

On July 14th, the entire family turned out at the Union Street Station to welcome Baird home on leave. Their anxious eyes swept the blue uniformed men disembarking from the train that sat throbbing massively on its tracks, occasionally blowing a blast of cinders into their eyes.

Dan-Pete caught sight of him first.

"There he is, look! There's Bay on the third car!"

They all saw him then. His white blond head a bright spot in the dingy station, towering above the other men crowding down the ramp. He saw them almost at the same moment and began grinning and waving. His beard was longer, his face thinner. His dark eyes caught Caroline's, the glance clinging. She smiled nervously and waved. The old feeling of constraint and embarrassment went sweeping through her.

Then he was beside them. He tried to swing the boys high into the air, but was quickly reminded of his broken ribs. He hugged Ann and Kemink, and slapped a hard embrace on Bromley. Caroline hung back, heart set at a wild beat. The children were talking in shrill, high-pitched exclamations, Ann was babbling happy words of welcome, Brom mumbling his own accompaniment. The train drowned everything out by letting off a screaming burst of steam.

Bay looked above the aggregated heads at Caroline. Self-consciously, she came forward and stood on tiptoe to give him a quick hug, a brief kiss on his cheek.

Fly was dragging at his hand.

"Uncle Bay," she said in a clear, penetrating voice, "Do you still have bugs in your beard?"

"I think I got rid of the last one!" Bay laughed. "But if you notice any suspicious wriggling, be sure to tell me."

Everyone else laughed too, except Caroline who felt humiliated and at once began to lecture Fly on the niceties of etiquette.

"Darling, you *know* better. You made the people in the station look at Uncle Bay and wonder if he had vermin. You could have hurt his feelings badly—"

Bay put one arm around her waist and picked up his valise with the other. "No scolding today—" he decreed, "even for the worst breaches of etiquette. Onward to the Bromley Thornton stronghold and Kemink's roast duckling!"

*   *   *

Just before Baird's return to camp the Sanitary Commission held its ball. The organization had outgrown its first quarters on Henry Street. The building there was being used as a hospital for the wounded and a large new edifice had been constructed to house the commission. Various bazaars, fairs, and balls were constantly being staged by patriotic ladies to raise funds for the Union armies. Notables of the stature of U.S. Grant and William Lloyd Garrison were procured to give stirring speeches and keep the home spirit kindled and the money flowing to support the war.

Beneath buntings of red, white, and blue and flags that hung motionless in the still, heavy air, the hall was packed with garrison soldiers from Camp Douglas, soldiers on leave, visiting dignitaries, Chicago socialites and business men, and the cream of the lovely ladies of the city. Their wide skirts embellished with flowers, ruffles, laces and ruchings swayed like pastel flower bells in the wind as they floated gracefully in the arms of their partners. The smell of pomades, crinoline, floor and boot wax, wilting flowers, tobacco and powder made a rich potpourri of the air that was both heady and debilitating to breathe.

There were cheers and tears at the moving oratory of speeches, but the trembling lips and moist eyes were swiftly replaced with laughter, gay sallies, and extravagant displays of wit and claims of love when the musicians once more took the podium.

Caroline had felt distressed the year before when Bay had not chosen to dance with her at Ann's ball. Now she found it more disconcerting when he chose to dance with no one but her. His dark eyes, waiting to catch her glance each time she looked up, were not laughing and teasing as they had always been before, but deep and unreadable. He held her lightly and it was as if a hot magnetic current flowed from him touching her with an awareness that made her cheeks burn. Between dances, he kept one of her hands locked in his and adroitly maneuvered her away from other men who approached, seeking her as a partner. He said little and to her chagrin she felt tongue tied and awkward.

She was relieved when intermission was called to raffle off cakes and antiques for the Union cause, and Bay had to excuse her to help with

230

the proceedings. When the final ivory-handled umbrella and maple-cinnamon cake had been handed down to the highest bidder, and the leader of the orchestra once more picked up his baton, Caroline carried several items, carefully tagged, to a side room where they would be claimed later by their owners. She took out a handkerchief and blotted her face. The night was desperately hot; there had been constant rumbles of thunder and now, quite suddenly, a storm broke. Fingers of mist poured through the windows. Caroline drew close, lifting her hot face to the mist, trying to sort through her sense of confusion and agitation—afraid, somehow, to go back to Bay.

"Why do you always run away from me?" It was Bay's voice behind her.

"I felt so warm—giddy," she apologized. She held a hand out to him to join her. "Look, Bay, at the rain. Each little drop falls as though it were floating—isn't it beautiful?"

"Yes—beautiful," he said, but he was looking at the moon-silvered outline of her face and bare shoulders.

She gave a breath of a sigh. The rain had stopped as suddenly as it had begun, and the moon was peeking out upon a glistening world.

"Oh, Bay, it looks so quiet, so peaceful now, with raindrops dripping from everything. It's hard to believe that right this minute the war is still going on somewhere—men are still being killed. . "

Sadness settled over her face.

"You look so pensive, Caroline. A penny for your thoughts," Bay demanded, after the silence had built into a mound between them.

"I can't help wondering sometimes if Adam is in the war—where he is—if he's all right—if maybe he's hurt or dead—" Her voice caught. "It's so hard not knowing. Even if you're separated from someone, you cannot entirely stop caring—the way you can pull an aching tooth and stop thinking about it. I lived with him for seven years—we shared our laughter and our tears. I thought I was right to send him away. I thought I had no other recourse. But now—sometimes I think—I think—Oh, Adam! He was suffering in the grip of such a terrible misconception. I should have tried to help—been more patient, understanding—instead of thinking he was a monster. My first duty seemed to be to protect Fly, but now I ask myself, in being a mother first, did I fail as a wife—?"

The curtain she had been holding back fell limply from her fingers and she turned back to Bay, contrite. "I'm sorry, Bay, forgive me. I don't know why I've been telling you all this—"

"Well, I do," he said in a cool, even voice, "and so do you, if you'll be honest. You know that any moment now I'm going to take you in my arms and you're invoking the name of Adam Quimby like a priest

231

holding up a silver cross in front of the devil, hoping I'll disappear. Only it's not going to work, Caroline. You can't write love letters to me for months and then expect me to turn into a friendly eunuch at the mention of Adam Quimby's name."

"Bay, I *never* wrote you *love* letters," Caroline denied in a shocked whisper, backing away from him.

"Oh yes you did," he said, laughing softly, advancing toward her. "It doesn't matter that there wasn't one word of love exchanged, every one of our letters was a love letter, and *you know it,* because we were writing to each other from the deepest level of our beings."

His hands captured her waist. She could feel the heat of each pulsing finger through the thin material of her gown, the bite of the thin metal stays in her flesh.

"Bay—" It was a small, gasping plea for release.

"Who do you think you've been sharing your 'laughter and your tears' with for the last year, Caroline? Not Adam Quimby—"

He gave her no opportunity to answer. He pulled her against him, laid his lips against hers. It had been years since she had known a man's love. She had sublimated her womanly desires in the care of the children, her school, incessant physical activity; they had gathered unused inside of her like a reservoir of oil, to which he had just touched a match. The half forgotten desires of the flesh resurrected in the form of giants raging through her. With a soft whimper, her body strained against his, her lips parted, her arms clung, a tremor akin to pain raced through her—but in the next instant she was horrified at the depth of her passion—terrified by his. She could feel a niagara surging through him, a wild untameable force.

"No—" she cried, twisting her face away, trying to escape. But he had felt that first quick response, and he would not let her go. He pulled her back so hard and close she could feel the beat of his heart. He brought his mouth against hers again and she felt another quickening convulsion of desire. It so filled her with panic that she burst from his arms with a super effort and shoved him away.

The shove pushed him against a large vase sitting on a table. It tottered and fell, crashing to the floor in a crescendo of shattering glass and crystaline thunder that cracked and echoed through the building.

For one unbearable moment, they stared at each other over the smashed wreckage, her eyes dark with emotion; his smoldering, his color high with the pounding rage of his passion. Then he shrugged and laughed softly and deprecatingly.

"Well, I guess your Reverend Quimby must be quite a man—or you not half the woman I thought. I've searched half my life for a woman

232

I could love. Now, I've found her and for reasons of her own, she doesn't care to requite my passion. My brain told me before I left for the war to forget you, that it was hopeless, but my heart insisted I play the game. *Goodbye,* Caroline."

"Bay—!"

Ann came hurrying into the room drawn by the loud explosion of the falling vase.

"My dears—whatever happened?"

Bay bowed in his usual charming manner and kissed her hand. "I'm afraid I accidentally broke a vase, Ann. I'll see the organization gets a check to cover a replacement."

Then he was gone with quick strides.

Ann turned to Caroline. "What happened? Did the two of you quarrel?"

More people were crowding forward to learn what the noise had been.

"Ann, not now—" Caroline pleaded. She picked up her skirts and ran after Bay, but she was hampered by the crowd, by her billowing gown, and her shorter stride. His cab was already leaving, the side lanterns winking through a renewed mist of rain.

"Bay—" she called, "Bay—!" But he did not hear her. She stood staring into the darkness, pearls of rain settling on her dark hair until at length Ann came out and found her there.

"Caroline—*you're soaked,*" Ann scolded, putting her arms around her sister and drawing her back toward the hall.

"I want to go home, Ann."

"I'll get Brom."

"No, please, just get me a cab."

"Caroline, don't you want to tell me about it?"

"Not yet, Ann, please."

Seeing tears in her sister's eyes, Ann bit back her questions and helped her into a cab.

When she arrived home, Caroline dragged herself wearily up the stairway. Kemink's door was ajar. She paused, hesitated. Her Indian friend heard her steps slow and halt and called, "I am not asleep. Come in if you wish. I'll light the lamp."

"No, please, leave it dark—" Caroline said. She went into the room and sank in a wilting rush of skirts beside the bed. In halting, broken sentences she told Kemink what had happened. "Oh, Kemink—I'm so confused. I'm filled with so many tumultuous, unsorted feelings. I do care about Bay, Kemink, I do—but how can I say I don't love Adam anymore? Am I really a horrible, wicked person—? Did I really lead Bay on with my letters, as he said and then—and then slap his

233

hands? Now he's going back to the war—and I've hurt him. I know I have—and hurt myself. But I couldn't—I'm still married—I'm so miserable, Kemink!"

She leaned her head against Kemink and cried for a long time. Her friend stroked her hair as if she were a child and said, "One cannot find a flower by tearing open a bud—or a butterfly by breaking a chrysalis. Calm your heart little friend—when the apple is ripe, it falls."

But for once even Kemink's counsel could not still her heartache. *Perhaps when the apple falls, there will be no one to pick it up,* Caroline thought; the finality with which Bay had said *goodbye,* was echoing through her mind.

49

A letter arrived with a check covering the broken vase—after that there was no word from Bay.

Each morning Caroline paused by the silver letter tray and searched through the stacks of papers, bills, and social invitations hoping to see Bay's handwriting. As days lengthened to weeks and weeks to months, her anxiety grew.

Ann, grown accustomed now to the war, ate her shirred eggs and sipped her breakfast tea with equanimity, while Brom read aloud the latest accounts of battles and casualties. It was Caroline who laid her toast aside, and grew pale.

Stonewall Jackson, West Point graduate, veteran of Mexican wars, teacher, Presbyterian deacon, sucker of lemons, a pray-er of silent prayers before battle had pulled off another victory over Union forces with his almost legendary troops on August 9 ten miles south of Culpepper.

Lee had followed up the success by dividing his army in half. He sent Jackson and Jeb Stuart (of the colorful uniforms and plumed hats) to flank Pope's forces and destroy the Federal depot at Manasses, but Pope failed to make good his bombastic brags. After two days of fierce fighting and the loss of 16,000 men, he stuck his tail between his legs and led his men in retreat. For the second time the Union forces came limping into Washington, tattered survivors of a major defeat at Manasses Junction, Bull Run. Pope whined as loudly in defeat as he had boasted in victory. A disillusioned Lincoln returned McClellan to command.

Desperate for food and supplies, Lee undertook an invasion of Union territory.

On September 17, McClelland's men and Lee's men met on the opposite sides of Antietam Creek near Sharpsburg, Maryland. In the bloodiest single-day battle of the war up to that point, Lee's advance was halted. He was forced to retreat back to Virginia.

Heartened by Lee's repulse, Lincoln issued a preliminary Emancipation Proclamation five days after Antietam. Chicago was jubilant. Ostensibly, the war was being fought to preserve the Union, but the issue of slavery had always been the canker sore beneath the saddle. The city, hotbed of abolitionists and Free Thinkers, rejoiced. The Union cause regained zeal.

Still prospering from distributing supplies and manufacturing wares of war, Chicago was swelling in population, waxing rich, extending its borders, but the death lists published daily were monotonously long and the swaths of grief left in their wake spared few families.

"The Battle of Antietam—12,410 Union troops killed, wounded or missing in action—" Bromley read.

It isn't like Bay not to write—even if he's angry with me. I can't believe he wouldn't send a few lines to Brom and Ann—

"Munfordville, Kentucky—4000 Union troops captured—"

But then he can't be dead or wounded, can he, or surely we would have received some word—

"Seven hundred and eighty-two Union men lost at Iuka, Mississippi—"

And where is Joshua? We don't hear a word from him either. His mother is frantic. And Adam, oh dear God—Where is Adam?—

"Dysentery, typhoid fever and pneumonia are killing twice as many of our forces as gunshot wounds—"

Bay, don't do this to me—please, please—

She wrote twice—uncertain, diffident little notes. There was no answer. One of the letters came back.

At last Caroline dropped all pride and presented herself one morning at the residence of Nelia Fitzpatrick. That young lady, who had been breakfasting with her aunt, received her graciously in the morning room and served her tea. Nelia was wearing a morning coat of pale yellow peau de soie and her long red hair streamed loosely over her shoulders, catching the sun in gleaming auburn strands.

235

How lovely she is! Caroline thought, noting that there were no lines around *her* lips or eyes. Her skin was flawless.

After a few polite civilities, Nelia began to probe to discover the reason for Caroline's visit.

"We haven't heard from Bay for so long," Caroline confessed. "We've been worried. Our letters come back. He must have a new address. I thought perhaps you might have heard from him."

"Oh, of course! I hear from him all the time," Nelia said, with a flurry of laughter. "In fact, Bay and I are engaged."

Caroline's spoon slipped from her fingers and rattled into the china saucer. She felt her face redden with embarrassment. "He is all right then?"

"Oh, quite. Of course he's been in a few battles, but he says lots of time his regiment just sits around and waits. You know how Mc-Clellan is."

"I'm very glad—" Caroline said faintly.

"I'm delighted I could relieve your worries. Bay is a naughty-boy not to have written to you. I shall have to scold him. Ah—Caroline, I would appreciate it if you wouldn't mention our engagement to anyone—not even Ann."

"You're keeping it a secret?"

"Well, yes—you see, Bay felt I should be free to continue going out socially in his absence. He's so generous. He really felt, in fact, that it was my patriotic duty to see that the soldiers on leave are entertained—you know, taken to the opera, have someone pretty to dance with and all. And Caroline, dear, you know how narrow-minded some people are. It seems, all things considered, wisest."

"Yes—" Caroline said automatically, though suddenly Nelia's prattling seemed far away and difficult for her to follow.

"I don't have my engagement ring yet anyway. Bay has to get it from the family vault. It belonged to his own dear mother, a family heirloom—"

"Oh. He never mentioned his mother to me, only his step-mother."

"I'm sure there are many things he hasn't mentioned to you," Nelia said archly.

"I'd better be going. I'll be late to school. Thank you so much—" Caroline said, wanting desperately to be out of that sunny room.

"Oh, dear, I can't think where I did put his latest address," Nelia moaned. "Why don't I send it to you when I locate it."

"That would be fine. Or let us know from time to time how he is, would you?"

"Of course!" Nelia said.

All that matters is that Bay is all right—Caroline thought, as she settled herself in the carriage. *That's all that matters.* She nodded to the driver. The autumn wind felt cold and everywhere leaves were falling—the streets cluttered with their dry and dying forms. They rasped hoarsely under the feet of the horses and gasped in brown eddies against the curbs.

Caroline's throat hurt. *I'm glad Bay found someone young and lovely to love,* she thought—but then she had to find her handkerchief to stifle a flood of tears that would not stay back.

*   *   *

Since the Battle of Antietam, McClellan had been licking his wounds. Pressures to return to battle were met with refusal on the grounds of inadequate supplies. The President towering above the tallest of his officers in his stovepipe hat, visited Little Mac and entreated him to press the action now that Lee was on the run. McClellan remained obdurate. At the end of his patience, Lincoln turned over the command to General Ambrose E. Burnside.

Thirty-eight year old Burnside felt inadequate to the task. Twice he had declined the command. Now it was forced upon him. He decided to move the Army of the Potomac to Fredericksburg, Virginia, cross the Rappahannock and strike Richmond rather than making Lee's army his objective.

By December of 1862, Lee had brought his army to Fredericksburg to meet the challenge. Burnside had hoped to cross the Rappahannock before Lee could take up strong positions of defense. The War Department had failed to supply the needed pontoons on time. When they did arrive, they crossed into the perilous fire of Lee's well entrenched army. The December 13th battle was suicidal for the Union soldiers, ending with 1300 of them piled in rows, while hundreds of others lay wounded in the cold, praying for stretcher bearers who seldom came.

The Union Army had suffered another disastrous defeat.

Caroline, the newspaper shaking in her fingers, searched through the Qs, the Ls and the Ms of the casualty list and closed her eyes with a prayer of relief when the names she was terrified to see were not there.

"Caroline, you've got to start eating more," Ann scolded. "You're getting so thin your clothes hang askew—or maybe you should stop going to the prison. It's too much to work at the school all day and then spend half the night at the hospital—"

"Ann, you know we can't stop helping at Camp— you know how great the need is," Caroline sighed.

Depressing it certainly was. Winter had taken Chicago in its fierce embrace. The bare trees rattled in sheaths of ice, and as soiled banks of snow climbed to mountainous dimensions the temperatures dropped lower and lower. Camp Douglas, a world of frozen mud, tin roofs, bare board floors, and little heat became another cold version of hell. The Southern prisoners, poorly clad, thin of blood, unprepared in every way for below zero temperatures died by the hundreds. They died of measles, small pox, dysentery, pneumonia—and Caroline suspected sometimes of heartbreak.

Their Northern captors were moved to pity. The garrison soldiers dropped their rancor against the Rebs and tried to do what they could to relieve the rampant misery. For the most part, the condition of the guards was only a trifle less miserable than that of the men they guarded. Nor were the nurses or volunteers immune. Caroline's fingers were chapped raw. The metal bedpans, urinals and washbasins were like ice. Water froze solid in the glasses by the bedsides. She had to wear flannel underwear beneath her pantaloons to ward off the frigid air that came blasting up through the splintery wooden floors.

The physical discomfort she gladly bore for those few hours each night but the emotional equivalent tore her apart.

One of her patients was a man in his forties. He had been a brave, handsome officer who had distinguished himself in numerous battles and earned respect from his men and his superior officers. Even the Union soldiers had afforded him a grudging admiration. Now in this dreary winter at Camp Douglas, blinded, one leg gone, suffering from dysentery, loss of blood and gangrene—out of his head with fever, he was reduced to childish whimpering. Whenever Caroline came near his bed, he would sob, "Mama—mama—" and grope blindly for her hand. When she in pity would give it to him, he would whimper, "Please, Mama, don't leave me, Mama—" and she, having to go on her rounds, could not control her weeping when she would finally wrench her hand free and his anguished cry would follow her—*"Mama, please Mama—don't leave me—"*

Doris Dormeister found her sobbing in the annex one night. She wrapped a sturdy arm around her and said, "Come on, let's go make some tea. It'll warm us up and we can bring some back for those who can drink it."

"We shouldn't take the time—"

"You need the time," Doris said shortly. "Ann hasn't got the stomach for this and you haven't got the heart. She's always heaving and you're always bawling."

"I'm so ashamed," Caroline said in a stricken whisper. "I hate myself for being so weak, but—" and the thought of the Southern major choked her up again. "I see all this—and I haven't heard from Bay—or Joshua—and I don't know where Adam is—"

"Come," Doris said again. She looped Caroline's shawl around her and together they crossed the dark frozen yard to the mess hall where there was a little pot-bellied stove on which they could heat water. In a short time the hot tin cups were warming their fingers while the tea warmed their stomachs.

Doris' bobbing curls were gone. Her hair was pulled back roughly and strands of grey showed boldly. Her face looked wrinkled and tired.

"So this is what it all comes to—" she said. "I don't know what to think anymore. I still believe every word I uttered before this war. I believe slavery is wrong. I believe if we condone it, it's as bad as engaging in it—but *Lord Jesus!* If this is the price—what is one to think? Can it still be worth it? You always seemed so interested in the spiritual, Caroline. Tell me—tell me, were we wrong? Did we try to right one evil with another? Did I—did I help to create this horror?"

Caroline answered in a faint voice, uncertainly.

"There have been times—mere instances, I suppose—when it was as if a wider view opened up to me and I was filled with the most profound joy because I *understood* that everything now is not what it seems—that no suffering is ever wasted. It's so simple, so marvelous— why didn't I see it before? But the revelation is beyond words and when one 'comes back', doubts come thrusting in and one thinks that perhaps it was only an emotional dream."

Doris shook her head in disappointment. "I've never been able to buy that 'someday' stuff as an answer. We'd better go back. Bring the pot and I'll bring the cups."

As they stepped back into the hospital barracks, they could hear some of the garrison troops singing, "When This Cruel War is Over."

"Weeping, sad and lonely,
 Hopes and fears now vain;
 When this cruel war is over
 Praying that we meet again—"

Unexpectedly, from far down the bedded corridor, a Southern voice picked up the refrain of the Union song plaintively—

"When this cruel waah is ovah—"

50

On Christmas eve, 1862, the Union Street Station was thronged with Chicagoans waiting to welcome home those soldiers lucky enough to have been given leave. Caroline, along with other members of the Sanitary Commission, had come to the station to make sure that no soldier was left lonely and unwelcomed on his arrival. She saw several familiar faces in the crowd. The Van der Hoefts and the McGintys were both expecting their sons home. The McGinty's son had written that he would be on crutches and Elaine McGinty kept warming a laprobe by one of the stoves. Outside, dray teams and buckboards, hansom cabs and matched geldings crowded against each other, the horses pawing the ice and sending wreaths of steam into the air with each breath.

The air inside was heavy with smoke from pipes and the green oak logs in the stoves. Everytime the door opened a wrong-way draft sucked smoke into the room. Some of the men, advantaged by the delay of the train, drank more than they ordinarily would have from bottles drawn from their inside pockets.

The women clustered together. Each mother's heart was glad for the other mother whose son was returning; strangers who had never seen each other before chatted like lifelong friends.

One woman sat apart in the corner, her face bitter and withdrawn. No one tried to penetrate her obvious grief, knowing it could not be lifted by words. Her black clothing and dry burning eyes made it clear that she waited not for a son or a husband, but for a coffin. The train that arrived with the living would also bring the dead.

Pausing here and there to greet a friend or to take a hand in comfort of those she knew needed it, Caroline made her way slowly to where a group of Union soldiers were sitting on their rolled up bags of gear. She was about to issue her invitation to any at loose ends for the Christmas holidays when her heart did a flip. One of the soldiers with his back to her was so tall, his back so broad, his hair so long and curly, that she was sure it couldn't be anyone but—

240

"Cricket!" she cried. "Cricket McGuire!"

The tall soldier turned and with a happy Indian yell, swept her above his head as if she were Fly instead of a grown woman.

"Miz Caroline! Miz Caroline Quimby! I can't believe my eyes. I knowed you was in Chicago, but I didn't niver think to set eyes on ye," he declared once he had allowed her feet to touch the floor again.

Everyone in the station was staring at them, but Caroline was too happy to care.

"I didn't know you had joined the army."

"Wull, I didn't 'till 'bout four weeks ago. I was out in California diggin' gold. But I promised my Ma before she died thet I'd look after my brother, and the whelp had to up n' join, though he hain't dry behind the ears yit. I figgered I'd better try n' git in the same outfit and keep an eye on 'im."

"Oh, Cricket,, it's so good to see you! You and all your friends must come home and have Christmas with us—"

"I cain't think of anything I'd ruther do, Miz Caroline, but we've had the hard luck o' being sent off on Christmas eve. We'd been gone 'fore now iffen the train hadn't been late. I guess we're going to be joinin' Gener'l Hiram Berry's forces down by the Rappahannock River."

"Oh, I am sorry—and disappointed that you can't have Christmas with us, but at least we can visit until the train comes. Could we sit down somewhere?"

Teasing and envious remarks from Cricket's companions followed them as Cricket took her arm and escorted her to a seat his friends yielded.

"Now you tell me how all you folks are," Cricket said. "I'll bet those boys o' yourn are so big I'd mistake 'em for bear—n' how's Kemink? She is some fine lady, thet one—"

"Yes, the boys are growing like something wild," Caroline said. "Danny gave up on the harmonica you gave them, but Dan-Pete's gotten quite good with it—well, at least he can play 'Old Black Joe'. And Kemink has taken Chicago in her stride."

"N' you, Miz Caroline?" His eyes probed her face, "You look real fine—"

"I'm busy, Cricket—I'm all right. I've started a school for children who have special problems—physical things like Fly had or not being able to learn easily—things like that."

"And how is that little lady? Bet she's growin' up pretty as her maw."

"Oh, Cricket, that's the greatest news of all. Her arm and hand are well now—" Caroline's voice grew husky. "If you see Adam—will you tell him that—that she's perfectly all right now?"

"I shore will."

"Have—you heard from him?"

"He was out in Californy diggin' gold with me, Caroline."

Her glance swept upward in surprise. "Adam?"

"Yes, Ma'm, I guess he's givin' up on the preachin'. He's in the war right now. Joined up the first thing."

"I *knew* it. I felt it. He's—he's all right?"

"The last I heard. But there is somethin' I think you got a right to know—"

"Yes, Cricket—?"

Cricket hesitated.

"He shoulda told ye hisself. I don't like being the one—still I think ye oughta know."

"What is it—?"

"Adam got an annulment."

Caroline looked bewildered.

"How could he do that without me? How could that be legal—"

"I don't know iffen it is legal, but he's remarried n' he n' his new woman got a nice little baby boy."

Caroline felt as if she were a sheet of glass shattering from the blow of a rock.

Cricket grabbed her hands in concern.

"Miz Caroline, you're whiter n' any ghost. I shouldn't a niver told ye."

"No, Cricket, no—you did the right thing. It's—it's just such a surprise. I'm all right now—" The moment had passed. She felt calm, remote.

"I'm glad for Adam. I hope he is happy," she said in a polite conversational tone as if she were speaking of a distant cousin.

"There it comes!" someone shouted, and at the same time the vibrating chuff-chuff of the approaching train could be heard and felt in the station. A cheer went up from those who waited, followed by a rustling of taffeta and silk over crinoline, the sharp echo of hurrying boots and the excited exclamations as the crowd surged off their benches, hurrying to line the platform where the passengers would disembark.

"Harry, is my bonnet on straight? Do I look all right?"

"You'd look like an angel to that boy if you had it on backwards!"

The woman in the black dress had buried her face in her hands and was beginning to sob.

Caroline shivered from the sudden blast of icy air drawn inward.

"Cricket, we've had such a short time. I'll write to you. Give me your address—" Her face still unnaturally white, she rummaged in

242

her purse for a pencil.

Cricket's face turned a dark russet.

"Miz Caroline, I'd like fer ye to write to me, more'n ye could ever know. But the truth is—I cain't read nor write, 'n I got myself such a horsehair case of the 'prides' thet I would plumb be humiliated to hiv to ask somebody else to read my mail fer me."

"I understand, Cricket—but here—at least take my address. If you ever get back to Chicago, please do come and see us. I'll never forget all you did for us that winter in Tomorrow River country."

"Didn't do nothin at all," Cricket disclaimed.

The train screamed to a stop, shooting red sparks and white steam into the black winter sky. People were shouting, crying, laughing in the joy of reunions.

"I'm real glad I had the pleasure to see you again," Cricket said, "n' more'n happy to learn Fly is all well." He felt inside the bag slung over his shoulder. "Here's a couple o' hardtack. Take'm home an give'm to the boys. Tell 'em those crackers show how tough us Blue boys is—cain't everbody chew nails—"

The train was empty of passengers now and the soldiers who had been waiting with Cricket were starting to board and take the emptied seats.

"I see the rest of the fellers is boardin'. I better git myself on thet train, too."

Caroline walked with him through the jostling crowd. When they reached the ramp, she stood on tiptoe and kissed him on the cheek.

There were whistles and loud chortles from the windows of the train. Cricket laughed.

"Ye jus' made me the most envied man in my company, Miz Caroline—probably in the entire regiment by the time those fellers get done spreading their stories. Ye take kere o' yerself now—"

Caroline watched with dazed eyes as the long, black train huffed into motion again, gathering speed, carrying Cricket's face and waving arm off in a blur. It took some time before she remembered why she was at the station. Almost everyone had gone home. Those with no place to go were easy to spot now. She saw several young, ruddy-faced boys in army great coats huddled together uncertainly by the stove.

"A leave and no family or friends in Chicago?" she asked dutifully."

"That's right, Ma'am!" They looked at her hopefully.

She took them back to the Thornton's with her—to hot cider and egg nog, roast turkey and plum pudding—a roaring fireplace, the green smell of the pitchy tree and melting candles—to laughter and music. Fly sat on their laps and the boys listened round-eyed to the tales of battle the fledgling soldiers manufactured on the spot. Ann and

Caroline danced with them. Bromley gave them wine and told them jokes.

To Caroline, the festivities seemed curiously distant.

Fly came running to her full of excitement.

"Look, Mama. Look what Aunt Kink made me!"

She held up two deerskin dolls dressed to resemble Dan and Dan-Pete.

"That's nice honey. Real nice," Caroline said, but her voice was flat. No genuine delight lit her eyes.

"Mama, is something wrong?" Danny asked, sidling up to her, looking at her anxiously with his serious, thickly fringed eyes.

"Tired—" she said softly, "just tired, darling."

She thought, *I should tell him about seeing Cricket, but then—if I do that, I should tell him about his father—not yet—not tonight—*

"We wish you a merry Christmas! We wish you a merry Christmas! We wish you a merry Christmas and a happy new year!"—the soldiers sang in lusty young voices.

*　　*　　*

The old year went out in a blaze of battles. One thousand seven hundred and seventy-six men were lost by the Union Army in an abortive attempt made by Sherman against the southern city of Vicksburg. The Union Army of the Cumberland and the Confederate Army of Tennessee grappled in a death grip at Stones River in central Tennessee.

The year of 1863 unfurled on a wave of liberty. On January 1, Lincoln officially signed and issued the Emancipation Proclamation. Jubilant blacks deserted their plantations and poured into the Union armies by the hundreds. Some cut all ties only to find themselves adrift and bewildered—unprepared for the freedom for which they had hungered.

51

Warm April rain sprinkled the roof tops, melted the snow, and kissed the barren trees back to bloom. Muddy banks and boulevards turned lush and green overnight. The shrill excited honk of returning geese blended with the songs of robins. But Caroline felt none of the swift quickening in her veins that she usually felt with spring. She felt tired and listless and found herself sharp and cross with the children.

"Soon it will be planting time!" Kemink, who loved the soil, exulted.

"And how do you think we can spare you to putter with a garden this year?" Caroline snapped.

"The children will work with me and learn much," Kemink answered, surprised at Caroline's tone.

"Oh, Kemink—I'm sorry," Caroline sighed. "I don't know what's the matter with me lately. I feel so *used up*. Old. Like a dry, dead twig!"

"Do you know why?"

"No," Caroline said, walking about restlessly, picking things up only to lay them down again. "Maybe I need a rest—a change. But I don't see how I can get away when I'm needed so badly at the hospital."

The prisoners had been cleared out of Camp Douglas in March, but those too sick to move had been left behind along with enough Union troops to guard them.

"Do you think that is all that bothers you?" Kemink persisted.

Caroline, her back to Kemink, laid down the sea shell she had just picked up from the mantel.

"You're right. I've been trying to run away from what's bothering me instead of admitting it. The truth is—Adam has obtained an annulment. It is truly and forever over between us. I could have loved Bay—but I sent him away—" She leaned her head against the mantel, "—and suddenly I feel old and empty. The children don't seem enough anymore. All that is bursting outside . ." she waved a wan hand toward the window where the silver sheen of leaves lapped in the sunshine like waves against the bluing sky—"and inside, I feel—I feel dead—dead—*dead*."

"You read to me from your Shakespeare book, 'The coward faces death a thousand times a day. The valiant taste of death but once.' Good words—but in a way, not true," Kemink said reflectively, "for

245

all of us, cowards and valiant, die many times in a lifetime. One Kemink died with Big Pete. A new Kemink had to be born, a different Kemink. Then again, when I left the land of my birth, my loved Tomorrow River country, one Kemink had to die and another be reborn. Like snakes, we must wriggle from our old skins, our old selves, to grow a larger spirit. I have watched our brother snake many times before the shedding of his skin. He grows torpid and without zeal. He no longer feels like whipping his slim body gracefully through the grass. His busy tongue does not seek food. He feels swollen and heavy. But one day he will burst from this state of torpor with a fine new skin, shiny as a wet bead with his bright new colors, his energy resurging like a river given great rains. Rest within yourself, Caroline. Accept your necessary grief—do not struggle to deny it—taste it, learn from it, but know that it will pass. Someday, as suddenly as the flash of a bird's wing, the 'dry twig' will flow again with sap and burst with bloom."

"I am fortunate to have you, Kemink," Caroline said. You never complain. You are always strong—always sustaining others. What an example you are to me! What would I do without you?" She added, half laughing and half crying, "Sometimes I wonder how you put up with me."

"Come, let us do some planting," Kemink urged. "There is healing in the earth."

Later, laying the first tiny seeds in the damp earth Kemink had turned, Caroline lifted her eyes to the April blue sky wispy with shy feathers of clouds.

"Everytime I get so busy with all the outside aspects of life that I forget that inward search, everything goes wrong," she thought. "I must go back to seeking—"

"Dear God, I must stop following my own will," she prayed from the depths of her unhappiness. "Now, at this moment, I give you my life. Use it as you will. Show me the way."

The sun shone warmly on her hair. A bee buzzed about her shoulders, rested for a minute on her collar, and then flew away. She could hear the quiet beat of her heart. The restlessness inside her stilled.

*   *   *

Late in January, General Burnside had gathered up his battered forces to once again try to force Lee from his stronghold above Fredericksburg. As had often happened in the past, the weather served the Confederate cause. A drenching two day storm left streams impassable

246

and the roads a morass of mud. Slogged to a virtual stop in the muck and wet, Burnside was relieved of his command on January 25. Like a frayed toy the Army of the Potomac was passed to yet another commander—General "Fighting Joe" Hooker.

As the warming sun of April greened the field and rashed the trees with buds, the Army of the Potomac began to feel a return of strength and spirit. Hooker had seen to it that they were better fed and better equipped. They had rested and licked their wounds during a long sedentary winter, and the monotony was becoming worse than battle. Hooker began to position his forces for attack.

Lee did not wait for Hooker to hit. Preferring to take the initiative, he daringly divided his own army into two parts and attacked at Chancellorville, (also known as the Wilderness) on the first day of May. The day's battle ended inconclusively, but that night a guide was found by Lee and Jackson who knew how to lead them through the tangled thickets of the wilderness.

By twilight of the following day, just as the whippoorwills began to cry their lonely song and the bursts from the rifle shells were starting to glow red against the gathering darkness, Jackson's men came pouring like hornets out of the forest to attack the Union forces being led by General Howard.

Jackson was wounded in the battle and died three days later. Lee wept openly.

As if some invisible force was working to even the score, General Hooker had been incapacitated as well when the battle was resumed on May 3, and by the end of the day his troops had been dragged back across the Rappahannock. This time a storm worked in the Union favor preventing Lee from following. Once again, Lee's brilliant generalship had defeated the Army of the Potomac with only half the strength. But the battle had cost both sides dearly. Seventeen thousand Union soldiers were killed or wounded and there were 13,000 Confederate casualties.

Among the Union soldiers wounded was Cricket McGuire. He had fought his third and last battle at Chancellorsville. He was hit first in the ankle and tried to crawl to a field hospital. He was stopped after a few dozen rods by a second bullet that struck his head. A third hit him in the shoulder; he felt too dazed and weak to go on. He lay unattended beneath the boiling sun. He could hear the other wounded around him crying for water. Some of them begged for death. He never forgot that it was a Johnny Reb, who crawled across the firing line to force his canteen of water between Cricket's parched lips and who crawled on to give water to more of the wounded in the area.

Later that day, his brother, whom he had thought to care for, found him and dragged him back behind the Union lines just in time to save him from being captured along with the other wounded who had been left on the field.

More fortunate than many, his foot was not amputated. He was taken to a Federal hospital in Washington to spend long months recuperating. He would limp the rest of his life and his shoulder had become a permanent weather vane.

52

Following Lee's successive victories over the Army of the Potomac, there was widespread hope in the south and fear in the north that Britain might espouse the Confederate cause. Two terrible battles in July ended in decisive victories for the North, burning out England's enthusiasm for such action and ending forever that Southern hope.

Grant had been doggedly attempting to take Vicksburg for months with the purpose of gaining control of the 250 mile segment of the Mississippi River controlled by the rebels. Time and time again victory eluded him.

After desperate attempts failed, including a plan to divert the Mississippi through a canal below Vicksburg, the Union Navy under Admiral David Porter sailed an armada of transports through two and a half hours of belching fire from the southern cannons. Grant had found his way at last to Vicksburg's vulnerable side. For forty-seven days he laid siege to the embattled southern city. The people were forced to take to caves and eat mule meat to survive before their commander, General Pamperton, finally surrendered on July 4.

Lincoln rejoiced, "The Father of Waters again flows unvexed to the sea—" The Union now had control of the Mississippi. The rebellious southland was hacked in half with one sharp blow.

While Grant had laid siege against Vicksburg, Lee pressed forward, the audacity of previous victories fueling his ragged troops' ardor to again invade the north. The grey hoard moved on like a swarm of locusts, chewing up York, taking Chambersburg, advancing on Harrisburg.

Finding that his plans for meeting Lee's new threat were not acceptable to the Secretary of State, General Hooker resigned. He was quickly replaced by General George Mead.

The two armies collided on the first day of July. The southern army forced the Union soldiers out of Gettysburg through a previously peaceful peach orchard, across a waving field of wheat onto the ramparts of rises known as Cemetery Ridge, Seminary Ridge, and Cusp Hill. For three days under the fervid heat of high summer the battle raged.

The ridges were not taken. The Union Army was fighting now on its own soil. Against monumental Southern bravery, the North prevailed.

It took weeks to bury all the Union dead, and the ambulance wagons of Lee's retreating troops stretched for twenty miles, rumbling through another scourge of rain to the accompaniment of sobs, groans, and screams from the wounded and dying who suffered agonies at each jolt of the rutted road.

There was little jubilation in the North. Nearly 30,000 Southern soldiers had died, but it had cost the lives of over 20,000 Northern men as well. The victory wine was bitter. New drafts were abrasive with the rich able to gain release from their obligations by buying substitutes; the inflationary prices were eating up the high wages and war profits. Everyone was sick to death of the war, and the Democrats were finding it a fertile time to cry for peace at any price and rail against the Republican incumbents.

*   *   *

When Cricket came limping back to Columbia in October, he was given a hero's welcome. Although everyone wanted to hear first hand accounts of the war, Cricket did not feel like talking about it. He sang war songs for them instead—"We're Tenting Tonight on the Old Camp Ground;" "Just Before the Battle, Mother;" "Tramp, Tramp, Tramp, the Boys Are Marching"—and he told them funny anecdotes about the other soldiers and camp life. He did not tell anyone about the horrors of lying for two days, wounded and bleeding his life slowly into the dust. He wanted to forget.

No one was more glad to see him than Sally Magee Quimby. She descended upon him with a squeal of joy. "Cricket McGuire, you got no idea how happy I am you're home! You jist got to come back where I can talk to you private—"

As Sally had written to Adam, she had "gotten her figger back," but her face had aged. There were black circles under her eyes and a puffiness around her jowls. Her hair hung in careless strands about her ears. She was looking at Cricket with such entreaty in her green eyes that he allowed himself to be drawn back to the room she still occupied in the back of "The Nugget."

"Cricket, look at him!" she said, frustatingly waving her hand toward a crib.

A little boy with round dark eyes and solemn face stared back at Cricket from between the bars of his bed.

"He's a right cute liddle fellar," Cricket said.

"Cute don't matter," Sally exploded. "Can't you see, Cricket? He's two years old n' he ain't even standing up. He's stupid, too. I got to change him like a baby. He don't smile. He don't talk. He don't do nothing normal 'cept eat."

"Well, mebbe you should take him to a doctor, Sally."

"I been to every doctor in San Francisco and the country round. They say he ain't never going to be normal. Cricket—I got to get rid of that kid—"

"Sally, you don't know what you're sayin'. You cain't jus' get rid o' yer own kid."

She was pacing around the room like a tigress about to whelp. "You know as well as I do that Adam left his first wife 'cause o' that kid of theirs. I'm not going to lose Adam because of—him." She whirled and pointed at the little boy. "I want you to get rid of him for me, Cricket. I don't care where you take him or what you do with him, just so long as Adam don't know."

"Sally, I cain't do thet. I hain't got no right to take Adam's son off somewhere and not tell him. What's Adam gonna say?"

"I'm gonna tell him the kid died."

"I don't mean to be unkind, Sally," Cricket said, "but war does strange things to a man sometimes. Did ja every think thet mebbe, well, mebbe Adam wouldn't niver *come* back 'less he thought the boy was here?"

"Yah," Sally said in a downhearted voice. "I know he ain't what you could say 'head over heels' about me. But—" Her voice lilted upward with a spurt of optimism, "I ain't gonna tell him the boy's dead until he *gets* back, and once he's back—this is gonna keep him, Cricket—"

She went to the bed, knelt, pushed a board loose and brought out a box.

"I'm rich, Cricket. See—it's filled with *gold*. The claim I bought for Adam turned out to be a mother-lode."

"Wull, I'm glad for ya about thet, Sally, but I still say it hain't right to get rid of Adam's little boy without him knowing it. You got all thet money. Why won't thet keep Adam here even if the boy hain't quite normal?"

250

"Cricket, you oughta know better'n anybody else that Adam's plumb touched on the subject o' that other kid. I ain't gonna risk it! You're gonna get rid of him for me."

Cricket shook his head. "I cain't, Sally."

"Oh, you're gonna do it alright," Sally said, "because o' this—"

She caught up several of the pouches from the casket—"Gold, Cricket —more'n you ever dreamed about. Ever' man's got his price."

"Thet's right as rain. But gold hain't mine, Sally. Ye better git someone else."

"I can't trust nobody but you, Cricket—" Sally suddenly turned pleading again. "Ever'one knows I'm rich, now. They'd blackmail me fer sure. Please, Cricket. You're the onliest one I can count on to do it secret."

"I'm sorry, Sally, but I just cain't. Wouldn't sit right with me. Adam n' me had our diffrunces, but we're still friends—"

"You'd be doin' Adam a favor! You know how that other kid riled him. If you care a nit about him, you'd be as frantic as I am to spare him knowin' about this one."

"Sally, I *cain't*."

"Well, I'm gonna git rid of him one way or another. If I have to drown him myself, then you can have that on your conscience, Cricket McGuire," Sally snarled.

"I hain't doin' it," Cricket yelled, "n' that's final."

He ducked out of the room just as she started throwing things.

But it wasn't final. Sally had an ally in Levi Jones, the only other person to whom she had confided her plans. Levi's claim was petering out.

"I mighta knowed thet ol' hornswoggler wouldn't a given me nothin' was any good," Levi grumbled. "Probably laughed his no good head off afore he died thinkin' how I'd sell out ever'thing in Wisconsin and come runnin' with 'm tongue hangin' out over a mine thet was all mined out—rotten, no good, connivin' weasel—"

Sally had promised gold to get rid of Adam's son, enough gold to keep Levi happy for the rest of his days.

"I want to go back to Wisconsin n' I don't even have the price o' passage," Levi whined to Cricket. "Ah'm jus' a poor ol' man who wants to die on his own soil—not in this parched, good-fer-nothing-but-snakes-n'-lizards country. I'm a poor dyin' ol' man, Cricket—"

"I'll find us a way back—both of us, without Sally's gold," Cricket promised.

"With thet bad limp you got, you hain't much better'n me," Levi observed. "Don't many folks want to hire a cripple."

Muscles fought in Cricket's jaw but he said nothing.

"She's right about Adam, you know," Levi went on slyly. "Pert near kill him to learn about thet boy. Might drive him plumb daft. Always figgered the other one was his woman's fault, ya know—"

"No! I hain't gonna do it," Cricket cried. But he tossed and turned all night. Levi listened with satisfaction and renewed his attack in the morning.

"Look, thet little boy might even git all right," Cricket shot back. "I saw Adam's first wife last Christmas n' she said his little girl is right as rain now. Purfect as she kin be."

That was a mistake because Levi soon had the whole story of the meeting in the railroad station and of Caroline's work with unfortunate children. Levi now had the lever he needed to lift the stubborn mountain of Cricket's will.

"Don't see how you kin treat a poor liddle child like that—" he mourned.

"I don't know what ye're talkin' 'bout," Cricket said, irritated.

"Ye're the only person in this world knows where this liddle fellar could git some help—n' you won't help him. You'd ruther let his mama git so desperate she'll just turn him over to any coyote who comes along hungry for some gold—"

"Levi—in the name of God, I cain't take *Adam's* kid to *Caroline*."

"She wouldn't niver have to know hit was Adam's kid," Levi said, chewing his mush with equanimity.

"She'd know," Cricket said.

"Now how's she gonna know?"

"She'd know. He looks like Adam for one thing. But even iffen she didn't—hit wouldn't be right not tellin' her."

"Aw right, you jus' let thet poor lil feller be shipped off with someone don't care two figs nor a holler—"

Suddenly, Cricket, who seldom swore, let out a roll of cuss words that made even Levi's eyebrows go up. He had reached his breaking point.

"All right! All right! I'll take thet poor lil kid to Miz Caroline because mebbe she can help him, n' it wouldn't be right not to give him thet chance. But I hain't promisin' I won't tell Adam iffen he asks me."

"Ya won't go tellin' him, 'less he is askin'?"

"No."

"Good 'nuff. Ye're a fine, humanitarian, heart o' gold man, Cricket McGuire."

Cricket looked at his partner sourly.

252

"There's one thing, Levi—on the trip back, *yer gonna change his pants*—" and he left, slamming the door.

Levi choked a bit on his last spoon of mush, looked thoughtful for a moment, and then mumbled to himself, "I reckon he means thet, but I guess I done a sight worse'n thet for a poke o' gold in my day. By cracky, I'll do 'er, iffen I have to."

Cricket and Levi left Columbia on a dark night in November. In the morning, Sally Magee Quimby announced that her child had died. A death certificate was signed by a local doctor who soon thereafter left town never to return. A small casket was ordered from the local undertaker. A wind storm blew dust and tumble weeds against the three or four dozen people who climbed up the rocky slopes of the hillside cemetery and watched Sally, dressed in black from head to toe, sob into her black handkerchief as the little casket was lowered into the ground.

Everyone said it was too bad, but then the child had never been quite right anyway and maybe it was all for the best. Then they hurried back to the saloon to wash the dust from their lips with the beer Sally had set up for the house.

53

In September the Union General Rosecrans and the Southern General Bragg had met on the banks of the River of Death, the Chickamauga. In the bloodiest fighting since Gettysburg, the Union had been forced into retreat.

The fortunes of the half-starved Union troops changed in November when Grant was given command.

Hooker and Sherman reached Chattanooga two days before Thanksgiving. Grant ordered construction of a road and bridge to Brown's Ferry. This "cracker line" soon had food and supplies flowing back to the besieged Union men.

The hills overlooking Chattanooga became battlefields as the two armies struggled for supremacy. When the smoke of the battle had cleared away, Bragg was in retreat to Georgia.

Northerners sat down to their turkeys with some satisfaction. If the South was not prone, she was on her knees. The Union had gobbled up the Mississippi Valley; stopped Lee's advance into Virginia, and broken Bragg's siege.

With fingers aching, faces raw, the shivering pickets of both armies trudged through mud and rain and snow. They knew only one thing for sure—it looked like another hard, cold winter.

* * *

The drawing room of the Thornton home was filled with fashionable ladies and gentlemen who had come to listen to Strauss waltzes being played by a fat and earnest pianist.

The musicale had lasted overlong and Caroline's mind had wandered into such a revery that she started when the little French maid, Valerie, leaned over a man in a checked waistcoat to whisper "Miz Caroline, there ees a gentleman to zee you."

With an apologetic glance, she made her way around the congregated gilt chairs and settees, stretched out legs and humped up knees.

"Did you ask the gentleman's name?" she questioned when they had gained their exit.

"He say Kreequet, I theenk," Valerie answered.

"Kreequet—?" puzzled Caroline, and then gathering up her skirts and rushing forward in sudden happy comprehension, "Cricket!"

She found him standing uneasily in the elegant foyer, a knapsack and guitar over one shoulder, a small child leaning against the other.

"Cricket, how good to see you!" she cried, clasping his hand. "And what have you here?" she asked, smiling at the little boy. The child instantly buried his head against Cricket.

"Ah'm afraid he's a present fer ye, iffen ye'll have'm,"

"For me?"

"He cain't walk n' he don't talk neither. I thought mebbe ye could help him like ye helped Fly. I got money—"

The child turned his head cautiously to peer at her. Caroline had the odd feeling that she had seen him someplace before. He looked at her solemnly. Suddenly the pupils of her eyes dilated until they blotted out the blue irises. She turned to Cricket. *"You've brought me Adam's son—"*

"Yes'm," Cricket said, sorrowful, ashamed and awkward. "I don't like to talk about it in front of the liddle fellar, but his Ma didn't

254

want him—"

The musicale had finally ended. The double doors of the drawing room burst open and a crush of people began to enter the hallway.

"We can't talk here, Cricket. I know—we'll go into the kitchen."

It was cozily warm in the low-ceilinged kitchen. Caroline added a few small logs to the fire.

Sensing the adult strain and tension, the child burrowed himself even more tightly against Cricket's big form.

"Are you hungry?" Caroline asked him, trying to overcome the emotions the sight of him churned within her.

He hid his face again.

"We ain't et since noon. I s'pect he is," Cricket volunteered.

Caroline heated soup and scooped strawberry preserves on thick slices of fresh bread. When the child saw Cricket dig in heartily he started to eat but continued to cast apprehensive glances at Caroline.

"You're not in uniform," Caroline said to Cricket, not able to discuss the child further until she was sure she was in control of her emotions.

"Got wounded and discharged," Cricket said.

"Oh, Cricket—"

He dismissed her quick sympathy with a wave of his hand. "I'm lucky to be out o' it. Hain't much fun."

Caroline sat down slowly at the table and looked at the child. "He's beautiful. He resembles—Fly."

"Yeh. He don't look none like his Mama. I guess I shouldn't o' brought him to ye, Miz Caroline, but like I said he needs help."

"His legs?"

"Same thing like Fly, only his leg."

"I see—" Caroline's voice trembled a little, "then Adam knows that—that it wasn't my fault after all—"

Cricket cleared his throat uneasily. "Adam don't know nuthin'. He hain't seen the child ever, n' his Mama don't want Adam niver to know. She knows why Adam left you n' she don't want it to happen to her."

"I see—" Caroline said again.

"She was willin' to pay well." Cricket drew a pouch out of his knapsack. "Ther's gold thar, Miz Caroline. Enuff to make it well worth your while."

"We can always use the money, Cricket—but it isn't a question of money. It's—it's—"

"I shouldn't a brung him to ye. Hit was stupid of me," Cricket grieved. "You're the last person in the world I'd want to hurt, Miz

Caroline."

"I know that Cricket. It's just that if Adam doesn't know, then I'm entering into a deception if I take the child."

"I ben through all thet maself, but I finally come to feelin' thet I had to think of the boy first. Adam's so all fired proud he'd niver bring him to ye for help even if he did know ye could mebbe do something. He's a nice liddle feller. He deserves some kinda chance too."

The little boy was drooping over his soup bowl.

"Ohhh, he's so tired," Caroline said with compassion. "What's his name?"

"She never told me, Ma'am, and somehow I niver asked."

"What's your real name, Cricket?"

"James. Jim."

"He's got to have a name. Would you mind if we called him after you?"

"Does that mean ye're gonna take him, Ma'am?"

Caroline sighed. "I don't know if it's right or wrong, Cricket, but he does need help."

She leaned forward and stroked the little boy's cheek. He drew back from her.

"His mama hain't been very patient with him," Cricket explained. "Hit takes awhile 'for he trusts someone."

"Come sit with me," Caroline coaxed. "He's so tired—maybe if I could rock him a bit—" she said to Cricket.

"C'mon, son. This's a real nice lady wants to hold you. She won't hurt ye none." He lifted the boy and sat him in Caroline's lap.

He looked at her with suspicious eyes, his body rigid in her arms.

"Do you still sing? Maybe if you would play your guitar and sing it might soothe him," Caroline suggested to Cricket.

Outside snow was falling. The fire made chuckling sounds as the wood collapsed. Cricket's fingers wandered across the strings, drawing out random cords, finally settling on an old Indian lullabye Caroline had heard Kemink sing.

"Little owl—little owl
Wide-eyed through the night.
Wink for the sun is climbing.
Wink for the sun is bright—"

After a while, the black eyelashes began to flutter, the small body grew heavier.

"Little owl—little owl

256

Dream of starlight
Close your wings on
the day's sunlight—"

"I think he's asleep," Caroline whispered.

"I'll play ye one I wrote myself while I was in the hospital,"
Cricket said, his face growing a deeper red. "I wrote it fer ye, Miz
Caroline. A man gets some funny thoughts sometimes when he hain't
got nuthin' to do but think fer weeks on end—"

He strummed softly across the strings.

"Bare limbs—grey sky—
I'm so cold in winter darkness.
Can't feel no spring comin'—Can't feel no spring comin'
Can't feel no spring comin'—niver.
Then I look into yer eyes—
I see lilacs n' butterflies
Blossoms burstin'—birds afly—
Suddenly the sun steals by.
Yer my springtime.
Yer my springtime.
In the dead of winter
Yer my springtime."

"That's beautiful, Cricket," Caroline said. Her expression revealed
how deeply she was touched.

"Like I said, a man gits foolish notions sometimes. I was thinking
about goin' back to Tomorrow River country, how it could be with—
with a woman ye really care about—"

"Cricket—"

He laughed softly, seeing how moved she was, how near to tears.

"Don't ye look like thet now, Honey-girl. Ye don't have to say
nothin'. When I come today and saw ye in this great fine house,
dressed all up so grand, I knew this was where ye belonged."

"Cricket, you're one of the most special people I've ever known.
Under different circumstances—"

"I know. Ye got all these kids to look after n' all. Hey—I think he's
gone to sleep all right. You want me to git him tucked in somewhere
fer ye?"

"I'll take him, Cricket. I'm afraid if we shift him to you it might
wake him. He's not heavy. Wait for me. I'll be right back."

When she came back, the kitchen was empty. Cricket was gone, but
he had left the sack of gold on the table.

54

Caroline's face was as fresh and red as a ripe strawberry within the folds of her dark winter hood as she stepped into the school room with her arms full of bundles and packages. The younger children, advanced in a pack to greet her.

"Wait—" she said, laughing, "wait until I set these down. I have a special surprise for you. How many of you have ever had a banana?"

"I have!"

"I never."

"Me neither."

"Are those those long yellow things? I think I did once."

Caroline turned from hanging up her cloak to draw a large bunch of fruit from one of the bags.

"Think of it! Bananas in February! And to think of the thousands of miles they have traveled to get to us. The clerk in the store told me these came from Ecuador. As soon as you find Ecuador on the map and globe for me, each of you may have one."

Danny did not join the scramble toward the map and globe.

"It seems sad, Mama, that we can have luxuries like bananas when the people in the South are starving. I read in the paper this morning that bacon is ten dollars a pound, and that people are making shoes out of their carpets. Why does God let people starve, Mama?"

"Danny," Caroline said, half laughing, half lamenting, "I think I shall almost be glad when you are grown up. Then maybe you'll be a preacher like your father so you can start answering the questions instead of asking them—"

The minute the words had left her lips she regretted them and sent a swift glance to see if the mention of his father might have wounded Danny.

When she had finally told him of Adam's remarriage, he had accepted it well. "I think it's better knowing he's never coming back. Thinking always that he might was like—like living with your shoe strings untied."

"Yes," Caroline had agreed, "I guess you're right." But her voice had sounded sad.

She had always believed in being open with her children, so she had told them that Jimmy was their half-brother. At the same time, she cautioned them that it must remain a family secret.

"Here it is! Here it is! That orange patch is Ecuador—"

258

"It's green on the map—"

Caroline bent over the globe to emphasize the long route the bananas had taken to arrive in Chicago.

Kemink was dispensing the fruit.

"Is goot!" Heine said, after the first dubious mouthful had convinced him.

"Mama, why does God let people starve?" Danny persisted.

"Ain't God's fault men are stupid," Dan-Pete said, "Indians never starve because they know how to use the food around them."

"No, that is not true," Kemink reprimanded softly, "there have been winters of great snows when our people did die of starvation, and summers of great drouth when even the wisest in the ways of the earth and field hungered."

"Why, Mama?" Danny pursued relentlessly.

"I don't believe God lets people starve," Caroline at last committed herself.

"But he *does*," Danny said with the passion of youthful anger. "People *do* starve. And He could stop it."

"Only if we ask Him, Danny. Only if we ask Him. That's free will again."

"Don't you think the Southern people ask Him? I read that General Lee prays all the time and that he believes he is fighting a holy war."

"I think that the Southern people who ask—believing—are supplied in one way or another," Caroline said. "Remember the manna in the desert?"

"But that was for His chosen people, the Jews."

"When we choose Him, we all become His chosen people."

"Mama, do you really believe that God answers prayer every time, if you pray right?"

"Yes, Danny, I do."

"I don't."

They stared at each other, mother and son, blue eyes meeting blue eyes in a tense communication more desperate than words.

"Why don't you believe, Dan?" Caroline finally asked.

"My father never came back—and—and Emily still isn't well. I've prayed for Emily every night for three years."

There was stillness in the room. The children sat with their half-eaten bananas forgotten, every eye on Caroline, even those of the tiniest who could not understand the scope of the discussion. All the childish faith the older children had in Caroline and the God they had been taught to believe in seemed to hang now in the balance of their watching, waiting eyes.

Caroline swallowed.

"Danny, your father has free will too. We can't pray to make some-one else do something he or she doesn't want to do. That is praying amiss."

"That's always what you say—*free will* is always the reason we can't have our prayers answered. I wish none of us ever had free will. I suppose Emily has free will too, and she *wants* to stay sick—"

"I don't pretend to have all the answers," Caroline said. "But I do know that 'faith is the substance of things not seen.' I *knew* Fly was healed long before it was apparent to anyone else. You have to believe it and to know it before it's visible to your eyes, Danny."

"Why does it have to be so hard?!"

"You'd like prayer to be a magic lantern we could just rub like Aladdin's genie?"

"Yes. Yes, I *would.*"

"Very few good things come without struggling for them. Perhaps it is the struggle that makes them so valuable."

"Can I have another 'nana?" Heinie asked, the fascination of the long conversation wearing off for him.

"I don't know if I have enough to go all the way around again, Heinie—" Caroline hesitated, wanting to be fair to everyone.

"He can have mine," Danny said, handing him his uneaten fruit.

"He can have Emily's. She isn't going to eat it. She hasn't even looked at hers," Georgio pointed out.

"Oh, Mama," Danny said, casting a heartsick glance at his en-chanted friend, "nothing can make something so wrong seem right to me."

"Danny—I think—I think faith *is* the magic lantern," Caroline sud-denly concluded. "Don't give up. Keep trying. Fly's healing took years, but it happened. She's healed!"

Danny's cheeks reddened. "Sometimes I wonder, Mama, if it wasn't something that sort of happened with Fly—that maybe would have happened anyway."

Caroline laid a hand on each side of her son's face.

"Danny, faith and its fruit are something each person must ex-perience for himself. Keep searching—keep believing and some day your magic lantern *will work.* The first few times you may still think it is possibly a coincidence—maybe an accident—but if you keep on, your whole being becomes stronger in its faith—it becomes like a strong tree growing in your heart, and the day comes when it is as difficult to not believe as it once was to believe."

Unexpectedly, Emily stood up. She not only stood up, but she picked up the banana that had been lying in her lap and set it in front of Danny. Everyone grew still again, holding their breath,

260

hoping that a miracle was about to happen.

There was a concerted whisper of disappointment when she sat down again, her eyes as blank and expressionless as ever.

"It was as if she *knew*," Danny said in a choked voice.

"Maybe she does," Caroline said. ' 'She looked at the stars. She pets the cat. Somewhere deep inside, she is perfect. You believe that, don't you, Danny?"

"Yes."

"At that moment when you can believe it more than you don't believe it, she'll be healed," Caroline predicted.

*   *   *

By a special act of Congress, Ulysses Grant was made a Lt. General in March and given a scope of power beyond any held by Union commanders up to that point in the war.

The former hardware clerk had his choice of field battle. There were advisors who urged him to remain where he had already proved his capacity for victory. He chose the greater challenge. He would take over the Army of the Potomac and face the titan, Lee. Sherman would be dispatched to attack Johnston in Georgia.

The Union forces had made their winter quarters one river down from the previous year. Grant had to cross the Rapidian rather than the Rappahannock to engage the enemy.

They began the tedious task of crossing via five pontoon bridges at midnight. There were over four thousand wagons of supplies and munitions as well as the soldiers and reserve artillery to transfer over. More than one man felt the hair on the back of his neck rise in expectation that Lee and his men would spring forth from the darkness at any moment to challenge their advance. All through the night the banks remained ominously silent. The wagons continued to jolt across with torturous slowness into the dawn, into the day, all day long. It was almost nightfall again before the last horse in the procession stepped off the pontoons and the bridges were destroyed.

The Army of the Potomac was ensconced in the Wilderness, that tractless overgrowth where Hooker had been surprised the spring before by Lee. Again Lee attacked with his entire force.

The almost impenetrable Wilderness made a battleground on which cannon and cavalry were virtually useless. For two days, men struggled in terrible hand to hand combat, Log breastworks, erected as protection, caught fire from the fusillade and the thick choking atmosphere of smoke added to the sense of confusion and terror. There was no grace of rain as there had been at Gettysburg to dampen and put out the blazes. Dozens of wounded were burned to death in the under-brush fires.

The South called it a draw and waited for Grant to limp away to recover as his successors always had. Grant called it a victory—he had got his unwieldly train across the river; he had taken at least man for man and his enemy could afford the loss much less than he.

"I propose to fight it out on this line if it takes all summer," Grant wired to Washington, along with a report of casualties estimated at twenty thousand men.

The soldiers had cheered Grant when he had not retreated after the Wilderness foray. They had felt, "Yes, let's get it over with once and for all—" But the wire, soon well publicized, made them feel that Grant regarded victory more highly than their lives. He was ready and willing to expend them as individuals in a mass slaughter if that was the only way to triumph. It had a sobering effect on the men, and for the most, the respect they felt for Grant was now tinged with bitterness. They understood full well why morning reports were no longer taken as the battles continued. The losses were so staggering it was wisdom not to count out loud.

On May 10th, the Union forces had almost broken through Lee's line at his weakest point. The casualties were monstrous, but the South pushed the Union forces back and healed their breach.

Grant squinted through the smoke from the cigar clenched in his teeth and proved he meant his wire by ordering yet another frontal attack at Cold harbor. Seven thousand Union men died in the first half hour of *that* battle. The victory was Lee's at the cost of 1500 men.

A total of fifty thousand Union men had been lost during the campaign to this point and Grant had earned himself a new nickname. He was called "The Butcher."

He settled in for a long stay. The Union soldiers ripped up the railroad ties and burned them. Petersburg was under siege. Grant, "The Butcher," was prepared now to play the waiting game. If he couldn't demolish Lee head on, he would starve him into submission.

55

For three days, a miserable drizzly rain had turned the roads into rivers of mud, soaked the men to the skin wherever their ponchos failed to cover them, and left the mules and horses steaming from their own heat.

The sight of a fire glowing in the darkness, an accompanying odor of stewing beef and onions wafting their way caused Adam to rein his horse sharply. He listened for a cautious moment, hearing only the sound of dripping rain, the slight creaking of bridles from the men and animals behind him, and the low humming of a woman. He nodded his men forward.

An old negro woman, black as a stove pipe, arrayed in a variety of colorful, cast-off clothing which included a striped sunbonnet, was stirring a large black pot of stew within a shelter she had made from fence rails.

"Well, Aunty," Adam said, dismounting with the awkwardness of limbs stiff from the rain, "that stew smells like ambrosia from heaven, and that fire's a welcome sight."

The old woman glared at him and lifted her wooden spoon in menace. "Dis stew yain't fer no Yankees!" she snapped at him, "n dis fire yain't neither. Don' you Yankees know how to make yo own fire?"

"I'm afraid you're mistaken, Aunty," Adam said easily. "That pot has supper for my men in it—and that fire is surely going to warm their bones."

His men were dismounting, gratefully crowding near the small shelter; some of them already had their tin cups and mess kettles out.

"Dis food all me n' ma white folks got left. Yu'all snatched everting else away!" the old woman said with spirit, waving her spoon in Adam's face. "Yu'all ride out. Y'ain't gonna hiv dis food 'ness ovah ma dead body—"

She was one of those old black servants who had earned a certain status in her world. She was known for her vitriolic tongue and sassy ways; even her white folks had indulged her. They often had said laughingly, "Yu'all better watch out for Sary Ann if you get spots on that cloth" or —"if you track up that floor—". She fully expected the Yankee Captain and his sodden men to turn tail and run as two generations of white children had harkened to her strident tones. But Adam ignored her and approached the kettle.

"Yo'all git outta heah or ah'll push dis hot pot in yo face—" the old woman threatened.

Without a word of warning, Adam drew his pistol and fired. The old woman slid slowly down to the mud floor, a look of incredulous belief the last expression on her face.

Cavanaugh gave an involuntary cry of protest. Adam turned on him, cold-eyed. "You got a problem?"

The boy's mouth was trembling, the muscles in his throat jerking. "Cap'n, Sir. I thought we were fighting this war to free the blacks not kill them, Sir."

"We're fighting this war to preserve the Union. She was a Southern sympathizer. My job is to see to my men. That's what I'm doing. You might as well learn right now that this is the way life is, Beans. Learn it—or maybe next time you'll be the one on the ground. Now, seeing you're so concerned, you can bury her."

"Yessir."

White-lipped, Cavanaugh dragged the stringy old body off into the rain. There was only a small moment of hesitation, then the rest of the men crowded forward with their cups. They ate in silence except for the hungry smacking of their jaws and the sound of swallowing.

Cavanaugh buried the old woman in the Tennessee mud as he had been told. He did not eat any of the stew when he returned, and from that time on his letters home were no longer filled with worshipping accounts of Captain Quimby.

Adam felt no compunction. Grant had sent Sheridan to ravage the Shenandoah Valley. All through the war it had been a life saving bread basket for Lee's troops. The orders now were to strip it so bare that "a crow flying across the valley would have to carry its own provisions." He was doing what he had been ordered to do. Against the mountainous tolls of deaths he had witnessed, the death of one small, shriveled black woman signified little.

He had changed since Shiloh. He rode a fine white horse now. He did not engage his heart with this horse—or, for that matter, with anyone anymore. Where before he had been easily moved, he was now stoney and callous, given to acts of gratuitous cruelty. The long suffering struggle with his conscience was over. He had lost what he referred to as his "preacher mentality."

Only when he was drunk did something of the old Adam crack through. He was prone then to empty his heart along with his cup to whoever drank with him. He would tell of his early dedication to God and of how it was rewarded with the birth of a deformed and illegitimate child.

"I loved that woman—God how I loved her," he would complain,

264

"enough to hold out my hand in forgiveness—to forget. But she—she was defiant, rebellious."

The sorry tale would go on to Sally who, seeing his loneliness and heartbreak, had seduced him, only to prove a screaming shrew. The tale always ended the same way. Adam would point out eloquently how terrible the world was, the inequities and cruelties of existence, and man's helplessness. His listeners were invariably moved to agree with him, sharing a sense of despair and hopelessness.

Adam was still a great orator.

*   *   *

In Georgia, Johnston kept Sherman at bay by moving his men behind heavy fortifications and breastworks and fighting only at such times as Sherman would finally storm his bastions in frustration. These tactics had meant greater losses for the Union than the South, but they also meant that by the end of July, the movements of the two armies had crept to Atlanta's front door.

A complex of industries and railroads, Atlanta was a prize the South could not afford to lose. While she was under seige and constant bombardment, Sherman sawed at the jugular vein that pumped the life blood of food and supplies into the besieged city—the railroads.

By night, the sulfurous red glow of burning railroad ties shone in the darkness; by day, "Sherman's neckties"—rails melted in the red hot fires of the burning ties and twisted about trees and fence posts—marked his advancing progress.

The South fought back with guerilla tactics, destroying bridges and railways needed for Northern supplies. But Sherman, foreseeing such contingencies, had had duplicate bridges built ahead of time and had only to have them shoved quickly into place.

The Southern general acknowledged the extremity of his situation on September 1 by setting fire to his own munitions and government properties within Atlanta before escaping with his men into the night.

On September 2, Sherman marched into Atlanta.

He at once set about turning Atlanta into a military garrison and foremost on his list was the evacuation of all civilians from the city. He declared he would not tie up hundreds of his men in garrison duty to police a hostile population. Citizens of Atlanta, including the old, sick, frail women, babies, and frightened darkies were driven from their homes into a countryside so short of food that the Southern soldiers had been chewing sugar cane to sustain their lives.

The South was finally prone, but still her fighting spirit remained. On November 15, Sherman burned what was left of Atlanta's war industries and set off for "Savannah and the sea—" While Atlanta went up in flames beneath clouds of black smoke, sixty thousand Union soldiers marched off singing, "Glory, Glory Hallelujah." Their mission was to ravage, burn, steal and destroy without quarter, a sixty-mile swath through the South.

No other single event of the war was to cause such bitterness as this march of pillage and destruction. Yet, Sherman's supporters pointed out that it was as effective as any of the terrible battles in undermining the Confederacy and at much less cost of human life; only twenty-five hundred human lives were lost compared to the thousands that fell in battle. But no such reasoning could annul the seeds of hatred that were sown as the Yankees trampled the Southland.

56

Ann was as excited as a debutante. The Thorntons had been invited to Lincoln's Inauguration.

Lincoln, worn down under the attrition of constant criticism, angered over the enormous losses Grant had suffered in the spring campaigns, and the inability of his administration to smother the Southern rebellion after years of trying, had been pessimistic about his chances for re-election. He had gone so far as to draft a memorandum which stated, "—it seems probable that the administration will not be re-elected. Then it will be my duty to save the Union between the election and inauguration, as he will have secured his election on such grounds that cannot possibly save it afterwards."

He was referring to his opponent George McClellan, the general he had so repeatedly appointed and removed from command of the Army of the Potomac, now retired. The platform issued by the Democrats had been a peace platform, ready to appease the enemy, stating—"after four years of failure to restore the Union with war—during which public liberty and private right alike have been trodden down and the material prosperity of the country impaired—justice demands a cessation of hostilities with a view to an ultimate convention of all the states to restore peace—"

McClellan himself had bridled at the content of the platform, stating that he could not adopt it in full with regard to his old comrades in arms—but a forced appeasement had been in the air. The capture of Atlanta had changed the tide and Lincoln had swept in on a great popular victory.

Bromley had become increasingly active in politics and his loyalty and enthusiasm during the darkest period had not gone unnoticed. Still the invitation had been a surprise.

"Are you sure this gown will not look provincial?" Ann asked, turning this way and that the better to see herself in the pier glass.

"You will hold your own with the finest belle in Washington," Caroline assured her through a mouthful of pins. She was pinning up the hem of a pale yellow satin dress, "but I will never get this finished if you don't stand still."

Ann laughed. "I do feel fidgety. This skirt must be a hundred yards around."

"Maybe twenty. There—that's the last pin. You can take it off now and I'll hem it up for you."

"You'll do no such thing, darling. I'll take it to my dressmaker tomorrow. With all you have to do, I shouldn't have asked you to pin it, but I couldn't wait!"

"It is lovely," Caroline said with admiration.

"Do you think I should wear pearls?—or would the pendant Bay gave me be more striking?"

Caroline began industriously sticking pins into the plush pin cushion, a flush creeping up her throat.

"The pendant would be lovely—"

"I'm sorry I mentioned Bay, Carrie. I see it disturbed you," Ann said, looking at her sister intently. "I suppose you still worry."

"Don't you? No one seems to have heard from him or about him since he left."

Ann smoothed the shimmering fold of her skirt. "May be I'm just self-centered, but no—somehow I don't worry about Bay. I have an intuitive feeling that he's all right."

"Worrying does not help, so it's good you can feel that way," Caroline approved. "I imagine we all have tender spots. Bay is one of mine. Press it and it hurts."

"Were you in love with him?" Ann asked, unable to stifle her curiosity any longer.

"Bay is like a natural force," Caroline said with a wry smile, "stimulating, frightening, exciting—he whirled into my life and out again like one of Kemink's devil winds."

"Do you love him?"

267

"He's engaged to Nelia Fitzpatrick."

"I see," Ann said with a wise look.

"And what is that supposed to mean!"

"It means that I see more than you are willing to tell me, and so for the moment, I'm going to leave you in peace," Ann said laughing. "Will you unhook me first?"

Caroline started to oblige, but she was only on the third of the twenty-two tiny satin buttons that marched down her sister's back when Zoe interrupted the task.

"Mees Caroline, a messenger haz come from Madam Kemink. She ask urgently that you come at once."

"Zoe, will you finish unbuttoning Mrs. Thornton?" Caroline asked, her fingers suddenly incapable of the simple task. "It must be an emergency. Kemink would not disturb me over a trifle."

"Do you want me to come with you?" Ann asked.

"You would have to change. I do not think I should wait," Caroline said, hurrying for her cloak.

Charles was not pleased to be routed from his after-supper fireplace to drive her across town. He tugged on his galoshes and ulster with maddening slowness. Seated behind his sullen back, Caroline tried to keep her mind from cartwheeling into frightened swoops—could Millie have had another attack?—Or worse, it could be smallpox. There was an epidemic in the city—

Stop! she cried to her mind, but it slid away from her to run through another gamut of fears. Caroline had never laid a whip to a horse in her life, but she had a moment of wild temptation when she would have liked to have laid it to Charles. He seemed to deliberately let the horses plod along. To her sharp urgings he only mumbled that it was dark and the street was full of pot holes. When they at last arrived, she leapt impatiently from the carriage, not waiting for him to assist her.

Inside the building, everything seemed quiet and serene. A small lamp burned on the table with its checkered cloth. In the back room, the children rested peacefully, their faces beautiful as only the faces of sleeping children can be. But the expression in Kemink's eyes as she came to greet her told Caroline that something was gravely wrong.

"Kemink, what *is* it?"

"Louise."

"She's ill?"

"She has gone on."

"Oh no!—are you sure?"

Kemink picked up the lamp and Caroline followed her upstairs to Louise Louwain's apartment.

268

"She said she was tired and thought she would lie down before tea," Kemink said. "When she did not come down for supper, I thought I should check to see if she was all right. I thought she was sleeping, so I tiptoed away. But when she did not come down to hear the little ones' prayers—she always comes, and they asked for her, I went again to see if all was well—"

Gently Kemink pushed open the door to the elderly woman's bedroom. "I found her so—"

Louise Louwain had neatly hung her black dress on a hook and slipped into a flowered pegnoir before lying down. A half cup of tea was by her bedside. Her aquiline features, pale in the half darkened room, showed she was at peace.

Caroline felt the thin wrist.

"Somewhere still—she lives," Kemink said.

Caroline nodded, then turned away to stare from the window to the slushy street below.

"I don't know what to do without her."

Old and frail though she had appeared, Louise's supportive strength had insinuated itself into Caroline's life in a hundred ways. She felt a rushing sense of loss.

"We must do—things," Kemink reminded sorrowfully. "We must wire her daughter—call a doctor—"

"Give me a little time," Caroline pleaded.

Kemink nodded and withdrew from the room.

Death. The great imponderable. One moment a human being could laugh, talk, touch, cry—and the next she was gone, leaving only a waxen shell behind.

Caroline sat with her deceased friend—and the mystery of death—until the doctor came. Then she forced herself to say "goodbye" with one final kiss and descended to attend to the responsibilities that awaited her.

"I will not go to the inauguration now," Ann said with a woeful face as soon as she heard. "Bromley and I will both stay and help you through this."

"If you didn't go to the inauguration, I should feel doubly bereaved," Caroline answered. "Louise would be the first to insist that you should not deprive yourself of this great occasion."

"But we would miss the funeral."

"She would understand. You must continue with your plans. Everything will be all right here."

Ann and Bromley were finally persuaded to leave on schedule, but as it turned out, everything was not "all right." Louise's daughter descended upon Chicago in a rage. She had never liked the school. She had been jealous of the time and attention her mother had devoted to it. Marcia Wilhaven stepped off the train in a high fashion rustle of black silk, gold earrings dancing angrily in her ears, her dark eyes snapping, and began a barrage of accusations against Caroline.

"My mother's death is your fault! You worked her to death! A woman of her age had no business being burdened with squalls of screaming, snivelling children!"

Totally taken back, Caroline at first tried to tell Marcia how much she had loved her mother and how much her mother had loved the children. When Marcia continued her diatribes, she attributed her words to the excesses of grief and held her peace, no longer trying to defend herself. Nevertheless, the venomous attacks hurt.

By the time the funeral was over, Marcia's fury had run its course; her bitterness had not.

"I will give you two months to get everything out of this building," she ordered Caroline.

*   *   *

A radiant Ann arrived home, bubbling with the happy experience of Washington and the inauguration.

"Oh, Caroline, you can't imagine how kind Mr. Lincoln is—and how droll and charming. We hear so much about how weighted he is with cares and problems—and his face is always so sad in photographs—I was quite unprepared for him to be so witty and warm—and *funny*. He kept all of us laughing with his outrageous stories. Come and sit down with me, I must tell you the greatest, most fantastic thing of all—"

She drew Caroline to one of the blue velvet settees and clasped both her hands in her own, her eyes brilliant with excitement. "You will never guess—the President had the kindest, most wonderful things to say about Bromley. He said my husband's 'charm and good manners had become legendary in Chicago—' and that it was well known that Brom had 'that greatest gift of all—the knowledge of how to pour oil on troubled waters'—and he had *lovely* things to say about me, too—and—oh, Caroline, the conclusion of the whole thing is that he is giving Brom an Ambassadorship to Anlavia! Of course it's only a little independent country near Spain but we'll love it all the same—and we have only three weeks 'til we must leave."

"You mean—you are going away—?" Caroline said, stunned.

270

Ann sobered a bit.

"Oh, darling, I've been so excited I've not stopped to think of what all this is going to mean. I suppose you won't come with us because of the children. Cannot Kemink and Louise take care of them for a few years—?"

She broke off, covering her lips with her fingers. "How could I have forgotten about Louise? Here I am prattling on like a mindless six year old when you are in mourning. Forgive me."

"I should ask you to forgive *me* for not rejoicing with you immediately," Caroline said, patting her sister's hand, "only I cannot deny I feel rather as if someone had taken a large spoon and stirred my life all about. First Louise dying and now this."

She explained to Ann then what had happened with Marcia. "I don't know what to do or where to turn. The school has been making out financially, but only because Louise gave us her services and free rent. Several of the families can only afford a pittance and a few of the children I took on charity because their need was so great."

"Oh, but the answer is very simple," Ann broke in. "We'll be gone five years—you can move the children here!"

"You're a precious, generous *idiot*," Caroline said. "Can you see a bunch of sticky, rambunctious youngsters wandering about in all this velvet and crystal?"

"Well—we could strip some of the rooms down—"

"I love you for offering, but I couldn't do it, Ann. I know how much your home means to you. I've been figuring and figuring, and I think that if I can find a bigger place and take five more students, their tuitions might cover the new expenses. Only—" she ended with a sigh, "what do I do first? Do I dare rent a building until I'm sure of enough new students to supply the funds? On the other hand, do I dare to interview new students until I'm sure I have a place for them?"

For the next week Caroline tramped through grey slush, searching for a new location. Everything she looked at was too small or too large; too old or too new, too drafty or too airless. When she did find a few places that could have proved suitable, wartime inflation had skyrocketed the rents out of her reach.

Discouraged, she wrote to Marcia Wilhaven asking for an extension of time, but Mrs. Wilhaven was adamant.

Ann was in a flurry of packing. Trunks, hat boxes, and shipping crates were all over the house.

"We'll loan you any amount of money you need," Ann volunteered, full of sympathy for her sister.

"I know," Caroline said, "but I couldn't keep running the school at a deficit on your generosity. I'm sure God wants this work to continue.

271

There must be *some* way. What I really wish," she ruminated, "is that we could get out of Chicago—out into the country where we could raise our own vegetables and the children could have animals and run in the outdoors as they did in Wisconsin—"

Ann clapped her hands in sudden delight. "Oh, I *know* the place! I know just the place! But wait—I must talk to Brom—"

A moment later Caroline could hear their voices rising and falling in what began to sound like a quarrel.

She was at the point of intruding, for she wanted no altercations between them over her affairs, when Ann emerged triumphant.

"Darling, it's settled. We'll make a trip to Wisconsin to see it. There will be just enough time before Brom and I take passage."

"It sounded as if—as if Brom did not approve," Caroline said.

"This is the situation," Ann said. "It's a country estate near a small town called Peshtigo that a friend left in Brom's care while he is away at war. Brom was a little concerned because the man hadn't told him to rent it. But the man's business has gone to ruin in his absence, his funds have been depleted by inflation, and Bromley finally had to agree with me that if we could accumulate some rent for him in his absence, we would be doing him a service."

"I don't know," Caroline demurred. "The war could end at any moment. Brom said at breakfast that Admiral Porter had captured Fort Fisher, which would cut off the last Southern port. People in the South are already paying three hundred dollars for a barrel of flour and using acorns for coffee. The war *can't* go on much longer. We might barely be settled and he would return."

"Brom's friend is a single man. He never lived on the estate. He kept it as an investment. *Believe me*," Ann said with emphatic certitude, "he won't turn you out should the war end. Say you'll at least look at it."

Caroline agreed to inspect the property, but she had a disturbing sense that there was something Ann was not telling her.

57

The minute Caroline saw the estate at Peshtigo Harbour, she understood her sister's enthusiasm. As Ann had predicted, it was perfect for Caroline's needs.

The house was constructed of square hewn logs so nicely adjusted that they seemed a solid block, soft and grey of color and mellow to the eye. The building was over a hundred feet long and a story and a half high. On the western side, a long, low piazza faced the Peshtigo river.

A parlor and reception room opened off a small vestibule. A stairway to the upper rooms was visible from the adjoining dining room.

"Come see the kitchen," Ann called. "It's the best room in the house."

The kitchen had windows along one entire side. They had arrived late in the day and the windows framed a sunset that was twice glorious because it was reflected in the river, and flamed again in reflected splendor on the shining water of Green Bay. Darting game and soaring birds turned the scene into a living picture.

One wall of the room was covered with a fireplace and huge brick oven. A small hallway led to a storeroom and pantry.

Most of the furniture was simple and suitable for children, but a special room to the north had soft carpets, a mahogany table, sofas and chairs of finest damask and a sterling tea set. There was a bedroom off this with a canopied bed and a mahogany chest and chair.

"These two rooms are so tastefully furnished it looks as if the man did live here," Caroline said.

"He used to stay sometimes for vacations. The place was a tavern years back," Ann said. "Brom's friend said itinerant preachers, raftsmen and voyagers have sheltered beneath this roof at one time or another."

Outside there was a spring house to keep things cold, a barn and a chicken house where a few corn cobs could still be seen scattered on the floor. With eyes grown wise from Kemink's tutelage, Caroline noted that there would be wild honey, maple syrup and sugar, hickory nuts, black walnuts, butternuts and hazel nuts. As night approached, she could hear the hoot of owls and the howl of wolves that had become familiar in the Tomorrow River country.

"Oh, Ann, I *do* want it," she conceded. "It is perfect. But surely it's worth much more than I can pay, and then there would be so many other expenses—getting all the children here; buying horses and cows and it's so large, we'd need additional help, more bedding, and we'd have more heating expense—"

"Carrie, you've forgotten something, and in the bustle of getting ready to leave for Europe, we've all forgotten it."

"What's that?" Caroline asked puzzled.

"The gold. The gold your friend left for Jimmy's care. Brom still has it in the safe."

"How could I? How could I have forgotten—?" Caroline began to laugh, tears of relief running down her cheeks at the same time. "All these weeks of anguish and harried figuring—and all the time that gold just *sitting there*."

Both sisters suddenly quoted almost simultaneously, "God moves in mysterious ways, His wonders to perform—"

Still laughing, they waded through the snow back to the waiting sleigh.

*　　*　　*

The sisters had been so busy they had had little time to brood over their impending separation, and suddenly it was upon them.

Even Brom's glasses grew misty as he embraced his sister-in-law at the station.

"I'd still feel better if you'd stay in Chicago," he said. "I feel rotten going off and leaving you without a man to—"

"I'm a man now, Uncle Brom," Danny asserted; then when his voice broke comically in the middle of the sentence, added, "Almost—" and had to laugh at himself.

Brom thumped him on the back. "You'll have to be, Danny. You'll have to be," he said with emotion.

He turned back to Caroline.

"Are you sure you won't let Fly go with us?"

Caroline shook her head. "We'll write often—"

"Will you send me a jeweled fan from Spain like the big ladies have at the opera?" Fly wheedled.

"Ten of them," Brom said, swinging her into one last hug. She had always been his favorite. "To think you'll be thirteen—a young lady when I see you next—"

The train was sounding its bell and the Thorntons had to go. One last inarticulate round of hugs and they were borne off. Caroline and the children watched the train gather speed until they could no longer see it in the distance.

The days that followed were hectic for Caroline. Parents of her students had to be told of the move and reconciled to it. Some of them were not happy to have their children taken so far away, but since it was almost impossible to find another place where such good care and devotion were assured, in the end only one parent withdrew a child.

There were interviews with the parents of prospective students and interviews for additional help.

Many of the Thornton's servants had been with them for years. Caroline could not summarily dismiss them. Positions had to be found commensurate to those they had held. She invited the weeping Bridget to come with them to Peshtigo as cook, but she wanted no part of "those wilds where you can hear the wolves howl—" Charles, too, preferred to retire rather than to move where he might be "required to feed chickens."

The books and equipment of the school had to be packed. At least two trips between Chicago and Peshtigo Harbour would be needed before the move could be accomplished.

There was so much to do that it was the first of April before Caroline was able to attend to her last responsibility in Chicago, supervising the closing up the Thornton house. She found it a melancholy task, covering all the lovely furniture with dust cloths, shrouding all the windows, locking up the silverware and crystal, storing the clothes not taken to Europe. But while she was about it, news arrived in the city that Richmond had fallen at last. Chicago went wild.

People surged into the streets crying and weeping, shouting and singing. Bonfires flared and cannons boomed all through the night, while church bells pealed an accompaniment from a hundred belfrys.

Caroline, drawn irresistibly into the streets was swept along in the emotion-whipped crowds. She could not help but think of another night not unlike this one when Bay's strong arms had held her protectively and carried her off to safety.

The war was as good as over—and a period of her life was ending as well. Suddenly she found herself laughing and crying along with all strangers who shoved, jostled, embraced, pushed and screamed about her in that unforgettable night.

*   *   *

From the barred windows of the Libby Prison in Richmond, the event the Chicago citizens jubilantly celebrated appeared to Baird LeSeure as a veritable hell.

The departing Southerners had set fire to their warehouses and government properties. The flames had spread unchecked until the

275

Union Army arrived and began an attempt to halt the destruction. Lawless mobs had pillaged, wrecked and robbed. Drunkenness was rampant in the streets; wine ran as freely as had the blood of both sides.

On April 4th, when the key was finally turned in their prison lock, and Bay and his surviving fellow officers were released, the city was acrid and blackened, still smoldering, glittering with broken glass and strewn with debris of every description. At that it seemed a fitting enough end to nearly two years of prison horror.

In the heat of the afternoon, Bay watched with a sense of unreality, as Lincoln rode through the street, hosannaed by the negroes who saw him as a saviour.

When he stepped from his carriage, an old black woman threw herself at his feet.

Lincoln lifted her up, embarrassed by this near deification. "Kneel only to God—" he pleaded.

And Bay, every bone protruding sharply beneath his prison pale skin, wondered how anyone could still believe in God.

58

Richmond was in flames, and by April 7th, Lee's dwindling, exhausted army was almost encircled and near starvation. The Southern general knew that even if his men could maintain their morale against these impossible odds, their bodies could not. He agreed to meet Grant at Appomattox, Virginia, on Palm Sunday, April 9th and there he surrendered.

The Union soldiers were massed in firm, well-disciplined lines. The Southerners, their grey and butternut uniforms fluttering in tatters from their gaunt frames, were scarecrow figures as they moved with the sag of weariness and defeat to lay down their arms. Regiment by regiment they advanced to stack their guns teepee style and divest themselves of their cartridges.

The Union soldiers watched with gravity and respect as the battered, bloodstained Confederate flags were reverently folded and laid down.

276

Tears dripped without shame down the combat-worn faces of many of the rebel soldiers; a few sobbed outright.

With unexpected sensitivity to the sensibilities of the brave Southern remnant, Grant forbade a victory cannonade. This man who had been so hard, so intractable a foe, proved magnanimous in victory.

The Southern soldiers who had horses or mules were allowed to keep them. "They will need them to plant crops—" Grant said. The officers were permitted to keep their side-arms, and the Southerners were assured of complete cessation of bitterness—there would be no treason trials.

Though Kirby Smith would hold on for months yet—thousands would still die in battle at Blakely, Alabama—and Jefferson Davis, the Confederate President, clutching his archive papers would attempt to escape and keep the Confederacy alive in his own fanatically dedicated person until August—the war to all real intents and purposes was over. The United States would not be fragmented. They would reunite as one nation "from sea to shining sea"—and the black man had gained, at least on paper, his freedom.

Six days later, the stars and stripes was raised once more over Fort Sumter where the carnage had all begun. Strangely, on the same day the curtain came down forever on Lincoln's great role. A bullet fired by John Wilkes Booth at the Ford Theatre proved fatal.

*   *   *

Bay had had a recurrence of malaria immediately upon his return to camp in July of '63, severe enough to place him in the Army hospital in Washington, D.C. His step-mother was duly informed, but it was not part of the responsibility of the War Department to see that all of a soldier's friends be informed as well. So, while he had rolled in sweats of delirium, Caroline's letters lay unopened and unread. They were forwarded to D.C. just as Bay recovered, was sent back to join his regiment advancing on Fredericksburg. It was part of the fortunes of war that he never received them. He had been captured at Fredericksburg and spent the rest of the war interned in the dark Libby warehouse in Richmond which had been pressed into service as a prison for nearly a thousand Union officers.

Though hundreds of letters, packages and gifts arrived daily, the prisoners had received little of the mail. The South was too much in need to allow their foes to feast while they famished. Often the prisoners had seen their packages stacked outside the prison until their captors could take advantage of whatever spoils they contained. So Bay had speculated that he might have had packages or letters from the Thorntons, Caroline or other friends he didn't receive.

He arrived in Chicago the first of May and went directly to Bromley's office. He was not surprised to find everything locked and bolted. Many offices were closed for the day. Lincoln's body was lying in state in the city, and Chicago was in mourning. The city was draped in black, flags were hanging everywhere at half-mast, and endless processions filed slowly up the long marble stairs to pay their last respects to the deceased president.

Bay hired a carriage and gave the Thornton address, his heart beating harder than it ever had in battle. Two years had passed since he had seen Caroline. He wondered what life had dealt to her while he had stultified behind prison bars—in what ways she might have changed. At the same time, he began to feel a joyous impatience to see all of them, the Thorntons, Firefly, Danny, Kemink, Dan-Pete. They were as close to family as he had.

As soon as the carriage stopped in front of the Thornton Manse he sensed something wrong. The house had an empty, closed look. He walked to the front door with a gathering apprehensiveness. He could see now that the windows were shrouded, the walk unswept. *Perhaps they have gone on their summer vacation already,* he thought, but tried the door bell anyway. He walked to the rear of the house and tried the back door, hoping that at least one servant might have stayed behind. There was no answer. He stood for a moment in dejection listening to the twitter of birds and the rush of May wind in the newly budded trees. The soul-less feeling of the uninhabited house seeped into him with searing disappointment.

He tried Doris Dormeister's home next.

"Madam has gone to pay her last respects to the President—" the butler explained icily before edging the door shut in his face.

His next try was more fruitful. Nelia Fitzpatrick opened the door herself. She was wearing apple green silk and her red hair was piled high except for ringlets which dangled devastatingly in front of each ear.

Her green eyes widened to a stare and then she said tentatively, "Bay—?" and grasped his hands to draw him inside, *"Bay—it is you!* Dear man, you look terrible. You've shaved off your beard and moustache and you're so thin!"

"And you look as gorgeous as ever," he laughed.

"Bay, what did they do to you? You're nothing but bones! We've all been so worried—no one has had a word from you. Do come in and sit down. No—here, by me."

"I've been in a Confederate prison. Actually, I've fared rather well. I was one of the few officers who didn't lose any teeth. Some of them

278

lost all their teeth."

"Oh, I don't want to hear about it," Nelia cried, clapping her pretty white hands over her ears. "The important thing is you're back."

"Do you know where the Thornton's are, Nelia? I stopped at their house and it was all closed up."

"They've gone off to Europe. He's been appointed as an ambassador to some obscure country. I can never remember the name, but it's somewhere near Spain."

"Brom an ambassador—that's a surprise, and yet, I would think it would be his forte. How he used to enjoy a good political fray at his table, always without getting sweated himself—"

"Sweated—?"

"I beg your pardon, Nelia. A prison is not the greatest environment to keep a man's language socially polished."

"But we're not going to talk about prison or the war. Promise. It depresses me too much. It seems I've heard nothing else for years."

"All right. I promise. And Caroline—did Caroline go with the Thorntons?"

"Caroline?—oh, Mrs. Quimby. No, she didn't. She isn't in Chicago anymore, though," Nelia's long lashes fell like dark fans over her luminous green eyes. "I'm not sure—but yes, yes, I think her husband came back from the war and they went off somewhere—but I can't say where."

Bay was quiet for such a long time that the dark lashes swept upward again so the green eyes could study him.

"Aren't you going to ask about *me*, Bay?"

"Darling, Nelia, yes—tell me about *you*."

"I'm still not married—not even engaged."

"Unbelievable. How have you kept off the hoards of young men?"

"I've been waiting for you, Bay."

He shook his head and laughed. "You flatter me."

"Bay, don't tease me. I'm utterly and completely serious. All the men I know have seemed absolute boys after you. You're the only man who has ever really stirred me."

"Nelia, I never meant it to be anything but fun between us. Surely you can't have laid down your heart for me when there were always so many others, and when we both took our relationship so lightly."

"Well, there it is, my living breathing heart," Nelia insisted.

"I'm afraid I am anything but husband material right now. I am broke, my business will have to be resurrected from cold ashes, and as you say, I look terrible and I confess I feel worse. Along with weariness and cynicism I am suffering from malaria and malnutrition."

"Ahhh, no."

"Ahhh, I'm afraid, yes."

"Damn you Bay," Nelia said, leaping to her feet, "it's humiliating enough to have to propose to you, but to be turned down so tongue in cheek is insupportable."

"Nelia, be realistic. Everything I said is true. You would hate being married to a poor man and you'd despise a sick one."

She sighed. "Yes, it is true you look awful—and it is true I would hate being poor and I can't abide sick people—but tell me, then, why I *still want you?*"

"You only think you do."

"Tell me just one more thing, Bay. If you are in such terrible shape and are such poor husband material, why were you so anxious to know where Caroline Quimby was—?"

"I wanted to know where the Thorntons were, too."

"You're in love with her, aren't you? And you don't even care that she's *married.*"

"I care."

"If Caroline Quimby was so stupid as to throw herself at your feet as I have, none of the excuses you gave to me would stand in the way, would they, Bay?"

"That was a question as pointed as a stiletto, young lady, and at this point I am figuratively bleeding all over your Persian rug."

Bay stood up. He took Nelia's hand and kissed it. "You are right. I owe you a straight answer. Yes, I am in love with Caroline Quimby. I have tried for three years to quell my unrequited passion and still it flames. But if she were here this minute—and free—I wouldn't have anything to offer her. It seems you and I both want what we can't have. A typical human idiosyncracy."

All the gaiety had drained from his face, leaving it with a desolation Nelia would not have imagined.

"Bay, I didn't mean to hurt you when you've just come home—but after all, you've hurt me too," Nelia pouted.

"You're an adorable child, and I'm inconsolable if I've hurt you. I'm comforted only by the realization that you are much too lovely to languish long. In fact, I see two young men coming up the walk at this very moment—"

"Bay—will I see you again soon?"

"I think not. I believe I will go South."

"South?"

"I've had a letter from my step-mother describing herself in desperate straits and she must be if she is pleading with me to come home. There's your bell."

"Oh, bother! If you want to stay longer, I'll get rid of them."

"No, dear. I was leaving anyway."

"Bay—"

He turned back, hat in hand.

"I'm not absolutely sure about Caroline. I think I heard something to that effect," her eyes fell again. "I could be mistaken."

"All facts taken into consideration, I guess it doesn't make a great deal of difference, does it?" Bay said. "Goodbye and good luck."

"Bay—"

But he was already bowing to the young men waiting at the front door.

"Damn it, I didn't want you anyway," Nelia said, but her eyes were filling with tears of pique.

Pleading a headache, she speedily got rid of her visitors and retired to her bedroom. From the bottom drawer of a jewelry box she extracted a letter in Caroline Quimby's handwriting.

"—Enclosed you will find the Thornton's new address and my own. We would be so grateful if you will let us know of Bay's health and well-being as soon as you have word. We remain concerned—"

Nelia tore the letter into a hundred tiny pieces.

59

In his rented carriage, Bay unfolded and reread the letter he had received from his step-mother, not on the crested stationery of old, but penned in shaky script in faded homemade ink on fool'scap.

"My Dear Baird,

"I have received word from the Union government that you have been a Southern prisoner most of this long cruel war, and have now been released and are free to return home. I never hid my sentiments regarding your defection to the North, but I am ready to lay aside recriminations and past rancors and beg that you do the same— for we are in desperate straits here and unless you come to our aid, I mistrust we can survive.

"If you will not do it in the name of your dear father, who sacrificed more than you will ever realize or understand to admit you to your heritage, then do it in the memory of Lilliane, for whom you sincerely had affection, I believe, if for any of us.

"Ever since your terrible Admiral Farragut destroyed our protecting flotilla and took New Orleans, we have known nothing but suffering. The city has been under martial law with the Union General Ben Butler in control, known by all and sundry as "Beast" Butler, so despicable has he been. He went so far as to issue a proclamation that if our ladies did not beam and smile at their captors, they would be treated as common women of the street—and one man was hanged without clemency for no worse crime than affixing a Confederate flag to one of our public buildings.

"But the greatest blow this past year has been the desertion of most of our negroes. Those who have remained with me are so old or so young or so ill or so inept that they are a burden rather than a help to me.

"I'm an old and broken woman, Baird. I cannot plant the fields alone. We have no money, no fuel, almost no food. I would that I had died along with your dear father rather than live to see the day when the windows of Fairlane are broken, stuffed with rags for want of better repair and the roof coming apart above our heads. We have one pig left, no mules, no horses, no cows. I have pawned and sold priceless paintings, candlesticks and furniture for flour and corn to keep my remaining help alive. Except for a few pieces of furniture, everything, even my jewels, are gone.

"I beg you to allay old wounds and in the memory of your father and Lilliane to come to me in all speed, not for myself, but for those who depend upon me.

Importunately, your step-mother,
Roxelle LeSeure"

Bay folded the letter again with an audible sigh. He could well imagine how it must have galled his proud stepmother to write it. He was tired and ill. His lungs ached with each breath and at night he was subject to recurrent bouts of shivering, sweating malarial fever. The last thing he felt like doing was to take on the responsibility of a penurious and dependent Southern household, but he could not find it in himself to ignore his step-mother's pathetic plea. There seemed little left to keep him in the North. He gathered the meagre papers and resources still at his Chicago office and booked passage the next day on a steamship to New Orleans.

He felt as if someone had set a heavy weight on his heart—so heavy that at any moment it might simply stop beating. No one on the ship would have guessed it. Dressed impeccably as always, he made all the ladies laugh and blush with his extravagant compliments; he sang and played games with the children; drank and played cards and roulette with the men. Bay belonged to that line of cynics who, finding the world an unexplainable, bitter, and painful place, refuse to add their cavil and cry to the already overflowing kettle of anguish. His defense against poverty, heartbreak, broken dreams and the agonies of the world was laughter. He would take nothing seriously.

One older woman saw through his defense. Watching him in an unguarded moment as he stood at the rail staring at the passing river, she said, "Poor lad, he is so alone and so ill—" and those who only a moment before had seen him waltzing and laughing with the belle of the ship thought she was daft.

Bay had once alleged that he wanted no part of the South or her institutions. He had always felt alienated from his Southern peers, but he was moved by what he saw when he landed at New Orleans on the way to Fairlane. The roads were thronged with ragged soldiers, many mutilated, hobbling wearily back to homes that sat disintegrating in rank weeds. He gave several bewildered blacks a ride in his carriage. A few of them were on their way back to plantations they had jubilantly deserted only weeks before.

Roxelle had made a vain attempt to maintain a proud facade for his arrival. She had rouged her sunken cheeks and fastened an aigrette in her fading curls, but it is difficult to be regal and dignified in a shrunken dress that reveals flapping carpet slippers and bare ankles. His shock at seeing the frail, withered woman who had replaced his once elegant step-mother could not entirely be hidden. At the expression on his face, she started to cry and then did what she had never done in all the years before. She threw her arms around him, sobbing, "Thank God, you have come. Thank God, you are here, Baird."

Drying her tears on an old piece of flannel, she said, "I know that in the past we have had our differences and that I was often unbending and unkind, Baird. It was gracious of you to put it behind and to come—" then the tears flooded again.

"I'm doing you no favor," Bay said lightly. "I've got bronchitis and malaria and I need a place to get well or die—this seemed as good as any."

His step-mother's face was a study. She had looked to him for salvation. Was he after all going to be only another burden on her already failing strength?

Bay gave her shoulder a reassuring pat. "Don't worry, I'm ambulatory and I've got some money. Tomorrow I'll buy a mule and we'll start the spring plowing."

"Oh—yes! I had Hannah brew some mint tea. You all come and

sit a spell now and get refreshed from your journey," Roxelle said, like a little girl suddenly remembering her manners.

Slap—slap—slap—her slippers flogged the rugless floor ahead of him, leading the way into the parlor, shuttered dark, bare, stripped of all former luxuries as she had written. It was like seeing the skeleton of a once beautiful woman.

"It's dark in here," Bay said, fighting a stifling feeling of depression. "Let's open the shutters and let in some light."

"The windows are all broken," Roxelle said dispiritedly.

"Have Hannah bring some candles then. I'm not going to sit in the dark."

"We have only a few left."

"Bring them anyway. We'll buy more tomorrow—and we'll buy a twenty pound goose and invite all your friends over—"

Roxelle's eyes shifted evasively. "Well—I don't know, Bay—"

"That's what everyone needs," Bay declared, "a little joy and festivity. We'll invite the Precotts and the DeWeise's and your friend, Julia Lee."

Roxelle looked down at her bare ankles. "I don't think you quite understand, Baird," she said delicately. "There are those who aren't as forgivin' as I am—about you serving the North. You'll not let abusing tongues upset you overmuch, will you?" she pleaded. "I mistrust that anyone would come to any party of ours."

"I see."

Later she took him to Lilliane's old room. "You'd best sleep here. It's the only one left with a feather tick and no roof leaks."

The room was shadowy and cold. The flowers on the wallpaper that had once made it seem like a bower were faded to ghosts as faint and faraway as the two children who had once clung together there in tender and precarious friendship. There was little left of Lilliane's presence in the room. When his step-mother had gone, Bay ran a slow reflective finger over the jewsharp that still sat on the dresser. He picked up a small picture of Lilliane in its tarnished frame and looked into the eyes of—*Caroline*.

With a stifled cry he sank on the bed, his face contorted.

"I think her husband came back from the war and they went off together somewhere—"

He saw his own hands as if they were the hands of a stranger straining the bedspread in a grip so fierce that the cloth threatened to rip. He loosened his fingers and closed his eyes.

What madness, he thought to himself, *to go on loving her like this.*

He lay back on the bed staring up at the ceiling. He could hear a rush of rain starting outside falling across the earth. He could feel

the rush of fever starting to heat through his body again. His mind waded, struggled up through the burnished pain of soul and body—
Tomorrow he would buy a mule—

*   *   *

The final ascent to the cemetery was so steep and rocky Adam and Sally had to abandon the carriage and go by foot. Hardened by his years of combat, Adam easily reached the top and had to wait as Sally, hampered by her corset and high heeled boots, puffed her way laboriously to join him. He had not waited for her or offered assistance. He stood, a lonely figure on the hillside that smelled of the hot sun-struck rocks and the wild cucumber they had bruised beneath their feet.

"There it is," Sally said, mopping her forehead, and pointing at a modest white cross protruding from a small mound of rocks.

Adam drew closer. His face was grey as he studied the inscription burned into the cross. Garth Quimby 1861-1863. For a moment lines of bitterness distorted his handsome features. He looked like an old, old, man.

Sally stared at him frightened.

"Adam—you takin' it hard?" she blurted. "I never thought you even wanted him."

"I didn't Sally—and then I did," he said, in a dead, heavy voice. "—so that now—it's like a punishment. I feel as if I had killed my own son. Can you understand that?"

"How could you kill him? You wasn't even here," Sally said.

He turned away from her with a sigh and sank down on a boulder that had bruted it's way up through the hard-baked soil.

"For four years I've seen nothing but death, death and more death. I'm so sick of death, Sally. You come to wear an armour as a defense— a protection—and finally the armour grows so thick and tough it becomes another kind of death—a prison you can't get out of. When the war ended, it was early spring—green—living things sprouting all around us—everywhere new beginnings. I wanted a new beginning too, Sally—"

"Well, you got one!" Sally said in a rush of enthusiasm, throwing herself down by his knees. "Great Aunt Nellie, Adam—we're rich! We can leave this crummy town—go to San Francisco—buy us a big fancy house, be real so-cie-ty! There ain't nothin' we want that we can't have—"

He looked down at her flushed and eager face with as much compassion as he had ever felt for her, mingled with a private anguish as he realized that he could never convey to her—never make her understand—that the new beginning his soul ached for was not something that could be bought with money.

He took her hand with more tenderness than he had ever shown her before.

"Sally, I dreamed of bringing up the child to be—what I somehow failed to become. Well—anyway—we can have another child"

Now it was her face that turned grey. She stood up abruptly, shaking the dust off the ruffles of her skirt.

"It may be spring, but it's still chilly up here when the wind blows. Let's go down, Adam. Don't help none sittin' and lookin' at a cross anyway."

"I want him to have a stone," Adam said. "A fine granite stone."

"Sure, angels and doves and whatever you say—" she was already hurrying down the trail.

The Golden Nugget gave a big party that night to celebrate Adam's return. Champagne flowed as the band played "Oh, Dem Golden Slippers" and "Celementine."

Doctor Leo Jennet was one of the few people in town who did not turn out for the celebration. He preferred absinthe to champagne and his own company to that of the people who congregated at the Nugget. He sat alone in his office which was connected to his adobe house, a man of moldy elegance, everything about him thin and precise, summed up by the hair line moustache that traced his almost lipless mouth. Beneath a green shaded light he was reading. He started when the door to his office suddenly burst open. Sally Magee Quimby flurried toward him in a rush of red taffeta urgency.

"Doc Jennet—you've gotta take my appendix out—*tonight.*"

"What nonsense, Sally," he countered with a dry smile. "I examined you less than a week ago and your appendix was perfect."

"For cryin' out loud—don't be such a dumb ox," I want you to take care—of other things—while you're at it." She averted her eyes.

"An unwanted pregnancy—?"

She gave him a furious look.

"Whatdya think I am? A loose woman? I been true to Adam," she fumed.

"Ahh—well, forgive me dear lady. But you will have to explain 'other things'. I should hate to open up your abdomen and not know why."

"You gotta fix it so I can't never get pregnant no more."

"I see."

"Well, I don't know if you do or not. I gotta good reason. Adam and I had a kid before and it wasn't right. He had a kid with his first wife—same way. Now you can't blame me for not wanting no more bummed up kids. I ain't taking that chance."

"Yes. And Adam—how does he feel about it?"

"He ain't to know. He ain't never to know. I told him the kid was perfect. Y'understand? He never knew."

"Hmmm—yes," the doctor said noncommittally.

Sally plunged a kidskin pouch filled with gold dust on the desk in front of him.

"I want it done tonight and I want it called an emergency operation on my appendix. Y'understand?"

He picked the pouch up in his thin fingers and caressed it, smiling his thin smile.

"No trouble at all, Sally. I will take care of everything. We'll need a nurse. But not Mrs. Jameson. She's too well versed, too clever. Mama Tutu would do fine. Someone to hold the lamp and keep things washed up—"

"Will—will it hurt very much?" Sally faltered for a moment.

"Enough," he said, "but you've got lots of grit Sally and I've got lots of laudanum. Between the two we'll make out fine."

Sally Quimby's healthy pink appendix was duly deposited in a glass jar in an upper room of the Gold Nugget where the operation was performed. And like the doctor before him, Doctor Jennet mysteriously left town soon after.

Adam came and sat dutifully by Sally's bedside at intervals during her period of recovery, but he was sulky.

"Some homecoming. Couldn't you have had this taken care of before?"

Sally looked at him with eyes that were tired and blank.

"I never thought about it," she said honestly.

For several weeks she felt lethargic and listless. The operation had taken more out of her than she had expected. But when Adam finally agreed to her constant importunities to move to 'Frisco and tackle high so-cie-ty (as Sally always put it) she regained some of her buoyancy.

Early in July they left Columbia in high style. The mine would continue to pump out an avalanche of wealth to support them in a style to which they hoped to become accustomed. Sally was thinking about velvet portieres and French underclothes. Adam was thinking about a matched pair of chestnut geldings—and somewhere, far back in his consciousness, a weathering white cross on a sun-baked hill.

PART III

PESHTIGO AND HARBOUR HILL

Bring ye all the tithes into the storehouse,
that there may be meat in mine house,
and prove me now herewith, saith the
Lord of hosts, if I will not
open you the windows of heaven,
and pour you out a blessing,
that there shall not be room enough
to receive it.

Malachi

60

Caroline liked the Peshtigo area. Chicago society had never been sure what to make of her. As a woman neither single nor married, carving out a living at what amounted to a trade (a genteel trade, to be sure, but still a trade) some of the upper crust had never felt quite comfortable in accepting her on their own level. On the other hand, since she was the sister of Ann Thornton, it had been unthinkable to treat her as a domestic either. The fact that she had been seen openly with Bay LeSeure, unmarried and highly eligible, had added a tinge of the scandalous. No such qualms or niceties colored her acceptance in the Peshtigo area. It was a thriving, lively, growing lumber area. One could pause at almost any time of day and hear a hammer ringing somewhere. The Belgian and Scandinavian farmers who had fought in the Civil War were returning home full of plans and ambitions. New barns and houses and a grist mill were going up. Lumbering was turning into a large enterprise. A new mill had been built nearby by a family named Williamson, and logging companies were hiring men by the hundreds.

Caroline had learned to drive the team, and she enjoyed driving into town for supplies or to have chicken feed ground. The clerks greeted her as if she were a family friend, dispensing local gossip along with her kerosene or yard goods, exhibiting a keen interest in her affairs as well so there would be something to pass along to the next customer.

Soon after her arrival, a story had been circulated that she was the widow of a Civil War officer, and as she had never taken the pains to deny the story, it was generally accepted as fact. Several gentlemen had polished up and driven out with visions of courting the pretty widow, but after finding out, as one gentleman put it, "she had such a passel of children like you niver did see!" had returned discouraged.

The truth was that with or without twenty children, Caroline could have wed again if she had been inclined to. There were three men to every woman in this raw lumbering community and not all of them were as easily discouraged as the man in the story bantered about. But her heart was still tender from lacerations left by Adam and Bay and in a certain sense, even by Cricket. She wanted no more emotional involvements. She threw herself into reconstructing the long-vacant property, which the children had christened "Harbour Hill." There were moments of intense loneliness and burgeoning need—moments

291

when the moonlight shining in trembling bands across the river elicited a nameless hurt—but she learned these moments passed. She accepted the pain, endured it, knowing it would not last. As she told Kemink, twenty children, five pigs, two helpers, twelve cows, forty chickens, six geese and three horses, her life was full to the "point of rupture."

She was hearing the smaller children's lessons one summer day when she glanced out the window and noticed a ragged youth coming down the drive on a decrepit looking mule. "Another boy on his way home from the war," she thought. She turned to tell Dan-Pete to have the cook set something out for the returning soldier and then thought better of it. The least she could do was to tend to his needs personally.

"Enough for today," she told her little class. "The older children are making cottage cheese in the dairy if you'd like to watch."

They scrambled off giggling as Caroline made her way to the kitchen to see what she could find for the young soldier. She never doubted that he would stop. She had fed dozens of returning boys. Always they sought the back door, seeming to feel that their appearance did not justify their entrance into the front hall.

With quick instructions to Jenny, she prepared a cloth over the kitchen table and set it neatly. "The best," she thought to herself, "is none too good for these men."

Half listening for the expected knock on the door, she began to warm up the bit of left-over roast and sent Jenny to get some cream.

"These boys have not been too well nourished and this one looks as if he had been traveling for a long time," Caroline said. "Bring plenty."

Jenny hurried off and Caroline, pausing by the door the cook had left ajar, felt her heart beat with pity at what she saw. A young boy, not yet eighteen, was huddled on the bottom step. His mule grazed over the lawn as if it too was starved. She ran down the steps toward him.

Jenny halted halfway to her errand to turn back with a word of caution to her mistress. "Careful, Ma'am, you know how these boys arrive—so many vermin it's a wonder it's not carried off they are."

The boy looked up. His face was thin and wasted, covered with dust, but he gave her an engaging grin. The grin nudged the door of memory.

"Joshua!" she cried, "It's *you*."

"I come a far piece to find you," he said.

"Have you been home? Does your mother know you're all right?"

"Yup, I been home, but they wouldn't let me keep Jeremy."

"Jeremy?"

292

His white teeth shone again in the dust of his face. "My mule, Jeremy. You s'pect you could keep the two of us on a bit?"

The mule was chomping as if intending to eat the entire lawn.

Caroline felt a grin ease over her own face. "Of course we can keep you on. If you know how I prayed you'd get through all this without harm! Come in, come in, I've got the table set for you and the roast is probably burning. I'll call Dan-Pete and have him put your mule in the barn."

"Well, I guess not without special instructions," Joshua said, rolling his eyes. "That mule is a bit unusual."

"He seems content where he is for the time being," Caroline said.

Between gigantic bites of bread and meat and swallows of milk, Joshua explained about Jeremy.

"We was fighting by the Chicamauga in Northern Virginia trying to take a ridge. I got lost off from the rest somehow and whooee, there was grapeshot and balls flying every which ways. I swear I'd got killed sure if this old mule hadn't come traipsing out from some underbrush. He was a pretty skinny, sorrowful looking beast, 'n looked even worse cause he had this raggedy ol' bearskin coat strapped on him like a saddle. But right then he looked like Salvation. I pret near flew onto him 'n he took off like he knew somethin' 'n got us both outta there. I was pretty grateful for him saving my life that way, but the next day when I tried to ride him he like to killed me. I had taken that old coat off to use for a bed roll and it took me some trial 'n error 'fore I found out the only way you can ride him is with that moldy ol' coat thrown over him."

Everyone at Harbour Hill soon became attached to Jeremy, peculiarities and all. The little mule carried the youngsters docilely on his back—as long as no one broke the rule involving the fur coat. Joshua kept it hanging on a peg next to his stall and when anyone intended riding, he remembered to put on the coat or soon came dashing back out to the tune of Jeremy's heels. He could be a vicious looking creature with his ears laid back, eyes rolling and heels flying, but if his demands were met, he was a wonderful pet. Visitors sometimes thought it strange, a child riding about on a mule that had a moth-eaten coat for a blanket in the middle of the summer.

Joshua's spindly, wearied look disappeared rapidly. He enjoyed being the hero of the Harbour Hill brood. He told such blood and thunder tales of his war adventures that sometimes Caroline was tempted to stifle his eloquence for fear he would cause the younger children to have nightmares. But remembering earlier days when he could not have spoken two lines without stuttering, she held her peace and thanked God for his new confident flamboyance, though she suspected that most of his tales were made up. She had long ago noticed that those soldiers who had really been in the *thick* of the fighting at Gettysburg or Fredericksburg or other battles seldom cared to recount the experience. They had a certain look in their eyes and a reticence with everyone except those comrades who had shared their hardships. Caroline guessed that the closest Joshua had come to real battles was at Chickamauga where he had picked up Jeremy. But in his own way he had "seen the elephant" and she did not rob him of his glory.

"I wish I'd been there!" Dan-Pete said enviously.

"I'm glad I wasn't," Danny still insisted. His desire to be a doctor had gained impetus since they had come to Peshtigo, for he had met Doc Fleishmann, a local druggist, who doubled as a physician. Fleishmann, a quiet spoken, dark-eyed man, welcomed the boy's company on his rounds.

At Harbour Hill, Danny had his own "patients." Emily was still his special concern and he added Jimmy. Caroline had finally gained the trust of Adam's little son, but her responsibilities were so many and so varied she often lacked the time she would have liked to devote to him. Danny took up the slack. Since Jimmy was not yet able to walk well, Danny took him everywhere pig-a-back. It was a common sight to see Danny bringing up the cows or mending the fence with Jimmy on his shoulders or back.

The summer was a long one for Caroline, full of making hay, preserving, teaching, rebuilding. She had taken the elegant bedroom off the sitting room at Kemink's insistence, and sometimes at the close of the day when the children were sleeping and the moon was turning the river silver, she wondered a little about the man who owned Harbour Hill. The war was over. He might return at any time and what then? Would he take the estate away from them after all the hard work and improvements?

She felt his presence in the room. His books lined the walls—Voltair, Cellini, Emerson, Balzac. A white ruffled shirt hung in the closet. The drawers smelled of bay rum.

But summer drifted into autumn, winter came, spring, another summer, yet no one had come to take Harbour Hill away from her.

61

For the first time Danny, Dan-Pete, and Felicity attended a public school. Indian children in the Sugar Bush and Peshtigo area didn't attend school, and Dan-Pete was quickly subjected to the blunt, abrasive pain of prejudice. The young Indian boy had a passionate and sensitive nature, and he would have found the school climate insupportable if he had not had Danny as a staunch companion. Dan-Pete was able to remain untouched for many months by the jibes, petty cruelties and indignities directed his way. But a day came in late spring of his second year at the school when his simmering anger boiled up. He had coped with the attacks against himself, but one of the boys laughed disparagingly and called Kemink a "stupid old squaw."

That was too much for Dan-Pete. He landed on the detractor like a wildcat. He was a strong, agile and quick boy, but he had not realized that six or eight of the biggest white boys would counter his attack en masse. To make matters worse, Danny had stayed home that day. Dan-Pete was alone in his battle, outnumbered beyond hope.

Not content with bruising and beating him, his opponents dragged him to a sapling in the yard and "tied him to a stake" as they put it. They smeared his face with mud for "war paint" and stuck pine branches in his hair for "feathers," all the while mocking him and making fun of him.

Even that was not the worst. The worst was dealt to him not by his enemies, but by Felicity. Along with the other girls in the school who witnessed the indignities, she giggled and laughed. *That* was the spear in his side; *that* was the gall in his throat.

With a Samson-like burst of rage, he broke loose from the sapling and his tormentors. He leaped over the picket fence surrounding the school and ran down the dusty road with their derisive laughter trailing him like tin cans tied to a dog's tail.

When he had reached the sanctuary of home, this boy who had been taught since infancy never to cry buried his mud stained face in his mother's lap and wept.

"Fly laughed at me, Mother. She laughed along with all the rest."

Kemink's hands lay gently on her son's head. "To her shame, not yours, Dan-Pete," she tried to comfort him.

"I always stood up for *her*," he sobbed. "I always cared for her."

"I know," Kemink said, remembering that long ago time when,

hardly bigger than a tadpole, he had rushed out to try to stop Adam from carrying her off, "but Fly is still only a little girl, Dan-Pete. Her soul has much growing to do. Let your soul be large enough to forgive."

"I'll never go back to that school," Dan-Pete raged, done with tears. He bounded to his feet, his head flung back. "They call me a 'breed'."

Kemink nodded, a sad smile curving her lips. "There will always be people who will try to make you ashamed because two bloods flow in your veins, my son. But I am not ashamed of the love I felt for your father or the love he felt for me. Few people of any race are given the kind of joy that sang through us. The fruit of that joy and love cannot be less than good. Be proud Dan-Pete that in you are melded the strengths of two great peoples."

"I would cut the white part of me out with a knife if I could," Dan-Pete fumed.

"Do not condemn all white people as those ignorant boys condemn all Indians," Kemink chided. "When you were too small to make a choice, I made it for you. But all the same, I think it is time for you to learn more of your Menominee heritage. We will go this summer to my people. We will return for a time to Tomorrow River. You will learn the ways of your grandfather."

The shine of fury in Dan-Pete's eyes was replaced by the sparkle of excitement. "Do you mean it, Mother? Do you really mean it?"

"I mean it. Aunt Caroline is well settled at Harbour Hill now. She can spare us for a time."

When Felicity learned that Dan-Pete was going away for the summer, she was chagrined.

"I'm sorry I laughed at you, Dan-Pete," she apologized. "Inside I was ashamed. I know if Danny would have been there, *he* wouldn't have laughed."

He looked at her woeful face and knew she was truly sorry. All the same she had left a scar.

When they embarked in their canoe from the dock at Harbour Hill, Kemink had exchanged her white garb for a long doeskin dress. She looked much slimmer, more regal, in her Indian dress, a beaded headband securing her black braids only slightly streaked with grey. Dan-Pete noted with pride how expertly she handled the canoe, how straight her back, how graceful her stroke, as they glided down the Bay then into the Fox on their way to Tomorrow River and the Thunder people. He sensed how greatly his mother was moved to be going back to the land of her birth, traveling again on the fairy waters between green trees burdened with clusters of birds, surrounded with wind-swayed flowers. He felt his own heart swell with emotion as his eyes caught barely remembered landmarks at Weyauwega and Gills Landing.

On the last day of their journey, around twilight, they began to hear drums. Kemink turned to him, her eyes shining.

"I will tell you the message of the drums," she said. "The drums say, 'Behold! Down the River of Tomorrow comes the son of the daughter of the great Menominee Chief Pow-wa-ga-nien. Down the River of Tomorrow comes Kemink, mother of the grandson of the great Chief Pow-wa-ga-nien. Come let us honor those who carry the blood of wise Pow-wa-ga-nien.' "

When they came at last to the camp and a great assemblage was gathered on the bank to meet them, the bruises on Dan-Pete's soul were sweetly soothed. Whatever the white boys at the Peshtigo school might say or think, it was evident that in her own land with her own people his mother was a great and honored personage, and he, too, was not without honor.

They were greeted ceremoniously by Sashwatka, who had been given the leadership of the tribe in Kemink's place since Chief Pow-wa-ga-nien's only other issue, a son, had died.

Sashwatka's hair had turned silvery, but he was still straight and tall, his eyes fierce in their dark beauty. He had married a good natured, broad-faced young woman who had filled his wigwam with four sons. He welcomed Kemink and Dan-Pete warmly to his lodge.

That evening there was a feast of venison and possum in their honor, eaten by the flaring light of torches and campfires. Dan-Pete fell asleep on a bed of pine needles and wolf skins, exhausted and content. But Kemink's heart was too full for sleep. When the last campfire diminished to winking coals, she rose and walked along the edge of the water. She listened to the sad call of the loons and watched the quick-silver moon swim in liquid crescents to her feet. After a time Sashwatka joined her.

"It is good to have you here," he said.

"It is good to be here. This land replenishes me."

"Have things been well with you?"

"They have been well. And you?"

"Well enough. There is ever trouble with the whites. The hearts of some of our young burn. But there will be other days to talk about that—not tonight."

The loon laughed now—wickedly, and there was a flutter of owl wings above their heads.

Sashwatka looked intently at Kemink, his face carved out of the darkness by moonlight. She felt a strange wish to reach out and touch the strong, aquiline line of his nose and cheekbones.

"Mukuna has been a good wife to me. She has filled my lodge with laughter and sons. I am grateful to her. I would do or say nothing to dishonor or wound her—but because Mukuna is Mukuna, I know that she would want me to say these words that have been held long within me."

They stared at each other in solemn silence for a moment, and then as if her silence had given him permission, he went on.

"My heart is deep for you, Kemink. It has always been so. If you had not chosen otherwise, my greatest joy would have been to have you beside me in this journey of life."

The loon sobbed now, his cry ebbing into the sound of wind rustled branches and the hushed slap of water against the bank. Tears filled Kemink's eyes, sparkling but not overflowing. The loon cried twice more before she had control of herself enough to answer him.

"I have always known, Sashwatka—and the knowledge has meant more to me than you would imagine. Perhaps you have felt that the emotion you had for me was barren and without fruit. I tell you that it is not true. The knowledge that you cared has borne me up through many temptations and adversities through all my life. Your feelings have helped me to live with strength as nobly as possible, that I might never dishonor or diminish myself in your eyes. Through distance, through time, through long years, the fact that you lived has mattered to me. If it were not so, I would not have felt free to bring my son to you in his hour of need."

"He will be as my own flesh," Sashwatka promised.

For a moment longer their eyes held in an intimacy beyond any caress.

"Will you stay with us?"

"You know I cannot. But I spoke true words when I told you that all is well with me. In the house of Caroline the two great needs of life are met—I am loved and I am needed. She is not an ordinary woman. She has been given a great healing gift. The daughter of Pow-wa-ga-nien is proud to serve that gift. But she could not do so if it were not for Sashwatka into whose hands she can rest the destiny of her people without fear."

Sashwatka sighed, a sound as sad as the fading call of the loon. "The destiny of our people—there is much we must talk about concerning that, Kemink."

And as they walked back toward the sleeping camp, he told her of the many things troubling the Thunder people. He told her how the reservation Indians were being mistreated by the white people and how their band of the Thunder people who had stolen away and found refuge here on the banks of the Tomorrow River found less and less of a livelihood to cling to as more and more of the wilderness was claimed and eaten up by the farmer's plow.

Lumbering interests in the state had not been long in casting eyes upon the timbered acres of the Menominee Reservation. In the early sixties the Indian office had agreed to contracts that permitted the whites to cull dead and down timber from the Indian land.

"For a time, all was well," Sashwatka said. "Then the whites began to take our green and standing timber as well. We formed a tribal council to stop this and appointed Menominees to supervise the lumbering. Since then, great fires have raged through our timber, and we suspect they are being set deliberately by the white people to make more of our timber cull stock for their harvest. If it continues, our entire timber acreage will be destroyed within a few years—and the timber is all our tribe has left."

Sashwatka complained also of how useless the annuities paid by the government were to most of the Menominees.

"Though the white government has made it against the law to bring liquor on the reservation, the law is not obeyed. The liquor runners know when the Menominee annuity is paid and they come like wolves. To our shame, many of our people get drunk and are easy prey then for the white traders," Sashwatka lamented bitterly.

Most grievous of all to Kemink's old friend was the fact that the history and religion of the tribes was passing into limbo.

"Only a few of our people remain 'blanket Indians.' Almost all have adopted the dress of the white man. No longer do our old men dance the medelinne and our young men do not know how to dream the dreams of divination. They deliver their souls to the God of Firewater, and O-ge-maw-nee tells me there is not one Menominee left of sufficient purity to be entrusted with the medicine bundles. O-ge-maw-nee and the other wise ones grow old. Who then will keep the divine secrets and remember our history? Who will preserve our totems and our sacred dances? Into whose care will the powerful medicine bundles be given?

"I speak peace in our councils. I beg them to hold back their passions and their anger when the white men seek to steal our green timber, for I see that in other tribes that have fought with fury but without wisdom, great suffering and destruction have been the only result. But they steal more from us than our timber. They steal what can never be replaced—and my heart *bursts within me!*" Sashwatka cried as they walked that night along the banks of the Tomorrow River.

62

"I am so pleased my cousin, Lisamarie, is coming to visit," Roxelle LeSeure said, hurrying about the table to straighten the candles that had started to lean in the warm spring air.

"Do you realize, Bay, that this is the first time since the war that she's had enough money for the fare? Charleston might as well have been the moon for all we've gotten to see each other these past six years."

Bay smiled at his step-mother. "I'm glad she's coming. For years I've been trying to get you to have a party like in the old days. It's good to see you all dressed up.

"Well now, Baird, it's you who bought the new dress and the candles and the fixings. I don't know where we'd be without you—Oh, my land, I do believe that's her coming up the drive now. I think I'm going to cry."

Bay gave her his handkerchief and pushed her toward the door. "Go out on the porch and smile."

The black coachman was helping his passenger from the carriage. She was an old woman, thin as a rack, her cheeks wreathed in wrinkles, her eyes resting in circles so black that Bay could see them from the window, but her back was straight, her bearing queenly as she advanced into Roxelle's waiting embrace.

Bay turned away from the emotional reunion and went into the kitchen to help Tessie with the rest of the "fixings." She had not prepared a company meal for so long she was in a dither about everything.

"Ah usa hive six lil' gals jus' fer to run 'n fetch fer me when ah was cookin' fer yo papa. 'N now ah's s'pose to do ever'ting by ma own lonesome," she complained darkly to Bay, although the truth was she was very excited to once again have a goose in the oven and a pudding in the pan. She had been up since dawn shucking peas and plucking feathers.

Bay busied himself making a punch he thought would be suitable to the ladies' appetites. He could hear their laughter and snatches of their conversation from where they had settled in the parlor. Greetings and reminiscence gradually flowed into talk of mutual relatives and how they had suffered or fared at the hands of the "Damn Yankees."

"My dear, you know our cousin from Georgia, Marilee Beauchamp? She was living on the plantation quite alone, widowed by the war in

300

the first year, with the full care and responsibility of her tiny children and her invalid mother-in-law. They were having dinner one evening when the servants came to tell them that a body of cavalry were riding in the gateway.

"Marilee answered the door herself. The Captain in charge told her cool as a mint julep that he'd come to burn the place down."

"Oh my, no! That house has been in the family for a hundred years. Colonel Beauchamp had an invaluable collection of early Georgia history—why, things that couldn't possibly be replaced—maps and letters," Roxelle said.

"But my dear, those savages didn't care. Marilee faced them with true Southern courage. She said they'd have to burn the house down over her head and the heads of her helpless children. Then she went back and sat down at the table as if not a thing had happened. The monsters didn't hesitate one moment. They started pouring camphene and kerosene on the furniture, and curtains. Some of the soldiers walked right up to the table and took the silverware and cups and candlesticks. Marilee said her heart was beating itself hollow, but she couldn't give them the satisfaction of knowing she was the least bit afraid. She finished every bite of her meal, folded up her napkin, and then and only then, took the children and her mother-in-law out under the trees. But *she* went right back in and sat down at the piano. They had started the house afire and she could hear the flames crackling and roaring in the next room, but she sat calmly as if nothing were happening and played "Thy Will Be Done," on that beautiful old piano until finally, when the flames were roaring up the roof above her head, one of the Yankees picked her up bodily and took her out."

"Oh my, Lisamarie! How did they make out with the house burned to the ground?!"

Bay interrupted at this point with the tray of iced punch. Lisamarie leaned forward, her eyes narrowed, to look at him better.

"Lisa, you remember my step-son, Baird, don't you?" Roxelle prompted.

The other woman stiffened, sprang upright, her dark eyes taking fire. "Roxelle, tell me that I don't hear you right," she pleaded. "Tell me that I don't see a damn Yankee standing in your parlor with your blessing and your permission."

"Lisamarie—" Roxelle quavered, "—we were in such bad straits after the war—if you only knew what Bay—"

"Oh, I do know! I can see it all around me. Your fields are plowed. Your cotton is growing. You're wearing a new dress. I can smell rich food from the kitchen. I was rejoicing for you, little thinking that you, of all people, had sold your soul to a turncoat Yankee for a mess of pottage. I'd rather starve, and sometimes I do."

"Lisa, please try and understand—"

"I am sorry. I cannot stay under a roof that harbors a Yankee. I will be going."

"But you only just got here. Your carriage is gone."

"I will walk every step of the way back to New Orleans before I'll sleep under the same roof as a *Yankee*."

"I will get you a carriage," Bay said quietly.

"I would take nothing from you," the old woman snorted. She picked up her flowered valise as best she could manage and half tottered, half sailed from the room. Roxelle followed, pleading, but her cousin would not return.

Roxelle finally came back dusty and tear stained. "If she doesn't have a heart attack trying to lug those valises at her age, I imagine she will put up with the Stewarts for the night."

"I'm sorry this happened, Roxelle."

"Oh, Bay, it's not your fault. You've been so good. The war never seems to end, even now that it's ended," she said, sinking forlornly onto the couch.

"I think it's time for me to leave," Bay said. "No one is going to have anything to do with you as long as I am around. If I go away, they'll forget and forgive in time."

"Bay, I don't want you to go away. I don't know what I'd do without you. But it does seem like you wouldn't have to associate so openly with the Yankee officers in town and the carpetbaggers and that other riffraff."

"That 'riffraff' as you call them, are about the only people in the South who will give me the time of day. I've always thought of myself as a lone wolf, but I find that after all, I do need a little companionship now and then."

Roxelle started to cry. "Ohh, everything is ruined—and the goose smells so good and the table is beautiful—"

Bay patted her shoulder. "Come on, we'll eat anyway. It'll break Tessie's heart if we don't after all the work she's put into this."

"Bay, I'm sorry, but I couldn't eat a bite."

"Well, look now," he said, squatting in front of her, "in the morning you go down to Stewarts and tell Lisamarie that she's completely right and that she has helped you to see the light—you've sent that no good scalawag Yankee packing, and I think she'll find it in her heart to forgive past sins."

"But Bay, I don't *want* to send you packing. I was never right to you when you were a child and I don't want to treat you shabby now. Besides," she ended plaintively, "what would I do without you?"

302

"To tell you the truth, Roxelle, I never planned to stay this long. It's taken longer to put this place on its feet than I thought it would. But it's coming along well now. Sam is a good overseer, and I really believe I can do more for you by returning north. I've still got some timber land in Wisconsin, and with all the building going on, logging is becoming big business."

"I don't want you to go, Bay," she said like a stubborn child.

He stood up and moved to the window looking out over the neat, tidy, green rows of cotton. "I'll always see that you're taken care of," he promised.

The room was filled with her quiet sobs. He thought how strange it was that though she had called him home only through expediency, now she genuinely cared for him. Life constantly took unexpected turns. He laid his hand gently on her greying curls before he went upstairs to pack his bags.

63

Having Dan-Pete gone for the summer was hard on Danny. They had been an extension of each other for so many years that it was like losing one arm. He turned more than ever to his work with Jimmy and Emily. Though the sudden miraculous cure he had hoped for Emily had never come, there was no doubt about her gradual improvement.

Emily still spent hours drawn within herself. She didn't speak, but the glazed look in her eyes was gone. She now watched the activities around her and was aware of other people and things. She dressed and fed herself and combed her own hair. Though she could not be counted on to contribute on a regular basis, she sometimes did small chores. She liked to strew feed for the chickens and to dip the warm milk for the kittens into their pans at milking time. Occasionally she would bring eggs to the house. Often in the evening when the family was gathered in the parlor to sing and tell stories, Emily would lay her head against Caroline's arm or Danny's cheek in a silent gesture of affection.

The cat Danny had found for her long before died during the winter. Emily had wept. As she wiped away the tears and caressed the grieving girl, Caroline told Danny, "She's is beginning to let herself feel, Danny. Today she weeps and our hearts are heavy with her, but it also means that someday soon she will laugh."

"And talk?" asked Danny wistfully.

"And talk," Caroline said with conviction.

Jimmy too remained silent although he was around five years old. But he had learned to laugh. He loved to have Danny roll him down the hay mow and would squeal with laughter. At first when the solemnity of his face was broken by dimples and the sparkle of his dark eyes, Caroline had to turn away, so vividly did he bring to mind the young Adam. As time went on, this feeling passed and it seemed natural that she should be bringing up Adam's son. Since he still did not walk well, Jimmy was usually with her, when he wasn't with Danny, sharing in a thousand small activities from rolling pie crust to matching socks.

On warm days, Danny took Jimmy to the river where the cows watered and encouraged him to wade in the stream. He seemed to be able to walk better in the water, and they spent happy times there.

Danny's resolve to be a doctor was waning.

"Riding around with Doc has shown me all the bad things about doctoring," he told his mother. "It seems like one long round of enemas, sutures, irrigating boils, dressing putrified wounds and inducing folks to vomit. I don't think I'm soft. I believe I could put up with all of it to see people well, but so often there's nothing he can do but give them sugar pills and comfort. It's too sad for me. Everytime I go with Doc I marvel the more how he takes it all and does what good he can. I wish I had your gift for healing, Mother."

"God does the healing.

"Even Doc can't get over it, Mother. He swears that when you come and sit with a patient, the fever goes away. And he says he'll swear to God that you healed Jess Hawkins of smallpox overnight."

"*I* didn't heal him," Caroline disavowed. "Jess had enormous faith. His own faith in God cured him. Jesus gave us this faith."

"I just wish your methods were more understandable, Mother. Something I could learn like mathematics."

"I think it is, Danny. I think it operates on some kind of basic law, only I'm doing it blindfolded. Someday, someone will figure it out and put it all down in black and white—one—two—three—"

"I'll bet it would still be difficult. Like playing the violin—some people have the knack and some don't."

Caroline shrugged. "Hardly anything is hard once you *really* know how. Speaking of knack, you're the only one who seems to have the knack of getting that new calf to drink from the bucket—"

"Which is to remind me that it's chore time," Danny said, laughing. "Maybe I'll end up being a farmer."

One afternoon, when he came back from his rounds with Doc, he found Emily waiting for him by the gate. She took his hand and walked with him back to the house. He was touched. It was the first time she had ever shown any longing for human companionship. After that she would often be waiting for him. Each time he saw her there it was a small pleasure he hugged to himself for the rest of the day.

*   *   *

When Dan-Pete returned in the fall, he had grown in many ways. The two boys quickly fell back into their pattern of intimacy, but Danny soon realized that the things his friend had experienced while they were apart had subtly changed their relationship. They did not care any less for each other; but there was a growing realization that their boyhood entity had of necessity begun to diverge. They both felt a quiet sadness.

Danny listened enviously to Dan-Pete's tales of bow shooting, bareback riding, rapids shooting, but the ancient Indian rites Dan-Pete had undergone to initiate him into manhood were too sacred to discuss even with Danny. He confided only that what had transpired during those two days and two nights had been profound and would alter the course of his life.

I wish I could go with you next summer," Danny sighed, "but Georgio's going home. He'll be leaving this fall and mother couldn't do without all three of us. Josh can't make hay alone."

"Maybe something will work out so you can come," Dan-Pete said hopefully.

Nothing did. In the summer that followed, Dan-Pete disappeared into what Danny could only imagine as the wild and enchanted domain of "Tomorrow River country," while he was left behind with the heavy mundane chores of summer and a sense of restlessness and uncertainty about growing up. Admiring the new surety that marked all of Dan-Pete's actions, he sometimes thought to himself that he wished white people had some kind of equivalent rites that would almost overnight make him sure of his manhood and his destiny.

In truth, it was not that easy for Dan-Pete either. The first summer in Tomorrow River country had been idyllic. But in subsequent summers, when he had been accepted as one with the other Indian braves his age, he found the popularity and esteem accorded him as the grandson of the great Pow-wa-ga-nien had its responsibilities and costs.

There were certain young braves of the Thunder people smoldering with hatred for the whites, occasioned and fanned by all manner of insults and abuses that had grown through the years. They urged

Dan-Pete to assume his rightful leadership as their Chief, to prove that he deserved his name. Their dream was to be led in rebellion against the whites, to die if need be, to dramatize the victimization of the Menominee. Each summer the pressure they put upon Dan-Pete to not return to the white eyes grew greater. Dan-Pete found it difficult not to be swept along by their ardor, not to succumb to their hot-blooded urgings. He spoke to Kemink of the conflict within him.

"Why should I return to the land of the white man, my Mother? My people have need of me. They ask me to be their chief, to lead them and protect them—"

She could have protested, 'You are only a child!,' but she said, "Long ago when you were too small to choose for yourself, I made the choice for you that you would live in the world of your father because I believed it would have been his wish. Now you are a man, and the decision is no longer mine. You must choose, Dan-Pete. But take care not to be lured into promises of false glory. I know well what your young friends urge upon you. The winds of rebellion leave only destruction in their wake. Do not imagine that Sashwatka is a fool. If ought were to be gained by violence at this time—do you think he would hesitate?"

Dan-Pete stalked the woods alone for days. In the end, his mother's counsel prevailed. He loved Sashwatka as a father, and he came to see that his mother was right. If he chose to follow the dictates of the hot-bloods of his tribe, it would mean wresting the power from the grasp of the older man.

Around a smokey campfire in autumn he spoke to his would-be followers.

"I have not yet the stature of Sashwatka, my brothers. If I thought I did, I would show myself as having a head more empty than a rattle. I respect and revere him. I will not claim the staff of leadership from his hands. If Sashwatka says that we must bide our time and humble ourselves in peace, it is wise to do so. But—I promise you that if the day ripens that we must ride against our oppressors, I shall not fail you!—" He threw his lance into the ground as quivering testimony to his words.

His words were not what they had hoped to hear, but his 'I shall not fail you!' was spoken with such passion and bravado that they cheered him anyway. They were convinced that a rebellion against the white men who were robbing the Menominee of timber would come whether Sashwatka willed it or not. Dan-Pete would join with them when the time came and lend the prestigious weight of Pow-wa-ga-nien ancestry to their cause.

It was heady business for a boy not quite eighteen. All the same

306

there was much that drew him back to Harbour Hill, much that tore him apart between his two worlds.

On the day he returned to Harbour Hill, he looked not like a future great Indian warrior chieftain, but like any hungry young boyman when he sat down in the porch swing, in each hand a hunk of freshly baked bread spread thickly with blackberry jam.

The screen door banged softly as Fly came and settled beside him in a scented flurry of yellow dimity, the white satin ribbon that tied back her dark curls dangling down and tickling his shoulder.

"Seems like you've been away forever, Dan-Pete. You even missed the county fair."

His mouth full of jam and bread, he grinned in answer.

Felicity was thirteen that summer, budding swiftly into young womanhood and full of self-conscious airs and graces, half charming, half ridiculous, that some girls of that age adopt. She smoothed the ruffles of her skirts delicately, glanced sideways at Dan-Pete and deliberately deepened the dimple in her cheek.

"I suppose some of those Indian girls are real pretty, Dan-Pete."

"They sure are," he agreed, licking blackberry jam off his fingers.

Felicity started rocking the swing. "S'pose you're sweet on one of them."

"Sweet on all of them," Dan-Pete said, his eyes laughing.

"Dan-Pete, you've got *awful* manners," she said in sudden provocation. "You've dripped jam all over yourself. You'd think you were six instead of practically a grown man!"

"The thing about Indian girls," Dan-Pete said, scraping a bit of jam from his shirt, "is they not only have big, dark eyes and hair clear down to here, but they never peeve or fret at you like white girls."

Fly leaped up from the swing and gave it a savage push. "Well, why don't you just go back to your old Indian girls then? N' to think I fancied all summer that I missed you—"

She swept off the veranda in a swirl of skirts, but he was a jump ahead of her. He caught her around the waist and whispered in her ear, "Indian girls speak gentle as doves—n' they've got smiles white as new snow and happy as sunlight," his voice dropped a note, "but I sort of favor mean, ornery girls like you."

She had her face covered with her hands, but he could see the dimple deepening between her fingers.

"Dan-Pete, you're the worst tease in the whole, entire world!"

He laughed as she scampered off, dark curls and white ribbons flying.

It was good to be home, he thought—then he sighed. He was no longer sure where *home* was.

64

Adam Quimby was bored. At the moment he was bored to the point of irritation because he had been waiting for over half an hour for Sally to finish her toilette so they could attend a party. But his boredom went deeper than the present moment, greying his days and sucking at his vitality. When they had first come to San Francisco, it had not been bad. He had to design and build the house which he hoped would establish Sally and him as a prince and princess of San Francisco. That had taken three years to complete and had held his interest for at least two. Then he had tried gambling for a time, but he was too well-versed in the odds from his black jack years to find any real relish in it. He was not by nature a businessman. If he could have used the wealth produced by Sally's mine as a launching point for further investments, he might have found a wealth of interests, but he had no taste for it. The intricacies of their business efforts were controlled by a weasel-faced man appropriately named Mr. Ferret. His own natural talents, which would have made him a great actor, orator, preacher, or politician, were bottled up unused, and restlessness and boredom grew inside of him like a disease. On the other hand, he enjoyed the accouterments of wealth, the big house, expensive clothing, fine horses, power and prestige. He had long ago convinced himself that the cosmos itself was at fault for the hollow bitterness of life. The price of being intelligent and sophisticated was to learn the truth that every kernel one bit into was rotten at the core.

Now he smashed his cigar into a marble ashtray with savagery and strode to the carved doors of the master bedroom.

"Damn it, Sally, if you're not out of there in two more seconds, I'm going without you."

"Well, come in and help me with these hooks," she yelled back crossly. "It's your own fault anyway, sending Babe away early. How do you expect me to do my own lacing?"

"I get sick of servants milling around us like goldfish in a pond," Adam grumbled as he came in to do her bidding.

"Well you didn't send Melio away."

"Melio is less intrusive than the rest."

In the dim plushness of their bedroom he could see Sally's reflection in the rococo pier glass. She could no longer boast, "I hiv kept my figger—" Even laced in so tightly that her cheeks were red from the effort, her flesh had passed from voluptuous to billowy. But her

308

shoulders and breasts were still powder white above the black silk and lace gown, her hair had a dull gold glint, and in the semi-darkness the puffiness of her jowls was not so noticeable.

Trying to fasten the small metal hooks that pulled the back of the dress together further irritated Adam; he had to poke and probe at Sally's flesh to make each hook meet. She cursed at his roughness and the impulse he had had a moment before to tell her that she looked nice died unspoken.

"The party will be half over before we get there," he complained.

"I always believe in comin' late and making an entrance anyhow," Sally said, posturing.

"If you drink as much as you did last time—" Adam started out. He was interrupted by a discreet tap on the door.

"Yes?" Adam said, all his irritations embodied in the one tense syllable.

"I'm sorry to bother you, Sir," Melio murmured through the thickness of the door. "A man just brought you a message from the Commodore Hotel. He said it was urgent."

"Get your cloak!" Adam snapped at Sally. Then he opened the door to Melio, who stood waiting with an envelope on a silver tray.

"Who was the man?" Adam asked, only mildly interested in the message described as urgent. He had found since he was rich that most of the urgent messages directed his way concerned matters urgent to others, not himself.

"He said you wouldn't know him, Sir."

"Very well, Melio. That's all." Adam dismissed the servant with sudden weariness. Sally had appeared, ready now, pulling on long white kid gloves. Adam sat down on a lounge with deliberate and aggravating slowness. It pleased him now to make Sally wait.

The message had little meaning to him when he read it. His first thought was to flip it into the waste basket. The message was a plea from a man named M. Durwood to meet him at the Commodore Hotel. Durwood was unable to come to Adam due to a terminal illness and he begged Adam to hasten to him in his own self-interest. But then the mystery of it grabbed him. He already felt bored by the thought of the party ahead. At least the adventure would offer something different.

"I have to go to the Commodore Hotel on business," he told Sally. "I will send you on to the party and join you later."

"Oh, Adam," Sally pouted, "can't you go tomorrow instead?"

"No," Adam said shortly, finding a certain pleasure in her displeasure. 'As I said, I will join you later—and—" he added with a dark glance, "you had better be sober."

* * *

The old man lay propped against two pillows. His long gaunt arms were stretched out as if he had already died and been laid to rest. His sick eyes looked at Adam from sunken caverns.

"You don't remember me, do you?" the old man asked. His lips seemed to stick together with each word, and his tone was one of disappointment.

What does he want from me, Adam thought, and was sorry already that he had come. "I'm afraid I don't," he said curtly.

"Before the war—in Columbia," the old man said. "Remember I built you a locker for your clothes? I carved an eagle on it—"

"Why it's McCarty—old McCarty the furniture maker and undertaker in Columbia—I remember you now," Adam said. "Well, old man, what are you doing in Frisco?" *And what in the devil do you want with me*—was Adam's unspoken thought.

"I'm dying," the old man said with a grimace that was meant to be a grin.

And what am I supposed to do about that? Adam thought with sarcasm, but he forced himself to say politely, "I'm sorry."

"A dying man wants everything off his conscience," the old man went on. "I come here to be by my son; and when I heard ya was in the city, it's been a burden on me to tell you before I die. Seemed I couldn't rest proper unless I did."

"Tell me what?" Adam asked. He was beginning to feel restless in this room of sickness. The "adventure" was worse than the party. He wanted to leave.

"I was always a God-fearing man. Bothered me at the time. I didn't want to do it—but Miss Sally—"

"Do what?" Adam said, his attention arrested now.

"There wasn't no baby in the casket, Adam. All there was was a big doll. Miss Sally—she gave me lots of money and made me promise never to tell nobody. But all these years it's bothered me. It wasn't right. It was strange goings on. She especially didn't want you to know. 'N you was my friend, Adam. You said my eagle was a work of art. Nobody else ever cared about those extras I did—"

The old man was rambling on in a frail, high-pitched monologue, but Adam's mind was quickened now, trying to grasp the importance of what at first had sounded like gibberish.

"Whose casket, old man? What doll?" he broke in.

"Why the little fella's, your son's." McCarty Durwood said.

Adam's interest was at last fully engaged. "You mean, McCarty, that there was no body in the casket—only a doll?"

"That's right, Adam."

"But why would Sally do that—?"

"That's what I been askin' myself all these years. The question was always a festerin' at me. But I feel better now I tole ya."

"If there was no body in the casket—what happened to my son?"

"You'd best ask her—ask Miss Sally," the old man said. The effort of unburdening himself had worn him out. His eyes closed and the attendant who had let Adam into the room nudged him to leave.

"McCarty—thank you," Adam said. "I'm glad you told me."

"The eagle—" the old man murmured, "I remember the eagle. I carved him in full flight—" The eyes came darting back for one small moment, "D'ya remember the eagle—Adam?"

"I remember. You carved a fine eagle."

"The best thing I ever did—" the old man said, and then his lips glued into one line and the lights went back into their cavern and did not flare again.

Sally was waiting up for him, lying on the bed, still fully dressed, a decanter of whiskey nestled in her arm.

"You never came to the party," she said accusingly. "Where you been all this time?"

He did not bother to answer her. He merely stood and looked at her with burning eyes for a long time before posing a question of his own.

"Why did you put a doll in my son's coffin, Sally?"

Always white, what little color her skin possessed drained away. Sally looked suddenly like a specter seated in the winey richness of the bed alcove.

"Whoever told you such a lie?"

But he had seen the truth written in her blanching flesh. "Why, Sally—*why*?" He was moving toward her, his shadow moving with him like a menacing enlarged double.

"It's a lie," she shrieked. "Whoever told you such a dirty lie?"

He hit her.

"*Why*, Sally?"

She rolled, blubbering onto the satin coverlet.

He grasped her arms in bruising fingers and shook her. "I want the truth and I want it *now*—"

She wrenched herself free of his grip, backed herself away, crouched on the slippery satin spread, her eyes dark with hatred and fear.

"Awright, damn you, awright. He never died. He never died at all. *He was like the other one.* Do you hear? He was crippled *like the other one!"*

She had wanted to hurt him and she had the triumph of succeeding. His face twisted with anguish.

"Sally—" he whispered, his voice suddenly hushed, almost pleading, "you told me the baby was all right. A perfect baby—"

"I *lied,*" she was taking what pleasure she could in hurting him.

He had sunk down, his head in his hands, his body crumpled.

Sally regained the liquor decanter she had lost in the struggle. "Adam—you better have a belt—" she said, not without solicitude. She had wanted to hurt him. She was glad she had hurt him. But at the same time, she was frightened by this weak crumpled Adam.

"My fault—my fault all the time," he mumbled hoarsely. Not her— never her."

The rings on her plump hands flashed in the lamplight as Sally uncorked the decanter and poured some wine. She held it out to him, but he shook his head, so she drank it herself.

"What happened to—to Garth?"

"How the hell would I know?" she evaded.

"You'd better know." He was on his feet again, all the menace back.

Sally's lips drew away from her teeth. She still had weapons of her own. He was asking for it. She'd give it to him.

"I sent him to *her.*"

"Her?"

"Her."

"Caroline—?" dazedly.

"Who else?" bitterly.

"You sent Garth to Caroline?" He could not comprehend it.

"Cricket and Levi took him. Cricket said she got the other one well. We thought she could help him."

"And did she?"

"I don't know. I never heard anything about him again."

"What kind of mother are you?"

"What kind of father are you? You never tried to find out nothing about the two you whelped with *her,* neither. You ain't no holier than I am, Adam, so don't try that bull with me."

"Garth could be alive."

"I s'pose."

"I'm going to find him. I'm going to find my son."

"You hypocrite," Sally blurted drunkenly, "It ain't your son you want to see, it's *her.* It's *her!* And you finally got an excuse."

"You're crazy. I could have seen her anytime I wanted to. I came back to *you* after the war. Do you think I couldn't have gone to her?"

"No, it wasn't me you came back to—I ain't dumb," Sally jeered.

"It was the money, Adam—and it's still the money. You like being rich—"

She crawled off the bed, swaying toward him. He turned his back on her, staring out the window.

—"but then maybe it was *me*, too," Sally said. She slid from the dress and undid the corset, taking a deep grateful breath as her flesh expanded to normal dimensions. She tossed the dress and corset on a chair and advanced toward him, her flesh moving loosely now in her chemise. She leaned against him. He felt the heat of her body penetrate the thin shirt he wore.

"Go see her, Adam. I hope you do. How long has it been—fifteen years? In your mind she's still young—but *fifteen years*? She could be fat and old and married and have ten children—" She threw her head back and laughed raucously.

He wanted to hit her again, but he forced himself to stare stubbornly out of the window instead.

"But even if she ain't—" Sally said evenly, "I ain't afraid of losing you—*do you hear that*? You ain't gonna leave me. You're gonna stay with me for the same reasons you come back to me in the first place." She nuzzled her body against his back. "Money—and because I'm a lewd woman. Oh, I know I'm a lewd woman," she laughed in the same raucous way. "I oughta know—you've told me enough times. But what you ain't never admitted, Adam, is that you *like* lewd women. I can give you things she's never given you—"

"How could you know what she gave me—" Adam brooded. "The words for what she gave me aren't even in your vocabulary—"

She sank her teeth into his shoulder. He yelped, and then whirled and caught her in a brutal embrace, half dragging her to the bed. She was laughing drunkenly.

Yes, Sally, he thought—*lust, you're right, that's all I ever feel for you lust or pity or anger. That's what I settled for—money and lust and anger and pity.* They fell on the bed together.

When his lust had been satisfied, he lay in the acrid grey ashes that it always left in its wake, as far from Sally's large and sweating body as he could. Through her snores he could hear rain falling on the streets of San Francisco.

"I *will find Caroline and the boy,*" he thought. "*I will find them.*"

He felt a lump rise in his throat and spread into his chest with emotion so intense he prayed he could cry and release his misery. But he felt he had lost the gift of tears somewhere in the mud of Shiloh. He could only lie listening to the sound of rain outside, enduring the pain, dry-eyed.

65

The wind caught Caroline's pink gingham apron, billowing it and tossing the ties in a highland fling. It tugged curls loose at the nape of her neck and around her face.

"It's a good drying day," she said as she put down the wicker basket piled high with wet clothes. "I want you to learn to hang them in the right way because it saves so much ironing," she told Fly and Margaret, each with her own basket.

"Who's that coming down the lane, Mama?" Fly asked.

Caroline turned, shielding her eyes from the sun to better view the figure approaching down the dusty, winding road. She could see it was a man. He was wearing a tan frockcoat and a white hat, and there was something familiar about the way he walked. The pair of overalls she was holding in her hand dropped from nerveless fingers.

"Mama, he's turning in our gate—"

A blaze of tears blurred her eyes.

"Bay!" she cried, and with her arms wide, ran toward him.

If at that moment he could have caught her in his arms as frankly and passionately as she came, it could have brushed away a thousand nuances that stood between them, but he was completely unprepared, stunned to see her. He could only blurt, "*Caroline*! What are *you* doing here?"

And she, being greeted in this manner, halted, abashed, stumble-footed, red climbing up her throat and cheeks.

"Then—then you didn't come to see *me*?"

"I didn't know you were here. I thought you'd gone off somewhere with Adam.

"No."

They stood looking at each other awkwardly, the tension of suppressed and overwhelming emotions robbing them of speech. A muscle was jumping in his cheek, and her bottom lip was quivering.

She swallowed hard, started to laugh a wobbly little laugh.

"Well, my goodness—whatever has brought you here, we're very glad to have you!"

"This is my place."

"Oh." Conflicting emotions jarred her.

"You didn't know?"

She shook her head.

Now he wanted to take her in his arms, pour out his anguished love in kisses and caresses; but she was already turning aside, taking his hand to draw him along, and a flurry of children seemed to be descending upon them from every direction.

The laundry baskets were forgotten under the plum trees. Caroline drew Bay toward the house.

"Bay, you can't know how worried we were after the war—not hearing from you all that time. How could you have been so cruel as not to get in touch with us? For a time we thought you might be dead. But then, when I saw Nelia Fitzpatrick the last time in Chicago and she—"

"What has Nelia Fitzpatrick got to do with it?"

"You're not married to her?"

"No. Should I be?"

"She told me you were engaged, the two of you—I assumed—"

"She said we were engaged? That minx!" he laughed. "Well, whether she's married or not the next time I see her I've a notion to paddle her. She told me you had gone back to Adam. Is it true?"

"No!" Caroline was not amused. She felt a red haze of anger fuse through her. She would liked to have gotten her fingers about Nelia's little neck and shaken her to a fare-thee-well. She almost blurted out some impassioned words to that effect but stifled them with the realization that such an outburst might prove more revealing to Bay than her pride would permit. Instead, after a momentary struggle with her emotions, she said, "Oh! Ann and Bromley will be so glad to hear of you. They still inquire about you in their letters. Oh, yes—" she cried, her eyes widening in sudden comprehension, "—and well they might. *They* knew all along this place belonged to you and never told me. I heard Ann and Bromley quarreling once, and now I'm sure that's why. I'll wager Bromley wanted Ann to tell me!"

"They're still in Europe?"

"Yes. We were quite disappointed when they didn't come home as we had expected, but the President extended the appointment and they hate to come home until they see the fruition of their efforts. Ann is as involved as Bromley."

They had reached the house, and Caroline stopped, looking up at Bay, shaking her head.

"I still can't believe you are really here, Bay. I've been doing all the talking and I want so much to hear about everything that's happened to *you*. I guess I don't have to show you the house—it's your house!" She laughed. "But do come in and have something to eat and tell me everything. Do you plan to stay on?"

"For a time at least. I'm going to look into the lumbering business. I'm thinking of putting up a mill."

"We could use another in the area," Caroline said, holding the screen door open. "I'll have the older children take my things out of your bedroom."

"No, don't do that. I'd much prefer to sleep in the spring house. I remember how cool it is there."

"Are you sure? I don't mind if you'd rather have the bedroom. Honestly."

"I'm sure."

"Mother, I'll bet Bay doesn't even recognize me," Fly, who had been tagging behind, interjected at this point.

"Oh, Darling, I'm sorry. I was so excited I forgot everything. Would you believe this young lady is Firefly, Bay?"

"Felicity," Fly corrected quickly.

"Her Royal Highness, the Princess of Chicago, in exile," Bay said, catching her hands and kissing them lightly.

"Sometimes I think she feels that way," Caroline said, laughing again. "She loves the bright lights and the restaurants and the shops when we visit Green Bay on business. But Danny and Dan-Pete wouldn't give up one inch of this place for an entire city. Oh, Fly, do fetch Kemink and tell her Bay has come."

Secretly, Fly was piqued that Bay had not commented upon what a lovely young lady she was becoming but had instantly turned his attention back to her mother. She wanted to stay and exert her charms on him, but she went obediently to seek Kemink.

"And where are the boys—" Bay was saying.

That evening at supper, seated at the table, Bay faced numerous freshly scrubbed young people of all ages and varieties. They looked at him with round solemn eyes, each head, even the smallest, wondering in its own way what this tall, handsome man had to do with Caroline. Glancing away from the gauntlet of eyes to Caroline's face, Bay said, "It looks as if I'm going to have to prove myself to a lot of people."

"They will all love you," Caroline answered him confidently, and then added bravely, "—as I do."

He looked up at her quickly. "And how is that—like a brother?"

Her courage faltered. She did not feel that a declaration of love was in order before so many curious eyes. Her glance fell, which he took as affirmation that that was indeed the way she loved. He felt a sense of depression engulf him.

At least Caroline's prediction that the children would love him quickly proved to be the case. His old talents of singing and playing the piano endeared him at once to the girls. The boys welcomed a mature male who knew how to initiate them into such fundamental

316

masculine skills as the best way to break a colt or make a wagon hitch. Within two weeks it seemed to everyone that the place could not have run without Bay.

If there was anyone with reservations, it was Fly. She was still a little jealous of the attentions Bay paid her mother while he continued to give her the affectionate, but she felt condescending, treatment accorded a child. Besides, she was jealous of the attentions Caroline gave Bay. Since she already had to share her mother with twenty near-siblings; she did not welcome an additional attraction for her mother's attention.

Danny on the other hand, who had longed for a father all his life, spent every spare moment he could with Bay. It was not unusual for their conversations about the war, its aftermath, philosophy, and religion to last long into the night. Bay was the first male intellectual challenge Danny had come up against. He found it exciting to test his values and principles against those held by Bay.

*   *   *

Kemink was sitting in the shade of the grape arbor shelling peas. Bay was leaning against one of the arbor supports watching Caroline and a group of the smaller children strewing grain for the ducks and chickens.

Caroline's hair, which had been very dark when she was in Chicago, was banded now with sunburned streaks and further lightened with an intermingling of silver here and there. It caught the light around her head like a halo. Ann would have run for the Magnolia cream if she could have seen her sister's skin, browned to a mellow apricot, but it was attractive with her sun-lightened hair. Her faded apron, slick with starch, also caught a sheen of light and sun, giving her entire figure a radiance.

"Caroline has changed," Bay said, looking at her reflectively. "In Chicago I used to work hard to draw a smile from her. Now she laughs all the time."

Caroline, unaware of his scrutiny, was laughing with carefree abandon. She was seated in the grass with half a dozen baby ducklings climbing over her lap in search of the corn in her apron pocket.

"Yes, in the last few years Caroline has learned to walk in the sun," Kemink agreed.

"She is complete—happy. She doesn't need anyone else."

Kemink smiled. It had apparently not occurred to Bay that Caroline's present happiness might in part be caused by his own presence.

"We all need someone else," Kemink said, "but you should know, tall brother, that though it is difficult to swim upstream, the reward makes the struggle worthwhile."

"I'm afraid I haven't strength for much struggle," Bay said.

"You have sickness," Kemink observed calmly.

"Yes," Bay laughed as if they were sharing a delightful joke, embarrassed lest Kemink think he was indulging in self-pity. "Well, it does hamper things, you know."

"She is a healing woman."

"Yes—she's done wonderful things with these children, but mainly their problems were emotionally grounded. I'm afraid I can't believe that she can heal a body debilitated by years in prison. I wish I could."

"She claims no powers for herself."

"I know."

"Let her help you, Bay."

"I don't want her pity."

"Ah, yes—" Kemink said with understanding. "Above all you do not want her pity. Proud Bay."

'Kemink—I love her."

"I know. Swim the stream, Bay."

66

"Come on, Emily. Come with me and help plant this tree. When it's grown, I'll carve your name in the trunk," Danny coaxed. He stood, bare to the waist, holding the sprig of a tree wrapped in a wet gunnysack.

July had been hot. August hotter. September was searing. It had not rained for weeks. There was a taste of dust in the air and the bald sky shimmered with visible waves of heat. Danny had been carrying water from the creek by the bucketful to keep the garden alive, and he had dug irrigation ditches into the potato patch and the sweet corn field where the plants had sprung up wizened and yellow and threatened now to die fruitless. Everything was harder and hotter and more difficult than other years, but Danny was touched

318

with a certain awareness of splendor around him. The thrusting, insistent, determined attempt of creation to produce in spite of the conditions quickened something in his own spirit. For several weeks he had watched this tiny tree struggling against all kinds of odds in a soddy, parched site which caught the most savage winds. It had persevered gallantly, but the drought was beginning to win. He could see the little tree was losing ground and in an impulsive gesture, decided to replant it in the moist, receptive soil near the creek bed.

He held out his free hand imperiously. "Come on, Emmy!"

She continued to sit on the veranda swing, still as a basque figurine in her white plissé apron, her face innocent of expression. He knew she had heard him, though she did not betray it in any way.

He bounded up the shallow steps and caught at her wrist, pulling her forward, laughing.

"I know you think it's too hot to budge, but there's a breeze in the meadow. Here—you bring the tree, and I'll carry the bucket of water."

He waited, prepared to stand sweating under the sun all day if necessary. Perhaps she read his determination in the steady gaze of his eyes, the set of his mouth. With a sudden graceful motion she took the tree and rose to follow him.

The grass in the meadow barely brushed their ankles, but late daisies rayed their small sunburst forms in minute patches of glory. A tinge of pine filtered through the miasma of heat and dust.

"There's where I dug the hole—" Danny indicated.

He sloshed some of the water from the bucket into the hole and added a little of the soil he had dug out to make a tender base of mud in which to set the fledgling tree.

Emily sank languidly onto the grass to wait. A stray breeze lifted dark strands of her hair, played with them, and bore the honeysuckle scent of her skin to Danny.

Kneeling by the small excavation, one hand grasping the tree, he looked at her with a sudden lump of heartache rising in his throat, making his voice hoarse.

"Oh, Emily, I wish you would talk to me. I wish just once you'd say my name—"

Her eyelashes fell across her dark eyes. She bent her face away from him.

"Well, never mind," he said with determined cheerfulness. "Here, I'll hold the tree upright and you pack the soil around it. I want *you* to plant it."

As always, she hesitated, seemed unaware that he had even spoken. He laid down the tree, picked up a handful of the moist earth, uncurled her fingers and pressed it into her palm.

"Feel of it, Emmy—smell it—wet earth is like the smell of life itself. Don't you want to live, Emmy? Be part of all this around us—" his voice was pleading.

Her eyes flickered with some invisible battle, some mysterious inner conflict.

He waited with a curious terrible tenseness.

Slowly she rose on her knees, picked up the tree and handed it to him. His heart was beating with a strange ache as he lowered the sapling into the hole. Hesitantly she began to push the earth around the roots, filling the hole until the tree could stand alone. Then they began to pack the last of the soil together, an inexplicable joy and excitement bubbling up in them in laughter.

Their hands met around the base of the tree, their eyes met over the small feathery tip, and the laughter in them died. Danny felt as if he couldn't breathe for the nearness of her. It seemed the most natural thing in the world to lean forward and touch her lips with his. He was unprepared for her instantaneous response. Her arms closed around his neck, engulfing him in warmth and honeysuckle. Their hearts fluttered against each other like two wild birds.

"Danny!"

It was his mother's voice and there was a sting of reproach in it. Danny let his fingers slide from Emily's arms and looked up at Caroline, but he was in no mood for apology or guilt.

"I love her, mother—and she loves me." He was sure of it.

"She isn't ready for this kind of love, Danny," Caroline said in a troubled voice. "Did you forget you promised to go with Bay to Little Suamico to help him bring back the equipment he's bought for his mill?"

"I did forget. I'm sorry." He turned back to Emily, knelt by her again. He touched her cheek with his finger. "I'll be gone a few days, but remember I love you. *I love you.*"

She nodded.

"Did you see that, mother?"

"Yes. You'd better hurry, Danny. I'm going to pick apples. I'll bring Emily back with me."

The two women looked after the young man as he leaped through the grass like an exalted stallion. A frown of worry decorated Caroline's brow. Emily, lips moving silently, practiced his name. *Danny.* Her eyes filled with sparkling tears. Caroline, turning, saw the tears. She had no way of knowing that they were tears of almost unbearable joy. And when the girl threw her arms around her, weeping copiously, she could not know that the tears were necessary waves to wash away the bastions that had held the young girl prisoner for so long. Hold-

320

ing the sobbing Emily tightly and protectively in her arms, she could only think with a sinking feeling, "Oh, Danny, what have you done?—"

* * *

In that fall of 1871 sparse goldenrod and brown leaved wild asters bravely shot color amidst the dried, drab green of seasoned out grasses. Cattails lifted powdery spears of brown unlike the normal velvet of other years. Once dust was raised on rutted roads, it hung in the air, then drifted in the hot wind to lodge on the weeds and mullen stalks.

In the peat bogs, small fires began igniting spontaneously, adding a smell of acrid, bitter smoke to the unbearable heavy air. The air was becoming wrapped in an atmosphere of foreboding and fear. Women halted their chores uneasily to seek out their children and make sure they were near. Farmers paused nervously in their work to gaze at the faint whiffs of smoke drifting in the air. The entire world around them had become a tinder box. *One spark and—*the forbidden and terrifying thought was insinuating itself into everyone's mind and heart.

* * *

Danny and Bay were gone four days, picking up and unloading the mill equipment at the site Bay had chosen. When they got back, Emily was gone.

Caroline was in the summer kitchen scalding jars for apple jelly when her son confronted her, his eyes leaping like bonfires in a face gone white beneath his tan.

"Emily isn't here. Fly says you sent her away."

Caroline dried her damp hands on her apron. "I didn't send her away, Dan," she said. "Her father came to see her and *he* decided she was so much better, he wanted to take her with him.

"You let her go—" It was a cry of despair.

"Danny, I had no right to keep her here. Besides—I had been praying about the whole thing. I thought this must be God's answer. I didn't send for her father. He just appeared."

"Praying about the whole thing? Emily and me—is that what you mean?"

"I have been concerned, Dan. How could I not be? Emily isn't well enough to—"

With a sudden wild flail of his fist, Danny sent one of his mother's jars crashing to the floor.

"All these years, Mother, I've believed every word you said as if you were some saint or something. But you're a hypocrite, that's what you are! You tell me to believe that Emily *is* perfect inside—but you

321

don't believe it yourself. Now you tell me she's not well at all—she's *sick*—"

"Danny, that isn't fair," Caroline said in a shaken voice, shocked to hear her son address her with such words in such tone. "I love both of you more than words can tell. You know that I wouldn't deliberately hurt either of you—" She laid her hand on his arm, felt the hard, angry swell of muscle and realized with a pang that she was no longer speaking to a little boy but to an enraged young man.

"I'll never forgive you. Never—" He slammed out of the kitchen.

Caroline ran after him, but he went into the barn and bolted the door against her.

"Danny, please. We must at least talk about it," she begged through the heavy door. "Don't shut me away, Danny."

He wouldn't answer her. From the other side she heard the terrible sobs of a man-boy.

"What's the trouble?" Bay asked. He had been unhitching the team.

Caroline lifted hurt, lifeless blue eyes to his. "I let Emily go away with her father. Danny is inconsolable. He won't talk to me. Will you try to talk with him, Bay?"

"I'll do what I can."

"I never meant to—"

"No, of course not. Let me talk to him."

Caroline dragged back toward the kitchen and forced her hands to return to their task.

Bay waited a few moments, then called, "Danny, can I come in?"

There was no answer. The thought crossed his mind that the boy might do harm to himself in the throes of his pain. There was an opening several feet above the door, and with a little exertion, Bay hoisted himself up through it. When his eyes became adjusted to the dimness inside the barn he saw Danny leaning against one of the wooden stanchions, his head buried in his arms. Cautiously, Bay slid off the hay and went down the wooden ladder. Danny did not look up.

Bay sat down on an upturned barrel and waited, hoping Danny would choose to make the first move. The boy remained silent, his back a muscled barricade of resentment.

"She may have done the wrong thing, Dan, but she didn't do it on purpose. You know that," Bay said finally.

"She sent Emily away without even telling me. She knows how I feel about her."

"Your mother was afraid that Emily wasn't ready for a man-woman kind of love yet. The girl can barely handle the buffetings of everyday life. How is she going to be strong enough to cope with the most powerful emotions human beings ever feel? You're only thinking of yourself, Dan. Your mother was thinking of Emily as well. Forcing yourself on her at this point—"

"Forcing—I didn't force my love on her!" Danny cried, whirling to face Bay, face white with rage. "I laid my love at her feet, a gift for her to pick up or discard as she chose—and I'm glad I did. Glad! It was honest and good, and nothing that you or my mother can say to me is going to make me think any different. At least I had the courage to tell her, which is more than you have. You've loved my mother for years, ever since I was a little kid—every time you're near her the tension and yearning is so thick between you they could be cut with a knife, but neither one of you say a word. You'll go on living in the spring house, trying to shut out the sight of her lamp burning in the window of your bedroom—well, I think that's stupid—"

"Danny, shut up—"

"Why should I? It's all right for you to tell me what to do—but if I tell you what everyone knows, it's not permissible."

"It isn't as simple as you think, Dan. What have I got to offer your mother? I'm still a sick man and a poor one. I wouldn't have her marry me out of pity. When I've got something ahead again—"

"Hah!" Danny snorted, "Those are just excuses. You've gotten better all the time. You hardly cough or get chills at all anymore, and the rent my mother paid for this place has been piling up for six years. Excuses, that's all. The real reason you don't say anything is because you're *afraid*. You're afraid that she still loves my father, that she'll never love anyone else—"

Danny broke off as the older man rose to his feet. The expression on his face was frightening to the boy.

"Bay—I'm—I'm sorry," he faltered. "I hurt so bad myself I guess I just didn't—"

"It's all right, Danny," Bay laid a hand on the boy's shoulder, "You're right. That's the hell of it, you see. You're right."

He opened up his shirt and took out a pouch from which he counted a substantial amount of money.

"Go and find your love. Go anywhere you have to—"

"Bay—"

"Take my horse to the station. I'll pick him up later."

"You mean it? Right now?"

"You'll never start sooner."

"But how will I ever find—"

"You will," Bay said with a slightly twisted grin.

Caroline was stirring jelly in the kitchen when Bay opened the door. She had a white cloth tied around her hair and her eyes still looked hurt and tired.

"Did you talk to him, Bay?" she asked anxiously. He was standing in the doorway, the sunlight burnishing his hair.

"Dan did most of the talking."

"What did he say—"

His eyes touched her with a nearly physical force. She felt the spoon loosen from her fingers even before he began to stride toward her.

"He said it was high time that I told his mother that I love her."

He took her into his arms and this time there were no barriers of possible infidelity or indelible memories holding her back.

The apple jelly boiled up rosily inside the kettle, gurgled and popped in bright bubbles up to the rim, foamed over and rolled onto the hot surface of the stove then blackened and unfurled in rolls of black smoke.

Kemink came hurrying into the kitchen, nose twitching, eyes smarting. "What in the world—"

She saw Bay and Caroline then, locked in oblivious embrace. She stole past them, picked up the wooden spoon and began to stir the jelly down, shaking salt on the crusting overflow with the other hand.

Bay drew back from Caroline, his eyes full of light. "Caroline— let's get married right away. Today—right now."

Caroline shook her head, breathless, excited, confused. "But Bay— we don't have a license. I need a dress. The jelly—"

"Don't worry about the jelly. I will take care of that," Kemink assured her.

"What about Danny?"

"I gave him my permission to go to Chicago and look for Emily. He's saddling the horse now. You can still stop him if you disagree."

"No—if you think it's all right—but shouldn't we wait until he comes back—?"

"Let's go get the license now, today."

Caroline suddenly realized how ludicrous it was to wait half a lifetime for a man to ask you to marry him and then to worry about whether the apple jelly was cared for.

"Yes—" she said, "Yes, yes, yes, yes! Give me five minutes to slip into a fresh dress—"

But while she was pulling the rose sprigged dress over her head, she heard the rumble of a wagon in the doorway, and when she came out ready to go, she found Bay deep in conversation with a soot covered man.

"Caroline, this is one of Jim Conover's men. He says they have a bad fire and Jim's mills are in danger of burning. They're digging ditches around the town to try to stop the fire, but the sawdust around the mills keeps catching fire from sparks. Hendrink here rode all night trying to find help."

"I went to Green Bay first, Ma'am," Hendrink said, "n' you couldn't *hire* nobody to come and help. There's been so many brush fires of late, and so much smoke and burning jus' day by day, thet those fellars were plumb sick of it n' they wouldn't come iffen you begged them and piled gold coins to their knees. So Big Jim, he sez, 'You go fetch Bay from down Peshtigo way. He might know some fellars there, would come.' Ma'am we gonna lose jus' about everything we got if we don't get some more help in stopping these fires—"

"Caroline—I hate to leave you," Bay said, "especially since Danny is leaving and Dan-Pete isn't back yet. Besides—" His eyes caressed her face saying more than words could.

"Jim sure is countin' on you—" Hendrink said.

"Of course—you will have to go," Caroline said. She knew how generous Big Jim Conover had been in helping Bay plan and outfit his mill. "We'll be all right. Dan-Pete should be home any day now, and we have Josh and the hired man."

"Well—I should go—" Bay admitted, his eyes still regretfully tracing Caroline's face.

"Won't you have a glass of cider or buttermilk to refresh you?" she asked Hendrink. He looked so weary with his soot tinged face and drooping shoulders.

"No, Ma'am—our situation back there is urgent. The sooner Bay can round us up some men—"

"I can't promise," Bay said, "The confounded fires are so prevalent no one wants to leave his own home and business, but I'll do what I can."

"Bay—please come back to me safely," Caroline begged, as he gave her a goodbye embrace.

"Don't you ever doubt that for a moment!" he said.

The last thing he called to her as the wagon rumbled out of the yard was—, "Get yourself a dress—lasso a preacher—and *hang up the wedding bells*—I'll be back!"

67

Passengers and well-wishers mingling in crowded throngs at the Milwaukee station cast admiring glances at a young woman dressed in dove grey, who moved slowly through their midst on the arm of her father. Her beauty was such that few were able to keep from paying her the tribute of lingering glances. But without exception, embarrassment grew on their faces and they looked away uneasily, sensing something abnormal about the girl. The lovely face was completely passive, the eyes as blank as a china doll's.

A young man hurried through the crowd, his eyes a blaze of anxiety in his sun-scorched face. He spoke desperately to the attendant at the gate, his eyes never leaving the throngs headed for the trains. Receiving no satisfactory reply to his queries, he hastened down the narrow loading platform, staring up wildly at the train windows. A call escaped him. "Emily—Emily!"

Aboard the train, the girl's blank expression wavered. A light flickered in her eyes, reflecting the urgency of the young man jostled and harried by the crowds along the walkway.

She turned to the man beside her, gripped his arm in wordless, frantic entreaty.

"Emily—what is it?" he asked, concerned but not comprehending.

With futile pantomine, she tried to draw his attention to the figure struggling through the crowd on the platform.

"Did you leave something behind that you need? Is that it? Don't be disturbed, child. Whatever it is, we can buy you another when we get—"

She shook her head in an agony of frustration.

With a burst of steam and a ringing of bells, the train began to move.

A stifled cry burst from the girl. Struggling to her feet she grasped the frame of the window and leaned out, causing great alarm to her father who feared she would fall. Even as he pinned her arms to secure her safety, her inarticulate despair at last found form—

"Dan—nee" she called. "Danny!"

The boy on the platform heard. He looked up and saw her half hanging through the window.

"Emily!" he shouted back.

His teeth blazed a white banner of joy across his face as he caught the handrail and swung himself aboard.

*   *   *

Rain—*rain—why* doesn't it rain? The question etched in every brain, was exchanged with every greeting. Each day dawned anxious with waiting, eyes and necks craned in silent supplication to the ungiving sky.

Caroline's eyes strained down the road as often as they did at the sky. Where was Bay? She longed for the comfort of his masculinity and strength in this odd, ominous autumn in which smoke hung in the air like danger.

"Weather like this can't hold," she tried to comfort herself and the children. "We had better bring a big load of supplies in from town. When the rain does come, it will be heavy."

"It won't hurt to get the supplies," Kemink agreed, "but there will be no rain."

Caroline groaned. She had learned from experience that Kemink was usually right when it came to weather. When her Indian friend said "Rain," it rained; when she said "Blow," it was well for the young trees to tighten their roots.

"Last night the moon rose like fire—red and burning," Kemink said. "It is not a good omen. But the wind blows off the lake most always, and it would make it hard for fire to reach us here at bayside."

"I am glad Dan-Pete will soon be home," Caroline admitted.

Dan-Pete was due back any day from his summer sojourn in the Tomorrow River country. Danny had sent a telegraph message that all was well and that he would be staying briefly with Emily and her family in Chicago.

Before Danny left, he had apologized to Caroline for his harsh words.

"Bay gave me money to go and find Emily, Mother. Are you going to quarrel with me about it?"

"No, Danny. Go with my blessing. I never meant to hurt you so deeply. I hope you find Emily. They were shopping in Milwaukee and will be leaving for Chicago. Here is her father's address—"

"Mother, I'm sorry about the things I said to you—"

"I'm sorry too, Danny—"

They had held each other close, forgiving and forgiven.

68

Kemink had been wrong! It rained the following day but the joy that rampaged throughout the community was as short-lived as the rain. The sprinkle settled the dust in the air for a few hours and dampened some of the ever smoldering small fires, but it was not heavy enough nor of long enough duration to deeply freshen the bone hard earth and brittle dying foliage.

Dan-Pete arrived home, dirt-blackened and weary from his trip, to report that the railroad crews building a line from Fort Howard to Escanaba, Michigan, were digging ten feet down to find water in what had in other years been impassable swamps and bogs.

"My Indian brothers blame the white man," Dan-Pete said. "They say he has offended the spirit of the forests because he has cut down the trees as in a massacre and has not asked pardon of the spirits he so takes."

Caroline shook her head sadly. "And there are those of our race who blame the Indians for the constant underbrush fires. They say the Indian braves have come to this traditional hunting ground for stalking deer and gathering trout and that they do not put out the fires they ignite at night for protection against animals. In the morning, the fires go on smoldering and—"

"They can't blame the Indians alone, Aunt Caroline," Dan-Pete interrupted. "The farmers go on clearing and burning their brush, and the railroad crews I passed were the worst of all. You could trace their progress each day by the trail of burning brushpiles they left behind them each night."

"You can't wear a white dress to town," Firefly, who was fifteen now and very clothes conscious, complained. "The air is so smoky that you come home as sooty as if you'd been riding on a train."

"Speaking of soot, Fly," Caroline said, "we'd better gather in the sheets we hung this morning or by sunset they will look as if they had never been washed."

Fly nodded, but she lingered behind in the kitchen with Dan-Pete after her mother had gone.

"Dan-Pete, do you think a girl will go to hell if she kisses a boy before she's married?"

"Absolutely!" Dan-Pete said and made a wicked face at her. "I suppose now you've taken to kissing boys."

"Of course not," she said, tossing her curls indignantly, "but I can't help it if one kissed *me,* can I? It's not my fault if I'm irresistible, is it?" she added mischievously.

"You'll definitely go to hell for that," Dan-Pete predicted, "and they'll put you in the hottest place there to boot for being so conceited!"

Fly laughed merrily. "Well, George Peterson tried to kiss me, and I wouldn't let him, so does that mean I'm going to go to heaven?"

Though Dan-Pete had maintained a half bantering tone with Fly

328

during the conversation, there had been an edge to his voice and a rather dangerous gleam to his dark eyes that had pleased her.

"You're close to talking sacrilegious now, girl," he said shortly. He turned away from her and began to unlace the moccasins he had worn on his journey.

"Well, you think Emily is so nice and she let Danny kiss her. She did! Do you think that means she will go to hell?"

"I'm no preacher! Whatcha asking me for?" Dan-Pete growled in sudden bad temper. "Anyway, if Dan kissed Emily it was his fault; but I'd almost be willing to swear that if a boy kissed you it would be because you pranced back and forth in front of him and dared him to."

To his surprise her eyes filled with quick tears. "You really don't think much of me, do you Dan-Pete?"

"Oh, Fly, of course I do," he said, his voice softened. "I'm just hot and tired and out of sorts. I don't feel like talking about kissing."

She turned her back sobbing. "You always say mean things to me— talk hateful."

"Don't cry," he pleaded, touching her shoulders gently. "I didn't mean to be mean to you—"

She turned her rosy face to him, tears still dripping down her cheeks, but a smothered giggle escaped from the softly pursed pouting lips she offered to him. "Now *you'll* have to kiss me to make me feel better."

She was playing a game. They both well knew it. She was waiting for him to explode, to offer to "bottom-end her," to chase her around the porch or throw a dipper of water at her. But somewhere over the summer he had grow past games.

"Don't Fly," he said in a tone of voice that filled her with a hard hurting sadness. "We aren't children anymore."

She felt her eyes filling with tears again, and she realized that the other tears had been real too. She had only pretended they weren't.

"You'd better go help your mother with those sheets."

For one more second she looked at him with tear-swimming, reproachful eyes. *Why,* her eyes pleaded wordlessly, *did you throw our innocence away? Why are you forcing me to be grown up and responsible and full of pain?*

His dark eyes looked back, sad, impenetrable, unreadable.

Her lips hardened with pride. She walked away from him into the heat outside. Usually she poured everything into her mother's lap, but now she was silent, gathering the sheets with fierce gestures, stuffing them violently into the basket.

Watching, Caroline asked, "Is something the matter, Fly?"

The girl looked up at her, her cheeks red velvet, her eyes a scalding blue. "Mother, it's so hot! It's so *damn* hot."

She waited with narrowed eyes for her mother to react to the unheard of swear word from her lips. Caroline gave her a strange look as unreadable as the one Dan-Pete had given her. All she said was, "There is only one more line to go, then we can go inside where it is cooler."

*　　*　　*

Caroline's usually light step dragged as she walked across the veranda and sank down in a rocker by Kemink. She brushed a loose strand of hair from her hot forehead.

"The heat makes the children so restless. By the time I had carried drinks to the last of the little ones, the first ones were asking for water again."

"But they are all asleep now?"

"For the moment."

"The boys have gone to help put out a fire in the Sugarbush."

Caroline fanned herself with her apron. "That's the third time this week they've been fetched. It's getting worse."

They had almost become accustomed to the rings of fire that smoldered all around them in the darkness each night, to the feverish touch of the occasional wind, and the nauseous gassy scent that drifted from the marshes and hung in the thick air.

"Strange," Caroline ruminated. "The older the children grow, the more I seem to miss their not having a father to help share the responsibility. Do you suppose having Bay here for even this short time has spoiled me? I wonder now at my audacity in taking all these other children to raise without a father." She told Kemink of Fly's unhappy mood and unwillingness to communicate what was bothering her. "For years I never even thought about it—and now I wonder how I dared."

Kemink chuckled. "When one is walking a tight rope, it is best not to look down."

"Dan-Pete often seems very tormented, too, Kemink. Do you ever regret having let him return to the Menominees? He seems so torn at times between his two worlds."

"The beaver sharpens his teeth by chewing wood," Kemink answered. "Our young sharpen their hearts, their minds, their souls against difficulties. I would not deprive my son of the currents in the river."

"Ah, Kemink, so you are one of those who thinks perfection would be stagnation."

"No, I believe in perfection," Kemink said. "I have known much perfection in my life. At its best, an apple is perfect. So are a strawberry and a wild rose perfect, and the moon at its full, and the sound of one's love returning when one has waited long—"

Caroline went on rocking, not getting the full impact of what Kemink was saying to her.

"—and the sound of one's love returning when one has waited long—" repeated Kemink.

Caroline turned to her friend with widened eyes. "Bay—?"

Kemink nodded. "Coming across the bridge now."

"Oh, Kemink, how I envy you those Indian ears. But are you sure? How can you—"

Kemink laughed. "I have Indian eyes as well as ears, and who but Bay has hair that gleams like silver in the night?"

Forgetting the heat, Caroline gathered up her skirts and ran off the veranda and down the path to greet him. The moment he dismounted she was in his arms.

"Oh, Bay, I'm so glad you're home. You were gone so long—I could not help worrying."

He held her close, stroking the tension from her back. "I'm sorry, darling, I never thought it would take so long. The situation isn't good. I would have been home earlier, but when I came through Peshtigo, there was a fire there, too. The men who had gone with me to help at Suamico expected me to give a hand. It was nip and tuck, but we did get it put out."

He bent and kissed her troubled face. "Don't look so worried, little one. The fires may have been something of a blessing. All the small brush around Peshtigo is burned off now, which should afford the town some protection."

"And at Suamico?"

"We saved the houses and mills with bucket brigades but—" he shook his head, unable to hide from her the fact that he found the situation serious, "—two of the railroad camps burned to the ground. I don't mind saying I don't like that."

"Bay—do you think the children are in danger here?" Caroline asked anxiously.

His eyes remained troubled, but he tried to comfort her. "All we need is one good rain. Now, let's not talk about it anymore tonight. What I want to know is—have you found us a preacher?"

"I have."

"Then we'll get the license tomorrow."

He looked over her head at the house and buildings faintly silhouetted in the night. He smiled, his teeth white in his soot-covered face.

"Do you know I've owned this place for ten years and this is the first time I ever thought of it as *home*? It's a good feeling to 'come home'."

He touched her cheeks, her lips, her hair, gently as if to reassure himself she was real, and then with a small groan, gathered her against him and kissed her for a long time.

She was silent as she walked with him toward the barn. With one hand he led his horse, the other he kept around her waist. He, too, was silent, and she sensed that there was still something bothering him that he hadn't mentioned. As they reached the barn, he turned to her—"Caroline—Adam Quimby is in Peshtigo. He wants to see you."

69

Caroline, clad only in her petticoat, looked out the window of her bedroom at a new day smothered in dust and heat before it had scarcely begun. The chickens dragging across the dooryard looked soiled and spiritless. The vegetation was so shriveled it was like a silent scream.

She dipped a washcloth into the basin of water and held it against her face an extra second, savoring the coolness. Somewhere deep inside of her there was a small shudder. Today was the day she would have to see Adam. She had agreed with Bay that it was useless to try to hide from him.

She opened her closet door and surveyed her meagre wardrobe. She was feminine enough to wish to look well in Adam's eyes. The rose sprigged voile?—but she didn't want to look so dressed up that Bay would think she was preening for Adam.

She finally chose an everyday dress of copen blue, unaware that it did more for her tanned skin and blue eyes than any dressier frock would.

In the yard, Bay was readying the wagon. Ordinarily they would have taken the carriage, but he had agreed with her that it might be well to bring back an extra stock of supplies. Jimmy was helping him with all the inefficiency of a ten year old, his hair glossy in the white hot sun.

Bay turned to his small helper.

"Run to the house, Jimmy, and tell your mother we're ready. Tell her to take a parasol. It's mighty hot even this early."

"Kin I come too, Bay?"

Not this time, Jimmy."

Disappointment darkening his face, Jimmy dragged his feet on his errand, watching little puffs of dust rise from his footsteps and hang in the air.

"Shucks and shuttles, I never hardly ever get to ride to town in the buckboard," he complained to himself.

Caroline was already on the veranda before he could deliver the message.

"Kin I go too?" he pleaded, looking up at her appealingly, hoping she would set aside Bay's edict. *"Please."*

"Next time," she said gently. Her eyes did not seem to be looking at him.

"You're supposed to take your parasol," he remembered to tell her.

"Run and fetch it for me, will you, darling?" she asked.

Baird lifted Caroline onto the spring bench seat at the front of the buckboard. Their eyes met.

"You aren't happy about seeing him again, are you, Caro?"

She shook her head.

He climbed up beside her and held her hand between both of his for a moment before clucking to the horses to start.

"We might as well get it over with. He won't leave Peshtigo without seeing you."

"I know. But I keep wondering *why* he would want to see me."

The wagon jolted ahead. Dust rose around them, a grey brown haze across the world.

The lane from Harbour Hill wound through the shore brush before coming out on the road to town. Elderberry bushes grew in profusion, holding lacy clusters of wizened fruit. In some places smoke weed and sedge grew in clumps.

Jimmy, clutching Caroline's forgotten parasol, ran as fast as he could across the bridge. If he was quick enough, he might still be able to head them off at the bend.

He emerged from the underbrush just in time to catch their attention with a vigorous wave of the parasol.

Bay drew the team to a halt and Caroline leaned to retrieve the proffered parasol. In one swift wiggle, Jimmy was in the buckboard with them, turning his eager, sweat-streaked face to Caroline.

"Please let me go too. I want to ride into Peshtigo on the buckboard more n' *anything*."

Caroline, who seldom reversed her decisions, found herself weakening under his hotly pleading gaze, but she shook her head at the sight of him. He had blackened his toes skirting the creek bed, his hair was pearled with grass seeds, and he was dusty all over. Besides, she was uneasy about the possibility of having Adam see the boy. It was this fear which had made her agree to meet Adam in Peshtigo in the first place. She had not wanted him to come to Harbour Hill and perhaps recognize the child as his own.

"Jimmy, you're not presentable."

Tears welled in his eyes.

"Well—maybe if he promised to stay in the buckboard out of sight—he did have to run hard to bring that parasol," Bay prompted.

"Promise?" Caroline asked.

He beamed, settling down between the two of them blissfully as Caroline unfurled the parasol, and Bay, with a slight grin jerked the reins and started the horses forward again. He cast an amused glance Caroline's way. "Softy—"

"Me!—" she began indignantly, and then she laughed too.

When they arrived in Peshtigo, they found the suffocating taste and smell of smoke and dirt had permeated the streets, but the foreboding of some approaching disaster seemed less evident here than in the hinterlands. Perhaps the residents were reassured by their success in putting out the fires that had threatened them four days earlier. The sawdust streets were thronged with the usual trade of farmers, loggers, housewives, workmen, and fancy women. Young people walked four abreast, laughing and jostling each other on the board sidewalks. The ring of cash registers and the jingle of harness mingled in the dead still air.

Bay drew the team to a stop on a side street and turned to Caroline.

"Adam has his wife with him. He wants to see you alone, so he's arranged for you to meet privately in the circuit judge's quarters. Just go up those stairs and turn one door to the right. He said he would be waiting for you."

She lifted eyes as dark as the smoke smothered sky. "Bay—aren't you going to come with me—?"

He shook his head. "Whatever he wants—it's between you and Adam, Caroline. I'll go take care of the supplies."

He took her parasol and gave it to Jimmy.

"Here. You're going to need this more than she will now. Watch the horses."

He lifted Caroline to the street. There was nothing she could do but go up the waiting steps. The heat squeezed around her. Her body felt damp, her lips dry.

Bay was watching her, waiting.

Resolutely, she turned and went into the building and started up the stairs. In those few moments as she mounted the worn treads, her fingers clutching the varnished rail so tightly they ached, she was assailed by a thousand memories.

She saw Adam again, shirtless, his black hair falling across his forehead, his smile dimpled as he watched a small Danny try to wield a shovel—she saw him come storming into the clearing on Ebonite, his head flung back, his white stock gleaming in the last light of day— she saw his profile, that handsome profile, outlined with moonlight beside her—

She shut her eyes tightly as if she could shut away the memories. They came anyway, thronging, leaping at her. She was lying in the dust again, where he had thrown her. He was lifting her up, tears running down his cheeks. He was holding Fly—smiling—*"She's dark like me"*—

Her heart was pounding so she stopped for a moment and laid both hands over it. She reached out for that inner divine strength she had come to know was there. With a renewed sense of composure, she continued her upward journey, turned to the right and paused before the dark varnished door, rapping softly.

"Come in!" said a voice. *His* voice—that strong, evocative preacher's voice.

She opened the door and for the first time in fourteen years, Adam and Caroline Quimby faced each other.

His first words were cruel.

"You're old—" he said. He said it because he wanted to hurt her for some reason but also because it was true. Caroline was not one of those women who seem impervious to the ravages of time. Laugh lines rayed abundantly from the corners of her eyes, pain lines bracketed her mouth, silver threads glinted in her hair.

"—but still beautiful," were the next words wrenched from him reluctantly, and they, too, were true. If Caroline was not one of those women whom times does not mark, she was one of those whom the patina of time makes only more captivating. Her face had become more transparent over the years, so that it was like a stage across which her emotions leaped and danced in endless fascination.

"You look much the same, Adam," she said.

His face was less marked by the passage of years than hers, but if hers had become more transparent, his had grown into an opaque mask through which he viewed the world with slitted eyes. In defiance of the heat, he was wearing a dark suit, opened to reveal a vest embroidered with white silk. Gold rings glittered on his fingers.

"Are you happy, Adam?" she asked.

"Of course not," he said sardonically. "Are you?"

"Yes."

"I don't believe you."

"Why did you want to see me after all these years?" Caroline asked.

He had been leaning against the desk. Now he stood up and began to advance toward her slowly. She drew back, feeling uncomfortable.

He was close enough to her now that he could reach out and touch her. His eyes burned dark in the white mask of his face.

"I have not been happy one day of my life since I left you. My dreams are filled with the sound of your name and I ache inside with a void that is worse than any possible disease. I have never stopped wanting you—loving you—needing you."

"No—no!" she shook her head, tears filling her eyes. "Adam, I didn't want to see you again! Bay made me—"

"*Why?*" Why didn't you want to see me again? Were you afraid? Afraid the magic would still be there? And we did have magic, didn't we? *Didn't we?*" he demanded harshly.

She nodded, blinking back the tears.

"Even after all this time, it's still there—"

Caroline twisted away at the same instant that she realized he was going to embrace her. His arm caught her beneath her breast, the other hand about her throat.

"I've never really loved anyone but you—" he whispered hoarsely against her hair. There was something rough and lustful about the fingers caressing her throat. She felt as violated and revolted as if a stranger had suddenly seized her on the street. He smelled of brandy, cigar smoke, strong cologne—odors she did not associate with Adam. She had a sudden, clear realization that *he was a stranger*.

"Let go of me!" She said it with such repulsion that he could not possibly mistake her emotion for anything but disgust. His fingers dropped from her as if he had been burned. He made a faint braying noise that did not quite pass for laughter and drew a supercilious expression of amusement across a face that, for a moment, had been naked of its mask and had revealed pure torment.

"So—you think you're in love with the tall pole with the French name."

The revulsion she had felt for him was replaced with a welling pity.

"Adam—if you had come back at the end of the war—even five years ago. But it's too late now. We're—we're strangers."

"Think about what we were to each other. I'm the father of your children! Then tell me that we can *ever* be strangers." His lips were jerking to keep his emotions safe behind the white mask.

"That young Adam and that young Caroline will exist forever in the limbo of the past. Nothing can take away what they were to each other that was good and holy and beautiful. But we aren't that Adam and that Caroline anymore, Adam. We're two different people."

At that moment the door which had been left ajar suddenly swung inward and Jimmy's face appeared, dusty, tinged with guilt, but smiling with hopeful appeal.

"I know I said I'd stay in the buckboard, but honest I'm gettin' baked like a turkey. Kin I go over to the park and get a drink?"

It would have been just an unwelcome interruption as far as Caroline was concerned, had she not been afraid Adam might recognize himself in the boy. But an expression of alarm flared across her face and her voice was too frantic and breathless as she said, "Jimmy—you get back to the buckboard this instant!"

"Wait a minute, son—come here," Adam said.

Jimmy moved hesitantly into the room.

"What's your name?"

"Jimmy."

"What's your last name?"

"Jimmy Quimby."

Adam beckoned him even closer, studying him. His fingers buried themselves emotionally into Jimmy's shoulders. The boy whimpered, frightened.

"I'm sorry, son—just wanted to see how tough you were. You look like a real Indian fighter to me," Adam said, all charm. "Where did you get that mole on your ear, son?"

"I dunno. I always had it."

"That's funny, so have I," Adam said, "and my father before me." He was looking over the boy's head at Caroline who had turned white.

"Jimmy Quimby, huh?"

The boy nodded.

"Here—here's a half dollar. You just run get yourself the biggest sasparilla in town."

"Hallelujah!" said Jimmy with delight, but then remembering he had to check with Caroline, he turned back and asked, "Is it all right?"

"Yes," Caroline said weakly. "Go."

"*That boy is my son*," Adam said the moment Jimmy's footsteps had faded on the stairs.

"Don't be absurd," Caroline said, her blood cold in the heat of the day.

"Jimmy *Quimby*."

"Don't forget that it's my name, too. He had no other name so I give him mine."

He came close to her again, his narrowed eyes devouring hers. "Look me straight in the face and tell me he's not my son, Caroline.

You never were able to lie."

"He's not your son!" *He's mine—my son!* she thought passionately. *I'm not lying. It takes more than blood—it takes love and sacrifice and devotion to make a child your own.* But her voice had wavered.

"It won't do you any good to lie. *I know.* That's why I'm here."

"No!" Caroline cried, covering her face with her hands.

His fingers were bruising her arms. "Admit it, Caroline. You stole my son!"

"The baby was like—like Fly. Defective, *you* would say. So you see, Adam, it was not my fault after all." The moment she said it, she was ashamed to have justified herself.

"I've known that for years. Maybe I always knew it deep inside," Adam said heavily.

"Your wife was afraid you would blame her. She wanted to get rid of the baby. Was determined to get rid of him. So Cricket brought him to me."

"She told me he was dead—the dirty—"

"Don't," Caroline pleaded. "She's your wife, Adam. She must have loved you desperately or she wouldn't have done it."

Adam's grin was sour. "You couldn't even begin to comprehend Sally, Caroline. But the important thing is—I want him. I want my son, Caroline! And I have a right to see my other children, too."

Hot tears ran down Caroline's cheeks.

"Adam, please don't do this to me. He's like my own child. I have loved him and raised him and helped him get well and strong. Why do we always have to hurt each other so much, Adam?"

"You have the other children. He isn't yours. And—he's all I've got. I'm not trying to pretend my life isn't bitter and empty, Caroline. It is. I want the child. He could make all the difference. And—I'm going to have him."

"I'll never give him up, Adam."

"I'll take it to court."

"You'll have to—"

Overcome with tears, she turned and ran down the stairs. Bay was loading the last sack of chicken feed into the buckboard. She flung herself into his arms sobbing.

"*Caro*—what is it?"

"Jimmy," she choked. "Adam is going to take Jimmy from us."

70

Sally Magee Quimby waited in misery for someone to answer the door at Harbour Hill. Her body had given way to fat and the only way she could maintain an illusion of a waistline was through merciless corsetry. Her flesh fried inside the canvas and whalebone contrivance. Why didn't these people answer their door!

She knocked again, furious. She could hear a piano—the sound of childish laughter—and at last footsteps. The door opened to reveal a slender woman in a white apron.

"Please come in. I'm sorry if you had to wait in the heat. We are all in the back kitchen, canning."

Sally mopped red cheeks. "I'd like to see Miz Quimby."

"I'm Mrs. Quimby."

Sally was astonished. *"You're* Caroline?" Cricket and Adam had referred to Caroline often as a 'lady'. She had expected silk and fashion, pearls and poufs, not a white apron and hair that escaped in wayward curls.

"Please come this way," Caroline said.

As Sally followed her toward the parlor, her eyes skimmed the scuffs on the dark floors covered with simple braided rugs, the windows curtained with muslin, a stone crock filled with the kind of bouquet a child might gather. The parlor, more luxurious with a gleam of silver and fine woods, was sparse and simple compared to Sally's "setting room" in San Francisco. Sally had portieres and Belgian carpets and lamps with crushed velvet shades and beaded fringe. She was puzzled then as to why there was a grace in this house that her own lacked.

Her stays creaked as she sat down on the sofa. She fumbled in her bag for a handkerchief to wipe her face.

"Wouldn't you like to take off your hat—it's *so* warm?" Caroline asked. She disappeared and soon returned with a tray of refreshments. She put it down and then seated herself. She looked at her guest with a certain curiosity and Sally realized she had not introduced herself.

"I'm—I'm Sally Quimby," she blurted.

"Oh," Caroline said, a world of sudden comprehension in that one small sound.

"Adam sent me. I thought maybe you wouldn't like me to come here. I didn't want to come—it don't seem right somehow—but when Adam makes up his mind about something, it's hard to go against him—"

"I know," Caroline said with such understanding that Sally thought; *Yes, she would know. If anyone else in this world would know how Adam is, she would.*

"He wants me to tell you that if you give us the boy without any trouble that I'll be good to him. That I do want him," Sally went on in a rush. She stared down at her hands. They twisted as if they had a life of their own. Then she looked up into Caroline's eyes. "I'd do anything to make Adam happy, *anything*. I do love him, you know."

"Yes, I'm sure you do." She said it with a compassion that made Sally want to cry, though she couldn't have said why. For the first time she had an inkling that being a lady meant more than knowing which fork was picked up first or whether one wore kid gloves. In a dim way, she understood that it was something *inside* of Caroline that caused Adam and Cricket to describe her as a lady, and she felt a new sting of bitterness as if she had been cheated in some fresh way. She had thought that she had become a lady when she and Adam moved to their San Francisco mansion and she had her clothes designed in Paris. She knew now that she still wasn't a lady and maybe never would be. At the same time, she felt an unexpected response to Caroline. She had never had a woman friend, a real one, except perhaps Mama Tutu. Adam was consistently sharp, sarcastic, and condescending to her. She hadn't realized how hungry she was for someone to say to her as Caroline had, "Yes, I understand—*I know*."

"It's real funny," Sally blinked back unexpected tears. "All these years I've hated you—hated the thought of you—because I felt Adam—well, I think he still—still thinks about you. But now that I've met you—I think—I think I like you."

"I hope what I'm going to say won't change that, Sally, but I have to say it. I love your little boy as if he were my own. I am going to fight every way I know to keep him."

Sally straightened. Her whalebone creaked. "I suppose you think I'm some kind of rotten person for giving him away."

"I'm not in a position to throw the first stone, Sally. We seem to sow what we reap, and I did wrong too. When I kept the truth about Jimmy from Adam, I became an accomplice. In my heart I knew that was wrong. Now I have to pay the price. In the event that Jimmy is—is taken from me," her voice broke, "the fact that you do want him and will be good to him will comfort me. But I repeat, I will do everything I can to keep from losing him. Go back and tell Adam we won't give him up without a fight."

"I suppose it don't seem fair to you," Sally said, "but you can't know how much Adam wants this kid. I—I can't have no more. I'd

340

give anything now if—but I can't."

"I'm sorry," Caroline said genuinely.

Sally had an absurd desire to lay her head on Caroline's shoulder and to break into sobs. She felt that Caroline understood everything in some mysterious way—the whole situation with her and Adam—the giving away of the child—and what was more, that she did not condemn or gloat, that she was sorry, truly sorry. The sobs were so close that Sally stuffed her handkerchief into the front of her dress and said, "I'd better go now. I done what he told me. There's just one more thing. Adam wants to see his other kids. He says he's got a right."

"Danny isn't here," Caroline said. "He is engaged to a lovely young woman and has gone to Chicago to visit her father. He won't be back for a week or so. But yes, I suppose Adam can see Felicity. You may come to dinner to-morrow evening, if that suits him."

"I'll tell him," Sally said.

Caroline walked with Sally across the sunbaked yard to where her buggy waited in the shade of an elm.

"Talk about the heat of the desert!" Sally complained. She fanned herself with her big hat as she struggled to get in. "Don't it ever rain around here?"

Jimmy was playing in the yard. He watched with curiosity as she drove off. "Who was that fat lady with the red face?" he asked Caroline.

She looked down at him, eyes full of pain. How could she say, *your mother*?

* * *

Dan-Pete drew the harmonica Cricket had given him years before from his shirt pocket and laid it against his lips. The tune he drew out was mournful and heavy. His shortness with Fly had been occasioned by more than the weariness and heat. He had brought bad news back with him from the Tomorrow River country and he was dreading the moment when he would have to tell his mother. He had put it off as long as he could and now in the oven heat of the evening he blotted his sweating face with his shirt tail and steeled himself to go find Kemink.

As if drawn by the intensity of his thoughts about her, Kemink appeared on the veranda, her apron a white oblong in the dusk.

"Any cooler out here?" she asked with a smile.

Dan-Pete shook his head. "There ain't no coolness left in this world no more. Even the lake water is warm as fresh milk."

His mother came and sat down on the steps beside him.

"Must be the smoke and heat have killed all the crickets," Dan-Pete said. "Other years the crickets would be making so much noise you couldn't hear your own thoughts. Just listen now, mother—how queer and silent it is—"

Kemink nodded. "Nothing feels like moving. I noticed cattle to-day—they barely ate. The grass is so dry and juiceless, and the heat makes them so tired that most of the time they lie in whatever shade they can find."

I'm just talkin' to hear myself talk—putting off telling her, Dan-Pete thought to himself. A sigh swelled his chest and burst from him, an explosion of sound in the utter stillness that hung about them.

Kemink's dark eyes studied him for a moment. "What is it, Dan-Pete?"

He buried his forehead in his clenched hands and rocked back and forth on his haunches still finding the words hard to form, impossible to launch.

"Tell me, child of my heart," Kemink said, speaking this time in Algonquin.

He loved the sound of her full deep voice in the darkness, the feel of her presence beside him. He hated to hurt her—to release words he knew would fly into her as an arrow.

"Sashwatka is—sick," he said cautiously.

There was a long silence while Kemink assimilated his words, his tone, the tension of his body.

"The illness is grave," Kemink surmised.

Dan-Pete nodded. His throat felt raw from breathing smoke filled air. There was an acrid taste of ash on his lips. He could not find any words to offer to his mother for comfort. Again he picked up the harmonica and played the heavy mournful little song. The melody seemed to hang in the air long after he had drawn his lips away.

After the heavy pause, his mother broke the silence. "Has he asked for Kemink?"

"He has."

"You should have told me at once, Dan-Pete."

"I know."

"I will leave tonight."

"I will come with you."

"No. This time I will go alone."

"Are you angry with me?"

"No."

"Then let me come with you."

"No."

Then seeing the suffering on his face, she added more gently in explanation, "When I am in great sorrow I have always found it necessary to be alone for a time."

As they stood up together, he enclosed her for a heartbeat in the young strength of his arms. He was remembering when his father died.

He released her, watched her walk away tall and proud. He wished she could have cried as Caroline would have. Then he lifted his shirt tail and blotted the sweat on his cheeks again—sweat that this time was mingled with tears. He knew he would not see Sashwatka alive again. He had lost his father for the second time.

71

Adam Quimby had never looked more handsome than he did by the mellow candlelight of the dining table candelabra. In deference to the continued heat, Bay had eschewed more formal attire for a light, open-necked shirt. Not Adam. He wore his boiled white shirt, white silk vest and matching cravat, complete with a dark coat, with as much ease as if it had been in the middle of the winter. Gold and diamond rings sparkled on his long fingers. His smile flashed continuously and always in Fly's direction. From the moment he had stepped into the house that evening, he had thrown all the magnetism at his disposal into charming Fly. She had floated down the stairs to greet him in her best white organdy dress, her dark curls lifted with a satin ribbon. Her eyes had been huge, her face grave, and she had said frankly, "I don't know how to greet you. It seems strange to shake hands with one's father, but it would seem even stranger to kiss you. Since you left when I was only a baby, I really don't know you."

"My heavens, you are a beauty!" Adam had declared, catching her hands in his, "Even more beautiful than your mother at your age. But what is this about my *leaving* you when you were a baby? Your mother *sent* me away."

Fly had turned to her mother with a confused expression, and Caroline, in turn, could not keep from sending a searing glance of reproach to Adam. He had refused to notice, riveting all his attention upon Fly.

Now at the dinner table, Fly's excitement was growing under Adam's all-consuming attention.

"You can't know how delightful it is to eat for once like civilized people," she was confiding to Adam in pear shaped tones, "at a normal sized table with candlelight. Usually there are about fifteen of us at trestles like a bunch of hogs. We're not a family—we're an army!"

Adam's laughter applauded and encouraged her wit, but Caroline, looking down at her plate, thought, —*she has been parading her small hurts to Adam all evening. I always thought we were so close, and yet I never suspected she resented the other children so much. I'm sure Danny doesn't. Why didn't she ever tell me?*

"At that, my dear, I should think an army would be preferrable to two lonely people," Adam was saying. "We hardly have scintillating meals at our house since we have no children, and my dear wife and I have so little in common." He twisted the word "dear" with a biting irony.

Sally had drawn fascinated glances from the young males of the house as she had passed through to the dining room, due to the extreme decolleté of her peach colored gown. Now she cleared her throat loudly.

"As your mother was saying yesterday, Miss Felicity, what you sow, you reap."

"Oh mother is full of those little old-fashioned homilies," Fly said airily. "But I'm sure *I* didn't sow all the children in this house!"

Fly's remark drew a new burst of appreciative laughter from her father. He had brought a bottle of wine as his contribution to the dinner, and he leaned toward her now, his eyes shining. "Let's drink to that. Certainly you're old enough now for a small glass of wine."

From habit she turned toward her mother for permission.

"You know I don't like spirits," Caroline said.

"Bay has wine whenever it pleases him," Fly said, pointedly. "But then you always cater to Bay's every whim, don't you?"

"Oh, come now, Carrie," Adam said, deliberately using the old diminutive of her name in a way that implied a somehow gross intimacy. "One little glass of wine isn't going to hurt her."

"Another glass wouldn't hurt me neither," Sally injected, pushing her glass toward him.

"The only people who are hurt by 'spirits' as you so quaintly call them, are the gluttons and intemperates of this world," Adam said, looking at his wife with open scorn as he spoke. He ignored her proffered glass and filled Fly's. Sally had looked flushed and miserable all evening, now her heavy chin trembled and her plump hands twisted her napkin into a tangle.

I can't let this go on, Caroline thought. *We can't sit here being a captive audience for Adam's and Fly's malice—.* She felt Bay's eyes touching her. His glance said he too had had enough.

Bay stood up abruptly. "It's too hot for dessert. Wouldn't you like to bring your coffee out on the terrace where it's cooler, Mrs. Quimby?"

344

"Yes," Sally said gratefully, "I sure would." As she struggled from the table she gave a burping grunt.

Fly giggled.

Bay's invitation was not altogether altruistic. He had a feeling that if he didn't get out of the room he was going to grab Adam and knock his charming smile down his throat as a beginning, and that his next project would be to give Fly all the spankings she had missed in her childhood.

Caroline gave her a reproachful look before saying, "I hope you will excuse me for a little while also. Tucking the children in for the night is a ritual."

"Mummy has to put her army to bed," Fly said, irrepressibly gay.

A muscle jumped in Bay's cheek and it was only with an effort that he escorted Sally from the room.

Caroline spent more time than usual with each of the children dreading to go back down. She sat for a long time by Jimmy's bed. He was not his usual loquacious self.

"Is something troubling you, Jimmy?"

His dark eyes stared straight up at the ceiling. "Somebody told me that the man and woman who came for dinner are my real mother and father and that they're going to take me away."

"Who told you that, Jimmy?"

"It don't matter. What matters is—is it *true*?"

"Yes, Jimmy," Caroline said, "the part about their being your real parents is true, but Bay and I are going to go to court to keep you with us—that is if you want to stay."

He bolted out of bed and into her arms, hugging her frantically. "Please don't let them take me away—*please*."

Caroline's eyes were red from crying by the time she returned to the parlor where Fly and Adam were sitting on the sofa together. Fly bounded off the seat with excitement when she saw her mother. Her cheeks were a wild, burning pink and her eyes sparkled.

"Mother, guess what? Papa has invited me to come to San Francisco and live with him and Sally for a while. He says if I come, he'll give me a debutante ball at the largest hotel in the city and he'll buy me a gown from Paris and a diamond necklace. Oh, mother, I'm so excited I can't bear it. Think of it, mother. *San Francisco!* From what I've read, it must be the most exciting city in the world. He's going to take me to the theater and operas and balls—"

Caroline turned her gaze from her daughter's transfigured face to Adam. He met her dazed and burning glance defiantly, a smile carved in the mask of his face.

At that moment, Bay and Sally came back from their sojourn on the terrace.

"Adam, I want to go home. I ain't feeling good," Sally complained. She did look warm and blotched, miserable, limp.

"Mother, please say I can go," Fly was begging.

"We'll—we'll talk about it," Caroline said faintly, not taking her glance from Adam.

"Besides, the sky is red all around with those horrid fires they got here all the time. It scares me silly. I want to go back to the hotel," Sally was importuning in a thin wail.

Adam was bowing over Fly's hands, kissing them.

"Why don't you come in and have dinner with us Sunday night at the hotel? I'll come and get you," Adam said to her.

This time Fly did not ask her mother's permission.

"Oh, Papa, I would love that!"

"Parting is such sweet sorrow then, until Sunday night."

He turned to bow over Caroline's hands and kiss them, but she pulled them away from his grasp.

I would like to kick you, Adam, she thought ferociously.

The corner of his mouth jerked with a smile as if her mental message had gotten through on target and amused him.

Bay escorted the guests to their carriage.

Caroline was too full of emotion to say anything to her daughter. She turned without a word and went into her bedroom, undid the sprigged rose dress and, with uncharacteristic untidiness, flung it across the bed. She slipped a dressing gown over her petticoat and sat down by her dresser, brushing her hair with agitated strokes.

There was a timid knock. "Mother?"

Fly's face appeared in the doorway. She must have had second thoughts about her behavior of the night, for her expression was contrite.

"Mother—I'm sorry if I seemed saucy tonight. To discover after all this time what a marvelous, wonderful man my father is, and then to find out that you sent him away! *You never told me.* I suppose I felt a little resentful to think of all the years I've been deprived of knowing my father."

A thousand retorts crowded to Caroline's lips, bitter as gall, scalding as lava. She bit them back.

Fly had come close to her now, was kneeling beside her, looking up at her imploringly.

"Please, Mother, let me go to San Francisco with him. Don't deprive me of my father a second time—"

Caroline put her hands over her eyes and a sigh shook her entire body.

"Please, Mother—" Fly persisted.

Again Caroline held back all the words she might have said. She reached out and touched her daughter's cheek. "Fly, It's been a long, emotionally draining day and night. It is unbelievably hot, I'm exhausted, and to tell you the truth, in a very cross mood. I don't think this is the time to discuss it."

Fly sprang to her feet with a sigh of exasperation. "You're not going to let me go. I can tell!"

"I didn't say that."

"You don't want me to go though, do you?"

"No, I don't."

"Give me one good reason. Just one!"

"Do you realize, Fly, that in the morning we are going to court because that man is trying to take Jimmy away from us?"

"Don't call him 'that man.' He's my *father*," Fly flared.

"All right. Your *father* is trying to take Jimmy away from us."

"Well, Mother, I don't think you've looked at it from his side at all. Is it his fault that horrible woman he married gave Jimmy away? He didn't even know about it. What kind of father would he be if he didn't want his son? Besides—" Fly hesitated as if she thought she might be going too far.

"Yes?" Caroline said testily.

"I think Jimmy would be better off with him. You have to think of Jimmy. Of course he feels bad right now. But he'll get over it. A boy needs a father—and Papa's *rich*. He can give him all sorts of things you never even thought of. Anyway, Jimmy has nothing to do with *me*. This is the most fantastic opportunity, Mother. Nothing like this will ever happen to me again. I'm going to *die* if you won't let me go! And besides, you haven't given me *one* good reason, not really. Why don't you want me to go, Mother?"

"I don't want you with your father. If you must know, I think he's become morally reprehensible."

"Hah!" Fly hooted. "Morally reprehensible—well, really. Who are you to judge? At least he *married* that Sally—"

"What is that supposed to mean, Fly?"

Fly flushed darkly. She had walked out onto a precipice and now she had to jump.

"Well, you must know what everybody in the country thinks about you and Bay living here together not married."

"Is that what you think too, Fly?"

"I don't know what I'm supposed to think," Fly said with a toss of her head. "You're hardly setting an example for me—"

All the held back fury of the night rushed through Caroline, sending her to her feet. Before she could stop herself, she had delivered a stinging slap across Fly's face.

Fly looked at her mother in disbelief. Her mother had never struck her before. Tears flooded her huge blue eyes. Her lower lip quivered like a small child's, but it was the woman who prevailed. Even as Caroline reached out to her in instant apology, Fly drew herself up stiffly.

"That makes up my mind for me. I'm going with my father to San Francisco whether you want me to or not!" she cried defiantly, and turning, ran from the room almost colliding with Bay, who had just come back from seeing the Quimbys to their carriage.

Caroline started up the stairs after her. Bay caught her gently. "Not tonight. You've had enough."

"Bay—oh, Bay," she said leaning wearily into his arms.

He drew her with him onto the terrace, hoping it might be at least one degree cooler, and she told him what had happened.

"Why didn't you tell her about her father? Why should you let him make you out the villain?" Bay protested.

Caroline sighed. It was a night of heavy sighs.

"Danny knew, of course, because he was old enough to remember. But neither of us ever told Fly that her father didn't want her. It seemed unnecessarily cruel. I didn't want her to ever feel that she was the reason for the breaking up of our marriage. And tonight—tonight I felt intuitively that this was not the time to tell Fly. Not now when she is so enamoured of her father. But—it will be all right. I know it will. The undertide of affection between Fly and me is too strong for any lasting breach. I know that in my soul. It's Jimmy who is tearing me apart. We don't have any legal rights to him, Bay—"

Bay looked down at her anguished face and now it was his turn to sigh deeply. "Caroline, what a Pandora's box of trouble Adam's coming back has brought. He still loves you, you know."

She let that pass without comment. "Bay—what Fly said about people talking about us, I suppose is true. Now that we have the license, I think we should try to get married before the trial tomorrow. It might make a difference."

"Well, Mrs. Quimby, the thing is—" he pursed his lips with pretended reluctance, "—I do have some apples to jell—and my boots are worn out—"

"Bay LeSeure, you wretch—" she cried. But he had said it so drolly that Caroline lost her sad face and had to laugh.

"I am proposing. Do you accept?" she insisted.

"A marriage of convenience, I gather?"

"Oh, no. A marriage of love. Decidedly a marriage of love."

348

"In haste?"

"In haste, if you will."

"I thought you wanted to wait until Danny got home?"

"I did. The trial changes everything. Are you reluctant, Sir?"

"Not on your life."

It was after midnight when they were married with the clergyman's wife staring at them owlishly from under her nightcap, and the clergyman himself valiantly stifling yawns between each series of vows. Dawn was breaking through as they drove into the yard at Harbour Hill. Streamers of light hung through the dark clouds, blessing the ground. The household was still asleep.

"Bay—it's, it's our wedding night—morning—" Caroline faltered in sudden realization. She was dead tired and the thought stunned her.

"Wedding morning, Mrs. LeSeure," Bay said cheerfully, "and you are going to get some sleep before that trial!" He lifted her out of the carriage, carried her into the house and settled her gently on her bed. Then he bent and kissed her with great tenderness. "Sleep, darling, *sleep.*"

She had never loved him more nor felt more loved.

72

The courtroom smelled of scorched varnish as if the heat was pressing against the wainscoting like a hot iron. The judge unbuttoned the top button of his collar and pressed a linen handkerchief against his jowls. Sally Quimby, dressed in plaid taffeta, flourished a palmetto fan vigorously but without relief. Streams of perspiration trickled visibly down her florid cheeks. There were dark circles beneath Caroline's eyes and her lips were pale. Bay sat on one side of her holding her hand. Jimmy sat within the circle of her arm on the other. It was time for the decision.

"Mrs. Quimby—I beg your pardon, Mrs. LeSeure—" the judge addressed her, "I would like to say before this court that I have had the good fortune to know you for some time. I am well aware of the work you have done with numerous children and this boy whose custody is in question in particular. The facts are indisputable that the child regained his health and the use of his limbs under your care and devotion. I do not feel I am remiss in admitting that my sympathies are entirely in your direction. However—"

The judge cleared his throat and the "however" hung ominously in the air.

"I do not feel that any man is wise enough to dispense justice at his own discretion and according to his own sympathies. I have always felt that while the letter of the law must be tempered with mercy, it cannot be dispensed with. And in this case, the letter of the law is clear. Mr. Quimby has demonstrated beyond all legal doubt that the child is his blood son and that this same child was taken by you without his knowledge or consent. In addition, since the child's natural mother now repents of her compliance and duplicity in spiriting the child from his father and is willing to make amends, this court sees no other recourse than to restore the child to his rightful parents."

"I won't—I won't go live with them!" Jimmy shouted. "They aren't my paw and maw! She's my maw," he clutched at Caroline.

"Hush, Jimmy—hush darling," Caroline pleaded, enfolding the child in her arms. He clung to her, his small shoulders heaving.

Bay leaped to his feet. "Your honor, we will appeal that decision."

The judge nodded. "I think quite properly so, Mr. LeSeure, although I doubt that any higher court will set aside my decision. However—" Again there was a clearing of the throat while the few participants in the drama waited achingly. "—however, in view of the pending appeal, this court will leave the boy in the present custody until the outcome of the further suit is forthcoming."

Now it was Adam who was on his feet, outraged. "We intend to leave Monday and take the boy with us."

"Sir—" the judge intoned with disapproval, "I am sure that your deepest concern is for your son. This must also be the concern of this court. While I do not anticipate an upset of the decision I have handed down, one must acknowledge that such a reversal could occur. I do not feel it would be to the child's advantage to be handed back and forth like a plate of pancakes. And in this instance, Sir," the judge added with a certain sharp satisfaction, "the law supports me." He struck his dock with the gavel. "This court is adjourned."

Jimmy suddenly squirmed away from Caroline and ran from the courtroom. Caroline darted forward to follow him, but Bay laid a restraining hand on her arm. "Give him a few minutes to himself, Caro."

"Adam, I'm purely going to die if I don't get something to drink," Sally whined.

Adam paid no attention to her. He was looking fixedly at Caroline. She had refrained from looking his way all through the trial, but now, almost as if compelled by the force of his gaze, she turned toward him. Her face was calm and her eyes met his without anger or resentment or even reproach. There was in them only a poignant sadness that infuriated him. He wanted her to be angry, hurt, indignant. He wanted anything but what he saw in that small instant before she turned back to Bay, lifting her face and eyes to him.

"I promise you I'll never let him take that child from you, if I have to kill him to prevent it," Bay swore.

"Don't Bay," Caroline said. "I shouldn't have taken Jimmy knowing that Adam was going to be told his son was dead. I knew it was wrong, but I did it anyway. I just want to go home, Bay. Please take me home."

"Adam, I'm thirsting to *death*," Sally complained more loudly.

Adam swore beween his teeth, but still under the watchful eye of the judge, it seemed best to play the role of solicitous husband. Grasping his wife's arm with a grip just short of bruising, he escorted her outside.

"Stay here," he commanded brusquely, "I want a word with Caroline."

But Caroline did not want a word with him. She was concerned because Jimmy was not in the carriage. Bay handed her into the rig and climbing up beside her said, "He's probably half way home by now—I've an errand to do and then we'll go home."

"Caroline—" Adam called.

Bay ignored him, cracked the reins sharply and set off at a good pace.

"Adam, I feel like I got sawdust in my throat—"

Adam was staring after the carriage.

"*Adam—*"

He whirled on Sally in sudden, savage anger. "Damn you, go get your rotgut!" He threw his wallet at her as if it were a rock.

She caught it with a grunt. "Jumping gophers Adam, what you so cranky about?" she asked plaintively. "You oughta be happy. You won didn't ya?"

"Come on, Sally," he said wearily. "Come on and get your drink."

*   *   *

Felicity's door has been firmly closed when Caroline had passed it that morning. It was still firmly closed, but this time Caroline chose to knock. After a moment, her daughter opened it. Fly still had on her blue morning coat and her curls looked uncombed.

"The judge awarded Jimmy's custody to your father," Caroline said.

"Well—I am sorry, for you, Mama," Fly said awkwardly, "but maybe—I don't mean to hurt your feelings—but maybe he will be better off with Papa. He can give him all sorts of advantages. You have to think of Jimmy, too, you know."

"We can't find Jimmy. Have you seen him?"

"I've been in my room all morning. Didn't you take him with you to the trial?"

"He ran away when the judge announced the decision. Bay thought he would probably come home. You're sure you haven't seen him?"

"I'm sure. Ask Dan-Pete. He's around here somewhere."

Dan-Pete had not seen Jimmy nor had anyone else. The entire household turned out into the sweltering heat to search for him.

All through the long afternoon they searched without success. Bay drove back to Peshtigo and made a house to house search there, up one street and down the other. His search was futile.

Caroline's anxiety grew as darkness approached. The constant fear of fire in the surrounding woods added an edge of terror to her concern. She was also torn between the wish to have every available person look for Jimmy and the fear that one of the other children might become confused and lost in the darkness.

When Bay returned from Peshtigo they decided the younger children should go back to the house and be put to bed. After they were settled the rest of the household continued to search. All night lanterns bobbed through the dark woods and barns and out-sheds.

Caroline called until she was hoarse. The heavy, smoke-laden atmosphere made their task more difficult. The searchers' lungs ached with breathing it, their eyes stung and watered making it harder to distinguish the movement of a wind moved branch from a small boy, a log from a hunched body, a moon struck stone from a human face.

Bay went back a second time to Peshtigo, and this time roused Adam from his hotel bed to aid in the search.

A good two dozen people came by wagon to help search the woods and around the house. Joining hands in a human chain they scoured the woodland but netted nothing. Jimmy was not to be found.

Morning came. The searchers straggled up to the house for food and then returned to the task. Some of the men, grim-faced, began to pole the river.

"You've got to get some rest," Bay told Caroline taking her arm.

She shook her head, "Bay, you know I can't rest until we find him." At his insistence, she did finally sit down for a moment, her face buried in her hands.

A half dozen of the Peshtigo women dropped the search to fix some lunch. Everyone was hungry and worn out. She could hear the rattle of dishes and the smell of frying ham. *Jimmy hasn't eaten since yesterday—perhaps the smell of food*—she thought hopefully. But lunch passed, the search went on, and still no Jimmy.

On a sudden hunch, Caroline climbed into the hayloft to investigate again. Others had been up there two or three times, but there was always the possibility that Jimmy could remain undiscovered, buried bodily in the hay. This time, she sat down and waited—

And waited—

And—suddenly, there was a sneeze.

"Jimmy," she cried, dizzy with relief. "Oh, *Jimmy,* why did you run away and hide. You've fretted us more than you can ever know!"

A pair of baleful dark eyes stared at her through a haze of straw. "Can't figure out why it should fret you none. You're gonna send me away, anyway."

Caroline sank down by the lump of straw and pulled enough away to reveal his doleful face.

"Jimmy—dear—" she began. She tried to take him in her arms, but his body was hard, resistant.

"You lied to me. You told me God never lets us down. But I heard the judge say he was going to send me with that duded up man and that fat lady with the red face."

"Jimmy—"

He turned away from her, his body compressed with grief.

She thought, *I should go and tell the others I've found him and he's safe,* but she felt a weariness such as she had felt only two or three times in her life. She felt she could not make the physical effort to move one inch further. With a long sigh, she lay back in the straw beside Jimmy. A few shafts of sunlight filtered through a broken board and touched them. It was warm and still. From some faraway world she could hear voices calling, "Jimmeee—Jimmeeee—"

After a time she felt his hand creep into hers and then his voice, muffled against the tension of held back tears, saying, "I don't want to leave you."

She turned, pulled the hard ball of rolled up little boy into her arms. "I *didn't* lie to you Jimmy. God doesn't ever let us down. Sometimes we just *think* he does. I suppose Joseph might have thought that God had let him down when he was left in a pit by his brothers and sold into slavery. But years later, he was able to tell those same brothers, 'You meant it as harm, but God meant it as *good.*' God can take things that seem dreadful and turn them into something good."

"But I don't want to leave you—" he was sobbing now.

She rocked him against her. "I don't want you to go, either, Jimmy. But maybe God knows that your father needs you even more. And—like Fly said to me, your real father is rich. He could probably buy you all sorts of things—"

"Even a pony of my own—?" for a moment a gleam of avarice outshone the gleam of tears.

"Very likely."

But his soul was not to be bought. The tears flooded back. "I don't care. I want to stay *here*."

"At any rate, you will be staying here for a while. We're going to appeal the case to a higher court, Jimmy, and the judge said you could stay with us until the final decision. And Jimmy, if you do have to leave, love is something that isn't stopped by distance. No matter how far away from us you go, that isn't going to stop us from loving you. And I don't think your father would forbid you to write to us. And another thing, it doesn't mean we would have to be separated for ever. You are ten years old. When you're twenty-one you'll be a man and can do what you want. I know that sounds like a long time now, but it isn't really."

"You're not going to send me away right away?"

"No—and I think we'd better go down now, don't you? Everyone else is still looking for you and worried about you."

"Well—I am awful thirsty—"

"Come on, then! We'll get some rootbeer out of the cellar for everyone."

"Look, young man," Bay said sternly, when the straw bedecked pair appeared, "I think you owe an apology to everyone in this household and in Peshtigo for pulling a trick like this. But I have a feeling that if I took a vote on whether you ought to be whipped or not, the verdict would be for leniency."

There was a cheer of assent from the dust streaked, weary searchers.

"Next time I'll take you to the woodshed," Bay promised. Jimmy beamed as if he had just received the highest praise and flung himself at Bay in a convulsive embrace.

Many of the searchers stayed to quaff rootbeer on the veranda, but some went back to Peshtigo to tell Adam and the other searchers there that Jimmy had been found. Caroline went inside to change out of her straw prickling dress. *Perhaps Fly would like some rootbeer, too,* she thought, and went up the stairs.

The hour near dinner found Fly sitting in front of her dressing table. She had on her white organdy dress and her hair was pulled up in a sophisticated manner. She jumped guiltily at her mother's step.

"Mother," she said defensively, "now that Jimmy has been found, I'm going out to dinner with Papa."

"If he comes—" Caroline said. Impulsively, she reached up and undid the filigreed lavaliere she wore around her neck. She slid it around her daughter's bare, beautiful young throat.

"This belonged to your grandmother. It's the perfect touch," she said fastening the catch.

"Oh, yes," Fly said, fingering the lavaliere eagerly. "Does that mean you don't mind, then, mother—about my going to dinner with Papa?"

"If your papa is still up to it. I will ask one thing of you. I will give you money to rent a room overnight in the hotel. There must have been a dozen small brush fires going when Bay and I came back from the trial and Oliver Dickinson said that over in the Sugar Bush area a burning tree fell across the road and blocked passage. I would feel easier if you would stay over in Peshtigo and we'll come in the morning and get you."

"Mother—I thought—I thought I might go with Papa tomorrow." Her eyes were downcast. She couldn't meet her mother's glance.

Caroline sank down in the wicker rocker. She was quiet for a long time, then she said, "If you really feel you want to go, Fly, I think you should. But again, I would like to ask one thing. Don't leave until Danny comes back. I think you should say goodbye to Danny before you go."

"Well—" Fly decided, "I guess that would be all right. I would sort of like to see Danny before I go. But you do promise—" She broke off to run and peer out the window at the sound of a carriage.

"Oh, he's here! I knew he would still come!" She turned in a flurry, "Do you think I'll need gloves?"

"No. It's much too warm."

She pirouetted. "Do I look—?"

"Beautiful," Caroline assured her.

"Mother—I do love you—."

"I know."

They embraced before Fly rushed off down the stairs. They had tried to "make up", but they were both aware that something painful and constrictive was still unresolved between them.

From below on the terrace, Caroline heard Bay's voice leading the rootbeer crowd in a ballad—"For my darlin' Annie Laurie—I would lay me doone and dee—"

She thought with a pang not unakin to that she had felt hours earlier—"It's our wedding night—"

And there was still so much to be done—chores—supper—the children to put to bed. She leaned her forearms on the sill of the airless window and looked down at the terrace. The tentacles of self-pity that had been closing about her, unclasped. Something inside of her began to sing. *Bay*—she thought, *Bay*.

73

Peshtigo was bathed in a dirty yellow light that gave an eery, magic-lantern distortion to the familiar, everyday scenes. The air was laden with smoke and a blizzard of fly ash drifted weightless in the unmoving air. The crisp organdy ruffles of Fly's dress were already wilting about her shoulders, and the curls at the nape of her neck and forehead were soaked with perspiration. She had looked forward to this dinner with her father so much, and now she found herself feeling uneasy and miserable as he helped her from the carriage.

Earlier in the day a couple of hundred men, imported from Chicago to lay the North Western line toward Marinette, had arrived in Peshtigo, and a large majority of them had found their way to the saloons. The village was raucous with the sound of their celebrating, and yet at the same time, gripped in a curious hush. This unnatural silence frightened Fly more than the eery light and the ribald shouts of the men who jostled and pushed each other on the board sidewalks. In that stillness there was a sense of waiting, an implied and unnameable threat that made her wish suddenly that she were back home with her mother at Harbour Hill.

Ahead of them on the sidewalk, one of the railroad men was playing "Turkey in the Straw" on a squeezebox while a companion did a spirited jig, jumping so hard on the boards in his heavy boots that splinters flew into the air. Six or eight other men urged the revelry on by slapping their knees to the spirited rhythm. Most of the railway men, like the lumbermen, were good to look at, fresh-faced from their outdoor labor, with great shouldered bodies beautifully muscled. But the man doing the jig looked more like a bear than a man. His face appeared to be nothing but beard and eyes, and black hair covered his arms like a rug. Fly gave a little scream as he made a motion to grasp her about the waist and include her in his dance.

Adam was instantly there enfolding her in the protection of his arm and saying, "Leave her alone!" with such authority that the railman staggered backward laughing. The sound of laughter trailed them into the hotel.

"All right?" Adam asked.

"Yes," Fly said a bit shakily.

Adam gave her a smile of reassurance. "I've had a special table set up for us. This way—"

A folding screen had been provided to afford them a sense of privacy.

356

There was a white cloth on the table, candles, fluted glasses filled with ice, a flower floating in a glass bowl. Fly began to feel better. This was more as she had envisioned it.

"I would have liked to have lobster bisque and champagne," Adam said as he seated her, "but in the provinces—"

"Ya take what ya git—" Sally said, as she joined them. She was wearing the plaid taffeta suit she had worn to the trial, but now it was crumpled and sweat stained. A bottle hung from one hand, and the uncertain way she was swaying made it evident that she had been drinking for some time.

"Am I invited to this party, or ain't I?"

"You were," Adam said coldly, "but now you're drunk."

"Pie-eyed," Sally admitted, plopping down on the chair Adam had just pulled out for himself. "I don't like you," she said conversationally to Fly. "It does beat all—I like your mother. I really like your mother. Doesn't that beat all? But I don't like you—."

"All right, Sally, that does it. You're going upstairs."

"Airs—" Sally said, ignoring Adam. "Airs—" She did a drunken parody of Fly's characteristic little habits of patting a curl here, straightening a ruffle there, the way she dimpled and fluttered her eyelashes.

Fly felt a choking lump rising in her throat. It was impossible not to recognize herself in Sally's drunken pantomime. "Oh, I wish I had never come," she thought, trying hard not to burst into tears. "She's right. I am silly and ridiculous and vain—"

Adam had taken a murderous grip on Sally's shoulder. He yanked her to her feet, his eyes slits of fury.

"I'm sorry, Adam—I'm sorry," Sally panted. "Lemme stay, Adam. I won't say one more word—not one. I'm sorry—"

"Please, Papa, let her stay," Fly begged hoarsely. The folding screen was affording only scant protection from the curious glances that were beginning to be cast their way, and she felt she would die of humiliation if Adam tried to wrestle his drunken mate up the staircase providing a free show for everyone.

Adam, also reluctant to create a further scene, loosened his grip on Sally and allowed her to collapse back in the chair, but his mood now was black and ugly. He realized that the evening had been damaged beyond repair.

"Papa—mother gave me money to stay at the hotel overnight, but I think I would rather go home tonight if it wouldn't be too much trouble—" Fly said in a small trembling voice.

"Darling—the evening has just begun. It's still going to be a lovely evening, I promise you," Adam tried valiantly. "See—here comes the wine."

The waiter appeared with the wine in a wooden bucket that would have been more appropriate for watering a horse, but it was well filled with ice and Adam extricated the bottle with a flourish and made a ceremony of uncorking it and filling each of their glasses.

Sally took a gulp of hers and made a sad hiccoughing sound. Fly, unaccustomed to good wine, was hard put not to make a face at the dry, bitter taste, but she managed a wan smile.

"You're like a rare gem someone has set in a crude brass setting," Adam was saying to her. "You don't belong in this rough place. How you will sparkle in San Francisco. My dear, your spirit will soar like a freed bird!"

Sally belched loudly. Adam gave her a malevolent warning glance.

"Papa—it's so queer—so still," Fly half whispered, her eyes roving uneasily about them. "It's as if there isn't enough air to breathe anymore, as if something terrible is going to happen any minute."

"It's probably going to storm," Adam said matter of factly. "It's often oppressive like this before a storm. God knows the area needs the rain. Put out some of these fires that fill the air with smoke and soot all the time."

Even as he spoke, a wind sprang up. The candles on the table guttered and the drapes throughout the room flew wildly.

"See, it's cooling off already," he encouraged, but Fly had sprung to her feet, her eyes enormous. She was filled with a rising sense of panic she couldn't explain. The breeze that was blowing up was not cooling. It was as hot as if it were blowing out of hell.

"Oh, Papa, I want to go home. *I really want to go home,*" she pleaded.

The candles flattened as if a gigantic hand had slapped them. The drapes billowed at the windows, the women's diaphanous clothing fluttered about their bodies. At the same time there was a noise. A low menacing rumble shook the tables and vibrated through their bodies, gathering rapidly into a terrible, stunning, thunderous roar. It sounded as if a million wild horses were stampeding toward the village in full gallop.

People surged from the bar, the tables, and the rooms above, flowing outside as if moved by one mind—terrified to see what was causing the paralyzing roar, yet more terrified not to see. Fly, caught in the throng, clung to Adam.

The sky was apocalyptic. A wave of fire seemed to hang above the trees, crested, ready to descend and engulf. No one screamed. No one spoke. Everyone was struck mute with horror. Then a building at the edge of the village literally burst into flames. One moment it was only a part of a dark mass at the end of the street—the next it was a torch against the night. Another ignited—and then another. Then there was a human scream and a woman with her hair streaming fire reeled in the street. Before anyone could run to her aid, she crumpled and blackened like a burning paper doll before their eyes.

The terrible scream jarred them back into reality. Everyone and everything began to move at once. People streamed from their homes, some dressed in nightwear, clutching children and possessions. Horses reared and screamed. The bells of the village churches began a frenzied ringing. Men, who were leaders in the village, shouted, trying to gather enough firefighters together to organize some attempt to save homes and businesses. Drunken railroaders fought each other to squeeze into boarding houses or saloons in hope of protection, while those in the buildings fought with as great panic to get out.

"To the river! To the river!"

"My God! Amelia's on fire!"

"Get a blanket!"

"The roof, George! The flames are on the east—"

There were screams and shouts and cries in the night, but in a greater sense, all sounds were so muffled beneath the great overhead roar it was almost as if the entire tumultous scene was taking place in virtual silence.

Fly clung to Adam, her throat so full of smoke she could not speak. He was trying to pry her fingers loose from his coat.

"No—no, no—" she finally choked, clinging more fiercely, wild with panic. "Don't leave me—"

"We've got to get out of here," Adam said, "It's raining fire. You won't get two feet in that dress. Fly, *listen to me*. I've got to get back into the hotel and get something to cover you with."

"You can't go in there. The place is on fire—" Sally, still drunk, said contemptuously.

"Fly, let loose of me," Adam commanded. He had to scream against the rising wind, which was practically lifting Fly off her feet. A woman's hat sailed past them, a cartwheel of flaming tulle and charring roses. Buildings were breaking up around them as if they were made of match sticks. Human beings were igniting as if they were gas soaked torches.

Fly's grasp loosened.

Adam half dragged her to the hotel hitching post. "Hang onto this. Wait here. Whatever you do, *don't run*. Wait. Wait for me, Fly. *Understand?*"

She could barely see him through the black rolling coils of smoke. She tried to nod. The wind was tearing her from the post. She locked her arms around it, falling to her knees.

"Damn you, Adam Quimby, you can't go in there, you stupid ijiot," Sally was screaming, brandishing her bottle.

Adam, trying to force his way through the doorway jammed with people struggling in both directions, waved wildly at Sally.

"Sally, stay out there. Wait for me."

Sally, using her bottle as a bludgeon, staggered after him, paying no heed to his instructions.

"Damn you, Adam—come back 'ere. This place is burnin' up! Can't you see this place is burnin' up—"

He disappeared through the throng of people. The next moment she saw him, a leaping figure on the stairway. She dropped the bottle, clutched the bannister unsteadily with both hands and started to follow him. She had gone two steps into the billowing, choking blackness when she heard the crackling noise behind her. Abruptly, she was stone sober. She turned to see a flowing sheet of fire moving toward her, but there was still an opening.

No man is worth dying for—the thought was as clear in her mind as if it had suddenly been chiseled in stone. *To hell with him*—

She gathered up her skirts and started back. The smoke funneled around her, blinding, choking her. She stumbled and felt herself begin to fall.

Holy Mary, Mother of God—from some long ago religious training the words started to form in her brain—then there were only the trampling feet and the burning fire—

"Fly!" Adam screamed from the upstairs window.

Fly, on her knees in the street below, looked up, straining to hear him.

"I'm throwing you a blanket! Don't wait for me! Wrap the blanket around you and head for the river. Get to the river!"

"Papa—" she called.

He looked down at her uplifted face illuminated by the fire and saw himself in it—not as he was, but as he had always intended to be— he saw himself, radiant, purified, glorified, mixed with some essence of Caroline, and for the first time in years, he felt clean. He could feel the wall of heat behind him. He knew fully now what the cost was going to be—and he was not sorry.

One moment Fly saw her father framed in the window, the next there was only a seething mass of flames.

She felt screams start to cascade from her lips. Maddened with shock and panic, she started to run, screaming, but strong arms caught her and a familiar voice said urgently but calmly, "Don't run, Fly. Don't run. With that dress, it's sure death."

"Dan-Pete—" She clung to him dizzy with relief.

He was wrapping her in the blanket her father had thrown to her. A meowing mass of cats ran past them. The wind was whipping her hair loose, beating it across her eyes. Her mind was trembling on the edge of utter madness. She knew she was still screaming, though she did not feel as if she was doing anything to make the screams.

Dan-Pete cupped her face in his hands. He was still speaking to her in that same low, measured tone.

"I'm going to get you out of this Fly. I'm not going to let anything happen to you. I'm not going to let anything hurt you. I love you— trust me. Do what I tell you."

She was shaking so she could not have stood on her feet even if the wind had been only one tenth as strong, but the panic within her was staunched. "Yes—" she said. "Yes—yes."

"We've got to get to the river," Dan-Pete told her. "I'm going to tie you to me so we don't get separated. You've got to do only two things. That blanket is your life. Keep hold of it and keep crawling. We're near the river. I'll do the rest."

She dug her fingernails into the blanket and began to crawl on her knees. The smoke was so thick she could not see Dan-Pete ahead of her, but she could feel the tug of the cloth he had tied from her waist to his own.

The streets were a boiling mire of people, fleeing animals, wagons, smoke, flying debris, and red hot coals. The sky above was a river of fire. Choking, coughing, half blinded, she crawled on her hands and knees, concentrating only on the tug of the rope. A dozen times the blanket smouldered where hot coals had fallen on it. Each time Dan-Pete stopped and knocked them off with his hands.

And then as a gale of wind cleared the smoke for a moment, they saw the bridge. It hung suspended between the two banks—a flaring necklace of flame. She hid her face against his chest.

74

Heat smothered Harbour Hill holding everything immobile. Nothing stirred. The children seemed to have sunk into a sleep of exhaustion in which they did not even move. Caroline listened for the crickets, the lowing of cattle—and heard nothing. Moving to the window, she lifted the curtain and looked out. The sky had the sullen red glow of an overheated frying pan. The smell of smoke was as omnipresent as ever.

There was the sound of a step. She could hear the sound of her beating heart as Bay smiled at her from the door.

She looked down in apology at her plissé peignoir. "I planned to have something lovely made—a trouseau of sorts—but there hasn't been time—"

"I never saw you before with your hair down like that about your shoulders. How young you look. How sweet."

They moved toward each other. A clean damp scent came from his just washed hair and body, mingling with the fragrance of her cologne.

He touched her shoulders.

"You're trembling." He laughed softly. "A less egotistical man might imagine you were frightened, but I know it's only eagerness."

He was teasing her, but she thought, *it is eagerness.*

"Oh, Bay—we've waited so long. I've wanted you more than you know." She thought of the times when he had passed close to her and she had felt weak at his nearness. Times when he had touched her and she could have fainted with longing.

"You—you won't be disappointed? We've repressed so much—how can two mere people begin to—"

His laughter seemed to close around her like warm arms. His fingers slid into her hair. He kissed her. His arms lifted her, his mouth still on hers. He laid her on the bed and the adventure and ecstacy began. She felt like a flower unfurling to the sun.

Her cheeks were wet with tears. He did not have to ask her why or to wonder. His own were wet with a joy too great to sustain.

"Listen Bay—" she whispered. "It's raining! After all this time, it's finally raining.

They could hear the hard splash against the trees, the wet breathy rustle against the shingles and roof. For the first time in months the curtains were lifting and blowing in a cooling, freshening breeze. They could feel the rain mist blowing across their faces through the open window.

"Do you want me to get up and close it?" Bay asked.

"Oh, no. It feels—wonderful—"

She turned back to his embrace.

If he had risen to close the window, he would have seen that the entire skyline was a raging river of fire. As it was, locked in the bliss of their embrace, they were unaware that Peshtigo was burning to the ground seven miles away in an unbelievable holocaust. They had grown so used to the glare of burning fires it did not occur to either of them to question the lurid light that filled the room.

*   *   *

On their knees, Dan-Pete and Fly crouched together and stared at the burning bridge. That way of escape had become an inferno, trapping men, women, horses, wagons, and pigs. People were jumping and diving and being pushed into the river, some of them flaming with fire as they fell. The screams of the drowning joined those of the burning as they sank beneath tornado driven waves.

The saw-dust streets were sizzling like firecrackers. Every house in town appeared to be burning. Fear crazed deer, rabbits and foxes vied for a pathway among the fleeing humans, bellowing cows, and squealing pigs. There was death behind them, death in front of them and fire raining all about them—still Dan-Pete felt such a fierce throb of life that he never doubted for a moment that he would save himself and the girl cowering in his arms.

"Fly, we're near the riverbank and we must roll over," he told her.

"I can't swim, Dan-Pete," she whimpered.

This took him aback for a moment. The river by this time was as terrible a melee as the land. Burning logs and flaming timbers sloshed about dangerously in the waves; nonswimmers already crusted the shorelines, some of them beating at flaming hair and clothing that continued to ignite unless they constantly submerged. Weakened by injuries and burns, even good swimmers were sinking beneath the waves. A little girl washed by clinging to the horns of a cow. The whole river was a violent red reflection of the exploding world.

"I won't let you drown," Dan-Pete promised. "When we get in the water, don't struggle and don't strangle me. Get it into your mind now that even if it feels as if you're drowning, you mustn't struggle and you must trust me."

"Dan-Pete, I don't know if I can," Fly panted. "I can't promise how I'll act if I start drowning."

The smoke was so dense around them now they could no longer see the bridge or the river. They were lost in a choking night. He grasped her around the waist and began to drag her. Fly couldn't breathe. She felt consciousness receding. Gagging, choking—she was not aware of rolling over the bank. The next thing she felt was the shock of the water, cold, terrifying, all enveloping. She gasped for breath involuntarily. Her lungs began to fill with water. She started to struggle and felt strong arms holding her, supporting her, lifting her from the water. Coughing, sputtering, she found air.

"You can touch here. Try not to breathe in too deeply. The air's so hot you'll sear your lungs." He loosened his arms.

"Dan-Pete, don't leave me!"

"Your blanket's floating away. I've got to get your blanket."

He edged off and grabbed the blanket. He held it above their heads like a tent. Other people were swarming in from the shoreline, forcing them into deeper water. She had a glimpse of the Catholic priest, Father Pernin, desperately clutching the altar tabernacle. A horribly burned woman floated past her like a dead fish. The water was cold. Her body grew more numb every minute, and she felt her will to survive weakening and draining from her. She could no longer stand up. Dan-Pete was supporting her, talking to her urgently, but she couldn't seem to understand what he was saying—people were pushing her, pushing her, pushing her into deeper water. She felt the waves slosh over her head and then lost consciousness again.

The next thing she felt was pain. There was a crushing pressure on her ribs, and she was vomiting. She felt the hot spill of it across her arms and opened her eyes but couldn't see anything, for the smoke. But she was on land again; she could feel herself being dragged roughly over the ground. Someone was smothering her with a wet blanket.

"I can't breathe!" she cried.

Dan-Pete pulled the blanket away but forced her back against the ground when she tried to rise. He dug furiously in the earth.

"Put your face by that hole. You've *got* to stay under the blanket."

A hot wind was blowing against them. The whole place was illumined as bright as day. Dan-Pete's face was glistening with sweat, blackened with smoke. There was a huge, red welt blistered along his cheek. There seemed to be something important she had to remember. Something even more important than this unbelievable Armageddon around them.

"Dan-Pete—" the words croaked through her raw, aching throat, "did you say—did you say you *loved me*?"

He was holding her down against the earth. "Yes, Fly—whatever else happens tonight, remember that—I love you." For one brief instant his mouth touched hers, smoke bitter, tender, utterly loving—

And there in that place of dead and dying, burned and suffering, half dead herself, in pain beyond anything she had experienced in her lifetime, she felt happiness flood through her. *He loves me.* She wanted to tell him that she loved him, too, but he was smothering her back under the blanket.

"Dan-Pete, please get under the blanket, too. You'll burn—"

"I can't," he said. He was forcing the blanket back over her head. She felt him pounding on the blanket and understood with a lurch of her heart that he couldn't seek safety under the blanket with her for fear they would both burn. He was putting out the sparks as they fell.

"No . . " she moaned, "no—" She tried to struggle but she was so tired, so weak, and there was so little air under the blanket that suddenly she felt everything going black again.

He felt her form go limp beneath the blanket. A blizzard of fire was raging all around them. His hands were a mass of blisters. He could not beat out the sparks anymore. His agony was too great. He laid his own body protectively over the small mound under the blanket. *He had promised her he wouldn't let her die.*

*   *   *

Where once there had been pine, tamarack, hemlock and spruce as far as the eye could see, now there was only a sea of raging fire, seething its way mercilessly over an area of a million acres. The air seemed to explode like fiery balloons in a continuing deafening series of detonations as sparks from the blazing, falling trees rose to collide with gas pockets.

The end of the world could not have been more terrifying to the simple immigrant farmers who had come into the Sugar-Bush-Peshtigo area with only their own strength, courage, and a few pots and pans to carve out a new life. For many it *was* the end of the world. They lingered too long trying to save what they had whetted out with hard labor and raw courage and lost their lives as well as their possessions.

An old woman with long white hair stood in one of the six area streams that offered a chance of survival to those fortunate enough to gain their refuge. She was singing in a wavering voice, "—One will

365

be grinding, grinding at the mill—One will be sleeping, sleeping sound and still. One will be taken and the other left behind—" Her rheumy eyes reflected the red horror all around her without fear. She was confidently waiting for Christ and his angels to appear at any moment out of the fire storm above the trees. Among faces twisted with fear, contorted with pain, blank with shock, hers was quietly rapturous.

75

Oh Bay—Bay—Bay your name sings through me like the chiming of church bells. When I awoke this morning, you were gone. I felt your absence like pain. I hurried from the bed—and then felt as if I were moving in warm honey, when I saw you from the window helping Willie bring up the cows for milking. I danced back to bed—I hugged the pillow you had slept on—I ran to lay my cheek against the shirt you wore last night and flung so casually on my chair. Then I ran down to set the table for breakfast—a table for the two of us alone. Will you notice I set my cup so it kisses your cup?

Everything in my life that is exciting is more exciting—everything that is beautiful is more beautiful—everything that is joyous is more joyous—everything that is intense is more intense—because I have you to share it with now. And God willing, the best part of all is the time stretching before us—Oh, Bay, there are so many things to share I can hardly wait. Do you realize I have never made soup for you? Oh, I make a most delicious soup, full of leeks and barley and good beef. You will love my soup. And I want to wade with you in the creek. There is a place upstream where there is a small waterfall and a great boulder to picnic on. And remember how you wrote to me once about the stars?—Oh, let's sleep in the meadow some night and watch them. I want to have your child. Will you teach me to ride horses? How you love horses—and your books, your beloved books—will you tell me about them? I want to know your deepest thoughts—but only when you give them to me as a gift—I love you so—

Caro—when I awoke this morning and found you beside me, I could hardly bear the joy I felt. How touching you were, asleep with your hair tumbled and your cheeks flushed and your fingers curled like a child—and you were smiling in your sleep, which pleased me wildly.

You have always had more faith than I about everything. It is beyond my power to believe that ecstasy—and God know, this is ecstasy —can last at such white heat for long—but however it changes, however it diminishes in the years ahead, I swear in my heart that I will never cease to love you, protect you, cherish you, be faithful to you.

I think I finally believe in God. In union with you, I at last felt a hint of the union with all things through an underlying power. I feel humbled and freed. Lesser and greater than I have ever felt before.

You are my love—my darling wife—my woman—

Caroline met Bay on the veranda. The sun wreathed her hair and brightened her eyes to a lake blue.

"I've arranged for Margaret to feed the children separately. This one morning I want to eat with you alone. I've set our table by the rose arbor." She lifted her arms in joy, "Isn't it glorious this morning? Did you see the rainbow?" She reeled into his arms, kissed his throat with a dozen, small laughing kisses, then slowly looked up, sensing something wrong.

He was looking down at her with tender regret.

"Caro, there is nothing I'd rather do than breakfast alone with you by the rose arbor—but I'm afraid there is something wrong."

"Wrong?"

"I don't want to alarm you, but look over there."

She turned her eyes in the direction he pointed. A dense pall of smoke hung to the west.

"There's always smoke—" she said faintly.

"And there are always ashes of late—but not like this. The breeze is bearing a ton of soot and a terrible odor—as if—"

"A major fire?"

"I don't know, Caro, but—"

"Oh, Bay, not Peshtigo!" she said with quickening fear. "Fly—"

"That's why I feel I'd better hitch up the wagon and see. Probably there's nothing at all to worry about, but I will feel uneasy until I've checked it out."

She nodded, trying hard to master her intense feeling of alarm.

He turned back to comfort her once more before going for the horses. "Whatever my private opinion of Adam Quimby, I'm sure he'd look out well for Fly—so don't go fretting without reason now."

"Yes—" she said, but without conviction. She began to pray fervently.

Before Bay had finished hitching the horses, a wagon inched into the yard. The horse pulling it appeared feeble and impaired in some way. The animal sank in the shafts by the gateway.

"It looks like Hank Jones—" Caroline said, straining her eyes. She ran behind Bay trying to keep up with his long stride.

It was Hank. His grey, billy-goat beard was burned to a black stubble on his chin. His left arm was oozing with raw wounds.

"Good heavens!" Caroline cried. "What happened, Hank?"

"Fire—" he croaked.

"Peshtigo—?" Bay asked, reaching up to help the old man from his perch.

Hank nodded.

"Fly—" Caroline screamed.

The old man's blackened face split into a grin. "I got her in the back o' the wagon—"

Even as he spoke Fly was pulling herself up painfully from the wagon bed. There was nothing left of her organdy dress but a blackened ruffle hanging in rags about her neck. There was no way of telling that her petticoat had once been white. Where her skin showed through the black smears of soot, it was scalded red. Her hair was singed and scorched all over her head. The shoes on her feet were so charred they looked as if they had been fashioned of charcoal. She half fell, half toppled into her mother's arms.

"Darling, darling," Caroline cried in a mixture of relief, distress, gratitude and anxiety. "Are you badly burned?"

"Mother—" Fly sobbed, "Peshtigo is burned to the ground. There must be thousands of people dead and oh, mother, I think—Papa's dead."

Caroline loved Bay. There was no doubt of it—Adam had become a stranger—worse—an enemy who threatened to steal away her children. But for one small moment, she was not Caroline LeSeure, she was the young, vulnerable girl who had given her heart to a man named Adam Quimby—and all that he had been to her and that she had been to him swarmed about her in a dizzying cascade of emotion. Then the moment was spent, and nothing mattered except Fly—and Hank—and all the people in Peshtigo who needed help.

"And mother—mother—" Fly was sobbing on, her whole body shaking in spasms of grief, "I think Dan-Pete is dead, too. He kept me alive—but he—he—he—"

Caroline was afraid her daughter was going to give in to hysterics.

She tightened her arms around her and started leading her toward the house. "Hank, come in, we'll fix your burns. Fly, sweet child, you're home now. You're safe."

With Bay supporting Hank and Caroline helping Fly, they made their way to the house.

"If I just had some nice cool buttermilk on these burns—" Hank was saying. "Now, I take a powerful confidence in buttermilk. Good for you inside and out."

The rest of the children were running from the house and barn to see what was happening and Bay and Caroline at once began issuing orders.

"No one has any food or water, Mother," Fly was saying. "Half the people are blind from the fire. They are wandering around, can't find their way."

"Bring out the surrey and the other wagon," Bay was commanding.

"Put all the sheets from the linen closet into the wagon, get all the bushels of apples you can fit in and some crocks of salt pork. Willie, will you get some hams and as many jugs of milk as you can find containers for? Millie, dear, get all the bread there is in the pantry and wrap some bowls of butter. Joshua, will you warm some water? Fly will have to be bathed—"

"Thet old horse o' mine's got cataracts so bad he kin hardly see—" Hank was saying. "I believe that saved my life. Horses what could see went plumb wild last night, couldn't do nothing with them. Most everybody had to flee on foot. But Angus—he's so deef, as deef as he is blind, 'n he jus' kept ploddin' along. Not that I didn't think we were goin' to meet our maker."

Caroline gently sponged her daughter's blistered and blackened skin and applied dressings to her burns.

"You're going to be all right, honey. I think you are mostly exhausted. We had a heavy rain. It's cooled off here. Climb into my bed and sleep. I can't stay with you with all those people in such dire need—but I will be back as soon as I can."

Fly looked at her mother with brimming eyes. "I'm going with you, Mother."

"Fly, you've been through a dreadful experience and you do have several deep burns. I think you should rest—"

"Mother, I can't. It's too horrible. You just can't know. And I never knew before what a silly, stupid, vain girl I was—and two men—the two most wonderful men in the world, died last night to keep me alive—so now, I have to be better some way. I have to make myself worth saving. I have to come and help—"

Caroline looked into her daughter's tear filled eyes and nodded slowly.

"Yes—yes, I see. Well, come then—God will sustain you—and all of us."

"I don't know if I can believe in God anymore, Mother. When you see—when you see—" She broke off, overcome with emotion.

* * *

"The rain saved our area," Bay said. For some five miles the forest about them remained unharmed. Outside that charmed circle they found total devastation.

The wagons, heavily loaded with food and supplies, jolted through burned and blackened stubble where once giant trees and virgin forest had reared. The roadsides were littered with the carcasses of animals, some of them still smoking. The air, acrid, bitter as bile with the smell of burned land and timber was permeated at times with the sweet but even more terrifying smell of roasted flesh.

For the most part they rode in silence, stunned by the blackened, surrealistic scene of death and destruction. Here and there a stone chimney rose, the only evidence except for the skeletons of cattle and pigs that a farm had existed in the area.

They stopped twice to pick up survivors, some so maimed and burned they looked like lepers in the last stage before death. Caroline climbed into the back of the wagon to cradle the head of one of the women who was moaning incessantly. Bay stopped from time to time to remove trees that had fallen across the road, or an animal caught in death.

Just before they reached Peshtigo, they came upon a dozen survivors squatting in a field, pulling raw turnips to eat. Their eyes looked dazed in their smoke covered faces.

Bay drew the lead wagon up. "We can fit you on somewhere—"

The tallest man shook his head. "Ain't nothin' up ahead. Nothin'. All gone, brother, all gone. Nothin' left."

Caroline stuffed some loaves of bread and a jar of butter into a basket. Bay swung it and a jug of milk to the man. They were gathering ravenously about it as the wagon jolted on.

At the outskirts of Peshtigo, Bay again drew the team to a halt. The man had not lied. Nothing was left standing but the studs of one lone house, the blackened ribs of some train cars and locomotives, and the stone foundation of what had been the woodenware factory.

Bay shook his head in horror and disbelief. "I saw Richmond burn after it fell. I was at Fredericksburg. But I have never seen anything to match this. Never."

370

The burnt sawdust streets were littered with shriveled, blackened bodies. Some of the corpses were postured in attitudes of prayer. The charred remains of many animals shared the space indiscriminately with the human dead. In the murky light of air still filled with rising ash, survivors wandered like lost souls searching for loved ones. Muted cries of anguish marked the moments when they were successful.

"I had hoped there might be some buildings still standing for shelter," Bay sighed.

"Oh, Bay—look," Caroline cried, stricken. She was already slipping from the wagon. A small, wiggling baby was lying on a blanket among several corpses. She came back with the child in her arms. The wagon jolted forward slowly. Ahead of them they could see a group of survivors congregated around what had once been a factory. Most of them had spent the night in the river. The day was cold and they were shaking pitifully, huddling around the still smoking pier and the factory foundation debris. Some, dazed and unmindful of anything but their extreme pain and distress, sat naked, drying their tattered rags of clothing by holding them out to the fire. Others lay full length on the ground, warming their shivering bodies in the sand which was still hot.

"Oh, God bless—" one of the women cried, "They've come with food and quilts."

At her cry, all those ambulatory and able to see began moving toward them and in minutes the wagons were picked bare.

Others crowded about them, tugging at their arms and hands, pulling at their clothing. "Oh, please, Ma'am, have you seen my mother. She's a tall woman with white hair—"; "Have you seen a little boy— red hair, one tooth out in front—he's only seven—"; "You wouldn't have some tea—?"

Bay pulled Caroline aside. "These people are in danger of pneumonia now. We've got to get them into some kind of shelter. I'll take those I can back to Harbour Hill—the children and those who are burned the worst. Then I'll try and bring back a load of lumber as soon as I can. There should be enough able men left to help Josh and me get some kind of barracks up."

"I'll stay here and do what I can," Caroline said.

Fly was ladling out milk. In their rush they had forgotten to bring cups; people were drinking it greedily from their doubled hands, but it was leaking wastefully.

"Bring cups—" Caroline called after Bay.

76

Some of the survivors of the fire had managed to walk the seven miles north to Peshtigo's neighboring city, Marinette. By one o'clock that afternoon, relief wagons from that sister city began to roll in and Caroline and Fly were joined in their ministering by a number of hearty women who came bearing crocks of hot soup and stew and coffee, warm clothing and cloth for bandaging.

"They say Chicago has suffered as terrible a fire as we—"

"Oh, no—" Caroline looked up from the child she was washing, brushing the hair from her eyes. *Please God—let Danny and Emily be all right.*

"Is there no doctor—" someone cried.

"The doctor is ill himself. They say one is coming from Marinette."

"Have you found mother?"

"No, I haven't found her."

"Where has the priest gone? There was a priest. My sister is dying—"

"Father Pernin is with someone else. Give her the final rites yourself—it is permissible."

"Ohhh, can I have a drink—will someone give me water?"

The cacophony of suffering never ceased.

Bay returned with a load of lumber, blankets and straw.

"Marinette didn't burn?" he asked, jubilant that it appeared it had not.

"By the grace of God—no, though it was nip and tuck all night," a man answered him.

"Can we get some of these people to your churches and halls?"

"Most of our public buildings did burn—but the proprietor of the Dunlap House is taking them in—still, there's hardly room left. If you've got timber, we'll help you put up some thing makeshift here—I've heard they've got help started to us from Green Bay."

"The Bay is safe?"

"From what I've heard."

As he lifted the two-by-fours for joists, and sank nails, Baird often followed Caroline with his eyes as she went among the suffering.

A stout woman in a checked dress sat on the ground rocking back and forth in a private agony, though she seemed unharmed physically.

"Emil burned right up sitting in his rocking chair. Emil burned up. Emil burned right up—" she chanted over and over. Bay saw Fly stop and shake her fiercely.

372

"Miz Wilson—Miz Wilson—"

"Emil burned right up—"

"Do you know how to make a sugar tit?"

Something in Fly's tone or the familiarity of the request got through to the woman.

"Why, yes—" she said in an almost normal voice.

The burns on Fly's arm had become unbearable under the weight of the baby she had taken from her mother. She thrust the infant into the other woman's arms. "Take care of this baby. You'll find milk and cloth in that wagon."

The woman accepted the peremptory order, took the baby and went in search of sugar and cloth.

By late afternoon, the misery of the refugees who had not been evacuated was compounded by a rainstorm—the rain that had been prayed for for so long—and that had come too late.

Bay and the other men who were helping to construct a shelter hurried to nail canvas to the leeward sides of the frame they had constructed, giving at least some protection. When Bay had driven his last nail, he sought Caroline.

"We're going home."

"Bay, we can't—"

"We have a whole houseful at home that need help, too. You can't expect Milly and Margaret to cope with everything there alone—and besides, you and Fly have got to have some rest."

A wagonload of fresh supplies and fresh workers had just pulled up in front of the makeshift hospital. Caroline gave in. "You're right, Bay, but Fly wants to—to look for Dan-Pete," Caroline explained.

Bay nodded. He put an arm around each of them and they walked through the drizzling rain.

"It was here, Mother—Bay—somewhere between the hotel and the river. I think here—I remember the stump. I was too afraid to look last night—" Fly said.

Caroline, walking slowly in the direction Fly was indicating, stopped suddenly with a sharp indrawn breath. She sank down to examine with dread the object that had caught her eye. Fly covered her face with her hands. Bay squatted quickly by Caroline's side and looked into her heartsick eyes.

"What is it?"

Caroline was smoothing soot from something small and metal. "A mouth organ. Cricket gave it to Dan-Pete years ago—"

"Are you sure it's the same one?"

She nodded, unable to speak.

A few feet further, they found the remains of a shirt that Kemink had made for her son, a special shirt with bead work trimming about the neck. The remnant of burned cloth lay near a charred pile of bones. There was no one else in Peshtigo who had a shirt like that.

They led Fly, sobbing and shaking, back through the rain to the wagon that was loaded with walking wounded, waiting to find shelter in the barns and outbuildings of Harbour Hill.

The wagon moved in a nightmare of rain and darkness and desolation, the mumble and moan of pain accompanying it.

Just once during the long journey, Fly lifted her hot wet face from her mother's comforting arms and shoulder.

"He loved me, Mother. Dan-Pete loved me. And I loved him."

Caroline, shaken more than by anything else that had happened that day, tried her best to comfort.

"He's with God now, darling."

"I don't believe in God anymore."

Bay laid an arm across his step-daughter's shoulder. "I know how you feel, Fly—I felt that way most of my life. I didn't believe there could be a God and a Fredericksburg, either. But I was watching your mother today—"

He broke off for a moment. There was nothing but the sound of the rain, the moaning, and the monotonous plop of the tired horse's feet.

"Today—I saw people twisting in pain grow quiet—I saw burned children fall asleep peacefully at your mother's touch—I saw a woman instantly healed of grief—"

"Yes—I know," Fly murmured. "Mother has some kind of gift—"

"No, I don't," Caroline denied wearily. Half her life people had ascribed a power to her that she knew she did not personally possess. The power was there and the only gift she had was using it when other people wouldn't believe it existed. There never seemed to be any way she could make people see that.

"There's *something*, Fly. Something—" and then, in what for Bay was a major and radical concession, he added, *"Someone—"*

Fly only buried her head harder against her mother and made no response.

As they plodded on in the darkness, Caroline thought of all the generations of people who had lived before them, asked the same questions and doubted the same doubts—of those who, like Bay and Fly, came to a point where they could not believe in any deity rather than believe in a deity who would permit the existence of evil. Then there were those (perhaps the vast majority) who decided to accept upon faith all they did not understand, and others who claimed they *did know* whether they did or not. She wondered if anyone in that

374

long line of seekers and finders had ever really found out and knew the whole and complete truth about human existence. She knew that she did not have the answers. She could not explain a Peshtigo. She could not explain the need for suffering. All the theologies she had ever heard were for her only a partial answer. Yet, there had been moments when she *had* known—not the answers, not quite, but a state of being—a wholeness, a transcendence into something beyond human experience during which she had been in the presence of something radiant and glorious and totally loving, beyond words— beyond thought. She felt her consciousness lifting above the darkness, and rain, and the groaning people behind her.

"Fly—" she said, flooded with conviction, "wherever Dan-Pete is, *he's all right*. I feel it."

"Mother—how can we ever tell *Kemink*," Fly moaned, breaking into fresh sobs.

As it turned out, they never had to tell Kemink. The first person they saw when they reached Harbour Hill was—

"Dan-Pete!" Caroline cried, "Oh, my dear, my dear, my dear." Tears spilled over her face as she hugged him again and again and again. "We thought you were dead. We found your shirt—"

"I gave it to an old woman whose clothes had been burned off. She died later anyway, poor thing—"

"And your mouth organ—"

"It was in the pocket of my shirt—"

Fly was standing up in the wagon, her face white. She was swaying as if she was going to faint.

"Hey!" Dan-Pete said, reaching up to catch her.

"Dan-Pete—Dan-Pete—" she said, "Why did you leave me last night?"

"I was dying of thirst. I went for water and when I came back, *you* were gone. I've been looking for you all day."

"There aren't words for how glad I am that you're all right," Bay said, touching Dan-Pete's shoulder, "but I better get these people out of the wagon. Some of them are in bad shape. And you have some bad burns that need care. Caro, can you take care of Dan-Pete?"

As he helped the invalids to the barn and the spring house, Fly stood unmoving in the rain, looking at Dan-Pete with parted lips. He was safe! There was a God.

"Mother—" she said, "Oh, Mother—" Her face shone like an opal in the darkness.

Dawn was breaking before Bay and Caroline finally went to bed.

Soon after they lay down Jenny came rapping urgently upon their door.

"I am sorry to call you," she apologized, "but another wagon of hurt and sick has come in—and I am not sure—but I think—well, I think you had better come—"

"What is it, Jenny?" asked Bay, following Caroline out of bed. "Whatever it is, I'll take care of it. Caroline's got to get some rest."

"Yes, please come—" Jenny said.

"You—go back to bed," Bay told Caroline sternly.

She went back to bed without argument, but she could not stay there. She got up and followed Bay and Jenny.

A man was lying on a stretcher at the bottom of the stairs. His hair and beard were burned off and half his face, shoulder and arm were hideously burned.

"Is it?"—Jenny asked.

"Yes," Bay said.

Caroline gave a small cry.

The man on the stretcher was Adam Quimby.

77

"How long we gonna have all those people in the barn? There ain't hardly room for the horses," Josh grumped.

Caroline reached across the lunch table and gave his hair an affectionate tousle. "Some are leaving today. We're taking some of them home and some to the boat. Quite a few have relatives upstream."

She leaned toward her husband. "Bay, I wish we could get a wire through to Chicago. Hank Jones stopped by again today, bless his heart, and he heard that almost the entire city went up in flames. I'm beginning to fear it is more than a rumor. I cannot help worrying about Danny and Emily."

Fly, coming in after carrying food to those in the barn, heard the last of her mother's comment. She smiled widely, her color high.

"Mama, you needn't worry a moment more. Danny and Emily are here. *They* were worried about *us!*"

Danny appeared in the doorway, Emily at his side and half a dozen smaller children entwined about him.

After tears and hugs and kisses of reunion all around, Danny sat down at the table and affirmed that there had been a terrible fire in Chicago the same night Peshtigo had burned.

"At first we thought we would be safe in Emily's father's townhouse. It is one of the few buildings in Chicago built of stone. But soon the fire was like a furnace, sweeping everything in its path and it seemed there would be no safety anywhere. Then General Phil Sheridan, who was recently given command of Army Headquarters in the city, ordered all the buildings on South Wabash Avenue near Congress street blown up. What a din and what a terrible spectacle! The explosives were almost more terrifying than the fire, but it did the trick and checked the course of the flames. He saved quite an area with his quick thinking."

"And what of the Thornton home?" Bay questioned.

"Looted," Danny said sadly. "We drove over afterward, as soon as travel was possible. All the windows were broken and everything movable had been carted away—but at least that side of the city didn't burn."

For a moment a lull fell over the breakfast table. They had many precious memories connected with that great old house.

"Do you think Uncle Brom and Auntie Ann will ever come back now?" Fly asked wistfully.

"Yes! I'm sure they will," Caroline said. "They will restore the house and we will all have wonderful times together again. To think of that lovely home being looted is sad, but we lost none of our dear ones, and with death hitting almost every family we should feel only gratitude and not waste a moment sorrowing for what can be replaced."

Bay laid down his napkin. "We were about to go into Peshtigo. Do you and Emily want to come along Danny?"

"Not now," Emily answered.

Everyone turned and looked at her in surprise. After her long years of silence, it amazed them to hear her speak. She flushed and smiled. It was still an effort for her to communicate with anyone but Danny.

*   *   *

"And God sent down His fire and His brimstone to destroy the unholy wickedness in this city as in Sodom and Gomorrah of old. He scourged it with bombs of fire and hails of red hot coals to burn the abomination He beheld here from His sight—"

The voice was clarion; the tone was passionate. The young revivalist in his crow black suit, waving his arms from a hastily constructed platform on the corner of a Peshtigo street, might have been Adam Quimby a decade or so before.

Caroline thought of all the innocent children she had seen, shriveled, suffocated, drowned; she thought of the pious old people, the burned claws of a corpse still clutching a rosary—*And if there be ten righteous men*—she thought—*and I can think of a hundred and a hundred more than that*—all the good, dear, hardworking people who had formed the core of Peshtigo—the Hank Jones's and the Oliver Dickinsons and the Father Pernin's —she shook her head.

The wagon almost ran into the dangling legs of a corpse. A man hung from a rough scaffold.

"Bay," Caroline gasped, "who could have done such a thing?"

He slipped a comforting arm about her shoulders. "I'm sorry, darling, I didn't see it until too late. There were a number of vultures who crept in to rob the dead of their valuables, rings, and whatever might still be on the bodies. I'm afraid some of the grief stricken have met outrage with outrage. That poor fellow for example."

Compelled against her will, Caroline looked back once more.

"Bay," she said hoarsely, "He looks like someone I knew long ago— I would almost swear—It's *Omar Pettigrew*."

"Try not to think about it," Bay advised softly.

* * *

Kemink had returned to Harbour Hill that afternoon. Though she had long been a Christian, something of her pantheistic Indian faith remained with her. To her, every spear of grass, every tree, every swaying wild flower contained within it the spirit of God. Caroline could feel how her friend had suffered when she saw Peshtigo. But she sensed that her friend's usual tranquility was torn with other grief as well; and as soon as they had an opportunity to be alone, she said, "You seem deeply troubled, Kemink. Is Sashwatka then *so* ill? Do you wish me to go to him? Do you think I might help?"

Kemink turned sad, luminous eyes upon Caroline, eyes that said much more than her lips. "Sashwatka has already gone to 'his land beyond the moon.' I shall not see my good friend on this earth again— and—my people face many hardships."

"I am *so* sorry," Caroline said, feeling the inadequacy of words.

"I do not wish my sorrow to flow outward from me," Kemink said. "There has been enough of sadness with this great fire. Let me bear this in silence, my friend."

Caroline respected Kemink's wish to bear her burden secretly, but her heart ached with the desire to somehow lighten her friend's misery.

*   *   *

By the first of November all the patients and refugees had left Harbour Hill, either by becoming ambulatory or being claimed by friends and relatives. The only remaining patient was Adam Quimby. Adam was still very ill. Like many of the fire victims he had nearly succumbed to pneumonia. His open wounds were slowly healing, but his body was in such a weakened and debilitated state it was evident that a long convalescence stretched ahead. For several weeks more his condition had demanded around the clock nursing from Caroline and Kemink, and his needs still presented a considerable nursing load. Bay brought up the subject as tactfully as he could.

"Caro, you need a rest. You cannot be up half the night for months on end and neither can Kemink. I think we should see to moving Adam somewhere else now."

Caroline, sipping a cup of tea, was standing with her back to him, looking out the window. She did not answer for a long time.

"Caro—?"

"Bay—there *is* no 'somewhere else' for Adam. He has no one. No one but us." She turned and gave him a pleading look.

"He's rich," Bay said, unmoved, "he can afford the finest hospital care—or special nurses at his home in San Francisco."

"Bay, he needs someone who cares right now. Otherwise—otherwise, he isn't going to make it—"

He tilted her face up to his.

"Do you care, Caroline?"

"Of course I care, Bay," she said without hesitation, "He's Danny and Fly's father—Jimmy's father—"

"And beside that—how much do you care, Caroline?"

"Bay, you're not jealous? Jealous of poor Adam?"

"Of course, I'm jealous. In his present condition he would arouse the sympathy of a fence post, and you're not a fence post."

"You're not jealous of sympathy, Bay LeSeure."

"I'm jealous of the hour after hour you spend at his bedside. I'm jealous of every touch you give his fevered brow. I'm jealous of all those years he had with you—"

Caroline started to laugh and drew him close to hug him.

"Oh, my darling. Bay, my crazy darling—"

"I suppose," Bay groaned, "Adam stays."

She looked up at him. "Please."

Adam stayed.

78

Winter began to stalk the land. From her window, Felicity could see sunset colors growing like sky flowers on the bare branches of the trees. She smoothed her brow with rose water before slipping into a cloak. A few minutes earlier she had seen Dan-Pete walking towards the woods. Now she went swiftly down the stairs, across the veranda, and in the same direction. Night sounds were beginning around her. She had never realized how sweet were the muted question of the owl, the dove's coo and the jackdaw's bark until she had seen that barren, burned world beyond their small circle of safety and felt the utter silence, the *lifelessness*. Swiftly, swiftly she went, vaulting over logs, brushing tree branches aside.

Dan-Pete whirled at the sound of a breaking branch.

"Fly—" he said, when he saw her framed in the swaying fir branches, "what are you doing out here?"

"Looking for you."

He turned his back on her. "The air is cold. Go back to the house."

"Have you been avoiding me, Dan-Pete?"

"No." He kept his back turned to her.

"You *are* avoiding me."

He said nothing.

After a moment, she sat down on a fallen tree.

"Dan-Pete—"

Still he said nothing.

"Do you remember what you said to me the night of the fire?"

"I said many things."

"You told me you loved me."

Silence.

"*I love you too.*"

Nothing. Only silence.

"Are you sorry you told me you loved me?" She was trying hard not to cry.

Suddenly, in one fierce bound he was on his knees in front of her. "Fly, it can't ever be. Please, just go back to the house. Do that for

380

me."

"*Why,* can't it ever be?"

"I'm an Indian and you're a white girl."

She laughed. "That's crazy, Dan-Pete. Your mother was an Indian and your father was a white man. I don't care that you're an Indian. Do you mind that I am white?"

"My mother and father were different."

"No they weren't. They loved each other—and so do we. You *do* love me. I know you do."

"Fly—" He touched her hair as if each strand were fragile. "Dear little Fly of satin ribbons and lacy petticoats, of lavender scents and flowered parasols—can you see yourself living in a teepee, cooking over an open fire, bathing in an icy stream?"

"But I wouldn't have to—" she protested. "You know Bay wants you to come into the lumber business with him. Not only wants you but *needs* you. He's going to make all kinds of money. We can have a wonderful life—"

"Fly—Sashwatka is dead."

She looked at him, not comprehending.

He stood up, his strong, beautiful body silhouetted against the sinking sun.

"I promised my people that if they needed me, I would come. I gave my word as a bond. Now that Sashwatka has gone, they have called me. Soon the annuities my people receive for the land sold to the government will run out. The Menominees must find a way to survive.

"The one resource we have left is timber. At present, it is the white man who prospers from our woodland. We receive only a small fraction from the lumber contracts. I want to help set up a lumbering business run by Menominees. The momentum for such an endeavor has begun. The new Indian agent is sympathetic to our council's plan. He is willing to help us, but our people are ignorant of the skills required in lumbering. I have learned those skills from Bay and Jim Conover by felling trees and damming streams and driving logs. The rivers are treacherous with rapids and falls which can jam a float of lumber into such a mass that only dynamite will untangle it. I have learned the secrets of floating the timber safely down stream. I have much to give my people."

Now she jumped to her feet passionately. "I don't care! I don't care! If I have to live in a teepee, I will—as long as I can be with you. *I love you*! Don't you understand?"

"Fly—it is not what I want for you," he said. "You were not made for such hardships. Your race is not the only one that can be cruel.

There are those of my people who would hate you for your white skin, who would do all they could to add to your misery."

He turned away from her.

"Dan-Pete!" she almost screamed, "Don't you walk away from me. Do you think I'm so shallow, so frivolous, *so nothing*—that I couldn't stand up to everything anyone might throw at me? Do you think so little of me? Your mother and my mother lived alone on the frontier. Do you think I am made of so much lesser stuff? *Dan-Pete—believe in me,*" she ended in sobs.

The next moment he was holding her in his arms, but even as he held her tight and hard against his body, his head was arched back as if he were in unbearable pain.

"Firefly—don't do this to me. If you truly love me—help me to do what I must do."

"At your side—in your arms, I will help you—"

He shook his head, looking down at her with an expression in his eyes that became branded on her heart.

"If I love you, I will never be able to do what may be required of me."

"Dan-Pete—" she whispered, "are you trying to tell me that you expect to be martyred or some such terrible thing?"

"I do not yet know what may be required of me, Fly. I only know that I will not be able to do whatever it is that I must, if my heart stays in the teepee with you."

"You're—you're saying that you love your—your stupid Indian struggle—or whatever it is, more than me!"

His lips were barely touching hers.

"Fly—" His eyes were filled with tears. *"If you love me,* help me to do the things I must do—be what I must be—"

"I do love you!"

"Swear—to help me."

"I can't."

"I can fight anything else in this world, Fly. But I cannot fight you, because you are my own heart. If you say to me this minute, *stay*—I will stay—"

She looked up at him. She could feel the hot, wild current of his body, the thrashing struggle of his soul—and young though she was she saw, however dimly, that if she told him to stay she would destroy him, and destroy as well the thing in him that she loved. She hesitated, and then with great effort said, "I swear—by my love—" She got the words out somehow between uncontrollable sobs.

"Fly—I will never love anyone but you." For one moment they clung, and then he turned and almost ran from her—ran from her

wracking, heartbroken sobs. And she turned and sank to her knees, her arms clasping a tree trunk.

79

In the long hours of his delirium and pain, Adam called Caroline's name again and again, and there was something in her that could not but respond to his tortured cry. As Bay had said, she was not a fence post.

In the dark hours of her vigil beside his bed she learned more about Adam than she wanted to know. In his babblings he disclosed the murder of the old black woman during the civil war, the long years of his tormented feelings for her, his unhappy relationship with Sally, his self-hatred.

She did not want to pry into the secret reaches of his soul. She was troubled and uneasy but there was no escape. For a time he was as dependent upon her as an infant, and that dependency forged its own bond just as it does with an infant. That too was troubling. She did not want to become re-involved with Adam.

But one morning in late November when he said her name it was with a difference. This was not the babbling of a man in delirium.

"Caroline?" He said her name very quietly and it was a question.

"Yes."

"It is you. I can't see you—but the smell of your hair—all these years—your hair still smells the same."

His eyesight had been destroyed on the badly burnt half of his face and he was still not able to turn over by himself. She moved to his other side.

"You've been taking care of me?"

"Yes."

He sighed heavily, as if the knowledge were almost unbearable.

"The fire. I remember. I was burned."

She winced as she saw his painfully burned hand grope across the scarred surface of his face.

He closed his eyes.

"Fly?"

"Fly's fine, Adam. Really."

"Fly's—fine," he whispered and went back to sleep.

The next time he woke up he asked about Sally. Caroline told him the truth.

"Poor Sally," he said, "poor, poor Sally." A few tears trickled across his scab stiffened cheek.

He began to gain a little each day. Caroline could feel him watching her with his good eye as she moved about the room, making his bed, washing him, setting out his food. He said little. He was still very weak.

One morning he said, "Caroline, bring me a mirror."

She was tucking in his sheets. Her hands stilled at the task.

He knows, she thought. *I know he knows. He sees what his hand looks like. He's felt of his face. He knows. It won't be a surprise—* But her legs felt weak.

"Give it a little time yet, Adam," she finally said lightly, "You still look pretty rough, you know."

"Please, Caroline."

She could not make him beg. She went for the mirror and gave it to him silently.

The face he saw in the mirror was not only livid with scar tissue, but the underlying formation of the flesh had been destroyed in places, so that as the wounds healed his mouth had been grotesquely stretched at the corner and his blinded eyeball indecently exposed. Adam—her handsome Adam looked like a monster. Caroline turned away to hide her emotion.

"Adam—" she tried to comfort him, "When your beard has grown out it will hide a lot—and I'm going to make a patch for your eye—and then when you have a hat on—" her voice dwindled off. She knew how puny and ineffective words were against what he was seeing in the mirror.

He had looked. He set the mirror aside. There was a strained moment of silence.

"Poetic justice, would you say?" he asked in a voice deepened with emotion.

Caroline couldn't speak.

"Don't," he said. "Please don't cry for me. Come sit here on the bed beside me for a minute."

Brushing away the tears, she sat down. He picked up her hand, giving it his full attention.

"All these years, I blamed you—I blamed God—I blamed Sally— I blamed the war—I blamed fate and chance and circumstance—and all the time I was to blame, Caroline. Me. 'Not in our stars but in ourselves'—"

Now it was her turn to plead. *"Don't!"*

384

"No, Caroline—it's good for me to face it. As long as we blame everyone and everything else we remain victims. If—if the fault is within ourselves, then at least we can try to do something about it, can't we? And there's some kind of hope in that."

"Yes, Adam. Yes."

His hand stole to his cheek again. "There is some kind of grand irony in this—I couldn't stand anyone else's deformity—what I did to Fly—to you—"

"Fly wants to see you Adam. She asks everyday."

"I want to see her too. But—will you bandage my face first? Not for my sake, but for hers."

She nodded.

The middle of December Adam began to get up, dress, and take a few steps. Fly spent many afternoons with him, reading and talking. Danny too, often took up his tray and joined him for supper or took time in the afternoon to play checkers with him. But in Danny's case the visits were the product of politeness and compassion. He felt very little for Adam. In his memory it was Bay who had written him letters, sent him Christmas gifts, taken him to the circus, stood by his mother. Jimmy refused to go into the room at all.

One evening when Caroline brought his tray Adam beckoned for her to sit down on the bed beside him.

"Caroline—there's something I should have said to you before this."

"Yes, Adam."

"I won't take them away from you. Jimmy and Fly. You're right. They are *your* children. You've earned them. I haven't."

"Adam—sometimes when someone has hurt us very much we think, 'someday you'll get punished'—but when something bad does happen to that person, we find we don't really want it to be that way. There's no joy in this for me—"

He stroked her cheek. "I know that. Whatever your little faults were, Carrie, malice and revenge were never among them."

His touch evoked long buried emotions. The man sitting beside her was not the stranger who had tried to roughly grasp her in the circuit office. This Adam was the Adam she had known long ago in another life.

"Oh—I'm sorry—" The voice was Bay's. He stood framed in the doorway, his face registering his feelings at seeing the two of them seated in such proximity, Adam's hand still resting on Caroline's cheek.

Bay turned and strode off. Caroline quickly rose and followed him. "Bay!"

He had just reached the stairs. He turned.

She went to him. "It wasn't the way it looked. Nothing happened.

I mean—"

"I know *exactly* what was happening in that room," he said, "and *I don't like it.*"

He pulled her against him hard and kissed her until she was breathless.

"That is to remind you that you are my wife, now," he said. "I was coming up to tell you that I would be late for supper. I have to pick up some things at the depot in Peshtigo. When I get back we'll talk more about this."

He bounded down the stairs, leaving her hot-cheeked and throbbing with a confusion of emotions. After some time, when she had composed herself, she returned to Adam's room to get the tray. She found him packing the few items of clothing she had bought him since the fire.

"Adam, you're not thinking of leaving? You're not nearly well enough," she protested.

" I have to go Caroline. You know I do."

His dark eye fastened on her with a complexity of passions that stilled all further protest from her.

"Yes," she said, defeated. "Yes. You must go."

She watched helplessly for a moment as he finished his packing.

"I'll let Fly go with you. She wanted to go to San Francisco so much. Remember?" Caroline brightened. "She can look after you until you're stronger."

"I'm not going to San Francisco, Carrie."

"What will you do Adam?—where will you go?"

"I'm going back to the Tomorrow River country."

"Back—back *home*?" the word slipped out. "You can't go back Adam—not in the way you're thinking."

"Maybe not. I only know I have to try. I lost some threads back there."

"What about Fly? Danny—and Jimmy—"

"Fly is the one who suggested it."

"She was?"

"Yes. We're very close, she and I. Strange isn't it? The one I wanted to discard as a misfit. Danny is polite, he tries, but it is Bay he loves and should love. And Jimmy—he doesn't want or need me."

"Adam—You aren't strong. Let me get Danny to help you down the stairs—"

"Caroline—"

She stopped by the door.

"There's something I want you to know."

"Yes, Adam?"

"I never stopped loving you. All those years, in spite of all that happened, all that I did, I never stopped loving you. Do you know that?"

She was crying again.

"Yes, Adam. I do know—*now*."

Later she stood on the porch with Fly and watched him leave with Danny who had hitched up the carriage.

"What is he going to do, all alone—?" Caroline faltered.

"He's going to preach, Mama," Fly said.

"*Preach?*"

"He's going back to preach in the Tomorrow River Country. He thinks he's finally ready to be a true minister."

"Oh, Fly—he can't. He's far from recovered. He can never."

"He's going to," Fly said. "It's all he has left. He has to do it, don't you see, Mama?"

"There's something I have to ask you," Jimmy said as Caroline leaned to kiss him goodnight. His eyes were worried.

Caroline settled down by him on the side of the bed. "What is it, darling?"

"You know I didn't want to go with *them*?"

"Yes—"

"And you said I should pray about it."

"Yes—?"

"Is that why they got burned? Did I make all that fire happen?"

"Oh, no, darling—no, no." She wrapped him in her arms, laughing, and hugging him. "Is that what's been worrying you? God wouldn't cause something so terrible to happen in answer to your prayers. I'm sure of that."

"But I *can* stay with you now, *always*?"

"Always—or at least as long as you want to. You like Bay very much, don't you?"

"Yah, and *he* likes me—"

"He *loves* you."

"And Danny loves me."

"Yes, and Danny loves you—and most of all, *I love you*." She kissed his eyelids. "Now go to sleep little one."

Before she could blow out the lamp and close the door he had obeyed.

EPILOGUE: PESHTIGO—APRIL, 1872

Once more the sound of hammers rang in the village and the smell of sawdust and new wood was sweet on the wind. Cattle lowed in the hollows where coarse green grass was forcing its way up through the burnt stubble of charred earth. Lambs gamboled on knolls where tiny creeping vines and hearty weeds were struggling to hide the scars of the fire.

Peshtigo was rising like a phoenix from its own ashes. Oliver Dickinson, who had lost a saw mill, his house, his meat market and a jewelry store valued altogether at a hundred thousand dollars had set the pace by rebuilding the first house. Since then, a good two dozen buildings had gone up with more being erected everyday.

Despite enormous losses, the Ogden Lumber Company also stuck with the town. They would rebuild in Peshtigo. Their lumberjacks now roamed the territory salvaging what pine they could. Where there were jobs, there was money; where there was money, there was trade; where there was trade, there was transportation; and where there was transportation, there was life. The village boomed into rebirth.

Caroline felt her heart swell as she looked at the raw studs of new buildings glowing gold in the afternoon sun. How tenacious mankind was—how stubborn—how glorious. Let others point out how inconsistent, stupid, sometimes cruel—there was that in man that thrilled her to the thought, *we ARE the sons of God!*

Bay caught her about the waist. "Lady of mine, are you coming or aren't you?"

Caroline held out a spray of tulips and appleblossoms to him. "I wanted to lay these on Sally's grave. Will you come with me?"

They were so close now that she knew he understood any lingering thoughts she had of the past and was not jealous. He took her hand and together they entered the cemetery and walked to the great mass grave where three hundred unidentified victims of the fire had been buried. She left one sprig of flowers there and went on to Sally's grave.

Sally Magee Quimby would achieve in death what she had never quite achieved in life—unity with Adam. He had ordered an ornate granite stone erected. It was engraved with both of their names. In death, he would rest by her side. Caroline laid the rest of the flowers on Sally's grave.

She was pensive for a short time as they rode homeward, but by the time they reached the gateway of Harbour Hill, her eyes were dancing and sparkling again with a secret excitement.

"Bay, draw up by the apple tree. There's something important I have to tell you."

"I already know," he said.

"You couldn't possibly know," she protested.

"But I do," he said, grinning broadly. Nevertheless, he halted the team in the shade of the apple tree.

"Well, if you're so clever then, what is it?" she challenged.

"We're going to have a child."

"Bay!" she squealed, "How *could* you know? I only found out for sure myself today."

He kissed her with more reverence than usual. "I always wanted to know from the moment of conception. I knew. I'm *very* happy."

"And handsome—and charming—and rich—so I suppose I shall have to forgive you for spoiling my wonderful surprise", Caroline said with a mock sigh. "Oh, well—Kemink is planting flowers by the veranda. I'll surprise *her*—"

"Was that John Anderson who just rode away?" Kemink asked of Felicity. "It seems he is here often of late. His intentions must be serious."

Fly leaned listlessly against the porch pillar. "I will never marry anyone as long as Dan-Pete remains unwed."

"Please do not say that, little daughter," Kemink said, "for though it saddens my heart greatly, I doubt that Dan-Pete will ever wed."

"Oh, he'll wed some day," Fly said with a touch of bitterness. "His tribe is avid for a little Pow-wa-ga-nien."

There was much that Kemink could have said, but she stifled her words. She and Fly had been over it many times before.

"Don't you care that he leads a life of terrible deprivation? You know he keeps nothing for himself. Everything goes to the tribe. He doesn't even eat decently and he dresses practically in rags. Don't you *care*, Kemink?" Fly raged.

"Do you doubt that my mother's heart might have chosen differently?" Kemink answered. "Do you think there could have been greater happiness for me than that he would have chosen to stay under this roof, any greater joy than that the blood of your mother and I, who have loved and honored each other so long, should flow into one vessel through our children? But the choice was not mine to make. He is my son and I love him and am proud because he follows his deepest heart truly. He is helping his people well in their need. A million feet of pine have been cut by the Menominees and driven down river to the mill at Keshena. The workers have earned over three thousand dollars for their families and five thousand dollars for the tribe this year."

Fly's long eyelashes blinked in her downcast face. "It isn't fair. I have lots of money from Papa and I'd give it all to the Menominees to please him, but he won't let me. He says 'We want no gift. We want to be self-sufficient.' But *he* can give away everything."

"It is different for him," Kemink said.

"I suppose I might as well go and help Emily stitch on her wedding gown," Fly said with a sigh. "At least *they* are happy. I'm glad for her and Danny."

"Happiness will come sniffing at your knee when you stop chasing it," said Kemink. "I know my words bring you no solace now, but someday you will know I speak the truth."

Fly was sure she would never be happy again, but she was ashamed of saddening Kemink. She dropped a kiss on the Indian woman's silver threaded head in atonement before she left.

Kemink dug deeply into the earth with her strong fingers, loving the thick velvety feel of it, the odor as ancient as the beginning of the world and as young, moist, and promising as tomorrow.

She could see Bay and Caroline, hands entwined, coming toward her. A halo of light seemed to hover about them, a symbol of their happiness. Caroline's body was as slender and graceful as ever, but something in the way she was looking up at Bay, something special in the way he was looking down at her, caused Kemink to smile to herself. *She is with child*—she thought with satisfaction. She tucked the flower bulbs deep into the waiting earth. *It is going to be a good year,* she thought. Kemink loved babies.